The Briefcase

Heath A. Dawson

The Briefcase

iUniverse, Inc.
New York   Bloomington

The Briefcase

iUniverse books may be ordered through booksellers or by contacting:

iUniverse
1663 Liberty Drive
Bloomington, IN 47403
www.iuniverse.com
1-800-Authors (1-800-288-4677)

Because of the dynamic nature of the Internet, any Web addresses or links contained in this book may have changed since publication and may no longer be valid. The views expressed in this work are solely those of the author and do not necessarily reflect the views of the publisher, and the publisher hereby disclaims any responsibility for them.

ISBN: 978-1-4502-4157-1 (sc)
ISBN: 978-1-4502-4158-8 (ebook)
ISBN: 978-1-4502-4159-5 (dj)

Library of Congress Control Number: 2010910807

Printed in the United States of America

iUniverse rev. date: 8/13/2010

www.HeathADawson.com

Acknowledgments

To Monica, my lovely wife and best friend: You have been a constant source of support while I chased this lifelong dream and I'll forever be thankful. I know it wasn't easy losing your husband for minutes, hours, and days at a time while he worked on his first novel. For that, I adore you. Thanks once again for encouraging me to accomplish this goal. Without you, it never would have happened. I love you!

To Ted Barnhart, my editor and friend: Thanks for lending an ear the past twelve or so years. You are the definition of a good friend. I know novels aren't your forte, but your time and efforts are appreciated beyond words. You helped make this novel the best it could be. I would also like to thank you for always being good for a laugh or two. Your sense of humor kept me going at times when I was ready to give up on this project.

To Dad (Tom) and Mom (Sherrie): I don't know where to begin. Although things were not always the best between us, God gave me a set of parents who loved me and always believed in me no matter what I did. Dad, I inherited the gift of gab from you and those words came to life on pages. Mom, you instilled in me the sense of never giving up, which helped me complete this novel. Hopefully, it's the first of many. You also gave me a great set of editorial eyes and I am extremely grateful for your help. I love both of you equally and hope I always make you proud.

To Kay Gowan (Harding University) and Dr. Bowen (Ohio Valley University): Had I never met the two of you, my journey in life would have taken a much different route. Thank you for saving me and seeing the potential in a procrastinating slacker. Kay, you will forever be in my heart and on my mind. Thank you for getting me through the times when I wasn't interested in being a college student, which was quite often. You helped me become something bigger than I ever imagined. My soul is grateful to God for putting you in my life. Dr. Bowen, you didn't have much to work with. For some unknown reason, you took me under your wing. Although you assigned projects, you had one yourself. Thank you for having faith in me when not too many people did. I have a deep love for literature and it's because of you.

To Brad Miller, my lookout: Milk was a bad choice! However, having you as a friend/part-time mentor has always been an excellent choice! You are one friend who will always be there for me and that's hard to find in life. Thanks for always looking out. By the way, keep up the good work on www.HeathADawson.com and thanks for the mug.

This book is dedicated to the memory of Wilma Rose Dawson
Nov. 9, 1926-Oct. 30, 1998

The Briefcase

Chapter One

HE ARRIVED FOR ANOTHER hectic morning at Stenson & Rhodes, a place he loved to loathe. He didn't have a reasonable explanation why he still worked there. Every morning was the same. He frantically hustled through the building's entrance, squeezed into an elevator, grabbed a quick cup of pick me up after exiting the elevator, and slid into his office at 8:00 a.m. sharp, not a second later or else he would receive a pink slip. His encased glass den was the only peaceful harbor to get away from the strange characters he worked with.

The workload piled a foot high on his desk was a drag, but what got under his skin the most was the endless flow of memos he received each day from Big Boy, a.k.a. Stenson—Harry Stenson. The poorly typed notes were closely followed by the annoying stench of cigar overpowering the rich mahogany smell on the top floor.

Stenson was the man in the penthouse. Despite being overweight and having a severe case of cigar breath, no one questioned his authority. He started the public relations firm in the late 70s and it expanded from a one-office operation with ten or so clients to a big-top circus conducting campaigns for every prominent business in Columbus and the Midwest.

Big Boy threatened to fire him numerous times, but knew he couldn't let him go. The young PR associate was one of his top workers. Also, Stenson and the associate's father had been teammates on the football field at the university in Oxford. Their friendship wasn't all they had in common.

"Preston O'Neil, you will never measure up to your father," Harry often said. Preston had heard the nonsense too many times to count.

The speech was tiresome, but if Preston left the firm, his dad would go on a lengthy tirade. Gary O'Neil had a temper and Preston literally pissed away loads of his money in college. Gary felt Preston was set for life and thought it would be a mistake if Preston did something he enjoyed instead of working at Stenson & Rhodes.

Preston, who resembled an Abercrombie & Fitch model, wanted to go into course management, but Gary didn't want a "fairy florist" in his family. Preston argued that studying horticulture didn't mean he would move to Massachusetts and tie the knot with another "pillow biter," as his insensitive pops liked to call them. Was going into horticulture such a bad idea? He wouldn't deal with flowers, nor would he have a pink cloud floating above his head. Gary had many derogatory sayings and wasn't afraid to use them. Preston wanted a superintendent position at a golf course and to live the rest of his days around the game he loved.

He was a good golfer in high school and college. At Columbus Central, he earned Division I state medalist honors his senior year and was offered scholarships to several universities. He decided to go to school in Athens because it was a place to have fun and get away from his father. His girlfriend of three years was headed to OU, too, making his decision easier.

He was the second best golfer on the team his freshman year and was all-conference during his sophomore campaign. Too much partying led to bad grades, which led to his dismissal as a junior. Preston and his girlfriend broke up during a tough third year at OU, so he transferred to Dayton and finished his last two years. He walked the stage in five years and was offered a job at Stenson & Rhodes. He turned it down initially so he could head to Myrtle Beach and land a job at a course, but his dad wouldn't have any part of his hopes and dreams. He was offered a considerable salary and was well on his way to earning six figures.

Preston didn't know what his father did to make a living. Gary told Preston he was a government official. Preston thought it was fitting because Gary could lie to anyone and was untraceable. His dad went in and out of the house at odd times. If his mother would have survived her accident, keeping a happy family together would have been impossible. She died when Preston was six, so his father raised him. Trevor, Preston's older brother, also died in the car wreck that resulted in his mom's death. Preston wanted to get as far away from his pops as he could, but Gary was the only family he had.

Dreaming of having a real family was a part-time hobby for Preston, but life led him down a different path. He had to play the hand dealt to him.

At 8:15, a ringing phone startled Preston. Stenson was on the other end. Preston thought Big Boy was ready to give him another crummy errand. The young associate got a lot of the "run this over to" or "make me a copy of this" type of jobs, which were supposed to be handled by the firm's interns. Preston didn't complain because his dad would hear about it. Most mistakes were reported to his father, making him feel like he was still in high school instead of a twenty-eight-year-old man.

"Preston, I need you to run over to the Arena District. Phil Seevers, a Buckeye Health representative, will meet you at Mehaffey's Pub on Front Street with information on a new campaign we are starting. They are ready to unveil new services and want us to do the advance PR."

Going to the Arena District wasn't so bad. It beat sitting in the office all day listening to gossip, the same 'ole hearsay that permeates in every office. Everyone has heard it.

"I can't stand my husband. I never should have married that bum. He's never been the same since the day he said, 'I do!' It's almost as if he said, 'I might!'"

"Did you hear about Claire and Mike in customer relations? They have been involved in an affair for the past three months."

"Can you blame him? His wife is a raging bedlamite."

"I feel bad for Claire's husband. He doesn't deserve that."

Yeah, everyone's heard it.

"What time do you want me to meet him?"

"He said he would be there around 11 o'clock. Preston, this isn't a usual job for you. I should be going, but I trust you. He's the Chief Operating Officer at Buckeye and pulls in a hefty salary. Make sure you do your best to impress him. Maybe he'll invite you to play golf with him. He's a member at Muirfield Village and regularly plays in the Pro-Am at the Memorial Tournament."

Preston had played at Muirfield, but it had been several years. He thought it would be an opportunity to promote himself. Aspirations of working on a course never left his mind.

Two hours had passed since he talked to Stenson. Preston worked on campaigns he was assigned to while killing time. As Preston gathered his things to head to Mehaffey's, his phone rang.

"Is this Preston O'Neil?"

"Yes."

"This is Phil Seevers. I'm running a little late. Instead of meeting at Mehaffey's at eleven, let's meet at Goodale Park at noon. I don't have time to do lunch."

Instead of telling Big Boy the meeting was pushed back, Preston left the office a little early. Any money he could cheat Stenson out of made him feel better.

Preston headed to the parking garage and got into his silver BMW 330ci. He pulled onto High Street and took off down the road. He was unaware his life was about to change. Instead of despising his place of work and trying to swindle Stenson out of a few bucks, he would have done anything to be replaced at the arranged meeting with Seevers.

WHEN HE WAS TWO, Preston's biological father was allegedly killed at a gas station during a failed robbery. After his father's shooting, the State of Arizona placed Preston in a children's home in Mesa, where Gary and Sharon O'Neil lived.

Gary bounced around several major cities across the United States and had met Sharon on a flight to Seattle eleven years earlier.

They kept in touch for the next year and decided to get married. They moved to Chicago for three years, stopped in Minneapolis for two, and then Dallas for a couple of years before heading to Arizona.

Trevor was four and his parents had been trying to have a second child for a few years. Failed attempts, including a miscarriage, led to frustration and concerns. A doctor told the couple they couldn't conceive another child. Sharon's urging led to an adoption.

When Sharon laid eyes on Preston, she immediately wanted him to be the second O'Neil boy. The couple adopted Preston and welcomed him into their home.

Sharon was an event coordinator for fashion shows. Sharon left the agency she worked for and started her own business in Mesa after she met Gary. It made things easier because she didn't travel as much, but Gary was still touring the U.S. He also made trips to Paris, London, Venice, and other big cities abroad, due to his job. Sharon enjoyed the fact her lifestyle had slowed down, but wished Gary's had as well. Keeping up with where Gary was day in and day out was Sharon's toughest task. He never told her what he did for the government and claimed he was fortunate to be married. She thought about leaving him several times, but never took that step.

Gary spent more time in hotel beds than he did his own. He also spent time in other beds that Sharon didn't know about, although she had suspicions. She never found out about his lifestyle outside their marriage or what he did to provide the extravagant things they had. Again, she had hunches, but Sharon had a dark secret of her own. Unfortunately, her life came to an end much too soon.

Gary was in Indianapolis the night Sharon was killed. She attended a summer party at the golf club in Mesa where Gary was a member. The couple's home was decorated with pictures of Mr. O'Neil and every golfer who played at the club. Those photos led to young Preston's fascination with golf.

According to witnesses at the party, Sharon wasn't drinking. However, police reports stated she had been. Many thought foul play was involved. Her car was found wrapped around a tree at the bottom of an embankment. Drugs were discovered inside the vehicle, which came as a surprise because Sharon was not the strung out type.

Rumors circulated that Preston's brother had been thrown from the vehicle, but he was never found. Witnesses said Trevor was with Sharon that night, but police filed it as a missing person's case. After a few years, most people forgot about the event. Gary couldn't get it out of his mind, so he and his boy moved to Columbus when Preston was in the fourth grade.

Preston spent most of his childhood trying to figure out what happened. His father wouldn't talk about the accident, which always bothered Preston. When he was a sophomore in high school, another parent asked why his mother never attended his golf matches. The parent didn't know Preston's mom had died in an accident. Gary went off on the lady, telling her it was none of her business. Preston didn't have a lot of memories of his adopted mom, but he knew she couldn't have killed herself with drugs and alcohol, especially with Trevor in the vehicle. He hoped someday he would find out the truth.

PRESTON GOT STUCK IN late-morning traffic, but arrived at Goodale Park at 11:45. He parked his Beamer, stepped out, and looked at his old friend.

The Park is a beautiful place. It is one of the oldest in the United States and the senior citizen among parks in Columbus. Goodale was transformed from a Civil War camp to a park in 1861. People still claim to hear Union soldiers shooting up Confederates. Others have heard voices or saw ghosts walking at night. Whatever the case, it was a serene getaway for Preston.

He and an ex-girlfriend, a five-six blonde beauty named Lauren Emory, spent hours in the park, which is over thirty-two acres of peaceful tranquility. There are nearly seven hundred trees, which offer residents a shady spot to take a nap during mid-summer days. Preston often caught himself daydreaming about those areas at Goodale while cooped up at Stenson & Rhodes.

It is appropriately considered the central hub of Columbus. Just about anyone can appreciate the social pleasantries Goodale Park has to offer. There are tennis courts, ball diamonds, grass-covered knolls, walking trails, basketball courts, pleasing aromatic gardens, and many other amenities for area residents and visitors to enjoy.

Many find old Goodale a perfect spot to take in views of Columbus' skyline. Preston had one of his most romantic dates there with Lauren. A horse-powered carriage dropped the couple off at the South Entrance where they walked past an iron gate held up by enormous stone pillars. Preston put his right arm around Lauren's waist and they strolled down a trail covered by rose petals. When the couple reached a spot near East Lake, Lauren was surprised by a dreamy candlelit picnic. The nighttime view of the skyline enhanced the mood that evening.

Lauren thought about saying yes the entire night, but Preston wasn't brave enough to pop the question. The words Lauren longed to hear never came out of Preston's mouth. That was one of their last great memories together.

Preston snapped back to reality after reminiscing for a while in the parking lot.

He lapped the walking trail encompassing the small lake near Park Street. He sort of knew what Seevers looked like because Big Boy had described him. Seevers was a thick, towering man with brown bushy hair, highlighted by a smattering of gray, which had also invaded his goatee. Preston recalled Stenson saying he e-mailed Phil a picture, so he expected Seevers to find him.

After a second lap around the walking trail, Preston still didn't see anyone resembling Seevers. He contemplated calling Stenson, but knew he would get the usual lecture about how he was undependable. Instead of calling Stenson, he waited.

A navy Lexus pulled into the lot three spaces down from Preston's BMW. Preston watched intently, hoping it was Seevers. When the man exited his car, Preston knew it wasn't Seevers. He looked like he was thirty, give or take a year or two. The guy lingered for a moment and went on his way.

Preston wondered if Seevers got tied up in traffic. Maybe Phil forgot he switched the meeting. It was time to check out the scene at Mehaffey's. When he arrived, the busty hostess at the door said Seevers left a few minutes earlier. Preston was frustrated and headed back to Goodale Park.

He noticed the Lexus was gone when he reached the park. It was 12:40 and Preston was ready to go back to Stenson & Rhodes, but decided to take another tour of Goodale.

His cell phone rang as he wandered around the trail.

"Preston, where are you?"

"I'm at Goodale Park. I received a call from Phil earlier today and he was running late. He asked me to meet him here instead of Mehaffey's."

"Are you an idiot? He told me he had been at Mehaffey's since 10:45 and you stood him up. Instead of wasting his day waiting on you, he went back to his office and said he would sit down with me next week. You're lucky we didn't lose the account. I told you he needed to be impressed and look what happened."

"I went to Mehaffey's and asked if he had been there. The hostess said he left a few minutes earlier."

"He didn't appreciate being stood up, so you have more explaining to do when you get back. This could be the nail in the coffin for you."

Instead of arguing, Preston listened to Stenson's verbal abuse. He agreed he and Big Boy needed to talk when he returned to Stenson & Rhodes. Not more than sixty seconds after he hung up with Stenson, Preston's cell phone rang again.

"Hello."

"Hey, this is Phil. Sorry about the mix up. My meeting this morning lasted longer than expected. I sent someone to the park to meet you. I told him you would be there and shouldn't be hard to find."

Preston remembered seeing the Lexus guy around.

"Do you know if the guy you sent was driving a navy Lexus?"

"Yes, that was him. He called and left a message that he stopped by Goodale Park. He didn't see anyone who resembled you. He said he walked around the trail near the parking lot a time or two, but eventually gave up and left."

"I was at the park. I saw him and thought you might have sent someone. I concluded the meeting was too important and you would rather handle the business."

"I've talked to Stenson and everything's all right. We're going to meet next week."

They said good-bye, but the conversation didn't sit well with Preston. He recalled the tone of Stenson's voice and knew he wasn't pleased. If Seevers talked to Stenson, why was Big Boy mad at Preston? He also wondered why the man wouldn't have approached him when he got out of his Lexus. The cars were only three spaces apart. Preston also made eye contact with the man. Things didn't add up.

Preston got tired of racking his brain and attempted to finish walking through the park. He was only twenty-five yards away from his car when someone called out to him. He turned around and it was the guy from the Lexus. Preston was a little cautious, especially since Seevers said the meeting would take place the following week.

"Are you Preston O'Neil?"

"Yes."

"I was here earlier to meet you. Seevers sent me because he was running late. I didn't see you the first time I stopped, so I took care of other business."

"I was here earlier and saw you. I thought we made eye contact. I talked to Seevers a few minutes ago and he said a meeting is slated for next week."

"Seevers called me as well and said you were still here, so I stopped by."

They walked closer and shook hands.

"I'm Matt Talbot."

His physical appearance and strong handshake sent notice that he probably frequented a health club. Matt was a handsome man. He had light brown hair gelled to perfection and his locks accented his perfect tan, one that wasn't achieved through a fake bake process. He wore black-rimmed reading glasses that made him look smart beyond his years. Preston thought Matt could pull a curled lock of hair down, discard the reading glasses, rip off the Men's Warehouse suit, and reintroduce himself as the man of steel.

After introductions were over, they sat on one of the benches and exchanged small talk. They discussed the Buckeyes, weather, traffic construction, and their night lives. Each man made a new friend.

The conversation lasted another twenty minutes. Preston realized he needed to get back to the office. He asked Matt if there was information or materials he needed to give him. Matt didn't have anything. Another red flag raised in Preston's mind. He wondered why Seevers sent someone unprepared to meet with him.

A black Expedition slowly drove by as they got up.

Matt looked like he had seen a ghost. His facial expression verified something was wrong. Preston asked Matt if he knew who was in the SUV and didn't receive an immediate answer. Matt watched attentively as the vehicle disappeared around the corner.

"In due time, you will understand what this is about. Those people who drove by are after me and have been for about the last ten days. I'll ask Seevers for your number and get in touch with you."

A thousand things ran through Preston's mind as he bent over to stare at the ground for a few seconds. Before he could formulate a sentence, the bench the acquaintances occupied suddenly got lighter.

As soon as Matt began jogging to his car, the vehicle roared around the corner.

"Run!" Matt demanded as he turned to the park.

Preston didn't have time to react. Matt disappeared as a trio of men got out of the Expedition and began chasing him. The black vehicle vanished as quickly as it appeared. Preston stood alone. He thought about calling for help, but didn't know why the men were armed and chasing Seevers' man

He also wondered why Matt told him to run since he didn't know the men. It was obvious they were after him for a reason. Maybe he was a gambler and owed sizeable debts. The men didn't look like average businessmen. All three of the ground troops were busting out of their shirts and didn't look like they made their money sitting in high-rise offices.

If Preston stuck around, he would find out what they did to earn a paycheck. It was time to leave. As he hurried to his car, he looked back and heard shots go off in the park. He wondered if Matt was alive, but knew it was time to get out of Goodale Park. As he peeled out of the parking spot, the Expedition rammed into the back left side of his BMW. The impact spun Preston's car around in the opposite direction. Unlike moments earlier, his reaction was like a sprinter responding to the starter's gun. He stomped the pedal.

Preston didn't know why he was involved, but whatever Matt did to them, they were incensed. He sped around the corner and darted into an alley. His heart was beating like a pencil or pen being repeatedly tapped on a desk by a nervous secretary. Preston sat in his car watching the road ahead and didn't see any of the men. After waiting a while, Preston raced to an adjacent parking garage. He pulled his ticket out of the toll, drove to the seventh floor, and parked his car.

His cell phone rang as he gathered his things.

"Hello."

"Preston, you have something we want. We are watching you and will be in touch."

He hung up, took a deep breath, and collected his thoughts. Preston didn't understand what the person was talking about. However, Preston knew he was in serious trouble if it was one of the 'roid ragers from Goodale Park.

Preston's thoughts about future danger would come to fruition.

Chapter Two

THE OFFICE WAS THE last place where Preston wanted to be. He wanted to turn around and fade into oblivion as soon as he walked through the double glass doors on the first floor. Seclusion seemed to be a reasonable choice after the afternoon's events.

As he rode the elevator, Preston thought about Big Boy and the trouble he was going to deal with during their conversation. Preston knew what happened would be hard to believe, but he had to tell Stenson everything.

Preston quietly ducked into his office and closed the door. It was a few minutes after 2 o'clock and he practiced his speech for Stenson a half dozen times. As he recited the notes scribbled on a piece of paper, there was a faint knock. He opened the door, but the corridor was empty. Preston looked left, then right, but there weren't any signs of a messenger.

A slight draft uplifted a small envelope as he was closing the door. Preston made sure no one was around as he picked up the mail. He peeked through the blinds before settling into his chair. He stared at the envelope for five minutes before opening it.

A hand written message from Matt was inside.

I told you that you would know what was going on in due time. What you witnessed at Goodale Park doesn't necessarily give you added insight. I didn't like putting you through that, but everything will turn out the way it is supposed to be.

You will continue getting clues about the situation. Part of this note was written days ago. You are probably wondering how I got it to you, but that doesn't matter. I know who you are and soon enough, you will, too. I'll see you soon.

Preston sat in stunned silence. He was well aware that he was a man who hated his job and was apparently in for the ride of his life, which appeared to be in jeopardy.

The page startled him.

"Preston O'Neil, you have a call on line five. Preston O'Neil... line five."

He was nearly hypnotized by the blinking light.

Preston grabbed the phone with a sweaty hand and hesitantly picked it up. He wondered if it would lead to more regret or if he could start putting pieces of the puzzle together.

He answered with a soft, nervous hello.

"We're looking for Preston O'Neil."

"Speaking."

"You know what we want. Give it back and you can return to your normal life. If you don't cooperate, you know where you'll stand. There will be consequences to deal with and you will have more to worry about than your job at Stenson & Rhodes."

Preston didn't understand what the voice on the other line was talking about. The sequences of the day flashed through his head in seconds. He thought the group of men felt Matt gave him something.

"I don't know what you want. I've never seen the guy you were chasing at Goodale Park before today. I was supposed to meet a gentleman named Phil Seevers, but he changed the meeting from Mehaffey's Pub to the location where I saw your men. As I was getting ready to leave the park, the man called to me and we spoke for a few minutes. Our conversation was over upon your interruption."

"Don't lie to us! We know you have it. Meet us at Tally's Hall. Give us what we want and we'll give you something you want."

The message was loud and clear. The missing item was probably in the possession of Matt when Preston and he talked at Goodale Park. The men thought it was given to O'Neil. They wanted it back so badly they were apparently willing to negotiate with him. However, Preston wasn't stupid. He knew he was in trouble regardless of whether he had the unknown item or not.

"I'll meet you, but I'm going to set the day and time."

"We want it back immediately. It's obvious we know where you work and we will get it back at any cost. If we have to show up at Stenson & Rhodes to retrieve what is ours, we'll go to that extreme. I think you understand it's best if this doesn't involve your place of employment."

The conversation ended as the man on the other end of the phone hung up. Preston wondered what "it" could be they were searching for and why they wanted "it" back.

A meeting with Stenson was next on the docket, but Preston received the only good news of the day from the secretary who paged him a few moments earlier. Stenson canceled the rest of his afternoon appointments, including the showdown with Preston, due to business needing his immediate attention.

Preston sighed with relief, knowing his meeting with Big Boy would at least have to wait another day. He went through papers piled on the corner of his desk and, as day slowly turned to night, decided to do some investigating of his own. The door closing behind him as he left his office was ironic because his old life had ended. The chance encounter with the mysterious Matt Talbot would change Preston's life.

As he exited Stenson & Rhodes, he said good-bye to the front desk secretary. As soon as he stepped onto the sidewalk, he noticed the dented black Expedition in a lot across the street. They would watch him at any cost. Preston fortunately left his BMW at the parking lot near Goodale Park, so they couldn't follow him in his vehicle. However, Preston traveled by cab during the afternoon and planned on catching one back to his car.

He knew he needed to get to his vehicle, but where would he go? If the group of men knew where he worked, they probably knew where he lived. Preston frequently ate at a sports bar a few blocks from where he worked. He was good friends with Clint Harbor, who was the owner, and knew he could slither out the back door.

He hurried over to Four Corners and slipped in the front door. As he stood in the entryway, he looked out the front window and noticed the black SUV parked next to the curb across the street. Two guys exited the vehicle and headed toward the establishment.

Preston pushed his way past waiting patrons and rushed to the bar where Clint was chatting with a few regulars.

"Hello. I saw you walk in and your drink's coming."

"Clint, I don't have time for a drink. I need a favor."

Before Clint responded, Preston showed his urgency by keeping the conversation one-sided.

"There are some guys after me. I don't know why. It's either a case of mistaken identity or they think I have something they want. I don't have time to brief you on the crazy events of my day, but I'll drop by soon and explain. Please, let me use the back door."

Clint saw the terror in Preston's eyes and knew he was in trouble. As he was set to reply, the door opened and Preston ducked around the bar before the two muscle heads caught a glimpse of him.

They scanned the place a couple times before one headed to the men's room and the other set up shop at the bar.

"What can I get you Arnold?" Clint said jokingly to the giant of a man.

"I'm not thirsty or in the mood for jokes, but maybe you could help me with something. A guy by the name of Preston was supposed to meet us here. He said you were the one to find when it came to paying off his debts. He has a big debt and I would hate to kill you in the middle of this bar. I'll say this once. We want what he has and we better have it by the end of the day or we'll be back for you."

"Listen! This is my bar and I know 85 percent of the people who walk through the front door. I don't know a guy named Preston."

While Clint finished trying to sell him on the lie, the other man returned from searching the men's room.

"He wasn't in there. He has to be in here somewhere."

Arnold, as Clint called him, stood up.

"We're celebrating Preston O'Neil's birthday tonight," he loudly announced. "I need to see a show of hands who knows the honored guest."

The place was full for an early dinner crowd. There were only two or three available tables and half the bar was full. The announcement seemed to be a crowd pleaser as several patrons in the establishment raised their hands.

"Tell me you don't know him again and I will blow your head off. Where is he?"

While the conversation was going on, Preston slowly crawled to the end of the bar, reaching the kitchen area. A few people recognized him when he stood.

"The place is being robbed by the big guys at the bar. Everyone needs to get out of the building."

Preston's news caused panic. While everyone scurried, he ripped off his suit jacket and threw it into the trash. He put on a chef's hat and an apron to blend in with the rest of the group. The kitchen door opened as they rushed out the back.

Preston reached the alleyway and yelled, "Run!"

The employees took off running with Preston. As they reached the end of the alleyway, a pair of husky voices called out to the group.

"Stop or we'll shoot!"

Half the group stopped, but Preston, along with a cook and three waitresses, kept running. Preston darted around the corner while the other man and waitresses took a left.

He looked over his right shoulder and one of the guys was on his trail. Preston was much lighter than the man chasing him and had a forty-yard head start. Preston pushed and shoved his way past people on the crowded sidewalk. He heard a bullet whistle past his head.

He didn't feel the pain of a bullet, but Preston didn't know what that felt like because he had never been shot. He looked himself over as he ran and didn't see blood. Preston was in range, but the chances of him being shot grew less the more they ran. He increased the distance between himself and the freak of nature to nearly seventy-five yards.

As they continued their sprint down the sidewalk, a couple was getting out of a cab. Preston quickly dove into the yellow and white vehicle before the man could shut the door.

"Drive!"

"Get out of this vehicle," the cab driver said in a Middle-Eastern accent Preston was barely able to understand.

As his pursuer closed in, Preston ripped out his wallet and threw a large wad of money at the driver.

"Please, step on it!"

Without hesitation, the cab driver laid a pair of impressive tracks on the roadway, leaving behind a strong odor of burning rubber. As they sped away, a bullet shattered the back window and struck the cab driver in the shoulder. The vehicle swerved into oncoming traffic and was somehow avoided. The cab slammed into a parked car on the wrong side of the street.

Preston didn't have time to see if the driver was OK. He painfully jumped out of the car and began a second leg of the marathon he didn't enter. The man chasing him stopped when he fired the shot, but Preston didn't look back until he ran another four blocks.

Out of breath, he stopped running. He didn't see signs of trouble, but it didn't stop the young public relations worker from constantly looking around. Preston needed to rest, so he went inside one of the pubs to get a drink or two.

After he spent an hour inside the dive, he decided to go back to Goodale Park to see what happened earlier in the day. As he was getting ready to leave, a TV grabbed his attention. The *WBNS* evening news was airing a live segment from the park.

"Jim, we don't know much about the victim, but we know the shooting took place around 1:15 this afternoon. Police said witnesses saw three men running after a man when shots were fired. Those on the scene said they began taking cover and heard a man yell out. The man was taken to OSU Medical Center and died minutes after arriving."

"Thanks Hannah. We will have an update when more information is released."

Preston knew most of what he watched on the newscast, but was unaware one of the four men was dead. Immediately, he thought of Matt and hoped he was OK.

He knew he couldn't get close to the scene, but it was time to go to the place that began his day of hell on earth.

WITH GARY NEVER AROUND, the O'Neil boys were close to their mother. Anyone who knew Sharon attested the boys were her life. They thought Trevor was her favorite because he was her oldest and only biological son. However, Sharon loved Preston just as much and it was evident to the boys.

When Trevor was in kindergarten, Sharon and Preston picked him up every day at 1:00 p.m. The following year, they picked him up each afternoon at 3 o'clock. As Trevor's first grade year passed, Sharon couldn't believe both boys would be in school in a few months. The boys kept her busy and filled the emptiness she felt from her marriage. Although a ring on her left finger reminded her she was married, Sharon felt like a single mother.

She took them to the park for picnics. They visited the zoo and were the last people to leave. The family, minus Gary, flew to Disneyland the week before Trevor started kindergarten. When the boys started playing T-ball and Coach Pitch, she got them ready for their games and drove them to the ball park. She even became the official scorekeeper for both teams.

The boys didn't have many fond memories of their dad, but they could recite the things their mother did with them, especially Preston, who was a lot more talkative than Trevor.

Most of the time, Gary was in a fancy restaurant in another part of the world with someone who wasn't his wife. However, on one particular night, he was at home with his family.

Sharon had an eye for fashion and also conjured up magic in the kitchen. The aromas found their way into every vent in the house that evening. It seemed like the three O'Neil males couldn't get away from them. They circulated throughout the house like a storm over warm waters in the Atlantic. Their tongues began dripping five minutes into her preparation and the anticipation of unleashing their taste buds on the various flavors was driving them crazy.

While the family was at the dinner table, Gary asked the boys, who were in third and first grade, about their games earlier in the week. Trevor's team lost, but he played reasonably well. Preston's Coach Pitch team didn't keep track of the score and it was probably a good thing. Preston wasn't interested in swinging a bat, but could smack a golf ball farther than half the hacks that hit balls into their back yard from a nearby course.

"Mommy gave that other guy a kiss."

As proven by millions of kids before, Preston blurted something that neither Sharon nor Gary expected to hear. Puzzled, Gary instantly glanced at Sharon.

"We need to talk."

Sharon didn't know how Preston saw her, but she wasn't going to add fuel to the burning fire by asking questions.

"Where did you see mommy do that?" Gary asked as he turned into a prosecuting attorney.

"I don't know where we were, but that man didn't want mommy to leave."

Gary had a tendency to scare the boys when he got mad and it was one of those times. He slammed his fist on the table and shouted, "What is he talking about?"

Preston started crying because he thought it was his fault Gary was angry. Trevor ran to his bedroom and hid in the closet.

Sharon calmed Preston and told him to go to the play room. She picked up her plate and went into the kitchen. Gary stormed in behind her as if prepared to unleash a furious combination of fisticuffs.

"I should have said something to you. A gentleman stopped by the office one afternoon after Preston and I picked Trevor up from school. He was in charge of a show and asked me to swing by the civic center to check things out. We stayed thirty minutes and he kissed me as we were leaving. The man didn't want me to go because he wanted me to stick around and help him put the finishing touches on things. Before you blow a gasket, he was gay. The boys made a big deal about it. I told them the man was a friend and it wasn't the same as kissing daddy."

Gary wasn't happy, but knew "twinkle toes" were often in contact with Sharon. He played it off as if it wasn't a big deal.

"I'm going to bed. I have to fly out early in the morning."

It was a fitting departure because both O'Neils had to make phone calls. Gary went to his office to make his. Everyone in the family knew they were not allowed to take one step into the forbidden room.

"I'll make it short and sweet. I want you to keep an eye on Sharon for the next few weeks. Something happened tonight at the dinner table and I want to make sure everything is all right."

Gary hung up and the voice on the other end began investigating the situation. He had been through the same rigmarole with Mr. O'Neil before. Although Gary was experienced at having affairs, the ole' hypocrite wanted to know what Sharon was doing at all times.

Sharon cleaned the table, put the dishes in the washer, and gathered the trash. She did most of the housework, including taking out the trash. She walked it to the curb and ducked into a shadow along their fence line with the only portable phone in the house.

"It's me. I don't have long because Gary's home. We were eating dinner and Preston revealed something that made me uneasy. He said I kissed you and you didn't want me to leave. I made up a story, but it's getting harder and harder to visit you. I thought Gary was going to hurt me. He is leaving tomorrow, but I don't trust the situation. I want to be with you, but I'm going to play it safe for a while. We have to be careful because I know Gary is a jealous person and he will be watching when I least expect it."

"I don't understand why you won't leave him. I know he has a great job and offers you a better material life than I can, but I can offer you love, which is something he doesn't have a clue about. I also realize there are two children involved, but I would care for both boys like they were my own. This has gone on far too long."

"I feel terrible about this, but it has to be this way until I can figure things out."

She hung up and dialed a wrong number so Gary couldn't hit redial.

Sharon spent minutes, hours, days, and weeks trying to come up with a plan. Due to her attendance at the summer golf party, she didn't have enough time to finalize the details.

THE PARK WAS A little quieter in the evening than it was during the day. Once the sun disappeared, it was a place for romance and star gazing. Preston found out it could also be a place of hate and soiling pleated Ralph Lauren's.

There wasn't much activity that night. The yellow police tape signaling trouble was visible from where Preston eyed the scene. He was still nervous from the day's events, but had to go back to the park to see if the item the jarheads were looking for was there.

After leaving the bar, he purchased a black Ohio State jogging suit at a High Street business. He hoped it would help him not look obvious while conducting his private eye work. Preston still had the feeling he was being watched and the hunch served him right. The muscle hounds weren't around, but a man watched with binoculars in a rented house across the street from where Preston was surveying things.

They didn't have plans to capture O'Neil that night—maybe a scare or two—but the spy game would be played out until they got their item back. They missed a golden opportunity earlier in the day and realized they needed things to die down, especially since one of their own took a bullet to the chest that afternoon.

Preston looked like a spectator watching Roger Federer and Raphael Nadal in the men's final at the French Open. He looked left and right more times than he could count. Another ten minutes of swivel head would send him to the chiropractor. Since he was worried more about keeping a lookout instead of investigating, it was time to go to his car and head home.

As Preston exited the stairwell and stepped on the concrete of the seventh floor, he knew more trouble was in store. He was certain he parked his car in spot G-19, but G-19 was empty, as was most of the parking lot.

They had Preston's car and he wondered how he would explain to Gary what happened to his luxurious ride. It was a gift from Stenson when Preston celebrated his first year with the company. Actually, it was from his father, but Preston didn't need to know that. Gary wanted him to work for Stenson & Rhodes at any cost and the gift was one of the things that kept him from signing on the dotted line elsewhere.

As Preston headed down the stairwell, he heard heavy footsteps coming up the flight of stairs. He knew it could be drunkards heading to their cars, but the steps sounded like thick marching and he automatically thought about Arnold and his crew. He reversed direction and went back to the seventh floor.

Preston, also a track star in his prep days, darted around the steep grade to the sixth floor and then to the fifth and fourth floors. As he stopped to catch a quick breather on the third floor, lights nearly blinded him. He tried looking through the windshield, but quickly found out why deer is a delicacy on Ohio's highways and interstates.

"Unbelievable," he thought. "I'm about to be a hood ornament."

The voice nearly gave him a heart attack. It bellowed from the darkness. Before Preston turned around, the lights in the parking garage were shut off.

The bright beams on the vehicle were flipped off, but they kept the parking lights on. They cast a shadow around the man speaking from the semi-darkness. He resembled a mob leader and Preston thought of gangster movies he watched growing up. He wondered if it was his fate. *The Dispatch* would read: *Young PR Exec gunned down in parking garage.*

"We know you spoke with that gentleman in the park. We've been trying to catch up with him for several days. Did he give you anything?"

They shook hands, but was a small piece of paper what they were after?

"No!" Preston declared.

"I'll make this clear. We could have come after you in the park, but we knew who you were. A little fender bender won't hurt anyone. All we're asking is that you cooperate. We will give you money if you hand over what we want. Do you have it?"

Two car doors opened as the question echoed throughout the parking garage. Preston thought he was seconds away from being reunited with his mother. He didn't have time to rationalize. He had pissed himself and shed fifteen pounds from the four gallons of sweat that had dripped onto the cold concrete.

"I might have it."

The timing for sarcasm wasn't good because a rough-up session was in store. Making them more upset by being a smart a'leck wasn't wise. They wanted Preston to know they meant business and if he got his hands on their prized possession, he was to return it at any cost.

"We know you don't have it and don't act like you do."

"Why don't you tell me what it is? Maybe I can help you."

Preston's offer drew a round of laughs. He didn't know he was a comedian. Maybe he could work on a routine and take his act to the Funny Bone. He could go on tour after gaining popularity and get as far away from Columbus as possible. But then again, he was about to take his last breath. Thoughts of a tombstone quickly returned.

Each guy grabbed him with such force that Preston thought his arms were broken. They lifted him off the ground, which wasn't tough, considering Preston was five-eleven and weighed 175 pounds. To the pair of extraterrestrials, it was like lifting a bag of apples. Indeed, Preston was about to be apple juice.

They carried him to the man in the shadows and he leaned forward to unveil a portion of his face. Preston didn't recognize him. He stared at him long and hard so the man's face would be a permanent memory in his mind, but the shadows made it difficult. The three-inch scar on his right jawline was the only feature Preston etched into his mind.

"You better hope this is the first and last time you see me. I want our item back. We know that boy has it and how he got his hands on it is still a mystery. If he gets in contact with you, we want to know. We will meet here every night at eleven-thirty until we get back what is rightfully ours. Once it's returned, you can return to your life, whatever it is you do for Harry Stenson."

After Mr. Shadow finished his speech, Preston took a blow in his ribcage and was on the ground coughing up what he thought was his insides.

"Let that be a lesson. Don't mess with us!"

As Preston was on the verge of passing out, he heard car doors open and slam behind the men. They pulled them shut with the slightest ease, but it sounded like cannons erupting when they closed the doors.

The men pulled off in the first car and Preston heard the voice behind the operation walking down the stairwell. Preston wanted to get up and follow him, but knew he wouldn't get far with several cracked ribs.

The garage was being watched from all sides. It took Preston fifteen minutes to gather himself off the pavement and lumber down the stairwell. When he stepped on the sidewalk in front of the parking garage, the street was dead. He glanced around hoping to spot anything out of the ordinary, but didn't want to look obvious. He knew it was going to be hard to give them the slip, especially without the services of his vehicle.

He walked to the corner and waited for a cab. As he waited, a chocolate sedan raced up to the curb. The passenger's door flipped open and Preston stared at a pistol.

Preston felt like he gazed at the cold steel for an hour. It was only seconds before he was sitting in the car weaving in and out of traffic. He didn't know where they were going, but they were trying to get there fast.

The voice behind him was unexpected, but recognizable. He heard the same voice earlier in the day at Goodale Park.

"Whatever you do, don't look back here! As you now know, I made it through that ordeal today. I'm not sure if you heard the news, but I shot one of those guys."

The fact someone was lying on the floorboard talking to him made the day stranger, but he understood what was going on. Preston was riding with a murderer who was trying to befriend him and God only knew about the driver's profile. The people after Matt were obviously the bad guys. Preston determined that after numerous cracked ribs in the garage.

Although the vehicle was traveling well above the speed limit, Preston could see what was going on. After riding in the car for ten minutes, things started getting fuzzy. The cars zipping by looked like streaks from a bad action snapshot taken by a throw-away camera.

It took another two or three minutes before he was knocked out. When Preston jumped in the car, the driver gave him a pill and a bottle of water.

"Take this!"

He initially refused, but the gun jammed into his side made agreeing easy. He also didn't know Matt was hiding on the floorboard in the back.

Matt could barely see the top of Preston's head when he looked up, but noticed he was trying to fend off a rapidly approaching nap. His neck snapped three or four times in thirty seconds. Preston finally gave up the fight and gently fell back against the head rest on the passenger's seat.

"Are they behind us or did you lose them?" Matt asked.

"I lost them about five miles back. We're only a minute or two away."

"When we get there, we have to make it quick."

"No problem."

Chapter Three

WHEN THE SEDAN REACHED the check point, Matt quickly got out and grabbed Preston. Matt placed him in the trunk of a gray Grand Prix and jumped in the back seat. Instead of lying uncomfortably on the floorboard again, he decided to sit up.

"Let's go."

The Grand Prix raced out of the parking lot. The driver of the sedan wheeled into a storage unit, got out of the car, pulled down the door, and locked it. He looked around to see if anyone was watching, but it was the time of day when activity was at a minimum. Matt's second partner then disappeared into the shadows.

After approximately a twenty-minute ride, the trio reached a mile-long access road. Worn down tire tracks and a grassy hump dominating the middle of the route were the main features of the unwelcoming path. The road was impassable after a solid rain. They had yet to encounter a battle with Ohio's sometimes severe weather, but Plan B was in place. They hoped hammers, cypress wood, and animal gathering wouldn't be necessary.

Woods lined both sides of the road as "No Hunting" and "No Trespassing" signs warned visitors that the supposed "No Outlet" route wasn't open to visitors. The linked chain attached to the pair of wooden posts on opposite sides of the road was adorned with another notice that read, "Owner will prosecute violators!"

Company obviously wasn't welcome on the property. The men escorting Preston didn't care what the signs declared.

Their routine was the same. They drove past the site and used a gravel lane about two hundred yards down the road as a turnaround point. While driving by, Matt jumped out and unhooked the chain. His partner turned the car around, flipped off the lights, and slowly pulled through the entrance as Matt reattached the chain to one of the posts.

After traveling across the beaten down road, or path as some called it, they reached and crossed the abandoned railroad tracks on the east side of the property. The road was supposed to end at a circular party site for hunters. However, the road extended for another quarter mile. When it reached the old railroad tracks, several steel plates had been placed over the rusty parallel beams so their vehicle could continue its journey.

A small grass field behind the gentlemen's temporary place of residence was on the other side of the unused tracks. They had torn down a portion of the fence, which didn't look much different than the rest of the crumbling barrier that once kept the facilities secure. They drove through the opening and into the backside of the deserted property. Johnson Road ran south of the land and into Route 23, the road that ran past the mile-long access path.

On the west side of the property was Gilbert Road, which led to a dead end where the employees' parking lot once stood. The address of the deserted property was 21522 Johnson Road. The site consumed over sixty acres. Most of the buildings looked like they should have been torn down decades ago.

A paved driveway led travelers to the security check-in building on the right side of the road. The double-gated electric fence appeared to be the only thing on the site that could be functional.

Inside the security gate, a pair of empty brick storage houses sat on the left. To the right was a good-sized garage. Two office buildings and four or five Dumpsters that should have been emptied years ago were at the end of the road. The centerpiece of the property was the warehouse. It towered over the office buildings and garage. It was a large structure and where the kidnappers called home.

They drove to the deserted warehouse and pulled inside. When Matt opened the trunk, Preston was still knocked out. They put him back there for two reasons. They didn't want him to see where their camp was stationed and didn't want him to go ballistic when he woke up from his nap.

The warehouse was a typical rundown business. It had been reduced to an ugly eyesore on the outside, but looked like the Taj Mahal compared to what was inside.

It was a gutted shell of its former self. The inside of the aged structure was old and creaky. Rusty pipes hung from the ceilings and were ready to burst without warning. Sections of the warehouse had collapsed and the rest of the structure was ready to give at a moment's notice. The remaining paint chipped beams couldn't provide support much longer. There were a few partially erected staircases, which had several missing steps, leading to the next floor. To top things off, the place was filled with asbestos.

The graffiti, courtesy of Columbus' destructive artists, was the only reason to look at the warehouse. The old tin roof had rusted due to years of Mother Nature leaving behind her acidic raindrops. Most of the windows were busted out by rock-throwing hoodlums.

It wasn't safe, but they didn't have much of a choice. It served as a location of security because it was a place no one had stepped foot in for the better part of two decades.

Preston opened his eyes and his body shook. He was startled by Matt and the other person standing over him.

"Are you going to kill me?"

"No. We're trying to help you," Matt said in a calming voice. "However, you have to agree to help us. We need you to be a player in this game against Stenson and his boys."

Preston wondered what Stenson had to do with what was going on. He knew he was a prick. He often sat at his desk daydreaming of ways to pay him back for the hard times he had given him.

"Stenson?"

"You don't need to worry about that. As I told you at Goodale Park, you will eventually understand what is going on. We are one step ahead of the guys watching us and that's all you need to know right now."

Preston recalled Matt telling him the same BS at the park. He also remembered Matt saying the guys had been after them for about ten days and weren't going to stop. The only way they were going to leave them alone was if Matt and his friend returned the missing item. There was also the option of death, which Preston wasn't interested in.

"What do you have?"

The question echoed throughout the warehouse. Both men gave Preston a dirty look and sat in silence for ten minutes.

He imagined every theory or scenario why the guys were after them and what "it" exactly was. He knew his first theory of the day—the gambling debt—was far from the truth. Preston got tired of trying to figure things out and decided to be brave.

"Tell me what they're after! If you don't, I'll tell them about this warehouse. I'm sure they have the resources to find you. I don't want to be involved."

"Listen," Matt pleaded. "You are the main reason for this mess. The meeting with Phil Seevers was a setup. Harry Stenson needed you to believe you were going to Mehaffey's for business, and Seevers will do anything for the money they're floating him. Buckeye Health is ready to start many new services, but Stenson & Rhodes will not conduct a new campaign for the company. I did some research and Buckeye Health conducts its business through an advertising agency by the name of Venture Media Corporation. Stenson & Rhodes has Seevers sign off on a few things each year claiming they provide services for Buckeye Health. He's not in the loop with what's going on, but he gets his side money and all is well."

Preston understood that Stenson & Rhodes was conducting illegal activities, but what did that have to do with him?

"Stenson wouldn't let you or his other young associates deal with an account like Buckeye Health. We're one step ahead of Stenson and we found out what was going on. Dane (who was informally introduced) bugged Stenson's office and hacked into his computer. He also has a tracking device installed in his cell phone and one on his vehicle. We retrieved your cell phone number. I called and posed as Seevers so I could switch the meeting. It's safe to say Stenson was fuming. Seevers, who was on a tight schedule, was irritated he was stood up, but didn't know what was going on."

Preston looked at the floor.

"It was a setup on both sides. You're probably wondering how you were being set up. You will find out soon enough. The reason I didn't talk to you at Goodale Park at first is because I wanted to make sure we weren't being watched by Stenson's thugs. I miscalculated and it almost cost us. We seized their item and they've been trying to repossess it ever since it became our property."

The more Matt tried to beat around the bush about what was going on, the more confused Preston became. He wished they would tell him what was going on. He knew Matt stole something from them and Dane was his technical support. What they had and where the item was at was anyone's guess.

"Let's get some sleep. We have to stay fresh to keep one step ahead of them," Dane said.

Matt and Dane showed him the former break room, which had been turned into a cozy bedroom, if that was possible in the old place. They chained one of Preston's ankles to a bedpost. They also padlocked the door from the outside so Preston would know he wasn't going anywhere.

"Trust us. We're going to make sure you're OK. That is why you're here with us."

Those were the last words Preston heard as he closed his eyes and quickly fell asleep after a long day.

STENSON WAS AT HIS office bright and early. He was briefed on the prior day's events. He knew Matt shot one of his men and kidnapped Preston after the parking garage episode. No one in Stenson's inner circle knew where Matt and his friend were hiding. They were searching for them, but didn't have any luck.

His secretary peeked around the corner.

"A gentleman is on line four."

The old gruff voice was familiar. It was a distinct voice that couldn't be forgotten. It sounded like the raspy voice of a mafia leader. Stenson and he rarely talked, but when they did, it meant business. They knew each other for quite some time, but each passing day was too long for Big Boy.

"What are you doing? Are you that incompetent? How could you let a couple of young guys possibly bring us down? Fix this mess or you will be the next target. I had to get involved and that upsets me. You know things get ugly when I'm upset."

The man on the other end hung up. Stenson had to figure things out quickly. He didn't have time to waste. He grabbed his coat and told his secretary to cancel his appointments and meetings once again. She tried to speak with him, but he disappeared behind elevator doors.

The ride wasn't pleasant for Stenson. He reached 315 and drove for what seemed like days. Big Boy didn't want to involve Gary, but didn't have a choice. He was going to Gary's house to fill him in on the situation.

He pulled up to the gate and pressed the buzzer. Within seconds, the gate opened and Stenson drove down the cobblestone driveway. O'Neil's house resembled the Playboy mansion. He moved there while Preston was in college. Preston was curious how his dad lived in one of the finest homes in Upper Arlington. Insurance money when Sharon died helped foot the bill.

Upper Arlington is one of the wealthiest areas surrounding Columbus. Upper Arlington is on the west side and there's more old money in Bexley to the east. Most of the new money is in wealthy areas that arc Columbus, including New Albany, Westerville, Powell, and Dublin. Worthington could be thrown into the mix and that's the ritziest areas around Columbus. German Village and Victorian Village are just north and south of downtown and offer residents trendy and hip lifestyles, but most people choose to live outside of downtown.

The next wave of cities includes Hilliard, Gahanna, Pickerington, and Lewis Center. A lot of upper middle-class families live there. The third tier of cities is Grove City, Reynoldsburg, Canal Winchester, and Galloway. The two least desired of the surrounding cities to live in is Groveport and Obetz. Like any big city, the suburban areas offer a lot of malls, shopping centers, and restaurants.

Gary O'Neil didn't care much for socializing. He wanted to hide out at his estate in Upper Arlington and steer clear north of downtown. Talk of Ohio State permeates three hundred sixty-five days per year and he grew sick of that rather quickly. He had heard enough O-H I-Os to last him a lifetime.

Before Stenson knocked on the door, Gary greeted him with a puzzled look.

"What brings you this way?"

"We have a dilemma on our hands. The boys have our item. We don't know where it is and we can't locate them."

"What do you want me to do?"

"That's not the entire story. We were tracking two men and were prepared to take one of them out at Goodale Park yesterday. The reason we couldn't gun down the Talbot boy near the parking lot is because he was talking to your son. Our guys chased Matt through the park and he shot Victor. We tried to follow Preston because we thought he might have the item, but after a parking garage encounter last night, we realized he didn't have it. We planned to keep a close watch on him, but someone kidnapped him as he exited the garage."

Gary sat in disbelief. He knew Preston was going to be his downfall. Despite the fact he raised Preston, it always bothered him he was not his biological father. He was starting to care less what happened to Preston and it showed.

"Do you think Preston will show up for work in the next few days?"

"Gary, they got to him and I'm sure he knows everything that has been going on over the last several years."

"I can try to talk him into coming here and staying. I know Preston is well-liked, but he doesn't have a lot of close friends. He has always been guarded because of what happened to his mother. Also, he and I haven't been the best of buddies. I'll try to reach out to him and make him feel like this is a safe place to be. At this point, I'm sure he doesn't trust anyone."

"Do you think they showed it to him?"

"If they went to the trouble to kidnap and hide him, I'm sure he knows what's going on."

"I'm sorry this is how it turned out."

The friends said good-bye and planned to stay in frequent contact.

THE BANGING ON THE bed frame finally got the best of Matt and Dane. They opened the door and Preston called them every name in the book. After five minutes of verbal abuse, Preston calmly sat on the corner of the bed.

"I don't care if you kill me. I want to know what is going on."

Matt decided it was time to let Preston know a little bit about who he was. They unlocked him from his chains and told him to take a seat on the rickety couch. The moment was tense so Preston decided to lie down and jokingly say, "OK doc, what's wrong with me?"

The three guys shared a laugh, although what Matt was about to tell Preston wasn't a laughing matter.

"This is going to be hard for you, but I'm asking you to believe every word. You might wonder how I know this information, but that's not important."

Matt delved into the story of Preston's biological father.

"Your real father's name is Kurt Carson. He was supposedly murdered at a gas station in Arizona when you were two years old."

Matt handed Preston a press clipping from an old newspaper that read: *Man shot and killed at local gas station.* Preston nodded as if to say he knew it was true. He did so while fighting tears.

"Gary O'Neil isn't who you think he is. Your adopted father told your mother he was a government official when in fact he was far from it. He traveled all over the world. Some of it was for pleasure, but none of it was to conduct business for the United States. Gary was and still is a hit man for Harry Stenson. He also works for someone else, but we'll save that for another talk. Stenson and his boys staged the attempted robbery of the gas station so they could accomplish one goal. They wanted to kill Kurt Carson. They discovered Sharon O'Neil had a dark secret of her own. Many times, she thought about leaving Gary because she knew he was living a lie. She never found out what Gary's true profession was, but knew he was putting their family in danger. She also felt he was spending time with other women."

Preston listened carefully to every word Matt spoke.

"She didn't believe in getting even, but that's what happened when she met Kurt. They met while Gary was out of town on business. It began innocently, but grew to a side romance in time. With orders from his boss, Stenson kept tabs on every person that worked under him. They also closely watched their families. They knew what Sharon was doing and eventually had to do something about it, especially when she made a startling discovery. They attempted to get rid of Kurt before Gary knew she was having an affair. They didn't want anything to cause problems for their operations."

Preston was stunned. He never expected his adopted mother to be a floozy. Doubts crept into his mind about what Matt was telling him, but he had been upfront since the moment they met. The fact he knew his father's real name triggered many thoughts.

What did he do? Where did he grow up? Did he know about him at the time of his death?

There were more questions, but one of them—why did Stenson have him killed?—was answered.

"Gary and Sharon were excited about adding another child to their family. After trying for several months, Sharon finally came back from the clinic with good news. Mr. and Mrs. O'Neil would be welcoming a second child. Throughout the pregnancy, Gary continued going out of town on business. Sharon kept seeing Kurt. Stenson, through his connections in Mesa, eventually caught on, well before Gary sought his investigative help. Stenson knew Kurt was the father and had to be eliminated."

Matt sat beside Preston to finish the story.

"It also wasn't safe to have Gary discover another man had been putting it to his old lady, which he nearly did at a dinner table discussion. If Gary found out Sharon slept with another man, he might kill both of them and bring unwanted attention to the Stenson & Rhodes' family. Stenson contemplated talking with Sharon about her private escapade, but knew she would tell Kurt and he would try to keep an eye on him. Whatever scenario he thought about, the safest way for the situation to be resolved was to get rid of Carson. The order was placed on Kurt."

"Was Gary the one who killed my real father?"

"No, and I'm not sure if he was involved. Police wrote it off as a failed robbery. The two goons involved were in and out of jail and the other man was a con artist who was on the lam from Texas."

"Why does Stenson need hit men?"

The question wasn't answered because Preston quickly asked another.

"So Sharon is my real mother and Trevor is my half-brother?"

"Yes."

Preston spent the next few minutes absorbing things. It didn't make sense that Sharon was his real mother. Why did she give him up for adoption and how did she keep it from Gary?

More truth was revealed over the next hour.

"In her seventh month, Sharon was having trouble with her pregnancy and Gary was going out of town more frequently. She needed someone with her every day and it was too dangerous to have Kurt spending time at her house. She decided to go to her mother's house in Fresno. Sharon told Gary she and Trevor were going to California for a couple months. Gary agreed with her decision. She packed her things and headed west, unknowingly accompanied by strangers. It was hard, but Sharon told Kurt he couldn't see her until after she had you. She mustered the courage to tell Gary things were over, but didn't want him flipping out and doing something that could harm her unborn child."

Preston slowly got up from the couch and said he was going to his room. They chuckled at the thought he wanted to go back to the place he fought so hard to get out of earlier that morning.

He sat down on the bed and wrapped his mind around something Matt told him in his letter. There was no doubt Matt knew who he was. Preston felt lost sitting by himself, but wanted to be alone. He spent twenty-eight years believing certain things and they were lies. Tears streamed down his face. He always wondered who his real mother was, but to find out the way he did was difficult.

Matt and Dane made brunch, but Preston wasn't in the mood to eat. He told them he wanted to be alone for a while. He spent ten hours in the bedroom thinking about his life and where it was headed.

At that moment, it seemed like it was going nowhere.

Chapter Four

A PAIR OF PHOTOS accompanied the white note card inside the manila envelope. The arrival of the unwanted correspondence almost sent Sharon into labor. She wondered how anyone knew her mother's address and who was on the other end of the cruel joke.

"Tell anyone you received this note or show anyone these photos and you will wind up sleeping with the fishes."

The photos were horrifying. Both pictures sent a clear message. Someone was watching and she didn't know what they wanted. One photo showed her having a good time with Kurt at their spot in Mesa. Sharon couldn't figure out how they discovered her secret.

Sharon hadn't told anyone about her fling with Kurt because she was ashamed. Her first thought was to call Kurt, but she figured they were watching him as well. She didn't want to chance it.

The second photograph was of Trevor. On the Polaroid, it read, "If you love your child, you will give up your child."

She didn't know what the statement meant. They could be asking her to get an abortion, which was inconceivable as far along as she was. Maybe they were asking her to give her child up for adoption or they wanted Trevor. She needed answers.

Gary called from Boston to see how she and Trevor were doing. She nearly caved in and told him the truth, but thought of them harming Trevor or doing something to her.

"I'm doing fine," she lied. "Trevor's also doing well."

"Put him on the phone."

"Hi daddy," the cute voice on the other end of the phone mumbled. "I miss you. When are you coming to grandma's house?"

It hurt Gary that he wasn't there for his son, but he never outwardly showed his emotions. He rarely spent time with his family, but that was a self-serving decision made years earlier. At times he missed Sharon, but his lady companions often kept him away from those feelings. He felt badly for Trevor, knowing he was going to grow up without the full-time presence of his father. Gary dealt with an abusive father when he was young and swore he would never be like his dad. Most men make that declaration, but there comes a time when they realize, "I am my dad!"

"I won't be home for a few more weeks. Do you want daddy to buy you something while he's here in Boston?"

"Yeah, I want some ice cream."

Gary laughed at the thought of sending ice cream through the mail. Sharon would swap a sticky, chocolate-stained piece of mail for the correspondence she received.

"I have to go. I love you!"

It was a typical conversation. He and Sharon's communication line was usually open for about thirty seconds and that was pushing it. She resented everything about Gary. She gave up her career to be closer to home and start a family. Sharon wished Gary would have done the same.

A few days passed and a second manila envelope showed up in Fresno. Sharon was supposed to be off her feet, but was checking the mail every day. She figured more unwanted mail was on the way.

Sharon went into the den and eased into a chair. Fortunately, there weren't any photographs, but what was in the envelope was worse. There were papers from an orphanage in Mesa. The note read, "You will give him up at some point. You know what you have done and we're going to fix the problem."

She understood they wanted her to give Preston up for adoption. She would never do that. She was weeks away from popping the little one out and knew Gary would be back from Boston. After days of thinking, she came up with a plan.

Kurt would raise Preston. Sharon was going to tell Gary she had a miscarriage and give Kurt the child. The blood test would prove he was Preston's father and the state would allow Kurt to raise the boy.

The only roadblock was Sharon didn't know who was sending the materials to her mother's house. They would know she didn't give her child up for adoption. It was obvious they were safeguarding someone. They weren't protecting her or Trevor, so Gary was the remaining choice. It was time to talk to someone about her problem.

Although it was well past 11:00 p.m., Sharon picked up the receiver and dialed a number she hadn't called since she left Mesa.

"Hello."

"It's Sharon. I'm sorry to call so late. I have a major problem and I need to talk about it. I received two manila envelopes this week at my mom's house. The first piece of mail included two photos and a note card. One of the pictures shows our naked bodies firmly pressed against each other and the other photo is of Trevor. The note says they will kill me if I spout a word. The message on Trevor's picture reads, "If you love your child, you will give up your child."

Kurt wanted to stop Sharon, but let her finish.

"I think Gary is affiliated with the mafia. They know about us and that's not all. I received a second piece of mail today. I expected more photos and six-feet under threats, but the envelope only contained four sheets of paper, all from an orphanage in Mesa."

He tried to calm her.

"It's not good for you to be so upset. What do you want me to do?"

"You have to leave Mesa! You're not safe. I screwed up. I'm not sure who is watching us, but they're not messing around."

They quickly got off the phone and Kurt peeked through the blinds in the front window. He didn't see anything unusual. He rushed to his bedroom and stuffed a backpack full of two or three day's worth of clothes. To be safe, he snuck out the back door. Kurt reached the halfway point in the alley behind his house and the explosion nearly launched him to the end of the crushed gravel roadway.

As he looked back at what was left of his house, ashes fell from the sky like rain. The blazing inferno glowed brightly and made the dark night seem like a full moon was overhead. Debris was scattered throughout the neighborhood as if a tornado ripped through the area. Every canine was barking like a group of mailmen had invaded their turf. Inquisitive neighbors were flipping on their porch lights one after another and Kurt knew he had to hide.

He had several scrapes and rapidly appearing bruises to go along with a massive headache. Kurt knew who they were after. He picked himself up and grabbed his backpack. The only way to get to the bus stop was to weave in and out of shadows, cutting through back yards.

It didn't take long to hear the faint screech of sirens. Kurt knew police and emergency crews were set to turn his block into a spectacle. He envisioned people walking up as far as police would let them on both sides of the street. He knew the people responsible for demolishing his house would keep an eye on things as well.

Kurt was within forty yards of the bus stop and noticed a strange man leaning against a wall. He darted behind Marlow's Body Shop and watched the man for five minutes. The guy had an athletic build and could chase Kurt down if there was a foot race. Kurt noticed him looking around more than he should have been. He also was on the pay phone twice in those five minutes. The Greyhound pulled up and when it disappeared, the man was still standing against the wall.

Headlights nearly gave Kurt's I-spy spot away. He made his way behind a trash bin and peered around the corner. The car stopped at the bus depot. The shady man looked around once more before giving up. He got in the car and the driver pulled away.

Were they looking for Kurt? It could have been a coincidence, but maybe they discovered he made it out of his house alive. He thought about going back, but didn't want anyone to know he made it out safely. Kurt noticed an old shed on the backside of Marlow's. There wasn't a lock on it. When he opened the squeaky doors, he saw a few tires and greasy spare parts. He moved a few of the parts aside and made a spot where he could lie down, using his backpack as a pillow.

Morning was rapidly approaching and he needed to rest before figuring out his next move.

PRESTON HEARD A CAR and wondered what was going on. He had drifted away while soaking in new information he received earlier in the day.

"Preston, it's 11 o'clock and we need to get you to your meeting at the parking garage."

"I'm not going to that garage again. I took one beating from them and don't want to experience another. They will probably kill me if they see me again. Why can't you give them their item and move on?"

"Because we don't have it," Matt stated. "And relax! You're not going to attend their meetings."

Preston was baffled. Matt told Preston he found the item a few weeks earlier and the men chasing Matt told Preston the same thing. If they didn't have it, who did?

"It's in a safe place with someone they would never expect."

Matt and Dane were taking Preston on a roller coaster ride and the twists and turns weren't going to stop.

They escorted Preston from his room and got in the car. They didn't like leaving at night, but they had to get close to the expected meeting.

They drove past the garage at 11:25 and Matt dialed Stenson.

"Who is in the garage?"

"What are you talking about?"

"Don't play dumb with me Stenson! I know you're planning on killing us if you get the chance. The man in the garage told Preston he was to meet them at eleven-thirty every night until they reclaimed their item. Do you think we're stupid? I have killed one of your boys. Don't make us drive in there and finish off the rest of your crew."

As they passed by a second time, Matt saw a green Pontiac Vibe pulling into the parking garage.

"If you're waiting on us, we're driving a green Pontiac Vibe."

Matt told Dane to pull over so they could watch.

After they nestled next to the curb across the street, a black Expedition squealed around the corner and raced into the parking garage.

"The trap is set," Matt said over a walkie-talkie.

As the Vibe made its way to the second level, the Expedition rammed into the back of it and pushed the green vehicle into a parked car. Three guys jumped out of the Expedition and surrounded the Vibe.

"Get out of the car!"

The couple in the car was terrified.

"What do you want from us?"

It was clear the couple didn't have anything to do with their predicament. The men contemplated executing them, but decided it wasn't worth the trouble or commotion.

However, the person stationed in the parking garage wasn't worried about causing a commotion. Bullets from the gun ricocheted throughout the garage and mowed down two of Stenson's thugs. The remaining henchman fired shots back as he sought shelter. He was able to reach the Expedition and slam it into reverse, leaving four black patches from the tires behind on the concrete. The noise from the gunfire was deafening and didn't make hanging around an option. The man hollered to the couple, "Are you OK?"

Both replied "yes" and that satisfied him. He stashed the gun into an opening of a broken block in the wall and darted into a stairwell. He reached ground level, slipped out the side, and scurried to the waiting vehicle.

"We have to get out of here."

Preston recognized the man who got in the car. He was the driver of the chocolate sedan.

"I got two of them, but one got away. He couldn't see me, but I guarantee they will be hot on our trail if we don't get moving."

They all agreed and headed back to the warehouse.

The group assembled near G-19 on the seventh floor heard the shots. Before they made their way past the scene on the second floor, police officers arrived.

Demands of "Stop the vehicle" and "Get out of the car" blared over a megaphone. The vehicle came to a halt and four men exited the vehicle with their hands in the air. One of the officers recognized the front passenger.

"Robert, you have some explaining to do. With your checkered past, I'm sure you were in the middle of the shootout."

"None of us were involved."

The man and woman who survived the incident verified Robert and his friends weren't involved.

"We were on the seventh floor going over business. We parked there earlier before going to dinner. When we returned to the car, we stood there about five minutes and then heard shots. We jumped in the car and hurried down here. When we turned the corner, we saw the same scene you discovered."

The lead detective arrived and questioned Robert and his crew. He decided they were innocent, but told them a visit to the station was possible if additional information was needed.

Robert called Stenson when they pulled out of the garage.

"What happened in there? Do you know two of our men were gunned down? We have lost three guys in two days. You have until the end of this week to find them and get this mess resolved."

While Stenson's group was flustered, Matt and his crew were enjoying what was going on. Preston still wasn't sure what to think. He was told Gary was a hit man and Stenson ran a dirty business. That seemed true, but Matt killed a man and the other person in the car finished off two of his own. For those keeping score, it was three to nothing in favor of the people Preston was involved with. He wasn't fond of associating with murderers, even if it was for a good reason.

Things were being answered, but not fast enough. Preston laid his head back and caught a quick nap.

When they reached the path, the chain was unhooked.

"Do you think some kids are partying?" Dane questioned.

"I'm not sure. We're not going down the path. Let's drive to Johnson Road and see if anything's going on."

The foursome turned onto Johnson and drove past the warehouse. There was a car at the entrance gate and it seemed their place of residence had been discovered. Preston tried to calm the intense moment.

"Boys, it looks like we have been evicted."

It drew a slight chuckle from Dane and the other man, but Matt didn't crack a smile. They would have to find somewhere else to stay. They passed Gilbert and turned around at the top of a hill on Johnson.

As they drove down the hill toward the warehouse, Dane flipped off the lights and eased over to the side of the road.

"Pop the trunk!" Matt demanded.

He returned to the car with night vision binoculars and surveyed the scene. Their nervousness was erased. They wouldn't need a new place of residence. It was a false alarm.

"What do you see?" questioned the unidentified man in the car.

"I'll let Preston tell you," Matt said as he handed him the binoculars.

Preston focused the lenses so he could take a look. When he had a clear view, it was obvious a motel room wasn't necessary. The lovers were going at it hot and heavy. They looked like a young high school couple, which answered whether there was a party near their usual entrance.

"What are we going to do?" Preston asked. "We can't sit here all night."

They decided to interrupt the couple. They pulled beside the rocking auto and all they could see through the steamed windows was a naked girl jumping off a boy. Matt shined a flashlight into their car and the boy didn't waste time. He didn't worry about getting dressed. He pulled onto Johnson and was gone in seconds.

They thought about calling the sheriff to investigate if there was a party on the dirt lane, but couldn't risk the sheriff discovering their entrance to the old warehouse. That option would have ended their stay at the paradise hotel. Matt wondered if some kids meandered farther down the path and entered the warehouse.

They decided to drive down the lane to see what was going on. As they crept to the entrance, Preston noticed the chain was fastened. They thought the passionate couple might have driven back to the party and told the rest of their friends what happened or maybe Stenson and his crew was on to them.

"What do we do?" Dane asked.

"We have to go to our second home until we can figure out what is going on here," Matt said.

"Great," Preston thought. If the warehouse was their main home, he couldn't wait to see where their weekend cottage was located. Maybe they would stay at a boarded up shack in one of the abandoned sections of town or possibly a roadside rest area. With his current running mates, anything was possible.

THE RINGING NOISE SERVED as an alarm clock. It wasn't a five-star hotel, but Kurt slept well in the old shed, until he was interrupted by the doorbell-like racket that served as a wake-up call.

Everything about Marlow's was old school. The coke machine that once served icy cold twelve-ounce bottles still stood. A rubber hose stretched across the entrance to the parking lot. As each car drove over it, a ding-ding rang out as both the front and back tires rolled over the hose. Old filling stations and body shops had those to signal when someone needed service or attention and Marlow's still conducted business that way. Too many vehicles needed attention that morning in Kurt's estimation.

He pulled himself off his make-shift bed and heard nearly every bone crack. Part of his aches and pains were from sleeping in the shed and the rest of his joints hurt from being helplessly launched in the air from the previous night's explosion.

Kurt closed his left eye and peeked through the slight opening of the shed. He didn't see anyone, so he quietly opened the creaky doors. He walked around the back of the building and looked around the corner. As he peered across the street where the man was picked up the night before, he noticed one of Marlow's mechanics walking toward him. He didn't want to be seen. It wasn't safe for anyone to know he made it out of his house. He scurried to the trash bin he hid behind the night before.

He heard a lighter flick a few times. His sense of smell took over. The aroma of the man's unwashed overalls could be smelled from twenty-five yards away. Most body shops employ the same kind of workers. They all look five to ten years older than their age. Despite looking like they couldn't whip their way out of a soaked brown bag, they have been in more bar fights than an army of men combined.

Most own two or three muscle cars or a motorcycle. Every Hank or Pete has a permanent stain of tobacco drizzled down their chin and a mouthful of teeth that make dentists cringe.

He probably had enough dirt under his fingernails to plant a nice row of corn and more grease on his body than a can of Crisco.

The next smell only added to the certainty he was a typical auto body man. The sound of the lighter being flicked was soon joined by a second sound—a small cough. It gave away what he was doing. A drag or two of what he was pulling on was exactly what Kurt needed.

He waited for the man to disappear around the corner. He scoped the scene and saw several semis being gassed up at the filling station next to the Greyhound stop. Kurt found an old beat up ball cap in the shed. He pulled it down to his eyes and walked to the station. When one of the drivers neared his rig, Kurt approached him.

"Where ya headed?"

"Fresno."

Kurt wasn't a religious man, but loosely believed there was an ultimate being. It was the first time he recalled thinking someone was looking out for him.

"Any chance I could hitch a ride? Just name your asking price."

"I guess I could use some company," the driver said. "You don't have to pay me. All you need to do is buy my lunch."

It was worth the price of admission. A ticket to ride the Greyhound would run him $25 or so. They hopped in the rig and drove off.

The driver wasn't talkative at first and it didn't bother Kurt. He hoped he wouldn't have to answer many questions. He didn't feel like being grilled about his personal life or giving a stranger his biography.

"Where were you coming from when I picked you up back at the station?"

"I got drunk last night with some friends. One of my buddies is getting married next month so he had a bachelor's party this weekend. I live in Fresno and I rode a bus here. I hate to fly and I'm not much of a driver. I usually take a bus whenever I go on trips. Most of us that got together are old college friends. Some flew in from Pittsburgh, Atlanta, Austin…"

The driver interrupted him as he spewed out the word Austin.

"That's where I'm from. I have lived there all my life. Hook 'Em Horns!"

They shared a laugh. Kurt wasn't a college football fan, but he wasn't stupid. He knew what that meant.

"We spent Friday night sharing old stories when we arrived in Mesa. We went golfing yesterday before hitting the town last night. We got wasted and that's why I look like I'm on a four-day drug binge. I went home with some woman from the last bar we visited. She lives behind the body shop across the street from the gas station. I wasn't sure how to get back to my friend's house. I tried to reach him and didn't get an answer. I saw the Greyhound station out the woman's back window when I woke up. I put on my clothes and headed over to get a ticket. The next bus headed to California wasn't leaving until 7:00 p.m. That's when I saw you."

It was one of the silliest big fish stories, but it satisfied the driver's curiosity. The story seemed to dot every *i* and cross every *t*. The only part he should have left out was his fictitious fling.

"I'm a God-fearing man. The Bible says in I Corinthians 6:18-20, 'Flee from sexual immorality. All other sins a man commits are outside his body, but he who sins sexually sins against his own body. Do you not know that your body is a temple of the Holy Spirit, who is in you, whom you have received from God? You are not your own; you were bought at a price. Therefore honor God with your body.' It's one of the hardest sins for a single person to avoid, but it's an important message. I'm not one to judge, but there is someone greater judging us up above."

His sermon wasn't necessary because Kurt had not committed that sin over the weekend, but he was certain the "judge" would declare him guilty of several counts over the years.

"Did you hear about the explosion while you were in Mesa last night?" the driver asked as he reached for the dashboard to grab a newspaper he picked up while checking out at the gas station.

The photo of his blown up house made him sick. He knew if Sharon waited another thirty minutes to call him, he would have been charcoal and facing the "judge" preacher man was talking about.

Kurt began reading the front page story. There were quotes from nearby neighbors who said typical things like, "It sounded like a bomb going off" or "I heard this loud noise that sounded like a car crash."

The story didn't offer many details, but the fire chief's comments bothered Kurt.

"We have ruled out foul play. It looks like it generated from the gas line. That's all I can say at this point."

Kurt knew someone was watching him and Sharon. She was receiving blackmail materials at her mother's house and someone tried to kill him. The fire chief shouldn't rule out foul play. That was the only possibility. A bomb detonated and he was saying it was a gas line. Kurt wondered if they paid him off. He wished he knew who they were. Without knowing who was responsible for sending letters to Sharon and attempting to kill him, there was nothing that could be done.

He knew he had to reach Sharon. They needed to find a place to hide.

The men stopped for lunch and Kurt picked up the tab. The driver's name was Jim Alexander. He was married and had three kids. They lived on a small farm, which Jim tended to on weekends. His wife and kids took care of it during the week. Those were a few facts Kurt learned about Jim during lunch.

Kurt never talked about himself. It was easy to ask questions and listen to Jim answer each one with a fifteen-minute reply. For a guy that didn't have much to say earlier, he made up for it after lunch. Kurt wanted to catch a nap before reaching Fresno, but it didn't happen.

When they pulled into town, Jim wheeled into a truck stop. Kurt offered to pay him, but Jim refused. They talked for ten minutes before parting ways. As Kurt headed up the sidewalk to a phone booth, Jim hollered, "I have something for you."

It made Kurt leery, but he went back to see what Jim wanted to give him. A Gideon's Bible was a possibility.

"If you're ever in Austin, please call me and come out to the farm. I would love to introduce you to my family. Our home is open to you any time you would like to visit."

"I appreciate it. Like I told you, I don't like to fly, but I enjoy taking road trips. If I'm down that way, I will make sure to come and see your spread."

Kurt put the piece of paper with Jim's number in his front pocket and said a last good-bye.

Chapter Five

BIG BOY AND HIS group reluctantly met at Stenson & Rhodes. Each hit man walked into the room and sat down, staring at the table. They didn't know the other assassins seated around the table. It was also the first time they had seen their employers.

The man identified as Robert was present and his look said it best. As Preston discovered in the parking garage, the man didn't mess around.

Who was the man Preston thought resembled a mob leader? His name was Robert Michael Rhodes. Like Gary and Harry, Robert and Big Boy were longtime friends. With each passing day, the less they became friends. They were more like associates than golfing buddies. They tried to stay out of the public's eye because it wasn't good for business if they were seen together.

Rhodes needed Stenson's help in the 80s. The pockets in every pair of pants, slacks, jeans, and shorts Robert owned were endless. Stenson helped him out of the jam for a nominal fee, but things never went away.

Rhodes' problems began innocently, but became worse the more he tried to fix them. The Hayes Carlson Company operated a magnesium and beryllium processing facility for the government in the 30s. The plant was used until 1943 when it was shut down.

In 1949, it reopened as an aluminum factory and survived until 1961 when it was purchased by Vandervort Tire Industries. The company was bought out by the Rhodes Tire and Rubber Company in 1973 and closed in 1987 as a new plant opened on the outskirts of Cincinnati.

Before the move was announced, Rhodes hired Stenson, who only had a few clients at the time. A campaign was conducted to help the company's image. It was beneficial to those who relocated their families and moved to Cincinnati. The campaign made a splash in Cincinnati and the Rhodes Tire and Rubber Company became one of the fastest rising companies in the Midwest.

Not only did the campaign help business improve for Rhodes, but the Stenson PR Firm grew nearly 500 percent over the next few years. It eventually became Stenson & Rhodes.

The main reason Rhodes closed the premises and moved to the Queen City is because several areas were found to have residual radioactivity exceeding criteria and beryllium waste. Employees were getting sick by the handfuls. The longer the company stayed near Columbus, the more sick time Rhodes Tire and Rubber Company paid out.

To avoid legal action from employees, Rhodes bought some of them out. It was costly and problematic, but it was only the start of his troubles.

Matt Talbot, and whoever was helping him, had become his biggest problem. Rhodes knew the problem, or problems, needed to be eliminated.

"The reason for this meeting is we're missing something that belongs to us. We also have lost three men—Victor, Marco, and Pavel. Jensen witnessed each shooting," Rhodes said pointing at Jensen. "We underestimated Talbot and his crew. They managed to get into the building and bug the phones. They also hacked into the network and kept tabs on what we have been up to. We had our vehicles searched and they found a tracking device on Stenson's. His phone had a tracer on it. We think they know everything we've done."

Rhodes walked around the table twice, collecting his thoughts.

"Earlier, we had the phones in the building replaced and installed new computers. There is a new cell phone in front of you with a different number. Place your old phone in the middle of the table and they will be destroyed when we leave. We're not sure if they still have inside connections, but with Preston out of the building, that should help our cause, with all due respect to you Gary. We also hired two security guards to watch the front door."

The lights dimmed and a photo flashed on the screen.

"All the things I mentioned are problems and some have been dealt with. If we don't get this back, each of us in this room and anyone associated with our group could be in trouble."

WITH THE WAREHOUSE UNSAFE, they had to go to their second hideout, which wasn't much of a safe haven. Matt hoped they wouldn't have to stay there for several reasons, but they didn't have a choice.

Fifteen minutes into the ride, Preston began wondering where they would end up. He decided to break the silence.

"Where are we staying?"

"At an old friend's house."

They drove another ten minutes and got off 270. A few miles down the road, they pulled into the Residents of Everett Wren apartment complex and cautiously drove around different sections. They passed through the complex and pulled back onto Morse Road. They circled around two more times before feeling things were safe.

They parked their car several units away from where they would be staying. Matt led the way as they walked around the backside of the apartments.

On a back porch overlooking a wooded area, Matt reached underneath a grill, pulling out a tiny magnetic box. He slid the box open and took out the key.

"Wait while I make sure it's all right to crash here."

He unlocked the sliding glass door and went inside. It seemed like they stood on the concrete slab for nearly an hour before Matt pulled the door open and whispered, "Come in."

A small trickle of light radiated from the only bedroom, but the rest of the place was dark.

"The tenant is getting us blankets and pillows. I'll sleep in the recliner and the rest of you can fight over the couch."

"Who lives here?" Preston asked.

He didn't receive an answer. While Preston tried to figure out where they were staying, Dane claimed the couch. Preston was reserved to pulling up a spot on the floor. Matt returned with blankets and pillows.

"It looks like you and Brock can cuddle."

It was one of Matt's bad habits. Preston received another odd introduction to one of his associates.

"Try to get some sleep. Preston, don't snoop around! You will understand where we are in the morning," Matt said before he plopped in a recliner.

Preston tossed and turned for an hour. He knew he was the only one awake because his captors had their chainsaws out. He got up and tip-toed down the hallway. He reached the bathroom, slowly shut the door, and locked it. He felt around for the light and turned it on. He quickly noticed there was a woman staying at the apartment. The products sitting on the counter and lavender towels gave it away.

There was a fuzzy bathrobe hanging on the back of the door and the shower curtain was aqua and pink. He opened all three drawers on the left side of the sink area. Q-tips, hair brushes, toothpaste, tampons, and other feminine things found in a bathroom were in the drawers.

He couldn't find items hinting a man stayed at the apartment. There weren't photographs of family or friends. There were a few scenic pictures of the beach on the wall, but that was it.

A slight knock startled Preston. He flushed the toilet and turned on the faucet. He washed his hands and toweled them off before opening the door. Matt greeted him with an inquisitive look.

"Is everything all right?"

"Yes. I had to use the bathroom."

"I'm making sure everything is OK. We need to get a good night's sleep. We have to get back to the warehouse in the morning."

Preston returned to the living room and covered up. He laid there for a while and eventually drifted off. Usually, he didn't remember his dreams, but the one about Sharon that night was surreal. Preston woke up and quickly realized it was a dream.

The second thing he noticed was the smell of a fantastic breakfast. He was more than ready for free samples. The sun was taking its time rising, but Preston saw signs of daylight through the transparent black curtains hanging from a rod above the sliding glass doors.

The kitchen light was the only one on in the apartment. The rest of the place was still dark, despite the sun making its slow ascension outside. He was lying on his back and lifted his head to see Brock was still knocked out. It was easy to hear Dane battling Paul Bunyan for lumberjack supremacy on the couch. He turned onto his left side and looked up at the recliner. Matt was up.

Matt heard Preston rustling and walked into the living room from the kitchen area.

"Breakfast is almost finished. You should take a shower before we eat."

Preston agreed and headed to the bathroom. The warm shower was his first in days. Like most showers after a multiple-day hiatus, his cleanliness made him feel like a new person. When he came out of the bathroom, he headed to the kitchen area with two objectives. The first was to see what was being served and his second goal was to discover who paid the rent.

The menu included most breakfast favorites—bacon, eggs, toast, and orange juice. There were also packets of instant oatmeal, bananas, and a box of Cheerios. Preston was pleased with the smorgasbord.

"Take a seat," Matt said while assembling his plate. "Dane and Brock, get up! It's time to eat."

As they slowly got up and lumbered to the table, Preston wondered if anyone else would join them.

"Is it just us eating?"

"This is it," Matt responded.

Preston couldn't understand why the person who lived at the residence was like Boo Radley. Matt had talked with her or him, but was it that important to keep their identity a secret?

Dane and Brock took their places at the table and Preston questioned them.

"Do you know where we're staying?"

"We're not at liberty to answer questions," Dane replied. "If Matt wants you to know, he will tell you. I know it has to be hard, but it's for your own good to know as little as possible."

Preston grew increasingly frustrated and reached his breaking point. He started screaming at the top of his lungs.

"Who lives here?"

"Why are you allowing them to do this to me?"

"Please, help me!"

It was too early for anyone to cause a ruckus. Matt jumped up from the table and pulled a gun.

"Stop hollering or I'll give you something to yell about! No one is here. They already left. Do you want to give us away? We're doing what's best for everyone involved. You're going to appreciate this when everything is said and done."

Preston acted like his tantrum was over. He calmed down and began eating. Five minutes passed and Preston jumped from his seat and raced down the hall. Matt, Dane, nor Brock were expecting the move and couldn't stop him.

As Preston reached the door knob and turned it, he discovered it was locked. He heard footsteps behind him and didn't have much time to react. He stepped back and kicked the door in. Preston darted into the room and stood in disbelief.

He tried to say something, but nothing came out.

The person sitting on the bed was also stunned. She knew he was there, but wasn't expecting an FBI-like raid on her bedroom. Dane grabbed Preston and pulled him out of the room, but it was too late. Matt was irate. He didn't want to stay at the apartment because of what occurred. Matt knew staying there was risky. Maybe they should have stayed at the warehouse and taken that risk.

Preston walked to the living room and sat on the couch. He heard Matt talking, but couldn't make out what he was saying.

"Dane and Brock, come in here," Matt said.

The men standing over Preston left him alone. The last time he was alone, he had a shackle around his ankle and was sucking in asbestos. He didn't count the hot shower because he was forced to leave the door cracked.

Preston could have made a second mad dash and ran out the back of the apartment. He was so shocked he couldn't move. He bent over and put his face into his hands. After sitting unattended for about ninety seconds, a second person joined him on the couch. Her touch was as soft as it had been years earlier.

"Before you say anything...I'm sorry!" Lauren said.

He rose up and couldn't look at her.

"You're sorry? Lauren, you broke my heart. I know you wanted to get married and expected me to ask that night at Goodale. We were too young. I loved you enough to know I wanted to be with you the rest of my life, but I felt we needed to wait until we were finished with college and established."

Lauren tried to interrupt, but Preston wouldn't allow it.

"Look at how things turned out. You ended 'us' and haven't tried to contact me since. You wouldn't take my phone calls and eventually changed your number. I e-mailed, but you canceled your account. I drove by your apartment and you had moved. I stopped by your work and they said you quit. I didn't believe it and sat outside for days. I never saw a trace of you."

"I'm..."

"I called your friends and Sarah told me you met someone and moved to Chicago. I drove to The Windy City and spent a month trying to find you. When I got back to Columbus, I went to visit Sarah again to see if she could give me more information. She was gone."

"I'm so sorry."

"I have thought about you every day, wondering if you were married and had a family of your own. I thought about the man you left me for and moved to Chicago with. I have asked myself over and over again, 'What made him better than me?'"

Preston could have poured his heart out for three days without taking a breath. Lauren finally started giving him answers. She sat something beside her on the floor and handed Preston a letter.

Lauren,

Your dad is very sick. We know he is having trouble making it to work because the cancer is slowly killing him. Your family doesn't have enough insurance to cover the expenses they are racking up. It's admirable you are working a second job to help pay for things. We have seen the benefits and golf outings in the newspaper to help raise money for your family. There is a way you can help your family. We have a blank check and are ready to put a two on it, which will be followed by five zeros.

You may wonder what you have to do to receive this money. It's easy. End your relationship with Preston O'Neil and a check will show up at the Emory residence. If you say no, you can watch your parents lose everything and probably say good-bye to your father. Would you rather say good-bye to your father or walk away from Preston? If you end things with him, you can't speak to him again. We will keep tabs on you and will know if you have even so much as looked at him.

We know this is a hard decision, but you have three days to make your choice. All you have to do is scribble yes or no on a piece of paper. You need to deliver it to a man at the Convocation Center on Thursday at noon. He will be on the side closest to the football stadium.

Good luck with your choice!

Preston was crying and finally looked at Lauren. She was also crying.

"I wish you would have let me know what happened. I wouldn't expect you to choose me over your dad. I have spent all this time wondering why you walked away and never explained things. This makes things a little clearer."

"I never went to Chicago, but I left Columbus for a few years. I was watched the first three years, but haven't seen anyone following me for quite some time. A guy I worked with posed as my boyfriend and that is why Sarah told you I left for Chicago. After she told me you talked to her, I gave her thirty-five hundred dollars to move and told her you were starting to get crazy. I also said you threatened to hurt her if I didn't come back to you. It was wrong, but I couldn't take the chance of losing the opportunity to save my dad."

"Did he make it?"

"Yes and no. He lived another three years before passing away. I wanted to find you after he went to be with God, but I got another letter in the mail. It said it didn't matter if my dad had died, I still couldn't be with you. Mom and I bought a new house in Dublin and that's where I lived until moving here a few months ago. I decided to move on with my life. That is when I met Matt."

"Are you together?"

Lauren laughed at Preston's question.

"No. We're friends. I was the first person he sought when he discovered what was going on. He told me most of the story and I was amazed at the things I heard. He told you some of the things I know and you will appreciate what he's doing for you."

Preston had butterflies as she talked. He felt like he had lost her forever, but felt life again as he sat there on the couch with her. Preston had not been on a date since Lauren ended their relationship. Lauren looked as good as the first day he saw her. He wanted to lean over and kiss her, but knew it would be inappropriate.

"Matt, would you like to rejoin us?"

The men exited Lauren's bedroom and walked into the living room.

"You have been wondering what we have. Look in Lauren's lap and you will know," Matt said.

Preston looked at the old raggedy thing and wondered why it was so relevant. He had gone through two of them at Stenson & Rhodes. Why would anyone care if they lost the ugly item sitting on Lauren's lap?

"Your hallowed item couldn't fetch five bucks at a yard sale. Why is that stupid thing so important to them?"

"Do you remember when I told you Gary was a hit man? He's not the only one," Matt explained. "We have killed three of them. Excluding Gary, seven remain, unless there are more we don't know about. The item sitting in Lauren's lap is how they conduct business."

Matt took the briefcase from Lauren and handed it to Preston.

"There is only one set of keys, but we found out where they were hidden. We stole the keys and made copies before returning them to the post office. We discovered where the briefcase was housed. It took time to get into the apartment, especially without being seen, but once we stole it, the cat and mouse game began."

Matt reached into his pocket and pulled out a key ring with three keys on it—one for the post office box, one to open the briefcase, and a third to open a compartment inside the briefcase. He handed the keys to Preston and told him to open the case.

Preston opened it and found a map inside. The numbers 16-9-24-11-3-18-10-3-21 were inscribed on the map and 11 was circled.

"What does this mean?"

"Keep going and I will explain it. Find the other key to open the compartment," Matt instructed.

Preston did as he was told. The only thing he noticed was a folder. He reached inside the folder and pulled out a photo. It was a picture of himself.

"What is my picture doing in this briefcase?"

"Here is how things are done. When we found the briefcase, we opened it and found the same things you did," Matt said as he handed him an old book. "Take the series of numbers and look through the first twenty-six pages."

Preston grabbed a pencil and jotted down the letters, which eventually spelled Columbus.

"What does this mean?"

He was instructed to look up the circled number in the index. Preston scanned the country list for 11. When he found 11 next to the United States, Matt grabbed the photo of Preston and ripped off the bottom right corner.

"Let's head to Lauren's bedroom."

The group went into her room and Dane closed the door. Lauren flipped on a black light on her night stand and Matt told them to huddle around.

"Dane, turn off the lights!"

The only thing visible in the room was the name Preston O'Neil on the torn piece of paper. Dane turned the lights back on and Preston had a curious look on his face.

"Preston, the city you live in is Columbus. The country you live in is the United States. It's obvious the glamour shot in the briefcase was you and that your name was stamped on the piece of paper. You were their next mark. That is where the meeting with Seevers came into play. We believe you were going to be gunned down outside Mehaffey's Pub. Just because we stopped them from accomplishing their goal of taking you out at that meeting...they will continue to hunt you down. The good news is only one hit man knows you are the next mark. We're sure Stenson and Rhodes know as well, but they may put out an APB and have everyone search for you."

"How am I going to avoid being killed?"

"I'll be honest. We're not sure we can keep you alive or any of us for that matter," Matt said. "We're all in trouble because of what we discovered and disrupted. We have a plan that could change our fortunes. We'll continue with our plans, but may have to accelerate things."

Of course, Preston wasn't tuned in to what those plans were, but Stenson and Rhodes had met their match. Matt and his crew were causing a living hell for the corporate big wigs. The chess match was becoming a true battle of wits.

They didn't know they were no longer able to eavesdrop on the happenings at Stenson & Rhodes and that was a problem. Matt, Dane, and Brock had stayed one step ahead of them, but Big Boy and his band of henchmen had evened the playing field, despite losing a few members from their team.

Everyone went back to the living room and, for the first time in a few days, relaxed and shared some laughs. The mood changed quickly. Lauren answered the phone and her look of terror said everything Matt and the rest of the guys needed to know.

The playing field was in fact even.

THE PICTURE ON THE screen in front of the room would have looked ordinary to someone who wasn't in the loop. Most business people are accompanied by one at their side. Some high-end professionals own two or three. They come in different shapes, colors, sizes, and price ranges, but the briefcase on the screen was not a run-of-the-mill case.

Black is favored by most working professionals. The fact it was brown made it different. Most briefcases look reasonably new, but not the one on the screen. It was once a deep brown that resembled a new Rawlings baseball glove and the exterior had a deep shine to it that screamed, "My owner is rich."

When the briefcase was opened, one whiff brought to mind the scent of a new car. However, the old tattered item showing on the big screen had seen its best days and looked like it needed to be put out to pasture.

The outside was scuffed, rendering it a shade of beige. If someone walked off the transit and left it sitting by their seat, it more than likely would be there the next day.

The new smell had been replaced. If lawlessness, deceit, treachery, evil, wickedness, murder, or any other synonym grouped with those words had a scent, that's how the inside smelled.

The contents of the briefcase were simple. The NRA would be disappointed because it didn't reek of gun powder or cold steel. Launderers would also be dejected because dead presidents weren't welcome. Only four things had a place in the old briefcase.

To find out what was in the briefcase, each hit man had to retrieve the keys to open it. A post office box was rented out and a forward was put on the box to Stenson & Rhodes. The bill was always paid, so the forward didn't draw attention. The only thing inside of the box was a set of keys. Each member of Stenson and Rhodes' crew had a key to the box to get to the keys. Upon receiving an assignment, they drove over to the post office around 5:00 a.m. and retrieved the set of keys.

The next destination was to a rented apartment on the west side of Columbus. The apartment wasn't in the best part of town, but that was by design. Rhodes paid the next year's rent and a handsome bonus in a Christmas card to the landlord, so he left them alone. Stenson always delivered the materials. The only time he showed up at the rental was to drop off information following a new assignment. They paid a couple of neighbors to keep an eye on things. "I didn't see anything officer" is a rule in the hood. With the money Harry and Robert were paying a couple of lookouts, their eyes were even more useless.

There were only a few things in the apartment, including a couch with an afghan thrown over it, and a table in the kitchen, which had a chair placed at it and a screwdriver on top of it. The briefcase also stayed there. The apartment was one of those that had an old furnace and grate-like registers on the floor. The briefcase was hidden in the empty bedroom. It was stashed in the register.

Once it was set on the kitchen table and opened, a map of the world was laid out in the bottom half of the chewed up black fuzzy interior. A series of numbers was written on the map. The numbers identified the country and the city where the assignment was to take place. After numbers were recorded, the person with the assignment unlocked a compartment in the top half of the briefcase.

It looked like a perfect place to store a handgun or a few greenbacks. However, it only contained a pocket, one that was in most briefcases. A folder was nestled in the pocket. The folder didn't contain private documents or secret instructions. A photo was the only thing housed in the folder. It was their mark.

They tore off the bottom right corner of the photo. The fourth item in the briefcase was a lighter. The map was burnt first. After studying the photo for ten minutes, the picture and folder were next to go up in smoke.

After placing the briefcase back in its hiding spot, the library was the next stop. It was one of the oldest tricks amongst criminals. Finding books that never left the house of geeks, another Gary O'Neil original, was easy. Anyone can visit a library and find a book that hasn't left the place in ten years or more. When the project started, Stenson and Rhodes spent two or three hours and found dozens that hadn't been checked out since the library opened, which was thirty-four years prior.

They decided on one particular book. It listed all the countries in the index, which is the main reason it was their top choice. Beside each country, they wrote a number. Of course, all the numbers were jumbled instead of going down the list in alphabetical order. For instance, Canada was 32 while the United States was 11.

The city where the mark lived was the hardest to assign a number. It took the two a lot of thinking until Stenson hatched an idea. All cities start with one of the twenty-six letters in the alphabet. Since Big Boy resided in Columbus, he pondered C first. He thought about Columbus and remembered the day he got his driver's license and backed into a neighbor's mailbox. Since you have to be sixteen to drive, he thought C could stand for 16. After that, he began assigning each letter a number. Once Stenson finished, he wrote the following numbers—16-9-24-3-18-10-3-21—on a piece of paper. Rhodes didn't know what it meant, but Stenson smiled.

He took the book and opened it. On the first twenty-six pages, Stenson wrote a letter by the number.

"Take the code and write each letter you see."

Rhodes turned to page sixteen and there was a C. He flipped back a few pages and there was an O. He continued on through page twenty-one until he had the word Columbus spelled out.

Stenson then rewrote the code and inserted 11, circling it.

"That will tell them the country and the other numbers are the city."

It was an ingenious plan. They identified the country and city of residence where their mark was living without mentioning either. They placed the book in a back corner of the library.

Each assassin visited the library and made sure no one was around when they took the book out of the case. They went to a private study area and solved the code. The book was returned to its spot and the last task took place.

Every hit man in the group had a black light lamp at home. The torn off piece from the photograph was held underneath the lamp and a name appeared. The mark was usually eliminated within two weeks.

"Gentlemen, I know we are not supposed to talk about the briefcase. Harry and I are the only two who can talk about it. Each of you seated at this table has adhered to that rule. However, I'm going to talk about it today in front of everyone. The briefcase is missing," Rhodes announced. "Someone entered the apartment and took it, which creates a problem. Harry talked to our watchdogs in the neighborhood and they didn't see anything. That's not our only problem. They also had a video camera set up and apparently recorded activity at the apartment. We found wires leading to an empty VCR in the attic's crawl space."

Each hit man gazed coldly around the room.

"I visited the library today. For the first time in over thirty-four years, someone took our book home. I asked the person working the desk and they didn't have a record of the book being registered at the library. In other words, it's like the book never existed. I don't know how this could happen, but we need to watch ourselves. There are some pricks screwing with us and I won't tolerate it."

Rhodes slowly circled the table twice before finishing what he had to say.

"For each of you, there is a $5 million bounty on the head of Matt Talbot. There are $2 million bounties on his associates. The last bounty is the hardest. Gary, we haven't discussed this with you, but I'm sure you will understand. We have placed a $1 million price on Preston's head. Usually, we don't conduct business this way. The briefcase system has worked for years and we would like things to continue until our final problem is solved from the old warehouse days."

The room was filled with silence for about ten minutes as each man took a while to soak things in. With video tapes, the briefcase, and the book, they had them by the balls.

Gary broke the silence.

"There are things that happened over the years I haven't agreed with, but I never said a word. Some of us lost our families and some have lost identities. I have raised Preston since he was a kid. He's the only family I have, but I know what has to be done."

Stenson stood up and shocked the entire room.

"I don't care who you knock off, you will get $5 million for each one."

Rhodes gave him a puzzled look and muttered, "It's about time you grew some fuzz on your nuts."

Preston, Matt, Dane, and Brock didn't know they were worth more than that day's lottery drawing, but the ante had been raised.

Although Talbot and his boys outsmarted Stenson and Rhodes, they didn't have the resources to stay ahead of them much longer. Matt knew they were running against time, but he had set out to bring down the entire operation and would stop at nothing to accomplish his goal.

Chapter Six

LAUREN TRIED TO ACT as if she hadn't heard from Preston or the other people causing major headaches for the person on the other end of the line.

She thought they decided it was safe to leave her alone, but the phone call verified they suspected she was involved.

"You need to cooperate with us if you have talked to them," Rhodes said. "They have killed three people while we have done nothing wrong. The people with your ex-boyfriend stole something from us and we want it back. We're not out to hurt them."

Matt noticed from Lauren's bedroom that a carload of men was parked outside the apartment.

"We have to get out of here," Matt whispered to Dane. "We have company."

"I haven't seen Preston since the help came for my dad. I did exactly as instructed. My dad passed away and I didn't search for Preston. I held up my end of the bargain, even though it hurt every day. I loved Preston and still do," Lauren said as she broke into tears.

Preston put his hand on Lauren's leg. She looked at him with approval.

"We know you have held up your end of the bargain. We have kept tabs on you over the years. You thought we ignored you, but we know what you have been up to. If you look out front, you will see we're still around."

Matt and the boys were trying to figure out what to do. They knew they couldn't bust out the front of the apartment. Sneaking out the back wasn't an option either. If Rhodes, Stenson, or anyone else in their group knew Lauren had visitors, she would be killed.

Matt grabbed a notebook and scribbled on a piece of paper.

Act calm and tell them you are willing to cooperate. Also, don't talk about caring for Preston. It makes it obvious you would help us if contacted.

Lauren nodded as she finished reading Matt's note.

"I know you feel I would help Preston if he was in trouble, but even though I still love him, I'm not in love with him. I moved on with my life, as I'm sure he has. When I agreed to say good-bye to him, I meant it. You tried to help with my father and I will always be grateful. My family comes first. The deal we agreed to was permanent. I will do whatever you need to help get your item back."

Lauren's voice didn't crack. She was precise and to the point. Her words made the voice on the other end feel at ease.

"I believe you would help us. We will keep a close eye on you. If they contact you, we want to know. There is a small silver stake in the flower bed next to your apartment. If they call or stop by, remove the stake. We will contact you if it happens. If you don't cooperate and we find out you have helped them or kept information from us, we will start killing members of your family."

The words were still echoing over the phone, although there was a dial tone. Lauren hung up and ordered everyone out of her apartment.

"Lauren, you have to relax," Matt said. "We know you're afraid and you have every right to be. We're all worried. Any of us could die because of what we have done, but look at the people who have been destroyed because of those rogues! My life is worth the risk. They need to pay for what they have done."

Matt paused long enough to give Lauren a chance to talk, but she stared through him.

"I'm going to do everything I can to make sure you're safe. This will be the last time we stay. We need to wait until tonight to get out of here. We will make our break then. You have to keep the same routine. Act as if nothing's wrong. They will watch you and notice strange behavior."

Lauren sighed and sank into the couch. Matt felt sorry for the people he involved, but there was nothing he could do about it. Revenge was on his mind from the time he woke up until he went to bed. He didn't want to see anyone else get hurt, but it was time for Rhodes, Stenson, Gary O'Neil, and the rest of their partners to go down in flames.

"I apologize for involving you," Matt said as he sat down on the other side of Lauren. "I knew I could bring you harm, but let my personal vendetta against them get in the way. I wish I would have done things differently. The things Dane, Brock, and I have done could send us to prison for a long time. We should have involved the police, but you know how our justice system works. They would have served minimal sentences after flashing their money for big time lawyers and politicians. We'll take the briefcase with us tonight and you will never deal with this again."

Lauren looked at Preston and said she needed to talk to him. They got up and went to her bedroom.

"I don't know how much they told you. Matt said they informed you about Gary and Kurt. I'm glad you know that part of your life. I want you to know I didn't find out about this until a few weeks ago. I also want them to pay for what they did. When I found out you were going to be killed, I agreed to let them keep the briefcase here and stay in case of an emergency."

Lauren closed the door before finishing her conversation with Preston.

"I want to help you, but I'm tired of feeling like I'm running from something. All of you need to leave, but I want you to know I love you. I have thought about you every day since we broke up. I would do anything for you. I know that seems hypocritical, but some of my family members could be killed. I'm in the middle of this and don't know what to do. They created your identity and covered up the truth about a lot of people."

Preston interrupted by pulling Lauren close to him. He gazed into her eyes as he held her hands.

"I didn't ask to be involved and know you don't want to be a part of this. However, if it's what it took to bring us back together...I don't care what happens to me from this point on. If we make it through this, I want to move to a place where no one knows who we are and start fresh."

Preston moved in to kiss Lauren, but she pulled away.

"Preston, you don't understand. If Matt and the rest of you continue interfering in their business, you will end up dead. You have to find a way out. Kissing me can't happen until the situation with Stenson, Rhodes, and your father is over. I'm sorry. I will not put my family in harm's way."

Preston let go of her hands and turned his back to her. They stood in silence for fifteen minutes. The room was eerily quiet. Lauren or Preston would start to say something, but decided the clicking of the clock said it best. They were in a race against time and the odds weren't in their favor. Stenson and Rhodes would use all their resources to find the briefcase and eliminate anyone who knew its dark secrets.

NEWS THAT A VISITOR was in Fresno nearly sent Sharon into labor. She didn't expect to see Kurt.

The fact someone wanted to stop by Fresno was a shock. Sharon spent years trying to talk her mother, Ava, into moving out of the city. Her mother always reiterated, "I was born and raised here, and I'm going to die here."

Since Sharon couldn't convince Ava to move to Mesa like she did years before, Sharon thought she could at least get her to move to Clovis. It's a part of Fresno, just on the northeastern side, which gets people closer to the Sierra Nevada Foothills. However, her mother didn't want any part of Clovis, Fig Garden, or the Tower District, which were also suggested as alternatives. She was staying put in South Fresno, come hell or high water.

Mrs. O'Neil was sure to take her inhaler, plenty of bottled water, and a weapon of choice when she visited. The air wasn't the most pleasant to breath. It made those with asthma feel like they stumbled upon the location where weeping and gnashing of teeth took place. It was hot in Mesa, but the heat was smothering in Fresno, despite claims of dry heat.

Winter was not the best time to visit. A winter fog, known as Tule Fog to locals, usually made things tough, but at least a snow shovel wasn't required, as migrants from the East Coast declared.

Living in Fresno in the late 70s was difficult. It was like every city in the fact it offered its fair share of crime. West of downtown and below the zoo was a caution zone. Shaw Avenue ran from 168 to 41 to Highway 99. Fresno State University was above East Shaw and the football players got into trouble from time to time. Some still say to steer clear of everything south of Shaw, especially at night. At times, people claimed there was enough gunfire to make a shooting range blush. Of course, exaggerations came with the territory, but the town could knock people around if they let it.

Owning real estate in the northern part of town was the way to go for those who chose to live in Fresno. Gated communities, shopping centers, and sparkling new cars were replaced by dilapidated eyesores, barred grocery stores, and broken down vehicles the further south of Shaw people traveled. Immigrants of the legal and illegal kind populated that part of the city.

Ava was used to the way of life in Fresno. She was one of those who lived below Shaw. She resided in the older part of town, which was known for its high level of poverty.

Sharon felt her mother was a prisoner of Fresno. She despised the fact there weren't any interstates or U.S. highways in Fresno, making it difficult to get around. Ava overlooked the lack of convenient travel because she wasn't into a fast lifestyle, thus the reason she stayed in South Fresno.

There were many things she liked and disliked, but the biggest thing she cherished was the abundance of locally grown fresh food. She was one of the few people on her block that had a mini-garden in her back yard. The biggest city in California's Central Valley was known for its agriculture and Ava's family had been farmers for generations.

Her family was one of several to lose farms and land because they wouldn't hire illegal immigrants, but she chose to stay put because she had friends who also shed honest blood, sweat, and tears in some of those abundant fields. She felt like she owed it to herself and the people who lost as much as she had to try to make Fresno a better place, even if it meant giving away one tomato at a time.

Kurt was in town because circumstances had changed. He was also homeless, which would allow him to fit in nicely in South Fresno.

He wrote a note to Sharon telling her where to meet him. He figured Stenson's men were watching her mother's residence closely, so he hatched a plan. Kurt gave the note to a boy riding a bicycle a couple blocks away from Ava's.

"Hey buddy, I'll give you twenty bucks if you take this to South Poppy Avenue. The house address is on the back of the note. It's a little yellow house with a green porch. You won't miss it. When you get there, tell Sharon that Kurt gave you something and you need to go inside to give it to her. If an old lady answers, ask to talk to Sharon. Here's a second note. If anyone stops you, give them this note. I want you to carry this in your hand, but keep the one you're giving to the lady in your pocket until you get inside. I will double your money when you return and let me know you delivered the note."

The boy rode down the street. The men spying from across the street paid close attention when he walked up the stairs. Just as Kurt assumed, they watched everyone who stepped foot on Ava's property.

Ava heard the knock and went to the front door. She peered out the blinds and saw a boy standing on her porch. She didn't care for candy bar peddlers or people offering to do chores for unreasonable fees. She cracked the door.

"I'm not interested."

As she was shutting the door, the boy said, "I need to talk to Sharon."

She opened the door a little wider and called to Sharon, "There is a boy on the front porch asking to see you."

Sharon was leery. She wondered how anyone knew where she was staying. She managed to get off the couch and mosey to the front door.

"What can I do for you young man?"

"I have something to give you and I need to do it inside. I'm not here to hurt anyone. I forget the man's name, but he gave me money to give you something."

Sharon knew her mother didn't need to hear what was going on so she asked her to get the boy something to drink.

"Come in," she said as she closed the door.

The boy reached in his pocket and then handed her the crumpled note.

"Can you remember if his name was Kurt?"

"Yes. That was his name," the boy said as he described Kurt's attributes.

Her mother returned from the kitchen and gave the boy a drink. Like most thirsty kids, he had the glass of cherry Kool-Aid gone in two gulps. Sharon opened the door and sent the red mustached boy on his way.

Sharon returned to the couch and sat down to read Kurt's note. Her mother stood in the entrance to the living room with a thousand questions running through her mind. She summed them up with, "What was that about?"

Her daughter blurted the first thing that came to mind.

"The boy said he didn't have any friends and wrote me a note asking if my baby will be his friend. He must have seen me get the mail or come into the house. What a sweet little kid."

The lie was ridiculous, but Sharon's mom was a gullible lady. Like most elderly folks, she was as innocent as the boy who dropped by unexpectedly. Asking, "How did he know your name?" should have been Ava's first question.

Sharon,

I made it to Fresno. It's not safe to visit you at your mother's house. I believe people are watching you and we can't involve your mother. You need to get out as soon as possible. Meet me at the Lighthouse Baptist Church on East

Kings Canyon Road at nine-thirty tonight. I'll take care of the people watching your mom's place.

As Zach made his way up the street, the man in the passenger's seat jumped out of the car and asked, "What do you have in your hand?"

The boy came to a stop and answered, "A note."

Once again, the boy was about to hit the jackpot.

"I'll give you $100 if you give me that note."

Zach knew he wasn't supposed to talk to strangers, but broke that rule by talking to Kurt and the two ladies. Going into a stranger's house was an even bigger no-no. He figured $40 was worth the risk, but $100 would have him retired at the age of ten.

He gave the note to the man and gladly pocketed a $100 bill. Zach peddled away and the man retreated to the car.

Sharon,
   Meet me in fifteen minutes at Aggie's Mini-Mart on East Church Avenue.

Kurt

The men didn't know the store's location and looked back to see where the boy was, but he had disappeared. Against strict orders, they pulled out of their spot and drove down the road. They saw someone mowing their grass and stopped to get directions.

Zach reported to Kurt and told him he delivered both notes. Kurt forked over a twenty and told him there was more work to do.

Kurt and the boy made their way over to East Church Avenue. Kurt had scoped the area after being dropped off by Mr. Alexander. He selected Aggie's because of the location, pay phone outside, and abandoned building across the street that had a stairwell leading to the roof.

Kurt called the cops and gave the boy more instructions and money, of course, before going to the rooftop.

Stenson's spies parked across the street from Aggie's. Within ninety seconds, several cruisers roared into the small parking lot beside Aggie's. A pair of officers bolted inside and told the only patron, "Put 'em up."

The cashier asked the police what was going on and they realized a robbery wasn't taking place.

"We were called about a robbery, so we rushed over here as fast as we could."

"Yeah, I know. Protect and serve," the cashier said sarcastically.

The corner grocery store had given out its fair share of free money over the years. Some of it ended up being rent money at the big house. Some of it went to veins, lungs, and noses. One thing was for certain, none of the money helped someone escape to the Cayman Islands for a lifelong retreat.

"The gentleman you were getting ready to arrest was shopping. He's a regular and wouldn't harm a soul."

The officers made a half-hearted apology and exited the store. Zach got a little more than he bargained for while doing what Kurt paid him to do and let out desperate cries.

"Help me!"

Both officers ran across the street and noticed a man getting into a silver Monte Carlo. The boy had steered his bicycle near the car and pulled a piece of paper from his pocket.

"I forgot to give you this a few minutes ago."

The men tried to get Zach to give it to them, but he refused. The driver angrily got out of the car. The man went up to Zach and wrestled the note away.

The man became more furious when he realized the paper was blank. He grabbed the boy by the arm and squeezed a little too hard. Kurt watched from the rooftop and was worried about his plan. The cops exited the grocery store just in time as Zach started screaming.

Before the officers could safely reach him, the Monte Carlo screeched out of the space it occupied. One of the officers got the license plate number and sounded it over the airwaves. Within six blocks, the police caught up to the Monte Carlo.

Had traffic not been congested, the spies would have made their way out of town, or wherever they were staying. The chase continued through town, with the scene playing out like a demolition derby at a county fair.

Eventually, the silver car slammed into the side of a delivery van on North Palm Avenue. The men tried to get out and run. By the time they crashed, three patrol cars had joined the chase. Officers surrounded them and forced them to the ground.

An officer who stayed behind assisted the boy, making sure he was all right. A small crowd gathered near the grocery store and a few people were hanging around the sidewalk where the boy had been screaming.

Kurt made his way down the stairwell while the cop talked to Zach. Frightened, the child saw Kurt and felt relieved. He ran to Kurt and asked for help.

"It's going to be OK," Kurt said.

He pulled the officer aside and told him he was a neighborhood child who liked to pull pranks. He told him he would walk Zach to his parent's house.

"Listen, boy!" the officer said. "We could take you to jail for calling the cops and reporting a false robbery. You don't want to spend the night in jail away from your mom and dad, do you? I'm going to let you go, but you better stay out of trouble."

The officer let the boy go. Kurt picked up Zach's bicycle and helped him back on his ride.

Kurt gave the officer a phony phone number and started to leave the scene.

"We will get in touch with you if we need anything else. Thanks for your cooperation. Be good Zach."

A SLIGHT KNOCK AT the door broke the silence. Matt opened it and peered in.

"Is everything all right?"

"Yes," Preston declared. "I want this to end. Part of me is ready to barge out the front door yelling, 'Here I am, come and get me!' The other part wants to put all of this together. I know there is a lot more I haven't found out. I feel it's time I know what's going on. You told me my adopted father is a hit man and revealed the identity of my real dad. I know about the briefcase, which you referred to as 'it' for the longest time. I know Lauren is involved. Dane and Brock were informally introduced, but I don't know who either of them are or why they're involved. While I'm at it, I don't really know who you are and why you're full of revenge."

Preston let Matt absorb the first part of his rant before finishing the rest.

"I don't want to be a pawn in whatever it is you're doing. I don't want Lauren to be in danger. If anything happens to her, I will be ready to take someone's life. You need to move on without us. Let us go and you can continue playing games with Stenson and Rhodes."

Matt asked Dane and Brock to join the three of them in the bedroom. They entered the room and Matt instructed Preston and Lauren to take a seat on the bed.

"Do you want to know why Dane and Brock are involved? Lauren knows why I'm involved, but that part will have to wait. I'm going to explain who these guys are so you can understand why the briefcase is such a big deal and why they're dedicated to taking down Stenson and Rhodes. In explaining who Dane and Brock are, I'm also going to reveal something to Lauren."

Lauren gave Matt a puzzled look and anticipated what he was going to say.

"In the 1930s, the Hayes Carlson Company operated a magnesium and beryllium processing facility for the government. The place was shut down in 1943. A grand opening of sorts took place in 1949 as an aluminum factory was housed in the facility and it operated until 1961. Vandervort Tire Industries moved its headquarters to the grounds and experienced twelve years of success, but was offered a lucrative buy out by the Rhodes Tire and Rubber Company in '73."

Preston sat wide-eyed as Matt shifted his weight while continuing the story.

"Rhodes kept his tire and rubber plant in operation at those premises for the next fourteen years. He decided to set up shop somewhere else and purchased a large piece of land near Cincinnati. Rhodes, being a smart business man, knew he had to leave town, but several of his employees were resistant to the change in scenery and were understandably causing a lot of problems for him."

Preston wanted to ask a question, but Lauren nudged him as if to say, "Let Matt finish."

"Enter Harry Stenson. He was hired to do the public relations work for the company. Stenson was working hard to get his big break in the business and to get the relocation campaign noticed. The campaign, which also involved a lot more than the move, not only made a difference within the company, but it drew major attention from outside the organization. From that point on, the Rhodes Tire and Rubber Company was on its way to becoming a monopoly in the Midwest. Rhodes added Stenson as a chairman for his company and the PR firm, which became one of the most recognizable in the Midwest, was turned into Stenson & Rhodes as Harry made Robert a partner in his business."

Lauren had heard the spiel, but Preston was hanging on every word.

"As I said, Rhodes is a smart man. He didn't want to make the move to Cincinnati, but was forced to. The reason he had to close the facility and move is because the grounds the Rhodes Tire and Rubber Company sat on were toxic dump sites. To be scientifically correct, residual radioactivity exceeding criteria was discovered, as was beryllium waste. All of that was seeping into the grounds, which in turn got into the water. Imagine sucking on a nuclear weapon like a lollipop and you get the gist of what was going on."

The words hit home with Lauren. She knew the history of the plant where her dad worked, but didn't know why the move to Cincinnati was made.

Her dad got sick several times while working at Rhodes and wasn't the call off kind. He was a hard worker and didn't believe in making money while lying on a couch. He often stood on his soap box and delivered messages of hatred for those who abused the unemployment and welfare systems. He felt everyone who could walk, talk, and move their arms should have a job. "Worthless trailer trash," he declared.

Lauren and her family knew something was wrong when his sickness confined him to bed. They didn't know the same thing was happening to several employees who worked at Rhodes.

"Are you telling me my dad got sick because the water he drank at Rhodes?"

"I have conducted extensive research. The number of people who died from cancer that worked for Johnson Aluminum, Vandervort, and Rhodes is mind boggling. Skepticism is expected because what family hasn't dealt with losing loved ones to cancer? However, facts are facts."

Preston put his arm around Lauren.

"The number of people who lost battles to cancer tripled from Johnson to Vandervort. It increased nearly sixteen times from Vandervort to Rhodes. The Rhodes Tire and Rubber Company also paid out more and more sick time each of the fourteen years before the move to Cincinnati. Not only were employees making additional doctor visits, but the number of birth defects and newborns who were dying was unbelievable. During the fourteen-year period Rhodes was housed on the contaminated grounds, one child per every twelve born to employees had some sort of birth defect. There were also twenty-nine babies who didn't see what the outside of a hospital looked like in those fourteen years."

Everyone in the room had tears in their eyes.

"Families organized a town hall style meeting at the company and nothing was done about the problems. A few months later, one of the guys who worked at Rhodes secretly talked an inspector into checking out the facilities. The outcome of his visit isn't known because no one heard from the inspector again."

Matt didn't know his suspicions were true. After the inspector assessed things, he went into Rhodes' office and gave him the grave news.

"I'm shutting this place down immediately. The water is heavily contaminated with radioactive materials. You and your employees could be knocking at death's door."

Rhodes reached inside the top right drawer of his desk and pulled out a .45, hitting him where the emerald or ruby is on an Indonesian woman. The silencer kept anyone from hearing a thing.

Rhodes knocked on his desk three or four times.

"You hear that sir?" he asked as he took a bite from his sandwich. "That's me knocking and no one is answering."

Inspectors who visited reported finding nothing because of incredible payouts they received. It didn't hurt that Rhodes had mafia backing—logical reasons why the tire company and Stenson's PR firm blossomed—and most people were well aware of the outside support.

Visits were always scheduled, but the inspector slumped over in the chair across from Rhodes was uninvited. At that point, the leather used to make the notorious briefcase was grazing in a field somewhere. A stable of hit men had not been assembled, although a few ruffians worked for them. Rhodes called his mafia buddies to help him clean up the mess. A pair of goons arrived that night and wheeled the inspector to their car.

Rhodes found it odd, but chuckled. He had hundreds of employees working hard day and night to assemble products, but two of his newest employees were taking something from his plant to be unassembled.

"What the inspector found was obvious," Matt said. "He discovered the same thing inspectors exposed years earlier. Vandervort was ordered to close, although it was the government's mistake from the start. Hayes Carlson was hired by the government to operate the magnesium and beryllium processing facility, but the company was government owned. If you look it up, Hayes vanished into thin air in 1943. Basically, the government owned its own business to dump toxic materials in a place they thought would never hurt a soul."

Matt slowly looked around at everyone to drive home the point.

"After Hayes vanished, the government-owned land sat unoccupied for six years and they figured everything was OK. Johnson purchased the land, once again off a fake entity, and the factory proudly opened its doors. It continually operated with people getting sick for no apparent reasons. Johnson closed its doors and relocated to Detroit in '61. Vandervort came swooping in, although the government wanted to repurchase the land and cover up the situation by turning it into a wildlife preservation area. Like the people, I guess they didn't care what happened to the animals."

Preston wanted to know more about Rhodes, but all he got out was, "Did Rhodes…"

"Vandervort took over, but it was more of the same. People were getting sick by the dozens and were beginning to die after two or three years of working there. Eventually, the government sent out inspectors and ordered the grounds to be closed due to contamination problems. The government was ready to pin everything on Vandervort. Rhodes was aware of the situation and his company was ready to take the next step. He needed a new piece of property to expand his business and was looking for cheap land. Vandervort, which wanted to save face, knew it was getting shut down so it gladly sold everything to Rhodes for a fraction of what the company and land was worth."

Lauren sat on the bed clinching her fists and shaking her head.

"Rhodes agreed to have cleanup conducted and regular tests done on the site. Rhodes hired a company to clean the land and adhered to strict rules. As time went on, tests became fewer and visits were always scheduled. Inspectors showed up, received large amounts of cash, wrote perfect reports, and were on their way."

Preston couldn't believe what he was hearing. He had doubts, as did Lauren, even though she knew everything, except the part about the radioactive materials that more than likely led to her father's death. Lauren knew her dad was in peak physical condition until two years after he landed a job with the Rhodes Tire and Rubber Company. As farfetched as things sounded, it added up. Once Matt finished the story, Preston and Lauren believed what he shared with them.

"Lauren, not only was your family affected, but Dane and Brock lost loved ones. Dane lost his dad while Brock lost his mother. Everyone around Columbus heard rumors about what happened, but once I discovered the truth, I realized it was time for something to be done. Through tons of reading and research, I found six or seven families that were affected. I wanted two people who lost parents to help me make Rhodes pay and bring light to the cover up. I met with three or four people and explained the story. They weren't interested in taking down Rhodes. They wanted to be left alone. I then met with Dane and he was in. His father refused to take a buyout and a few weeks later, he was gone. Brock's mom was also against being bought out and was a problem for Rhodes. She didn't last very long either. Brock wants to kill Rhodes."

Matt was ready to give Lauren another bombshell.

"A short time after the inspector was murdered, Rhodes owned new ground in Cincinnati and announced the relocation plan. Instead of facing lawsuits that would award families millions of dollars, the company began buying out employees. A year's wages and benefits were too much for people to turn down. By the time Rhodes left town, only 20 percent of the people headed to Cincinnati, including your dad. It was a steep price for Rhodes to pay, but instead of losing his company and paying millions of dollars in lawsuits, he put money in front of people's noses they couldn't refuse."

"Although I never worked there, I was one of those idiots," Lauren said.

"He had every person who took a buyout sign a contract stating they couldn't come back for more money down the road or sue him. It was a ploy that worked on some people. With the help of Stenson, he carefully crafted an ingenious plan and there wasn't much anyone could do about it. Lauren, you really got conned. They knew if you stayed with Preston, the two of you could have caused problems. Stenson and Rhodes couldn't risk you talking about what was going on. They decided to give you $200,000, knowing you could land a multi-million dollar settlement."

Lauren had done her fair share of crying, but was an emotional wreck after hearing the rest of the story. As Preston did when he sat on the bench at Goodale Park talking to Matt and when he was let out of the trunk at the warehouse the first night, Lauren had a thousand questions running through her mind. All she could do was put her face in a pillow and cry once again.

Her crying didn't last long as the knock at her back sliding glass door meant they were in serious trouble.

Chapter
Seven

HE HID IN THE darkest spot near the church. After thirty minutes, he saw a blue Oldsmobile pull in front of the building. Kurt pulled back some bushes he had tucked himself into so he could see who it was. Sharon had safely arrived.

She wobbled up four brick layered steps and started down the sidewalk beside the church. He waited until she reached the back of the church before making contact with her.

"Psst."

Sharon quickly turned her head and peered toward the bushes. To say she was afraid was an understatement. It was nine-thirty and she was in the south side of Fresno. Normal people were in their homes with one eye on the TV and the other peeking through curtains in the front window.

She thought the meeting was a setup. What if it was one of her unwanted pen pals calling out?

"Who is it and where are you?"

Kurt rustled the bushes back and forth to let her know where he was.

"Do not walk over here," he whispered. "I want you to call a cab and wait on the front steps. When the cab shows up, get in and drive around the block two times. Make sure no one is following you. If no cars are following you, stop and I'll join you."

Sharon wobbled down the sidewalk and reached the pay phone. She painfully squeezed into the booth and dialed the Yellow Cab service. After receiving conformation she would be picked up, Sharon walked to the church steps and waited. Within ten minutes, a cabbie showed up in front of the church. She got in and the driver asked, "Where to?"

"I have a strange request. I have a feeling someone is following me. I can't deal with the paranoia. I'm a member of this church and I would rather them harm me here than anywhere else. I didn't see anyone follow me, nor did I notice anyone around, but I still feel like they're out there. I want you to drive around the block two times. I want to watch if anyone is following us. If I don't see anyone by the second loop, I'm heading home."

"I can't do that ma'am. I can't put myself or this cab in harm's way. You need to involve the police if you think someone is following you. Please, get out of the vehicle."

Sharon handed him an envelope with $500 in it.

"Is that enough for you to make a couple of right-hand turns?"

The driver immediately pulled away from the church and Sharon heard the ticking from the timing mechanism on the old mechanical taximeter, which was replaced by electronic mileage meters a few years later. Kurt saw the cab disappear around the corner and exited the bushes. He made his way across the small parking lot and ducked into a shadow near the church.

Sharon looked around to see if they were being followed. The driver was also nervous and frequently scoping the surroundings. A few minutes passed and they completed their first lap. Sharon and the driver looked at the church and the area looked as peaceful as it had moments earlier.

"Keep driving!"

Kurt was standing against the building and pulled his head away from the red bricks to catch a glimpse of the cab as it made its way around the corner once again. Other cars passed in front of the church, but his plan earlier in the day eliminated any threat that evening.

The cab eased in front of the church once again and Sharon told the driver to pull up to the curb. Kurt stepped away from the building and appeared in front of the church. The driver was more than ready to punch it.

"Do I drive? Do I drive?" he nervously shouted.

"No. It is safe."

Kurt opened the door and didn't have weird instructions for the driver. He handed him a piece of paper with the location of a bus depot. Sharon looked at Kurt and he slowly shook his head no while telling her, "Shhh."

The cabbie dropped them off a block away from the Super 8 Motel where Kurt had a room reserved. He handed the man a fifty, thanking him for the ride. Sharon also expressed gratitude as the cabbie and Kurt helped her out of the back seat. They walked her to a bench beside a bus sign.

"I must say, this has been strange. If you don't mind me asking, where are you going from here?"

"There are people following us. I think we'll head to San Francisco for a few days and then go where the wind blows," Kurt replied.

The trio said their good-byes. Kurt and Sharon watched the yellow vehicle until the taillights disappeared into the night. Kurt helped Sharon get up and they walked around the corner to the motel.

"Don't ask questions yet. I will explain everything when we get to our room."

THE KNOCK STARTLED THEM, especially since it was coming from the back door. There wasn't anywhere for Matt, Preston, Dane, and Brock to hide.

Lauren walked to the edge of her living room and saw a shadow that appeared to be a man standing on her back patio. A second knock made Lauren flinch again. She wasn't sure what to do. She decided to run to her laundry room and strip down to nothing. She put a towel around herself and looked through the blinds.

It had been a while since she had seen or spoken to the man standing on her patio. He was someone she got along with, but knew the danger he presented.

She didn't know $20 million was in her bedroom. Usually some loose change in her couch or on the counter by the stove was all the money in her apartment. There was a pot of gold in Everett Wren that day and people were down the street buying lottery tickets with their fingers crossed. They would be at Lauren's apartment if they knew about the bounty on her visitors' heads. Unfortunately, neither Lauren nor the guys knew about the prices on their heads.

Lauren didn't have time to run back and talk to Matt. She hoped they were smart enough to hide in her closet, under the bed, or in the bathroom. At least they would be out of the way if the visitor glanced around.

"I was ready to take a bath. What can I do for you?"

"We need to talk. I'm not here to hurt you, but you have to understand the situation."

Lauren left the blinds slightly open so he could see her walk to her laundry room. She pulled the sliding wooden door shut behind her and quickly got dressed.

The boys were in the bedroom discussing who the visitor could be. Matt felt the person had to be one of the people who were after them. He peeked outside the bedroom window once again and the car that had been sitting there was gone.

Matt scanned the parked cars. He looked underneath all the vehicles and around each side. He looked on the balcony of the adjacent apartment buildings and didn't see anyone.

"I'm not sure if the coast is clear. This could be a trap. We have to hide in available spots."

Dane and Brock moved Lauren's big screen TV away from the corner. Preston got behind it and squatted down. Brock helped Dane get a spot in Lauren's closet. Several dresses flowed to the floor and he nestled into them. If anyone stepped into the closet, it would be impossible to see Dane unless they moved the dresses around.

Brock got underneath Lauren's bed and Matt stuffed himself into the linen closet in the bathroom.

Lauren opened the door and invited Gary inside. She knew why he was there. His eyes wandered around the apartment, letting Lauren know he was memorizing the entire scene. Men usually gave Lauren elevator eyes because she was an attractive woman, but Gary was only interested in her apartment.

"Please, sit down."

Gary took a seat on the couch and got to the point.

"Lauren, I need to know the truth. Have you spoken to Preston within the last few days?"

"I told the man on the phone...I haven't seen or spoke to Preston since the day I made my decision."

It was hard for Lauren to lie after the things she found out before he showed up uninvited. She wanted to tell him how disgusting she thought he was, especially since he was a big part of what happened to her father and several other people who worked for Rhodes. She remained poised.

"I'll be honest. Would I like to know how Preston is doing? The answer is obvious. However, I know what I signed up for and have adhered to the rules. I miss him, but I'm at a different chapter in my life. If you said, 'He's doing well,' it would make me feel better."

Gary paid close attention to Lauren, analyzing her body language. He mastered the art of reading people at a young age and it served him well. He saw a confident woman sitting beside him. He didn't sense nervousness and her words rang with honesty. For someone so good at knowing when he was being deceived, the wool had been pulled over his eyes.

"Preston works at Stenson & Rhodes here in Columbus. He graduated from college and wanted to move to Myrtle Beach. You know how much he loves golf. He loves that awful sport more than anything. I talked him out of moving south and into working for Harry Stenson. He has done quite well for himself. I don't know what he makes, but I'm sure he's around six figures."

Lauren was pleased to hear Preston was successful, but figured he was miserable not being on a golf course day after day.

"A few days ago, his life was turned upside down. A group of men kidnapped Preston. No one has heard from Preston since. I want to know if you have heard from him. I'm really worried. The men who kidnapped Preston stole something from Stenson and have killed three of his employees. They are dangerous and will kill Preston next, if they haven't already."

Lauren highly doubted they killed three people. Then again, she never asked Matt if it was true. What if they were the bad guys and made up everything? A motive was the biggest stumbling block to the theory. Murder, kidnapping, theft, and other misdemeanors were on their rap sheets. However, money was the only thing they could be after and that was unlikely. The briefcase proved they weren't lying. Suddenly, she realized the briefcase was sitting at the end of the couch.

"I know you need to get in touch with Preston and you're worried because he's your son. I'm worried about him, too. Maybe I can help you set them up."

Lauren didn't want to make that offer because she realized making deals with Stenson and his associates wasn't wise. However, she would say anything to get Gary out of her apartment.

"I want you to come with me. I have plenty of room at my house and want to keep you out of harm's way. If they kidnapped Preston, they could come after you."

Lauren didn't know how to respond to his slumber party invite. The thought of staying in the same house with him for a night or several nights repulsed her. She used to respect the man sitting beside her, although Preston talked bad about him all the time. Gary always treated Lauren like a lady and gave her great gifts during the holidays and on her birthday.

"I would rather stay here. If they're going to come after me, let them. I'm not afraid."

Her denial frustrated Gary. He jumped up from the couch and pulled out a gun.

"You are going with me, whether you like it or not."

"Shoot me! You took my life away from me years ago. I'm already dead. A bullet isn't going to do a thing to me."

Her scrappy attitude surprised Gary, but he dealt with people like her before. He killed a few women in his time, but didn't want to hurt Lauren.

"I'll ask you again. Have you seen Preston or any of the people involved?"

"I know you're not religious, but haven't you heard it said, 'Let your yes be yes and your no be no?' I told you, I haven't seen them."

"Then why are five plates on your kitchen counter? The rest of this place is spotless, but five plates sit dirty on the counter," Gary said as he walked into the kitchen.

Lauren quickly kicked the briefcase under the couch. Gary walked over to the laundry room and opened the door. There was a small basket of clothes and a usual assortment of detergents, bleaches, and cleaners.

He walked around the counter and into the living room.

"I'm going to look around the rest of your place."

"Go ahead. You won't find anything. Those plates were from yesterday and this morning."

The bright light coming from an open window caused Gary to walk past the bathroom and into the bedroom. He noticed the window and knew someone had been there. The obvious place to hide was more than likely where the ship jumper had been. Gary looked under the bed and there wasn't a thing underneath it. The closet was the next place he looked. A quick peek inside unveiled an organized area. He looked at the tops of the hangers and along the floor. He didn't notice anything unusual.

As he turned around, his cell phone rang.

When Gary entered the apartment, Brock heard his voice and knew trouble had arrived. He panicked and didn't know what to do. He knew Gary would kill him if he looked under the bed.

As he was lying under the bed listening to Gary and Lauren talk, he crawled from underneath it and took a glance through the blinds. He didn't see anything and decided to get out of the apartment. He carefully opened the window and popped the screen. Brock thought he made too much noise, but once he safely reached the ground, he wasn't worried.

He took off running for their car, which was parked in another section of the complex. When he reached the spot where they left it the night before, the car was gone. As he started back to the apartment, a disguised mailman pulled a vehicle over and two masked men dressed in black got out with guns.

"Stop or we will kill you! Where are the rest of your friends?" Brock stopped to answer them.

"I'm the only one staying at Lauren's. I'm the safety valve."

Brock saw the look in their eyes and knew he was going to die either way, so he decided to run. He made it ten feet before gunfire hit both legs. He tried to keep running, but pain dropped him face first to the ground. As blood gushed from both legs, he tried using his hands, elbows, and arms to pull himself along the ground.

The gunmen raced over to Brock and flipped him on his back.

"Again, where are the rest of your friends?"

"Go to hell!"

Those were the last words Brock spoke. The men popped bullets through his body like acupuncture. Blood spurted all over their black clothes and the brownish colored grass quickly turned red. A few tenants noticed the commotion, but none wanted to challenge the pair of thugs. They called the police, but it was too late.

They each grabbed one of Brock's legs and drug him to the mail truck. They shoved him in the back and sped around the corner.

"Hello," Gary said as he answered his phone.

"We have one of them. We were in the mail truck and saw him looking for the car we found this morning when we called you. He tried to run so we killed him. We have him in the truck with us."

"Drop him off in front and get out of here as fast as you can."

"Our car is parked behind the emporium and we will make the switch."

The truck screeched to a halt in front of Lauren's apartment. The back door flung open and they threw Brock Beckman's lifeless body to the ground. The truck was gone as quickly as it appeared.

"Lauren, I believe there is something you need to see," Gary said as he looked out the window. "That is the man who has been staying here, one you said you didn't know."

Lauren's shriek of horror nearly caused Preston and Dane to make a noise. Preston was potty trained years ago, but for the second time in days, a pair of Depends would have been nice. He didn't have to look outside to understand what happened. He heard Brock slide out from under the bed and pop the screen. Preston wanted to talk him out of it, but knew he had to remain silent.

88

"That is one of the men who stole the item and kidnapped my son."

"I thought you said they weren't the bad guys. Anyone who could do that to a person is straight from hell."

"Well, look at it this way. It's three to one, so figure out who's good and bad. All they want is their item and this can end."

Gary thought he would never see the briefcase again. He figured killing Matt and the rest of his crew would be the only way to resolve the situation. However, he was set to get a close up view of the briefcase.

"Make one move and your brains will reach that body lying on the pavement," a masked Matt said as he stuck cold steel against the back of Gary's head. "First, drop the gun. Then hold your hands in the air and put these handcuffs on."

He looked over Gary's left shoulder long enough to see Brock's body.

"That was a big mistake. Lauren, put the screen back in place so we can shut the window and close the blinds. The cops will be here any minute and we don't need unwarranted attention."

Lauren followed Matt's instructions and they went to the living room. Matt figured Gary knew twenty kinds of martial arts. He and Lauren had to be careful.

"Lauren, I want you to stay on the opposite side of the room. He could easily kill you if you get too close."

Matt reached inside Gary's sports coat and found a second gun. He took it and threw it to Lauren. He instructed Gary to untie his shoes and take them off. Matt then had him unbuckle his belt and remove it.

"Unbutton your pants."

Gary followed Matt's orders and his pants slowly slid down his legs to his ankles.

"Step out of your pants."

Lauren was embarrassed to look at a half-naked man who should be her father-in-law. She was able to hide her uncomfortable feelings because she knew Matt was making sure they were safe.

"Get him some water in a plastic cup."

She handed the cup of water to Matt, who pulled out the same bottle of pills that caused Preston's head to do several loops when they first met. Matt dropped three of the pills in the cup and ordered Gary to drink it.

Within minutes, Gary was heavy eyed and fell back onto the couch. Matt pulled the briefcase from underneath the couch and held it up. Gary forced his eyes to stay open long enough to take a look at the briefcase in front of him.

"Is this what you're after? We have it now and it's not going anywhere. We know what this is used for and it won't be used by you, Stenson, or Rhodes again."

Those were the last words Gary heard as he slumped over on the couch. When he was soundly asleep, Matt went into the closet and told Dane to come out. They helped Preston get out from behind the TV and went into the living room.

"We have to get back to the warehouse as quickly as possible," Matt said to Dane. "Cops will be questioning tenants in this area and we can't be here when they show up. I want you and Preston to take Gary back to the warehouse. Put him in the second brick storage house we set up."

Preston gave Matt a quizzical look.

"Preston, you have to trust us. We need it to look like you're a prisoner instead of our friend. From this point on, you have to be like one of Hollywood's finest. We need Gary to believe you are being held captive as well. When he wakes up, you need to be the first thing he sees. All you have to do is play your part and we will do the rest."

As Lauren got her car keys, sirens echoed throughout the buildings. It only took ten minutes and police had yellow-taped the area.

"It looks like we will have to go to plan B," Lauren said.

The fact cops were hovering around kept the men who killed Brock away from the scene. Matt knew it was a problem though because they needed to leave. If they left, the cops would question them. Explaining Gary's state of well being wouldn't have been easy. If they waited until the cops left, they risked the chance of dealing with Stenson's boys and not being able to see much of what was going on outside.

Things were unraveling and Matt needed five minutes of solitary confinement to come up with a new plan.

He told everyone to stay calm as he went into the bathroom and shut the door. The trio in the living room was stunned. Dane knew they could be killed, but Brock's murder heightened the danger they faced.

Lauren was shook up seeing Brock's body in front of her apartment. She paced around the room. Preston didn't know what to think. He took a seat on the floor and thought how he would trade that spot for the one back at Stenson & Rhodes. He chuckled about having a desire to be at his least favorite place in the world.

As he laughed to himself, Lauren was perplexed.

"What's so funny?"

"I was thinking how I would trade all of this to go back where I was a few days ago. I hated working at Stenson & Rhodes and was negative day after day. I would gladly take that life over the chaotic one I have now."

"I can sympathize with you. I hated my life as well. I always worried about who might be watching. I also thought about you a lot. My life has seemed like I have been on parole, but still looking through bars."

Matt returned to the living room and explained his plan. It was another off-the-wall scheme, but was expected.

Preston cocked his head and looked out the corner of his eyes at Matt.

"You are absolutely crazy. What if it doesn't work?"

"You should know by now," Matt said with a grin, "that everything isn't going to work according to plan. I think we have a shot at pulling it off, but it's a craps shoot. I'm hoping we roll snake eyes."

Lauren rolled her eyes.

"Luck isn't on our side. Look on the street. Copperheads, cobras, rattlers, and any other kind can be damned. The only thing we are is snake bitten."

Matt picked up the phone and started putting his new plan into action.

"Well, here's hoping getting the venom sucked out feels good," he said as he winked at Lauren.

THEY CAUTIOUSLY MOVED ACROSS a dimly lit parking lot to
a small corridor that led to B-24, which was the last room on the
backside of the motel. Kurt pulled out the room key and they quickly
moved inside.

"We only have fifteen minutes."

"Why?" Sharon asked.

"I got rid of my clothes and have an explosive in this backpack.
After I'm finished explaining what we're going to do, I'm blowing
the doors off this place."

"I don't want to be involved. Are you trying to send me into labor
early? I'm surprised I haven't had a miscarriage. Kurt, I made a big
mistake. I never imagined I could have an affair. I care for you, but it
was and still is wrong. Instead of meeting you at that church, I should
have went inside and met with God. I do not regret meeting you, but
I'm disappointed in myself for what I have done. I have put myself
and Trevor in harm's way. We have to end this situation."

"I know you feel badly for what we have done. An affair is a
serious matter," Kurt said as he recalled Mr. Alexander's sermon in
the rig. "You can't change what we have done and I will be a part of
the child's life. That is why I am doing what I'm doing."

"That doesn't justify taking matters into your own hands!"

"I met a kind man—Jim Alexander—who gave me a ride from
Mesa. During the ride, he told me a lot about himself. He lives on
a small farm with his family on the outskirts of Austin. 'Hook 'Em
Horns' he proudly said. He gave me his phone number and address.
I know it's a little soon to call him since we just met, but he knows
about my house explosion. He had a newspaper and I read about
my house being blown to smithereens. I know I could tell him what
happened and he would welcome us with open arms."

His confused companion wanted to leave Kurt and the affair in
her rearview mirror.

"Did you bring the photo?"

Sharon reached inside her purse and pulled out the small manila
envelope. She handed it to Kurt. He knew about the photograph, but
looking at the picture gave him cold chills. He placed the photo in
a briefcase and opened the door. He looked down the hall to the left

and right, making sure no one was around. Kurt took the briefcase and sat it next to B-18.

He returned to the room.

"It's time to leave."

"How can you do this? Don't you care about killing innocent people?"

"No one is going to get hurt. Every room in this wing is rented and they are empty. That is the reason it is so quiet on this side. It's also the reason there aren't many cars. The plastic explosives should only take out two or three rooms, but I don't want innocent bystanders walking around outside the room."

Sharon interrupted Kurt, but he quickly said, "They're not in my name."

She let the words sink in before responding.

"If the room or rooms are not in your name, whose name are they under?"

"I know most of this sounds unbelievable, but I planned this for quite some time. The explosion expedited things. I had back-up plans to back-up plans. As soon as Jim dropped me off, I asked around to find out where most of the prostitutes work. I caught a cab to a heavily worked area and talked with a few before I found one I liked for the job. We caught another cab to a local department store and I bought her decent looking clothes. We went to the motel and…no, nothing like that happened. I gave her an extra thousand for the desk clerk so he wouldn't ask questions."

The thought of Kurt hanging with a prostitute repulsed Sharon.

"I know it is costly, but I had her rent every room on B wing so no one will be hurt. Candy, which probably isn't her real name, didn't know what I, Tim to Candy, am planning on doing, but she finally got to earn money without degrading herself. She said they didn't hassle her because of the money she gave them under the table and it didn't hurt that Candy knew the man. She gave me the room keys and thanked me. We gave each other a hug and she went on her way."

"Who do the rooms belong to for the night?"

"The rooms are under the name Marilyn Garland," Kurt said with a smirk. "We are covered. I know the briefcase doesn't make sense, but it will."

Kurt peeked outside once more and there wasn't any activity. He walked into the bathroom, sat the backpack in the tub, and closed the door. He grabbed Sharon by the hand and they left. They reached the bus stop at 10:28. A bus was scheduled to swing by that spot twenty-four/seven on the hour and half past the hour.

As the bus rolled to a stop, the explosion echoed throughout the block like a bomb going off in the Middle East. Glass, lumber, and remains of the motel quickly littered the area. Kurt and Sharon were startled, even though they knew it was coming. The dozen or so people on the bus looked around with curiosity. The couple paid their fares and sat near the front of the bus on the opposite side of where the explosion took place. The bus driver looked at them like they did something wrong, but dismissed their involvement when he saw Sharon's rounded belly.

The Greyhound station was five minutes away. Sharon didn't look at Kurt on the way there. He told her about the possibility of heading to Austin, but didn't say it was a definite plan. Kurt had plenty of money to purchase two bus tickets to the Longhorn State. He would put them up in a hotel until he contacted Mr. Alexander, but calming Sharon when he told her they were headed to Texas would to be difficult.

They reached the bus depot. Kurt looked at Sharon and said, "It's time for everything to fall into place." Sharon argued with Kurt when they got off the bus.

"I don't know what is going on, but I'm not going anywhere. What about my Oldsmobile? It's at the church. I'm calling my mother to pick me up. I know you are trying to fix things, but blowing up a motel and putting me in the middle of it isn't my idea of the right solution," she said a little too loudly for Kurt's liking.

He pulled her aside and explained they would go to prison if anyone heard her talking about their involvement in the motel explosion.

"You have to calm down. Your mother can't pick you up. I'm not sure what happened to the creeps watching your mom's place earlier this afternoon. The fact they didn't follow you to the church proves something happened. They could be back in front of Ava's house.

They also could have made a call to the bullpen and their secondary crew is watching now."

Sharon looked at Kurt with disbelief.

"It's set up. They believe I died in a house explosion and the only way the photo got in the briefcase near the motel was by you. It's also going to look like something happened to you. When your mother hasn't heard from you, the police are going to search for you. When they find the briefcase and open it, it's going to look like someone was trying to blackmail us. The person they will be after is Stenson. I placed one of his business cards in the identification tag inside. Don't ask how I got it. I guarantee they know everything about us, especially if they're sending you photos and other unwanted materials to your mother's house. If you continue staying in Fresno, Ava and Trevor could be in trouble. We don't know what they do, but we have an idea."

She didn't care what he had to say when they stepped off the bus, but knew he was right. They had to get out of town. Stenson and his crew attempted to kill Kurt and failed. In their minds, they succeeded. If they knew Kurt was alive, they wouldn't fail a second time. They watched Sharon for a few days and she felt lucky there wasn't a gas leak at her mother's house. She knew it was time to leave Fresno. However, Mrs. O'Neil couldn't bear the thought of leaving Trevor, despite the fact he loved his "Mamaw".

"How long will we be in Austin? When am I going to get Trevor? I can't have my mother thinking I'm dead."

"Once Stenson is contacted by police about the briefcase, he will think you died in the explosion. However, we'll type a note saying you have been kidnapped. We will send one to your mother's house and one to your house, assuring them you will not be harmed and Trevor is to remain with Ava. We're going to tell them you will be safely returned to Fresno once you have the baby and it is sent to a waiting European family that paid big bucks for the child. The only way to avoid sending the child overseas is to send $400,000 to Stenson, who will give the money to us at the appropriate time. Once we, meaning the kidnappers, have the money, you will be released."

"You are trying to cause problems for that man. He deserves it. He has been a part of our lives since I met Gary and I wish I would have never met him. For that matter, I wish Gary had never met him in college. The only problem with the story is Gary's going to confront Stenson, who will rightfully deny involvement. What if they go to my mother's house and see the second note and blame her?"

"I'm going to sign it with a false name and place it at different spots on the bottom of the page so it could not have been duplicated. It will at least buy us some time. Who cares if Gary and Stenson go at it? Maybe they will kill each other, which would be a blessing. As for our baby, you're going to leave it in Austin with me. I know it will be hard, but we will figure that part out as we go."

It was time for them to leave California. They purchased their tickets to Santa Fe and were on their way. They would purchase two more tickets at another depot in San Antonio and head to Austin.

It was scary for them, but it was at least a plan. Sharon was impressed with Kurt's careful planning. Some of it had been luck, but nature was on their side for the time being.

She leaned back against the head rest as Kurt turned off their overhead light. Her eyes got heavier and heavier as she ran through the events of the day. Kurt watched Sharon lose the battle. Before they reached the next town, she was fast asleep and dreaming about a new life.

Chapter Eight

ROACHES WEREN'T THE ONLY things crawling around the motel. The blast attracted emergency crews, cops, news teams, and bystanders to the scene. The dimly lit lot was a disco from the red and blue flashers spinning around.

Investigators went room to room trying to figure out the cause of the explosion. At the check-in desk, the clerk let police look at the log book. They found it strange the entire B wing was booked, but only a handful of rooms were occupied in the A wing. They doubted Marilyn Garland existed, and if she did, she had not signed her name on the dotted line for twenty-four rooms that night. It was an alias.

The clerk claimed a woman requested the entire back section of the motel earlier that day.

"She said a reunion was taking place."

Without pictures of the lady, the police didn't have much to go on. The description the clerk gave them wouldn't help because Candy didn't have black hair and green eyes, nor was she five-three.

Guests staying in the A wing were questioned, but no one saw a thing. One guest said he walked to an ice machine on the B wing because the one outside his room was out.

"I walked back there about twenty minutes before the blast took place and it was a ghost town. I didn't see lights shadowed on the curtains. I guess the reunion the clerk told you about was for a bunch of spirits."

After looking through the rooms on A wing, including the five that housed guests, the search moved to B.

The explosion only moved the briefcase a few feet. The inspectors noticed it lying on the sidewalk near B-18. An expert reached the briefcase and looked it over with care. He placed his ear against it and didn't hear ticking. He examined the lock to see if it was rigged and determined it was safe.

He handed it to an officer, who took it to the main office.

The search on B didn't produce evidence until they reached B-24. The room was nearly gone, but investigators determined it is where the blast occurred. After a few hours, they established a bomb was placed in the room, but couldn't come to a conclusion why someone wanted the room destroyed.

In the main office, an officer sat the briefcase on the counter. It wasn't locked so it was easily opened. A photo was inside.

They showed the photo to the desk clerk and asked if the woman signed for the rooms. Sharon stayed at the motel for about fifteen minutes, but she wasn't Marilyn Garland, a.k.a. Candy the prostitute.

"No, that's not her," he said with a pompous attitude because Sharon didn't have black hair and green eyes.

Police and investigators were frustrated. They had one possible suspect and followed that lead until it produced a roadblock. Weeks passed and the case was put in a box and tucked away in a room with other unsolved work.

The motel received a facelift and all the rooms were rebuilt. The blast was talked about for the next year or two, but was eliminated from small talk after a few years passed.

Stenson couldn't stop talking about what happened. Someone had screwed with him and it was the first time he was forced to play defense. Usually, he and Rhodes were on the offensive side.

Once the investigators reached their downtown office, Stenson was their target. The briefcase made him their only suspect.

The phone rang at Stenson's home in Worthington at four-thirty the day after the explosion.

"Hello"

"This is Captain Luango with the Fresno Police Department. I'm trying to reach Harry Stenson."

"Speaking."

"I'll get to the point Mr. Stenson. Last night, there was an explosion that ripped apart a portion of the B wing at a local motel. We are investigating the situation and have one suspect...you!"

"That's crazy. I wasn't in Fresno last night. I was home with my wife and kids."

"We would like to discuss things with you in person. We found something at the scene we think belongs to you. Your name is attached to it and there is also a picture we would like to ask some questions about."

"I would like to know what you found."

"You will find out when we sit down and talk. We're going to fly you to Fresno tomorrow. We're putting $400 into your bank account for your airfare and we will pick you up at the airport. If all goes well, you will be able to return home when our chat is over."

"Whatever happened, I'm not involved."

They hung up and Stenson called his bank. The caller on the other end followed through with his promise as there was $400 more in his account than what his bank book read.

He drove to the bank and withdrew the money. After purchasing an airline ticket, Stenson heard a knock at his door when he returned home. He went to the doorway and looked outside. Two officers stood on his porch.

"What can I do for you gentlemen?"

"Is your family home?" one of the officers asked.

"My kids are home from school, but my wife won't be home for twenty minutes or so."

"We would like to speak to your kids about your whereabouts last night," the second officer told him.

"Is this about the phone call I received before you showed up?"

"Yes. Fresno police contacted us about an incident that occurred last night and we waited for you to return home. We're here to validate you were home last night. We have to make sure you don't try to skip town if you were involved."

"If you discover I was home last night, why do I have to fly to Fresno?"

"If your alibi checks out, you should be in the clear. They want to find out why something belonging to you was at the scene."

Stenson walked to the kitchen counter, grabbed his flight confirmation number, and showed it to the officers.

"This proves I'm not going to run. Kids, I need you to come here for a few minutes."

It didn't take either of the Stenson children long to make their way to the front room because they were eavesdropping on the trio's conversation. Harry told his kids to tell the officers the truth and excused himself to the family room. One of the officers accompanied him to watch what he was doing while the senior officer sat at the kitchen table with Stenson's kids.

"I need to know where your dad was last night."

"He got home after I did, but we were here together from that point on," his fifteen-year-old son Harry III said. "It was a usual night for us. We ate dinner around 6 o'clock, watched TV, and then dad went to his office to do some work while mom got her lesson plans together for school."

The same story was reiterated by Summer, Stenson's thirteen-year-old daughter. About the time she finished telling the officer about the previous night, their mother walked in the door with a look of disgust.

"What has your father done now?"

"Hello Mrs. Stenson. Officer Jones and I are here to question your family about Harry's whereabouts last night. The kids told us what went on and we need confirmation from you."

She sat her things on the floor and told the officer about dinner, TV, and the rest of their evening.

"I don't know what he did after I went to bed around 10 o'clock, but he certainly didn't fly to California, blow up a motel in the middle of the night, and return to make me coffee by five-thirty."

The officer chuckled at her sarcasm and was satisfied with their accounts. Harry was definitely at home during the explosion. The officer walked into the family room and told Stenson his alibi checked out.

"I know you weren't in Fresno last night, but they still want to go over some things with you. If we need anything else, we'll contact you."

June watched the car make its way off their property and then started with Big Boy.

"What's going on now? You are always involved in something. I am tired of it. You will say, 'Look around! Could anyone else give you this?' I don't care, Harry. I won't be subjected to this anymore. Having our kids interrogated by the police is terrible. Did you have something to do with that motel being blown up?"

"I wasn't part of that. I haven't been to Fresno and didn't have anything to do with what happened."

The family sat and talked about their unexpected visitors and what took place in Fresno. They were interested to know why Harry was being questioned. The biggest thing Stenson was worried about was the picture and item they found.

After another typical night, Stenson tucked himself into bed and was asleep before he thought about the next day.

MATT HUNG UP THE phone and told everyone to get ready to leave. They gathered up what little they had, including the briefcase, and sat it by the back door. They walked to the back porch and laid Gary on the concrete slab behind Lauren's apartment. She looked at them with disgust and Preston didn't know what to think.

"What if this plan doesn't work?" Lauren asked.

"We can't risk dragging him across the parking lot," Matt pointed out. "If you can come up with a better plan, I'm all ears."

Lauren and Preston realized they couldn't improvise like Matt, so they agreed to follow instructions.

"Lauren, walk around to the entranceway and wait for the ambulance. If the cops see you, start walking. When the ambulance arrives, tell the EMTs to go behind the complex. If they insist on going to the front, tell them it's OK. I gave them the wrong apartment number if we have to go that route. Preston, stay here with Gary. You need to keep the EMTs occupied until we're able to seize our opportunity."

Fifteen minutes passed and they saw the ambulance's lights twirling around near the entrance to the complex. They saw Lauren talking to them and pointing in their direction.

"I think it's game time," Matt announced.

Matt and Dane stepped inside Lauren's apartment and pulled the sliding glass door to a crack. They also pulled the curtains shut.

"Preston, you have to stick to the plan."

The driver of the ambulance pulled up to Lauren and asked if she was with the party who called for an emergency squad.

"Yes, but you can't go in the front door. There was an accident earlier and the police have things taped off. You will have to go to the rear."

They nestled the ambulance next to the apartment building and the EMTs jumped out. Lauren watched as they rushed around to possibly save a life.

They reached Gary's body and rapidly asked questions.

"He's been unresponsive for the last several minutes," Preston said.

The EMTs looked at one another after checking on Gary. His color was fine and he wasn't having difficulty breathing.

"What did he eat today and has he been active?"

"I'm not sure," Preston answered. "I'm a neighbor who's trying to help. The man's son is inside making phone calls to relatives. He was panicking and didn't know what to do."

Preston cracked the sliding glass door, leaning forward to put his head inside.

"Hey Mark, can you come here?"

The plan was working to perfection. Matt and Dane waited for their cues to go into action. Preston stood at the door waiting for a response.

"I'll be back."

Preston moved the curtains back and stepped inside. While the EMTs tried to figure out what was wrong with Gary, Lauren began to cry.

"I don't know what's wrong with him," she said with a whimper. "He was fine nearly an hour ago. My boyfriend is shook up and I don't know how to help him."

"Relax Miss. Everything is going to be all right. His vitals appear to be fine. Maybe he took one too many sleeping pills."

"I'm going to see if Mark is coming."

Lauren opened the door the rest of the way and stepped inside. She pulled back the curtains and moved out of the way. Matt and Dane rushed out and took the EMTs by surprise.

"Don't move," Matt said through the mask he had slipped on. "We don't want to hurt you. All you have to do is cooperate. We don't want medicine or money. We need a ride and we're taking this man with us."

The EMTs dealt with bizarre circumstances, but nothing like their current situation. The trio trembled as Matt pointed a gun at them.

"The accident out front has a bit to do with us. Three men killed one of my friends and dumped him in front of the building. They are prepared to kill us. The man lying here had a gun jammed in the girl's side until I overtook him. You're right. You could say he's a sleeping beauty. As much as we would like to, we don't want to hurt him. We want to safely get out of here, but don't want to answer questions."

"What do you want us to do?" the female EMT asked.

"Trust me, I would like to show you," Dane joked through his mask.

"We need the three of you to go inside and take off your uniforms," Matt said. "We would like you to do it quickly. Paul (Preston's alias), stand outside and keep watch. Whistle if you see anyone."

Matt took the male EMTs to Lauren's bedroom and made them strip down to their boxers and undershirts. He took their uniforms and handed them to Dane, who was hoping to see the female EMT strip down.

"Put this on!" Matt said to Dane.

"All right, honey. It's your turn. Come in here with her," Matt said to Lauren. "Boys, you need to head to the living room. She didn't invite us to watch the peep show and I at least have that much respect."

"Thank you," she said as she walked into the bedroom.

Lauren, who held an unloaded pistol, gave the female EMT a T-shirt and sweat pants. She took off the uniform, handed it to

Lauren, and put on Lauren's clothes before going to the living room. By that time, Dane had one of the uniforms on.

"You mean I missed the show?"

"You could pay me $1,000 with the theatre sitting empty and the show would be sold out," she said to a round of laughter.

"We hate to do this, but we have to. Each of you need to take a seat at the kitchen table," Matt said.

The male EMTs slowly walked to the table and took their spots. Dane had them place their hands at their sides and he wrapped duct tape around the chair and their arms. He taped their ankles to the legs of the chair. Although he received objections from the men, he placed gags in their mouths and told them not to worry.

"Someone will be here later tonight to let you go," Dane said to ease their minds. "I know it seems like we're evil, but we don't want to harm you. OK toots, you're next."

Lauren returned to the living room with a uniform on and they were close to leaving.

"You need one of us to call over the radio," the female EMT said. "When we leave a site, it is protocol for us to check in. I'll go with you."

Matt pondered her offer for a few seconds and agreed.

"There are two conditions. Don't do anything stupid and stay away from him," he said nodding at Dane, who showed his disapproval.

"Have Paul put the last uniform on and keep watch," Matt said to Dane.

Preston went inside and slipped into the uniform. As he exited Lauren's bedroom, he heard officers approaching the front of the apartment.

"We need to get out of here. We're about to have company."

The group hurried outside. They closed the back sliding door and Matt and Dane took off their masks.

"What are you doing?" Preston said as he noticed the female EMT memorizing every square inch of their faces.

Matt asked her name.

"Savannah. That isn't a fake name either."

"Savannah, if the cops see us, this is your dad and I'm your fiancé," he said while looking at a sparkling ring on her left hand.

"Get the stretcher and we'll place Gary on it. We need to get him to the ambulance as quickly as possible."

They raced to the ambulance and pulled the stretcher out with enough clangs and bangs to make anyone watching feel badly for the ride Gary was about to take. They reached Gary and hoisted him onto the stretcher. They were lucky to have Savannah helping them because they didn't know what they were doing.

She strapped him onto the stretcher and made sure he was secure. As they wheeled him through the grass, they heard a faint knock on Lauren's front door. They kicked it into high gear and began pushing Gary toward the ambulance like a housemother who won a shopping spree at a local grocery store.

They reached the ambulance and were set to lift Gary into the back when an officer called out to them.

"Is everything OK over there?"

"Yes officer," Lauren assured him. "We have a mild stroke victim, but he's going to be all right."

"Carry on."

It was a close call, but the group's plan worked. The officer didn't get close enough for a good look at them. They placed Gary in the back of the ambulance and Dane jumped into the driver's seat while Lauren got into the passenger's side.

They pulled onto Morse Road and let out sighs of relief. It was another risky move, but it turned out for the best.

TRAFFIC ON THE WAY to the airport was a predictable bumper-to-bumper pace. Thanks to years of practice, he managed to weave in and out of cars on the city's outer belt like a NASCAR champ. He parked his car at an overnight lot in case he was asked to stay in Fresno longer than desired. Big Boy put on his rain coat and walked to the shuttle bus.

He made his way inside the airport and grabbed his ticket while getting a carry-on bag tagged. Stenson passed several shops and magazine stands before going through security, which was a fiasco due to his flashy jewelry.

Although trouble possibly awaited him in Fresno, it didn't show in his demeanor. Stenson strutted through the airport with his usual walk, one that said, "I own this place."

When he reached Delta's terminal, he took a seat and waited for the boarding call. The announcement blared over the intercom. Stenson walked down the ramp to the plane and found his seat.

He spent the flight preparing for questions they could ask. When the plane touched ground in California, Stenson felt he was ready for the onslaught. Big Boy and authorities knew he wasn't in Fresno two nights prior, but that wouldn't stop them from pinning everything on him.

He got off the plane and looked around when he exited the ramp. Stenson didn't see anyone who appeared to be searching for him. He didn't know what to do so he took a seat outside the terminal.

After five minutes, two men approached him.

"Are you Harry Stenson?"

"Yes."

"We're the investigators on the case. I'm detective Rick Shields and this is detective Joe Reynolds. We're going to grab a bite to eat and head to the office to run you through some questions."

Lunch was at a local dive, one that served good food, as most local dives do. They small-talked each other while they ate and drove to the station when they finished. The mood changed when they made their way inside the interrogation room.

Captain Luango and other officers sat inside a small room to watch the show. It's almost as if they paid big money to view what was going to take place. The luxury suite was missing beer, greasy food, and a couple attractive hostesses. Coffee, doughnuts, and sweaty counterparts would have to do.

Stenson flopped into his chair with an aura of confidence. He didn't have anything to conceal and certainly wasn't going to let a few men hiding behind badges scare him.

The interrogators didn't pull punches. The first round bell sounded and they came out swinging like Mike Tyson in his "Kid Dynamite" days.

"We know you weren't in Fresno two nights ago, but we're certain you ordered the motel to be blown up. Tell us why you wanted that to happen!" Shields demanded.

"I don't know why the motel was blown up. This is the first time I have been to Fresno. I don't know anyone who lives here and I didn't order anyone to make a stop in Fresno. Why would I want some five-and-dime motel blown up in this crummy city? I think the fog has clouded your viewpoint on things."

"Everyone at the scene of the crime, which is what took place, said your name didn't ring a bell. However, the desk clerk said you stayed there quite often," Reynolds said as he displayed a common characteristic of a good interrogator.

"I'm not stupid. You can come up with every lie in the book to get me to admit to something I didn't do. It's not going to happen. I told you I wasn't there and didn't have anything to do with the explosion. We can call my lawyers if this is how the afternoon is going to go. I'm more than happy to answer questions and I'll do it truthfully, but I won't be accused of something I didn't do."

The investigators leaned in and whispered to one another for a few seconds. Stenson rolled his eyes and sighed to let them know he was perturbed. He looked at the black glass window in the middle of the wall to his left. For fun, he waved and smiled. His sarcasm missed its mark on the other side of the wall.

"He is an arrogant prick," Luango said. "He might not have anything to do with it, but I would love to see him charged because of his attitude."

Back inside the interrogation room, Shields reached down and pulled the briefcase from underneath the table. He placed it on top of the long table and pushed it toward Stenson.

"Have you seen this before?"

Stenson pulled it closer. He wanted to say yes because it was a top of the line briefcase. It looked like a shoe shiner in Mississippi or Louisiana spent time with it. The briefcase had a few scuffmarks, which were more than likely from the ride it took during the blast, but the polished shine made it hard to ignore.

As soon as Big Boy opened it, the scent hit him like a skunk on the side of the road. However, it was a pleasant aroma. It made him think of a new Buick. The black fuzzy interior also made him think of something that was still a little taboo. It resembled a floor rug in one of the porno movies he had watched.

He looked inside the pocket and it was empty. He didn't know why the briefcase linked him to the explosion.

Reynolds and Shields grew impatient waiting for an answer while Stenson took his time looking over the briefcase.

"Well, have you seen this briefcase before?"

"No, but I would like to have it."

The gentlemen began a second round of whispering before sliding a second item Stenson's way.

Once again, Stenson picked it up and looked it over.

"I won't allow you to waste your breath this time. I have seen this before," said a laughing Stenson, who held up the business card with a sense of pride.

"Explain why your business card was in the identification tag inside the briefcase."

"Maybe the briefcase is mine. I know the two of you, along with the rest of the people on the other side of that glass, are trying to do your job. My job is to make sure I'm not charged because I'm innocent. I'm as curious as you. I would like to know how one of my cards got inside this briefcase."

As he finished talking, reality sank in. He knew he had something to do with Fresno because two of his boys were watching Sharon's every move at her mother's house. He hadn't heard from them since the day of the blast. Either they were discovered and eliminated or they were the cause of the blast.

He concluded they wouldn't set him up so he figured it was Sharon.

After Shields walked over and handed him a folder, Stenson knew she was involved in the explosion.

He wouldn't open it because he knew what was inside.

"Open it!"

Stenson slowly opened the folder and tried not to let his face prove he knew the person in the photograph. It was one of two pictures sent to Ava's house as a scare tactic. Stenson tried forcing her to end the rendezvous with her mystery lover, who he hoped was eliminated.

Despite Stenson trying to hide the fact he knew her, Shields landed another punch.

"We knew you would deny knowing this woman. We found the place where you had the film developed and they described the same picture you're looking at now."

Stenson hired someone to follow Sharon and take pictures of anything suspicious, but didn't know where the film was developed. The film was processed by the man he hired in a dark room at his house. The lie worked and forced Stenson to talk.

"I don't know who took the picture, but I know who this woman is," Stenson admitted. "I know Sharon is having an affair, but that isn't something you bring up like the weather. Maybe someone is trying to get money from her."

"So we're supposed to believe a briefcase you claim to never have seen shows up unaccompanied at a motel, one of your business cards somehow gets blown a few thousand miles left and inserts itself into the identification tag, and a photograph that depicts an attractive woman getting it on joins the party?"

Shields laughed at the question, as if to say, "You're screwed Big Boy!"

"If you think I did it, lock me up and put me on trial. You might prove the briefcase is mine, which it is not. You might prove I put one of my business cards inside the briefcase, which I did not. You might prove I sent the picture, which I didn't take, develop, or send. Like any case, it comes down to how elaborate the story is linking evidence to a particular individual. Yes, it looks like I could have been involved, but I wasn't at the scene, so I won't be charged with blowing up a motel. If I'm charged with owning a nice briefcase, so be it. If I'm charged with trying to get a little business, so be it. If I'm charged with stalking, so be it. I know I didn't take part in blowing up that motel, so let me walk out of here or put me in jail. Either way, I'm done talking. You can talk to my attorneys."

"Some of this might be circumstantial, but someone you know did this. Maybe it was the two gentlemen we have locked up."

As he finished talking, the door opened and Jackson and Ryule walked in. They took their seats and Stenson looked at them, sending a signal through his eyes that said, "Don't say a word."

"Do you know them?"

"No."

"These gentlemen were arrested yesterday after a felonious high-speed chase through downtown Fresno. Guess where they're from!"

"Columbus."

"You guessed it," Reynolds said. "Why would two shady guys from Columbus be in town for what they called business, especially when they weren't dressed like they were going to an important meeting? We caught them harassing a little boy outside a corner store in South Fresno and when we approached them, they sped off. After several minutes, a bad crash stopped them dead in their tracks."

"We had to accompany them to the hospital to get treated before bringing them to the station," Shields added. "Neither one had much to say, but sitting in this room for several hours has a tendency to make someone talk. Business turned into investigative work, which turned into keeping an eye on someone, which turned into working for...Harry Stenson. If you don't know these men, how do they know you by name and claim to work for you?"

Stenson stared at the table thinking about everything he had been asked. He tried to collect himself before answering in haste.

"Maybe I lied about not having business here in Fresno," Stenson confessed. "Although I had two guys working for me in Fresno doesn't mean I had anything to do with what took place at that motel."

Shields grunted in response to Stenson's matter of fact attitude.

"Here is how I know these gentlemen. I discovered Sharon O'Neil, who lives in Mesa with her husband Gary, was having an affair. Gary and I went to college together and are lifelong friends. He is the kind of guy that snaps. He's a good guy, but has a wicked temper. I knew if he found out his wife was sleeping with someone else, he would flip. I knew the other man involved could be killed and Sharon as well."

Reynolds sat back in the black leather chair and shook his head at Stenson's feeble attempt to justify his actions.

"We put Sharon under surveillance, thus the investigative work. One of the guys following her took a few pictures of Sharon and her lover. Sharon moved to Fresno to live with her mother while finishing her pregnancy, due to Gary being on the road so much. I lied about the photos. We sent them to Sharon in an attempt to stop the affair. They have a little boy and another on the way. I was trying to protect a friend and a family. As far as money, she can tell you we didn't try to extort any from her. I don't need it and neither do they. I have a successful public relations firm and it's growing by the day."

His reasoning sounded logical to both investigators, but it didn't explain why they were in Fresno and what kind of business they were conducting.

"Why are the two of you here?"

Stenson interrupted before they responded.

"I sent them to Fresno to keep an eye on Sharon. After we sent her the photo, I wanted to make sure she was keeping to herself."

"And if she wasn't?" Shields asked.

"We were going to cross that bridge when we reached it. She wasn't going to be hurt, but we were going to make sure it didn't cause problems for our business. I didn't want one of my employees involved in a vicious crime. It would be bad for business. Gary is one of my top executives and how would that look? I guess we would have told her we knew and were going to tell Gary unless she ended things with her lover. We knew he wouldn't take the news well either way because he is a bit possessive of Sharon. The whole thing is a mess."

"Let's get off the Sharon O'Neil topic. For the betterment of this day, we'll buy into what you're trying to sell us. We know none of you were involved in yesterday's blast because you were on the other side of the country and the two of you were behind bars. However, we want to know how the explosion happened."

The three men not wearing badges looked at each other with clueless looks. Finally, Jackson spoke up.

"We were outside of that store yesterday because we were trying to track down a man by the name of Kurt. While we were waiting, a boy came by and threw a rock at our vehicle. It upset me, so I got out and grabbed him by the arm. He started kicking me and I got rough with him. That's when the officer came out. I panicked and jumped back in the car and we took off. We saw the same boy earlier in the day and he gave us a note that was from Kurt to Sharon saying he was going to be at that store. If you search our car, you will find the note. The boy asked for money, but we didn't have cash on us. I gave him a briefcase instead and told him to sell it."

As Jackson rambled, a detective entered the room and sat a box on the table.

"If you take a close look, the man Sharon is on top of is Kurt. Apparently, an explosion took place at his house. No one knows if he's dead, but I have a suspicion he's behind both explosions. I have a feeling the boy gave Kurt, assuming he's still alive, my briefcase. The only way the picture ends up in the briefcase is he placed it there. Sharon could have access to one of Stenson's business cards and put it in there to frame Harry. I know it sounds ridiculous, but it's the truth."

While Jackson tried to weasel out of trouble, Shields pulled a Ziploc baggie from the box. A note found inside their vehicle was being stored inside the baggie as evidence.

Sharon,
Meet me in fifteen minutes at Aggie's Mini-Mart on East Church Avenue.

Kurt

Kurt was in Fresno and knew Sharon, so Jackson's story added up. A third whisper session took place and Shields left the room.

He walked into the small room where the captain was watching things and discussed the interviews.

"They know more than they're telling us. I don't trust those guys, but they weren't at the scene of the crime, which eliminates them as our bomber."

"I agree," the captain concurred. "The one admitted it was his briefcase. That entirely eliminates Stenson. His business card was in the briefcase and the picture ties him to what happened as well, but I don't believe he's involved. Keep them locked up until they post bail."

Shields walked back into the chilly room and took his seat.

"Stenson, we're letting you go, but be available. You will be staying here to face charges filed against you," he said while looking at Jackson and Ryule.

Stenson's men were escorted from the room and the investigators led Harry to the front door.

"We'll keep in touch," they said. "One of our officers is waiting to take you to the airport. Enjoy your flight home."

Harry walked to the patrol car.

"I'll be back."

He walked back inside the station and dropped by the front desk.

"I want to post bail for two men."

The old lady on the verge of retirement at the window was offended by him interrupting her Solitaire time. He told her who he wanted to bail out. She took his money and told him to be seated. Within minutes, Jackson and Ryule were escorted out by an officer and both investigators.

Reynolds and Shields knew they made a mistake by allowing Stenson to walk, but their hands were tied. He legally had a right to bail out anyone in the jail.

"Don't mess with us Stenson or you will all be in here and won't get out."

"You know how to reach me," he said as he smiled like he dodged another bullet.

The three men walked out the door and got into the officer's cruiser. The officer tried to start a conversation, but no one said a word. The ride to the airport was like a funeral procession. In Stenson's mind, it was. He had replaced his right-hand men before and would do it again.

Chapter Nine

THE BUS PULLED INTO Austin and, for the first time in days, Sharon and Kurt felt a sense of relief. Neither had been there before, but they fell in love with the city in the first ten minutes. The Central Texas Hill Country has that effect on visitors.

Even though they were in a place where no one knew their faces or names, Kurt knew Stenson and his crew would look for them. However, finding them would be nearly impossible. Kurt and Sharon were needles in haystacks.

They got off the bus at the depot and didn't know where to go. Kurt noticed a phone booth so they walked over to it and looked for lodging. They found a fancy hotel located on the Colorado River that overlooked downtown Austin, which is still the pulse of Travis County. Their room was located near the top of the hotel and the views were breathtaking.

They saw people walking on a trail nestled beside the river. The Mesa lovers saw shoppers making their way along sidewalks in a bustling downtown. If they looked hard enough, they could see politicians getting their hands dirty and lining their pockets at the capital building.

The visitors didn't leave the premises the rest of the day. They visited the hotel's restaurant to get lunch, but retreated to their room when they finished eating. Sharon was worn out and needed to get all the rest she could.

It wouldn't be much longer before she burst. The problem with Sharon leaving Mesa was she left her family doctor behind. She was referred to a doctor in Fresno, but was on her own in Austin. Sharon and Kurt knew she wasn't supposed to travel and their child could be in danger, but they didn't have a choice.

After an afternoon of relaxation, Kurt tried to contact Jim. He reached inside the pocket of the shirt he had worn for days and pulled out Mr. Alexander's phone number. He placed his fingers into each number and circled around the rotary phone.

"Hello."

"Is Jim there?" Kurt asked the woman on the other end.

"He's out right now. May I ask who is calling?"

"I'm an old friend. When do you expect him to return?"

"I'm not sure. He's in and out. If you give me your name and number, I'll make sure he returns the call."

"If he's out on the farm, I can call him later tonight. If he's on the road, I'll try again in a few days."

It was obvious to Mr. Alexander's wife the man knew her husband. She somewhat let her guard down after Kurt's last comments.

"He's on his way back from Fresno and is supposed to be home Thursday. Jim's typically home for the weekends. What did you say your name was?" she asked in one final attempt to get his name.

Since she was open and honest, he told her who was calling.

"Kurt. Who am I speaking with?"

"This is his wife Elaine."

"Tell Jim that Kurt is in Austin. I'm staying at a hotel for the next few days. While I'm in town, I would like to see him. Maybe we can get together Friday or Saturday."

"Jim loves to have visitors, especially old friends. Make sure you bring a healthy appetite. When you're traveling, a home-cooked meal always hits the spot. I'll give him the message you called. Where can he reach you?"

"I'm not sure what the number is here. I'll get in touch with him when he returns."

They ended their conversation. Sharon had closed her eyes while Kurt was talking and dozed off. Kurt wanted to tell her about their possible trip to the Alexander farm, but didn't want to wake her. He turned on the tube and watched TV until his chin was buried in his chest.

Neither of them moved the entire night. It was the first time they slept comfortably for a while. Kurt woke up first and went down to the restaurant. He meandered through the breakfast buffet line and loaded up a Styrofoam box for each of them.

Sharon slowly opened her eyes when Kurt sat their breakfast on the table near the window.

"Good morning. I have breakfast."

"You know how pregnant women love to eat," Sharon laughed. "I could smell it as soon as you were outside the door."

Sharon slowly wiggled her way out of bed and wobbled to the table. Kurt sat pillows on her chair and she plopped down to eat. He pulled back the curtains and they ate in peace while taking in the beautiful morning God created in Austin.

"We have a couple days to spend here," Kurt said. "I will go stir crazy being cooped up inside this room. I don't know if you are up for a little sight seeing."

"I won't make it much longer. I have to get to a doctor soon. I saw Dr. Singh in Fresno last Wednesday and he thought I might go into labor sometime this week. I don't think walking around would be good for me. I'm supposed to be off my feet and have ignored those orders. I don't want to be locked inside this room for the next few days either, but walking to the restaurant yesterday wore me out. I would like to save my energy for traveling to Jim's house over the weekend."

Kurt agreed and they kept a routine for the next few days. He got breakfast for them when he woke up. They ate and watched TV until lunch, then spent time doing crossword puzzles from a book Kurt purchased in the lobby. A nap soon followed and then it was time for dinner. Kurt went to the restaurant and returned with their meals. More TV watching ensued until time to hit the sack.

The calendar rolled to Friday and it was time for Kurt to contact Jim. He finished his morning bacon, eggs, and toast before retrieving Jim's number off the night stand.

Unfortunately, the invention of the cell phone was years away so Kurt waited for the rotary phone to slowly work its magic.

"Alexander residence," Jim proudly said.

"Is this Jim?"

"Speaking."

"How are you? This is Kurt."

"The fellow I picked up in Mesa earlier this week?"

"Yes. I hate to take up your invitation to visit so soon, but my friend and I needed to get away from California for a few days. I told Sharon how you passionately talked about Austin so we traveled to Texas. We're going home Sunday."

"Elaine said you called, but it didn't register you were who she was talking about," Jim said in his twangy southern drawl. "I have a lot of work to finish this afternoon and in the morning. Come over tomorrow for dinner around 6 o'clock."

Kurt didn't know how to get to the Alexander farm, but Jim solved the problem.

"We need directions from where we are staying."

"A cab ride wouldn't do the drive justice. I'll have Colt, the oldest of my three children, pick you up in front of the hotel at 5:00 p.m. and he will give you a mini tour of Austin on the way."

"That sounds good."

"We look forward to having you as guests. We'll see you tomorrow."

Kurt would rather have their reunion that night. He was more than ready to see something besides flowery wallpaper and old Westerns. Kurt explained the details to Sharon when he got off the phone.

They continued their routine until the next day. After catching a few Zs, they woke up and got ready. At 4:45, they closed the door behind them and walked to the lobby's entrance. While Sharon sat reading one of the latest fashion magazines, Kurt kept a close eye on the carport.

At 4:58, an old Chevrolet pickup pulled up to the curb. Kurt saw a male in his early twenties driving the vehicle. Country music blared from the speaker system and the exhaust echoed throughout the carport. The driver turned the music down and got out. He looked inside the hotel, but couldn't see Kurt or Sharon behind the dark glass. He glanced around the parking lot a couple times before Kurt decided it was Colt.

"I believe he's here," Kurt said to Sharon.

He helped her get off the couch and they exited the hotel. They approached the truck and Kurt and Colt made eye contact.

"Are you here to pick up Kurt and Sharon?"

"Yes. I'm Colt Alexander," he said as he extended a hand to Kurt.

A firm handshake took place and Colt noticed Sharon was pregnant.

"It looks like you're about to pop ma'am."

"I'm supposed to be relaxing, but I need to get away from this hotel. It could happen any moment. Let's hope it's not over dinner."

"My family has helped deliver many calves, but I'm not sure how we would do bringing a little tot into the world."

The men helped Sharon get into the truck. Once she settled in, they pulled out of the carport and the tour of Austin began. As Colt showed them several landmarks and historic places, Kurt wondered how they were ever important. It seemed the only reason each place was significant was because a Texas Longhorns flag adorned their exterior. Colt drove past Armadillo World Headquarters and there was a burnt orange flag flapping in the wind.

Colt continued driving around town. They passed the Deep Eddy Pool, Driskill Hotel, and Texas State Capitol. Nearly every car had a University of Texas bumper sticker. Every other person wore Texas Longhorns clothing and the ones that didn't we're certainly viewed as outcasts. Nearly every billboard had a UT logo on it. Kurt discovered people were nuts about their Longhorns. It made sense why Jim stated "Hook 'Em Horns" when they met earlier in the week.

Colt decided it was time to venture away from downtown. He drove west out of the heart of the city and the roller coaster ride began. As flat as the other half of Austin was, the western side of town certainly made up for the other half being like an undeveloped chest on a woman. They made their way out of the city and began down a scenic state route.

"We don't live in Austin," Colt said. "We live in a small farming community. We tell folks we live in Austin because it's easier to say. They should change the names of these small towns around here to Austin. Every person within forty-five minutes says they're from Austin anyway. I hope my driving isn't making you sick. I should have warned you things were a little hilly."

After fifteen minutes on the winding route, they turned right onto a lengthy unpaved road.

"That's part of our farm on the left. The land to the right is owned by the Parsons. Mr. Parson and my dad are good friends. We help them in times of need and they do the same for us."

The mile drive down the dirt road reached a T. A white farm house sat directly in front of the stop. There was a cattle barn to the right of the house and a pair of silos towered behind the barn. The road to the right went down a sharp hill and a large pond sat on the right hand side of the road.

"If we turn right, the road goes back up a hill and comes to a dead end at the top. The Parsons have a few chicken houses and horse barns on top of the hill (or heel in Colt's drawl). The pond at the bottom of the hill has the biggest bass you will find in all of Texas. I have seen bass pulled out that would make a marlin blush."

Since going right wasn't an option, Colt turned left and started down a gradual slope towards his family's farm. They passed a small cemetery on the right side of the road, which made Kurt and Sharon look at each other.

Colt saw their puzzled looks when they passed the cemetery so he gave them a history lesson.

"That is the former Calvary Baptist cemetery. There used to be a small church next to it and a lot of the members are buried there. My dad's great grandfather used to be the pastor. A tornado wiped it out in the early 1900s and the congregation met in a horse barn until the church was rebuilt in 1931. It survived two more tornadoes and a historic hailstorm. In 1975, a couple city slickers were on a drunken rampage and lit the place on fire. My grandma was the first to discover it and called the Parsons and other nearby neighbors.

Everyone banded together to try to save it. One of the church members had a truss collapse on him and they didn't get him out in time."

The oft emotional Sharon fought back tears.

"Once Mr. Burks died, everyone decided the church needed moved to a different location. He is buried in the cemetery and nearly every land owner who passed since then has a plot. It's a revered place around these parts. A few years ago, kids I went to high school with went in there on Halloween and tried to conjure up spirits. The only thing they stirred up was a few angry farmers. My dad fired a shotgun blast and it scared those kids so badly they thought ghosts were shooting at them. I think they were out of there within ten seconds. The story has been distorted to the point those kids were actually chased out of the cemetery by dead farmers and one of them fired a rifle from the Texas Revolution. It's funny stuff."

Colt put his truck in neutral and coasted to the bottom of the hill. He pulled into his family's driveway on the left side of the gravel road.

THEY KNEW LAUREN HAD to go back for her car. Their vehicle was impounded by Stenson and the rest of his evil empire. Trouble waited if they were caught in the ambulance. Matt instructed Dane to drive past Easton. Nearly two miles down the road, a small vacated shopping complex gave them the opportunity to ditch the ambulance and wait for Lauren.

Dane wheeled the ambulance into the parking lot, which served as a place for drug drop-offs, lot lizards, and occasional napping spots for coppers. They drove around the backside of the complex and parked the ambulance. Matt called a cab and the vehicle arrived in three minutes.

Matt walked Lauren to the entrance of the complex and begged her not to screw them over.

"For the first time, this operation is in someone else's hands. Please come back to get us."

Lauren got into the cab and thought about telling the driver to take her to the airport so she could board a plane and get as far away from Columbus as possible.

"Residents of Everett Wren please."

The driver obliged. The five-minute trip wasn't nearly long enough. It seemed like she had fifteen seconds to think about things before they pulled into the back entrance. Lauren paid the driver and walked to the back of her apartment.

When she reached the back door, Lauren noticed it was opened. She was frightened because she knew they shut the door when they left.

She slowly leaned inside, but couldn't see anything because it was dark. She wanted to go in, but was afraid of what awaited. She faintly heard police wrapping up their investigative work so she thought she was safe. She felt around for the light switch on the wall and discovered another terrifying scene. Both male EMTs were gone.

She panicked and didn't know what to do. Maybe the cops were waiting to arrest her. Maybe the EMTs were kidnapped by Stenson and Rhodes. Lauren knew her time was limited. She had to slip away as quickly as possible.

She went to her bedroom, stuffed a few of her belongings into an overnight bag, and hustled out the back. She walked around the side of her building. Once Lauren reached the front, she pretended like she was going to work.

"Stop!" an officer shouted. "Where are you going?"

"I'm headed to work, sir."

"Before you go, we need to ask a few questions."

They decided Lauren was free to go after questioning her for fifteen minutes. She told them she slept all afternoon because she worked a twelve-hour night shift. Both officers bought her story.

Lauren reached her car and dropped the keys three or four times because she was nervous. She finally quit fumbling around and found the right key. She started the engine and pulled out of her space. The cops waved her through and she turned out of the complex.

The drive down Morse Road should have ended in a collision. Lauren spent more time staring in the mirror than focusing on the road. Someone was following her, or so she thought. The trip ended as she reached the parking lot and pulled next to the ambulance.

"What took you so long?" Matt asked.

"When I arrived at the apartment, the EMTs were gone. They weren't inside and I didn't see them outside. I gathered a few things and went straight to my car. An officer called me over and I spent fifteen minutes trying to give them the run around. We're lucky they let me leave."

"Let's get moving," Matt said. "We need to get things set up at the warehouse."

Lauren got in the back and Dane took the wheel. The drive to the warehouse was uneventful. They approached the access road and things looked normal. Matt jumped out, unhooked the chain, and knelt in the weeds. Dane flipped off the car's lights and drove to the turnaround lane. He turned the car around, drove back to the access road, and pulled in. Matt attached the chain and rejoined them.

Preston was happy to see how things worked instead of being stuffed in a trunk while knocked out cold. Lauren was also observant, but Preston was really interested in what was going on.

Dane pulled the car past the circular party site and drove over the railroad tracks. Despite the apparent high school fiesta, everything was OK. They eased through the fence and pulled into the warehouse. They were safely home, as Matt and Dane dubbed the warehouse. Savannah wished she hadn't offered to accompany the group of strangers.

They popped the trunk and pulled Gary out. He was slowly coming to his senses, but they still had twenty minutes or so.

"This is where we need you the most Preston," Matt said. "You're not going to like some of this, but we need you to play along."

Preston was uncomfortable, although he was briefed on what was going to happen. He agreed to play his part and walked across the road to the storage houses.

"This place is creepy," Preston whispered.

Matt and Dane dragged Gary by his arms to the door of the second storage building and let him fall face first to the ground. He moaned when they dropped him, but was still like a town drunkard.

Dane unlocked the door and Preston's eyes swelled to the size of golf balls when he caught a glimpse of what was inside through the small crack in the door. He couldn't believe what he saw.

Before Preston turned around to argue, Matt shoved a needle in his left triceps.

"What are you doing?" Preston said as he pushed his way past them. "I'm finished with this. You could go to the law, but instead you trespass, kidnap, steal, and play a part in having one of your friends killed."

After venting, Preston turned and started running across the road. Before reaching the other side, he started feeling dizzy. He staggered toward the warehouse and fell to his knees before slumping on his right side.

Preston was in for a long few days, but if he performed admirably, it would get them one step closer to payback.

COLT GOT OUT AND walked around to help Kurt ease Sharon out of the pickup.

"Hold on a second," Colt said.

He returned with a small step stool.

"This should make it easier."

Sharon stepped onto the stool and made her way down three steps, hoping it was the last time she attempted the task.

As Colt, who obviously received the gift of gab from his father, rambled on about their farm, both visitors checked out the Alexander landscape.

Their small white house sat on the bend in the road, which continued to the next farm about half a mile away. A road veered to the left beside the Alexander's house that ran into a state route almost a mile up the road. On the right side of that road was a milk barn, which was home to a few cats and dogs.

Behind the milk barn was an enormous pasture full of dairy cattle. A bull was on the hillside staring down at the cattle as if to say, "Which one of you Bessies are going to get it today?"

A tractor and another truck sat in front of Colt's pickup. An aged barn housing the family's station wagon, tractor and car parts, tools, and other various items sat nearby. Jim was making his last pass in the hayfield behind the barn when he noticed Colt was back with their visitors.

He waved to them and pulled beside the barn. He shut his John Deere tractor off and made his way over to Kurt and Sharon.

"Howdy," he said as if to signify he was a southern farmer. "Did Colt's driving get the best of you?"

Kurt thought Colt's driving was up to par, but his talking could have been minimized.

"You have raised a fine young man," Sharon said. "I hope my children grow up to be as well-mannered."

Sharon was a pretty woman and her words made Colt blush.

Jim knew Kurt was bringing someone with him, but never imagined Kurt's friend being a pregnant woman.

"I'm Jim," he said to Sharon.

"It's nice to meet you. I'm Sharon."

"Let's go in the house and see what Elaine cooked for us."

As they made their way into the house, the smell of barbecue ribs filled their nostrils and made each of their mouths water. The house was quaint and country-like. The living room was the first room visitors walked into. Despite the old hardwood floors not giving off their best shine, Elaine had a rug near the front door for footwear.

Jim and Elaine's bedroom sat to the left of the living room and Kurt saw a gun rack hanging on the wall. He wondered if one of the guns was involved in the Halloween scare.

Once they took their shoes off, they made their way through the living room and into the kitchen. Elaine cooked a masterpiece that included ribs, sweet potatoes, okra, freshly picked green beans, cornbread, and two pies, one raspberry and the other apple.

"We don't drink much around here, but Colt has a beer or two with his buddies from time to time," Jim said. "Colt picked up a six-pack in case you wanted a beer. Elaine and I drink sweet tea."

"I'm Elaine," Jim's wife said as she hugged Sharon and then shook Kurt's hand. "I hope you like what I prepared. I haven't been out of Texas so I'm not sure what they cook out there in California. If you don't like it, you don't have to eat it. We have a pizza shop five minutes down the road."

As they sat down, the front door swung open. Jim looked at his watch and shook his head.

"Right on time," he grumbled.

The youngest Alexander boy, Tyler, and their daughter, Chelsea, kicked off their shoes and joined them.

"Boy, take off your hat and introduce yourself," Jim said. "You too, young lady."

"Hello. I'm Tyler Alexander."

"And I'm Chelsea Alexander."

The introductions were over and everyone dug in. Jim and Colt did most of the talking, which came as no surprise to the rest of those seated at the table. Okra was a first for Kurt and Sharon, but they enjoyed it. Sharon ate more than Kurt, until dessert was served. Kurt ate two slices of Elaine's homemade apple pie, which was baked with apples from the trees in their side yard.

The conversation centered around their trip and the weather in Austin. Jim was proud of the fact Austin averaged about three hundred days of sunshine per year. However, it rained a good bit and the Alexander farm, like many on the edge of the Texas Hill Country, was subject to flash floods. When the skies opened, severe thunderstorms were commonplace.

Jim and Elaine were inquisitive about Fresno. Since Kurt didn't know much about Fresno, he let Sharon do the talking.

She told them the bad things about Fresno first, which didn't leave her much to talk about. Austinites boasted about their safe city. While crime was on the rise in America, Austin and its expanding suburbs remained some of the safest places to live in the country.

Sharon couldn't report that Fresno was equally safe. She explained about the gangs, drugs, and crime. Breathing difficulties and extreme heat were also problems. Texas was hot, but Fresno put Austin to shame.

Like Austin, Fresno didn't deal with miserable winters. Sharon told them about Tule Fog, which fascinated the Alexanders. She praised the roadways around Texas while bashing the lack of means to get around in Fresno.

It didn't take the hosts long to figure out they weren't missing much in California.

Although Sharon spent the better part of twenty minutes tearing down Fresno, she saved the best for last. Since they were eating in a farmhouse, she knew the Alexanders would appreciate the best Fresno had to offer. She intentionally waited to tell them about the agriculture and wealth of fresh food grown locally.

Sharon explained how the largest city in California's Central Valley was well known for its crop growing, cultivation, farming, and gardening. She also talked about her mom and shared her family's roots in farming.

By the end of the conversation, Sharon had the family laughing about some stories from her childhood. It was safe to say the Alexanders were taking to Sharon, who received looks of condemnation when she arrived.

They got up from the table and the Alexanders took Kurt and Sharon outside to show them around. Sharon wasn't feeling well, but knew they were proud of where they lived and what they had. She wasn't going to show she would rather stay inside.

Jim took them around the side of the house and they walked down to a small pond.

"We have decent fish in there, but nothing compared to the monsters in the Parson's pond," Colt pointed out.

Elaine showed them her apple trees and raspberry bushes, but Jim and Colt provided commentary. She cut a rose from her flower garden for Sharon. The longer they were outside, the worse she felt. She wanted to excuse herself and go inside, but Jim and Colt didn't leave much of an opening for anyone to talk.

Not one car passed since Colt pulled into the driveway. There wasn't a reason to look left, right, left, and right again. Jim trudged into the roadway without a care in the world.

Kurt noticed Sharon looked pale. They made it across the road and reached the outside of the milking barn when Sharon's legs became weak.

"Are you feeling all right?" Kurt asked Sharon.

"I don't know. Ever since we came outside, I have felt nauseous. I'm not going to make it."

The words barely left Sharon's mouth before she wailed in pain. The Alexanders froze with concerned looks on their faces.

Although he knew what was going on, Kurt asked the obvious. "What's wrong?"

"I'm in pain. I think it's happening."

"We need to get you inside the house," Elaine said. "Jim, call Doc Badnarik."

Before Jim ran across the street, Sharon cried out in pain a second time. The severity of her agony dropped her to the ground. It was obvious they weren't going to make it inside.

Elaine ordered Chelsea to get blankets and towels from the house. She went into the barn and cleared out a spot in one of the stalls where they delivered newborn calves.

Kurt, Jim, and Colt lifted Sharon and gently sat her on top of a small hay bale. Chelsea returned with the supplies her mother requested and Elaine spread blankets on top of the spot she cleared. The men eased her onto the blankets and Jim ran to the house and called Doc Badnarik.

Chelsea grabbed a silver bucket and rinsed it out. She filled it with lukewarm water and placed it near Sharon, who was in labor. Elaine asked Jim and Colt to stand outside the stall so Sharon could have privacy.

Doc Badnarik pulled up to the house and walked to the barn. Despite giving her pain medication, the next two hours were difficult. Sharon screamed in agony and there wasn't a thing anyone could do. Kurt held her hand as he sat beside her while Doc Badnarik, and Elaine and Chelsea, who served as nursing interns for the evening, were telling her to push, push, push.

She finally hit the home stretch. Every birth is different. Some women go through a long, drawn out process while other deliveries happen quickly. It felt like three weeks to Sharon, but her delivery of Preston was fast, which brought double the pain.

At 11:03 p.m., Preston popped his screaming head out of his mother's body. It looked like Jim and Colt had competition because Preston didn't stop for an hour.

"Great! A feisty little booger," Kurt said.

Preston finally wiggled his way into the world, thanks to intense pushing by Sharon. The doctor checked him and everything was fine. They used the water Chelsea placed beside Sharon to clean Preston. Elaine wrapped him in a towel and handed him to his exhausted mother.

Jim and Colt popped their heads into the stall.

"You got your wish. At least you got to eat a peaceful meal," Colt said as he remembered Sharon's words when he picked them up at the hotel. "I guess you can add baby delivering to the Alexander's resume as well."

Colt's comments drew a grin from his dad, but he elbowed him as if to say, "Enough of the jokes."

Jim didn't know it, but Kurt saw the rib shot he gave his son.

"It's OK. A little humor is needed right now. I'm ready to look outside to see if a trio of men is standing there with gold, incense, and myrrh."

Jim and Elaine were religious and knew Kurt was trying to be funny. They knew he in no way was saying Preston was Christ's equal. He was making light of the fact that not too many kids are born in a barn.

It was closing in on 2:00 a.m. and the Alexander children retired for the night. Doc Badnarik was also ready to go home. He would return in the morning to check on them.

"Good job," he said to Sharon, who was on the verge of falling asleep.

"Thanks for being here," she barely mumbled due to the medication.

Jim and Elaine went to the house as well. They shut off all but one small light in the barn and said their good nights. They sent Doc Badnarik on his way and retired to their bedroom.

Within ten minutes, the noise died down and Kurt was the only one awake. He sat in the semi-lit stall proudly holding Preston. His life was hell at times since he met Sharon, but it was worth it.

He knew what he did was wrong. Engaging in an affair chewed at his conscience for months and even more so since Rev. Jim's lesson on the way to Fresno. Looking at Preston made those guilty feelings go away.

Kurt looked up to the ceiling of the barn and said, "I will make this up to you. If you're listening to a bad person like me, thank you for this little guy."

Preston was as peaceful as could be. Kurt pulled him in a little closer and laid his head back against the stall. Cows would be shuffling in and out of the barn in a couple of hours, but time no longer mattered to Mr. Carson.

Chapter Ten

GARY AND PRESTON MOVED to Columbus as the Rhodes Tire and Rubber Company was set to close its doors. Gary didn't travel as much as he did when Sharon was alive. He wanted to work, but had an obligation to raise Preston. His mother was alive, but she and Gary weren't close when he was growing up.

Although Matt and the rest of his crew thought Gary was a hit man—they were correct in their assumption—he was much more.

Gary only took a job on a mark when he was pressed into duty. At times, some of the work wasn't done the way he liked and he stepped in to get the job done. He turned the gun on a few associates over the years because he felt they were sloppy. That was the least favorite part of his involvement, but he did whatever was necessary to keep a lifestyle he dreamed of having as the middle child of an abusive father and a workaholic mother.

The main role he played for Stenson and Rhodes was simple. Gary O'Neil was a recruiter. He had been to London, Athens, St. Petersburg, Paris, Rio de Janeiro, Venice, Hamburg, Sydney, and several other big cities around the world. He also visited obscure towns in the middle of nowhere to recruit the best assassins in the world.

Victor, who was killed by Matt in Goodale Park, was one of his best recruits. He took the news about his murder harder than anyone, but it came with the territory. Gary was like a college football coach. He took pride in recruiting and his recruits. He got so caught up in it that he pitched it as, "We would like you to join the program."

Since Gary had played football, he understood what it was like to only have four years of eligibility. He implemented the rule when asked by Rhodes and Stenson to recruit for them. Stenson knew what was going on, but Rhodes took the initiative to get rid of problems the old fashioned way.

Gary decided how long each hit man was involved and five jobs was the maximum. Each mark brought a handsome reward. Once their eligibility was exhausted, they were removed from the program, either by a bullet or relocation to obscurity.

Victor's last mark was Preston. He was supposed to take him out at Mehaffey's Pub. Circumstances forced Stenson to call an audible. Pavel, Marco, and Jensen were summoned individually to find Matt Talbot and whoever else stole the briefcase. It was against their doctrine, but the four were partnered by Rhodes and Stenson through Gary to take care of the situation at Goodale.

The first commandment in the Stenson and Rhodes' crime syndicate was never talk about the briefcase with anyone, including any level of law enforcement. The second rule was each hit man worked alone. They weren't allowed to know who they worked for and friendships with their co-employees were forbidden. Gary was the only person each of them knew.

When an order was placed on a mark, Gary was called. Rhodes and Stenson conversed about the problem and Big Boy then called Gary. The conversation was always the same when an order was placed.

"Hello."

"Hey, it's me. What about this weather today?" Stenson said to cue Gary he was to spring into action.

They talked about normal stuff for a few minutes in case anyone was listening. They said good-bye and Gary made his assignment. Stenson did his part and visited the apartment.

There wasn't a need for the operation until things started going south at Rhodes Tire and Rubber Company.

Melvin Clarke, who was Dane's father, didn't want to move to Cincinnati, nor did he want a buyout. He wanted a settlement. His family was part of a group that organized a town hall meeting. Rhodes hired men to play the part of inspectors. They visited the facility and tried to ease the situation by telling employees and their families things were being done to improve the situation.

Mr. Clarke didn't buy their lies. He was the one who talked to the inspector, the man who served as target practice for Rhodes in his office. Robert spent several weeks trying to find out who talked to the investigator, but employees banded together and kept quiet.

The reason only 20 percent of Rhodes' work force moved to Cincinnati was due to people being fired without cause. Many of his workers never got an opportunity to choose a buyout. Despite record profits, layoffs were announced and Rhodes got rid of anyone who talked about inspections or anything to do with them. He also fired several employees for insubordination, but it was because they wouldn't give him information about "The rat".

Rhodes wanted to know who talked to the inspector and offered a reward for information. It was evident someone would eventually crack so Melvin dropped by to speak with Rhodes.

"May I come in?"

"My door is always open."

"I know you don't know me, but I'm one of the employees in the warehouse. I work on the stamping line. My name is Melvin Clarke and I have worked here six years. I know you offered a year's wages and benefits as part of a buyout package. I'm one of the few who turned it down."

"That was dumb."

"People taking buyouts and signing contracts your lawyers drew up are foolish. You might have done your homework, but so have I. You make eight figures per year, but that doesn't make you better or smarter. I want what is rightfully mine. I have used all my vacation, sick, and personal days this year. That's not unusual, but each day was spent in bed, on the couch, at my doctor's office, or in the hospital. I'm sure you don't care, but I do and so does my family. I was diagnosed with cancer two months ago and I'm not sure how long I have to live. I want to make sure my family's taken care of after I'm gone. Do you think one year's pay and benefits are going to help with what I'm facing?"

Rhodes' body twitched as he let out a slight laugh that was heard through his nostrils.

"I won't be blamed for you getting cancer. My father died of cancer several years ago. I have a twin brother who dealt with the disease two years ago. I care what happens to my employees. I think I have been fair. I know a lot of people have been sick around here. We had inspectors come in and there were some red flags. That's part of the reason we're moving to Cincinnati. However, we did everything we could to keep people safe while at this site."

"I want $1.5 million and not a penny less," Melvin demanded. "I also want full benefits for my family until I die."

"You're nuts. I'm not giving you that kind of money. One year and benefits is a good deal. I'll double it for you. You're the only person who will be offered this deal. If you want to involve lawyers…be my guest. We'll drag this thing out for three or four years. Who knows, by that time we could all be dead."

"I'll gladly oblige if you want to play this out. You will be sorry you didn't take my deal."

For the second time, Rhodes was ready to decorate someone's forehead. No one missed the inspector, but he couldn't explain the absence of Mr. Clarke.

Melvin walked out of the office and Rhodes envisioned a bullet entering his back. Mr. Clarke turned the corner and Rhodes sat in his chair wondering how he could remedy the situation.

Early that evening, Rhodes called Big Boy and asked to meet with him. Stenson rarely drove to the facility, but knew the situation was desperate. The meeting had to take place.

A FEW WEEKS PASSED and investigators were baffled by the motel explosion. Only two people could be linked to the explosion. Jackson was the first suspect since he said the briefcase was his. Stenson was also linked to the crime because his business card was in the briefcase, but investigators knew he was in Columbus the night of the blast.

When Stenson returned to Columbus, he talked about eliminating his pair of screw-ups. However, he didn't want the briefcase sitting in Fresno. As long as it sat in an evidence room, it tied him to the case. He decided to keep Jackson around because he told them the briefcase was his, even though it wasn't. The briefcase belonged to Kurt, but he wasn't returning to Fresno to pick it up. A prison sentence awaited him if he claimed the briefcase and raising a child was the only thing on his mind. Stenson needed Jackson around to return to Fresno, but it was time to get rid of Ryule.

The need for rule number two came about because of Ryule. He and Jackson were among a handful of guys who worked for Stenson and Rhodes in the early going. Jackson and Ryule worked together. When Jackson realized Ryule was gone, he became suspicious and feared for his life. Stenson gave Jackson a spiel about Ryule needing to return to his country because his mother was ill. Jackson wouldn't stop questioning Stenson, Rhodes, or Gary about Ryule's return or how he was doing. It was obvious their operation couldn't function like a human body. Their muscles needed to work independently.

Stenson called Rhodes and told him they needed to get rid of an associate. He agreed it was time to say adios to their Brazilian hit man.

Ryule picked up Stenson and they drove to a meeting spot near the state fairgrounds. When they arrived, Rhodes waited in a limo with Gary, who was visiting Columbus to take care of a few problems. Gary had a bungalow near downtown and stayed there when he visited the state's capital.

Stenson got out of the car and told Ryule to wait. One of the limo doors opened and Stenson got inside.

"Why did you tell him we are here?" Rhodes asked.

"I told him we are discussing business."

"Do you think he suspects anything?"

"You never know what someone else is thinking, but he didn't seem cautious," Stenson replied.

"Gary, say good-bye to Mr. Dominguez," Rhodes said.

They popped the trunk and Gary exited the vehicle. He subtly looked over the top of the limo and made eye contact with Ryule. He walked around to the back and took out a duffel bag. He closed the trunk and went to Ryule's vehicle.

Ryule might not have seemed cautious to Stenson, but was aware of the business he was involved in. Ryule was packing heat and had his piece drawn. He was prepared to put a bullet in Gary.

Gary read Ryule's nervousness and tried easing the situation.

"How are you this evening? We'll be ready to roll in a few seconds."

Ryule didn't hear Gary's words. He had a gun pressed against his right leg and slowly pulled it to his chest, aiming the weapon at Gary's head.

"You pull anything funny and it's good-bye to you my friend," Ryule said.

"Relax! Nothing's going on."

"What's in the bag, my man?"

"It's a bonus from Mr. Rhodes. Gary opened the bag enough for Ryule to see the greenbacks wrapped around what he truly was carrying. Open the trunk."

Ryule, along with Jackson, screwed up the assignment in Fresno, but wasn't clueless. He was always on guard and for good reason.

Stenson and Rhodes intently watched what took place. They realized something was wrong.

"Head back to the vehicle. He suspects something," Rhodes said.

Stenson got out of the limo and played up the scene.

"Yeah, we'll be in touch. I'm sure Ryule will appreciate it. Take care," Stenson said loudly enough to be overheard.

As soon as Ryule heard Stenson's words to Rhodes, he eased up and lowered his gun. He reached under the steering column and popped the trunk.

"I'm sorry. I'm just a bit nervous tonight."

Gary walked around and placed the duffel bag in the trunk. As Gary and Stenson brushed past each other, they stopped and embraced. The driver of the limo rolled down the passenger's window and claimed Rhodes forgot to give something to Big Boy.

Gary opened the back door and got in the limo. He left the door open so Ryule could see inside. Stenson walked to the limo and Rhodes handed him an empty envelope. It was strictly a ploy to get Stenson into the vehicle.

"Get in," Rhodes whispered.

Stenson stood next to the vehicle and peered inside.

"I could always use a little extra myself," he chuckled.

As soon as Stenson said that, he quickly got inside and closed the door behind him. Ryule knew something was wrong. He didn't have time to process what he saw the previous ten minutes. His first reaction was to get out of there before they jumped out and sprayed his car with bullets. He shifted into first gear and hammered the gas.

As the limo driver nonchalantly pulled away from their meeting at the fairgrounds, they heard the explosion behind them. Stenson, Rhodes, and Gary peered out the back window and saw the fireball across the parking lot.

Ryule's instincts were correct. However, he saw money in the duffel bag when Gary unzipped it. The homemade device was wrapped in $20 bills. Had he asked to investigate the contents of the bag, he might be alive. Instead, his ashes floated in the air with half burnt Andrew Jacksons.

"It looks like we need a new meeting spot," Rhodes said with a huge smile on his face.

They drove off like nothing happened. It was just another day at the office. The limo pulled into Stenson's driveway and they agreed to talk about their next move the following morning.

Stenson phoned Jackson when he woke up and said they were going to Fresno to retrieve the briefcase.

Jackson tried to call Ryule as soon as he got off the phone with Stenson, but didn't get an answer. The private employees of Rhodes and Stenson were to be available at all times. They were given a five-hour window of free time on Sundays, starting at 9:00 a.m. They were allowed to attend church or get their errands done in that time frame.

Since it was Thursday, Ryule should have answered on the third ring. They were aware Jackson would be concerned with Ryule's whereabouts, thus the reason the trip to Fresno needed to be made sooner rather than later.

Stenson arrived at Jackson's studio apartment an hour after he called. Jackson was surprised Big Boy was paying him a visit. Usually, Gary was the only person who stopped by his residence.

"Get some things together," Big Boy demanded. "We need to get going. If we don't get that briefcase, I'm afraid we're going to be tried for the bombing. It's been three weeks and I have expected visitors each and every one of those twenty-one days. They can't finger any of us, but they know we were in Fresno. You and Ryule were there in body and I was there because of a business card in the briefcase. You both have to face the music because of your participation in the Fresno 500. Do you think they're going to let that crime go unpunished? They have three people who can somewhat be linked to the crime scene and they'll make up anything to pin the blame on us. We may not be allowed to leave Fresno this time, but I'll take that risk to get the briefcase."

Jackson introduced himself to the man who accompanied Stenson, but he wasn't as cordial.

"We're going to be late for our flight. If we miss it, I won't reschedule," the man said.

None of the men said a word on their cross-country flight. They landed in Fresno and went straight to police headquarters. Stenson didn't care to see the grumpy old lady again.

"What do you need?" she asked in an agitated tone.

"We're here to see Shields, Reynolds, or Captain Luango."

"The captain is on vacation and won't be back until Monday. I'm not sure if Shields or Reynolds are in the building. Have a seat and I'll check."

Her area was about the size of a ticket booth at a movie theater and she disappeared through a side door. The waiting room sat directly in front of her reception booth. Besides the front double-doors that led into the building, there were two doors—one on the left and one to the right—leading to different areas. The door on the left led to the jail area. The door on the right led to offices and investigation rooms.

The buzzer to the large door on the right sounded and Shields walked out.

"What can I do for you gentlemen?"

"We're here to retrieve my briefcase," Jackson replied.

"That's a key piece of evidence."

"You can't keep it," Stenson said. "He was locked up, so he couldn't be the one who triggered the explosion. He has a legal right to the briefcase."

"No he doesn't. The briefcase belongs to us."

"Hello. I'm Quincy Spargrove and I represent these fine gentlemen."

The fact he was a prick at his apartment and during the flight from Columbus was suddenly all right. Jackson didn't know who he was, but his profession served him well. He looked like the Harvard-educated type.

"We'll leave this place with the briefcase today," he said in a confident manner.

"The briefcase is in our evidence room. It won't be leaving."

Quincy expected that type of response. He sat his briefcase on the coffee table while Shields was talking and pulled out a document. Quincy handed him the notarized document.

Detective Shields was more disgusted the further he read.

"I'll be back."

"What is going on?" Jackson asked.

"He'll return in five to ten minutes and you will be asked to sign a form that allows them to release your item to you. You'll sign the release form and we'll be on our way."

As Quincy predicted, Shields returned to the waiting area with the briefcase in one hand. He was holding a form in his other hand.

"Read this and sign it."

About one-third of the way down, Jackson looked at Stenson, who looked at him as if to say, "Sign the form now!"

He finished the last two-thirds of the form in about ten seconds and signed his name at the bottom.

Shields took the form and handed the briefcase to Spargrove.

"Stay close to the phone, Stenson. Jackson, we'll see you soon," Shields said with a big smile.

Stenson got a kick out of Shields' parting words because he knew it was the last time he would see Jackson.

The trio headed back to the airport and was in Columbus before midnight. Stenson had what he wanted and Jackson was no longer needed. If they knocked him off that night, it would look suspicious, so they waited.

Over the next few days, Jackson became increasingly bothersome. He called Gary six or seven times per day asking about Ryule. Stenson finally stopped by Jackson's apartment and ordered him not to ask about Ryule. He told him about his sick mother in Brazil and that still didn't ease Jackson's concerns.

He called Rhodes. When he didn't get the answers he wanted from Robert, he drove to the facility the following week. His fate was cemented when he crossed that boundary.

His actions taught them a valuable lesson. They didn't hire anyone they knew, nor did they employ anyone from the United States. The assassins from other countries, except Ryule, had a different demeanor and it was something Rhodes appreciated. Jackson was steady in the early going, but his growing paranoia became a hindrance for the work they wanted to accomplish.

As soon as Jackson left the impromptu meeting with Rhodes at the plant, Robert phoned Stenson, who dialed Gary.

Jackson walked into the apartment and put his keys on a stand near the doorway. He was always cautious when he returned home. It was as if he expected company. That night, he did.

He turned on the shower and grabbed a few things from his bedroom. The five-minute cleansing would be his last. He slipped into comfortable sweat pants and an old T-shirt, and settled onto the couch.

Gary could see him through the louvers of the pantry door. Jackson was watching a movie on HBO. He quietly opened the pantry door and took the phone cord from his right jacket pocket. Gary cut the line while Jackson showered and removed the phone cord from the wall.

As Jackson watched a man have his way with a bimbo on the tube, Gary took an end of the phone cord and wrapped it a few times around his left hand. He looped the rest of it around his right hand, leaving him two feet of cord. Gary knew it would fit around Jackson's neck.

He crept behind the unsuspecting man like a lion going after his prey. After tip-toeing the last few steps, he reached over Jackson and had him turning purple within fifteen seconds.

Although Jackson was a skilled fighter, he wasn't going to overpower Gary, who was seemingly chiseled out of granite.

Jackson kicked his legs and tried to turn himself sideways, but Gary had a tight grip around his neck. Jackson attempted to use his arms to fight off his attacker, but Gary walked around the right side of the sofa where Jackson was sitting and moved him face down.

Gary, with his left knee planted firmly into Jackson's back, knew it was only a matter of time. Jackson's arms soon went from flailing to waving. Gary held his opponent in a sleeper hold and it reminded him of old time wrestling. After three arm raises and no response on Jackson's part, the imaginary referee declared Gary the victor.

All signs of life were gone once Jackson's right arm fell to his side. Gary kept the hold for another thirty seconds before letting go. He flipped Jackson on his back and a grape-colored face proved all he needed to know.

Gary walked into Jackson's bedroom and retrieved the briefcase, which was in his possession because they wanted him to think he was still part of their crew.

Mr. O'Neil walked into the living room. He turned off the TV and all the lights. He didn't mind killing someone, but hated wasting electricity.

He immediately drove to the facility and presented the briefcase to Rhodes, who would keep an eye on it.

After a brief visit with Rhodes, Gary walked to an incinerator and discarded the gloves, phone cord, shoes, and light jacket he wore at the apartment.

He went to his car, put on another jacket, and left. He didn't think twice about what took place.

STENSON PULLED INTO THE driveway and waved to the security guard at the entrance. He motioned him through and Big Boy slipped the man a large bill as he drove by.

After parking in his usual spot, Stenson entered the plant and strolled into Rhodes' office.

"Have a seat," Rhodes said while skipping the greetings. "His name is Melvin Clarke and he is going to be a thorn in our side if we don't take care of him. People are talking and he's one of the biggest reasons why. It's only a matter of time before we're finished. We have to do something soon."

"What do you propose?"

"I have thought about that prick all day and how to get rid of him, but we're going to deal with several problems over the coming months or even years. Moving to Cincinnati will alleviate a few problems and buying out some employees will get rid of several headaches. However, we have to deal with people like Melvin."

Stenson listened to Rhodes' voice and sensed a sign of fear for the first time.

"Call some of your mafia buddies and have them whack the guy."

"It's not that easy. They whack the guy and then we owe them a favor. I don't like owing favors. Don't you remember those goons they sent to get rid of that inspector a while back? The next time they visit, they could be here for us because I didn't return the favor in a manner pleasing to them. Listen! Unless you're Joe Pistone, you won't infiltrate the mafia. There are always rats, but they keep pretty quiet about their business. I like that fact, but we can do the same thing and not owe favors to anyone. I have some ideas and want to see what you think."

Rhodes opened a closet in the corner of his office. The briefcase was on the floor. He pulled it out and sat it on his desk. Stenson hadn't seen it since the day they visited Fresno a few years earlier.

"Someone used this to cause problems for you. Now, we're going to use it to get rid of our problems."

They talked about putting the target's information in the briefcase and hiring someone to carry out the task. That, like several ideas, wouldn't work.

It took them a while to mastermind their final plan, but they knew it would work. They had a list of things to do in a short amount of time.

Rhodes scoured the classified section before finding an apartment on the west side of town. Rhodes sat outside the building two days and kept a close eye on the neighborhood's activities. The rundown section was perfect for what they hoped to accomplish. Robert met with the landlord. He gave him a tour of the place, which proved better suited for their cause than they hoped. He paid rent through the following year and the top priority was finished.

Robert found an old couch and a kitchen table at a flea market. He bought both items and placed them inside the apartment. He put the afghan his grandmother knitted for him as a kid on the sofa and slid one of the four chairs up to the table in the kitchen. The briefcase was placed in the register in the bedroom and the screwdriver was the final decorative touch.

Harry rented a post office box. Duplicate keys to the apartment and briefcase were made and placed inside the box. Once Stenson and Rhodes completed their tasks, they gave Gary several keys to the box and informed him about the recruitment program. Loose guidelines were set, but two rules had to be followed. The rest was up to Gary.

The hardest part of the plan was coming up with the code, but Stenson wasn't at the top of his class in college without reason. Stenson talked Rhodes into visiting the city's library. He told Robert about the code and they found a book for their assassins to solve it.

He wrote a series of numbers and had Robert decipher what they meant. When Rhodes completed it, he just shook his head. It was brilliant.

They went to extremes to make sure everything would work. A few days later, Gary told them about his plans and everything was set into motion.

It was time to get rid of their first headache. Melvin Clarke didn't know it, but he was about to be a guinea pig.

Chapter Eleven

GARY AND PRESTON AWOKE in identical fashion. Waking to a whiff of freshly brewed Columbian coffee or greasy bacon frying in a skillet was their preference, but their return to consciousness wasn't pleasant.

They winced because of the blaring music being blasted through the soundproof storage house. The tunes weren't good for a headache, one that topped a Saturday morning pounder from a previous night on the town.

"Tall Paul, he's my all. Tall Paul, he's my all." The words sang by Annette echoed back and forth, up and down, and all around. Preston enjoyed early 90s grunge while Gary was into a little of everything—The Beatles, Stevie Nicks, KISS, and Ted Nugent.

Without the wadded rags in their mouths that were duct-taped tightly around their heads, they would agree the 50s tune on constant repeat was driving them crazy. It was Matt's goal, at least for Gary.

They were shocked to see their surroundings. Gary couldn't believe who sat fifteen feet in front of him. His adopted son was in a duplicate situation.

A single drop light protruded from the ceiling above his child. The light, which hung from a two-foot linked chain, produced enough watts to hit every nook and cranny in Rhode Island. Gary's skin was hot so he imagined Preston felt warm from the fake rays as well. The elder O'Neil loved tropical paradises that produced the same kind of warmth, but the dirty dungeon they sat in wasn't a place for fanny flossers or suntan lotion.

Gary thought about wiggling his way onto his side and using his feet to drag himself to Preston, who could untie him or vice versa. However, Gary and Preston weren't going anywhere.

The antique chairs they sat in were made for looks, not for sitting like a king. The old rickety wood was ready to give, thus sitting still was a top priority. Like Gary, Preston's legs were free to swing and kick around any way he wanted, but doing so wouldn't be wise, not just because of the squeaky timber.

The storage house tenants sat on makeshift stages. The circular stage had a circumference of seven feet and didn't rise more than two feet off the ground. Its best feature, or worst depending on the perspective, was it could be spun like a merry-go-round.

The stage wasn't meant for belting karaoke or turning in thespian performances. Its existence had one purpose. The stage was intended for terror.

Shoes and socks would be a blessing. One, to keep their feet warm in a room Matt kept at a chilly fifty-six degrees and two, to avoid the danger of lacerating one of their hoofers.

Matt paid a visit to Hamilton's Junk Yard. He purchased three broken windshields, which Milo Hamilton thought was strange. However, his curiosity wouldn't keep his grubby paws from a little cabbage.

When Matt and Brock returned to the warehouse, they crushed the glass and carefully laid it on each stage. The only part not covered with an inch-thick layer of glass was a spot barely big enough for their feet. It was up to Gary and Preston if they wanted to chance stretching.

If they moved and their chairs gave way, their feet would be the least of their concerns. Both men were stripped down to their skivvies, thus rolling around on glass wasn't an inviting thought. They couldn't move their head and moving their eyes was almost too much movement. The duct-tape keeping the rags in place was also wrapped around the headrest of the chair. Staring at one another was about all they could do.

The rest of the surroundings gave the room a mafia-like interrogation vibe. Although Preston knew what was going on, he was afraid. He agreed to help Matt make Gary believe he was also a prisoner. There must have been fine print Preston overlooked on the contract because he didn't sign up to be a Guantanamo Bay resident.

In the corner of the room near Gary was a wooden desk, similar to one a kindergarten teacher has, with a chair placed at it. Two iron contraptions were bolted to the top of the desk, which had a light hanging over it.

On the left side of the desk, which faced the center of the room, there was another wooden chair. Next to the chair, an old milk crate was turned upside down and a gun sat on top of it. Fortunately, for Preston's sake, Gary couldn't see it. Worrying about cuts would be an afterthought.

Gary focused on the corner of the room near Preston, who couldn't see what his father observed.

A garden hose was wrapped neatly and hanging on the wall. A small metal bath tub, one reminiscent of Wild West days, sat on wheels next to the hose. The cement floor in that corner of the room sloped to a drain. "The aquatic center" was Matt's nickname for the corner. Gary knew a bath was in his future, whether he liked it or not.

The last items, which were on the left side of the room (Preston was closest to the door so his vantage point was the room's compass), they saw were a stove and an old rusty box spring. The stove was adorned with boiling pots. They made Preston think of food, but Gary knew the silver pots weren't for boiling taters or noodles. The box spring wasn't suitable for a nap and lying on it would require a tetanus shot.

A visitor interrupted their imaginations and examinations of the room.

Matt walked in and didn't speak for ten minutes. Preston didn't recognize him. The black plastic mask he wore was unlike any he had seen in a slasher flick. It was almost satanic and gave off a "You're gonna die" look. The black hooded satin robe and black boots he wore made it creepier. The youngest O'Neil wondered if they would be bludgeoned to death.

He unwound the duct-tape from Preston's head and did the same to Gary.

"This isn't Halloween and do you think you scare me with that outfit?" Gary questioned after the lengthy silence.

The person who slowly paced around the room after taking their gags off was agitated by Gary's comments. He walked to the door and motioned for back-ups. Two people walked into the room and were dressed the same, except they wore different colors. Dane was dressed in maroon and Lauren in forest green.

"What's it going to be?" Matt asked as Preston recognized his voice. "How about the Tucker telephone? I'm sure there are some Arkansans who would pass on that. A little Iron Maiden would be great, and I'm not talking about the rock band boys. The ole' Judas Chair for you Mr. O'Neil? That would be fitting because you are going to tell us what we want to know and we won't give you thirty silver pieces for your betrayal."

It was evident to Gary the man had done a little torturing in his time. Matt's research on the subject made it appear as if he had two graves dug up in a nearby corn field and would deposit the bodies once he retrieved his information.

"I don't know what you want, but you don't frighten me with your tactics."

Matt knew Gary wouldn't compromise at first. Patience was necessary, but he was going to break him. He walked over to Preston and started a conversation.

"Little O'Neil, will you tell us what we want to know?"

Preston shook his head no while giving Matt eyes instructing him where to go.

"All we want to know is how the briefcase works. The first one that tells us can walk out and we'll let you speculate about the remaining tight-lipped O'Neil. The rat race is on."

Preston acted like he was ready to say something, but paused. Matt approached him and tilted his head.

"Do you have something to say?"

"I don't know anything about the briefcase and have repeatedly told you that for the past few days. You kidnapped me and brought here under the assumption I have secret information. You have subjected me to this torture long enough. It's time to let me go."

It wasn't worth an academy award, but Preston performed admirably. Maybe the stage was for a thespian after all. His response captured Gary's attention.

"We know you're aware how the briefcase works," Matt said as he pulled out a fake document from the pocket of his robe.

He put the piece of paper about a foot in front of Preston's face. "Read it!"

Preston,

I know this will come as a surprise, but I have to let you know about your dad. He's a hit man for Stenson. Harry and I have been involved for several years, but they will try to pin everything on me. I won't keep up this façade nor turn my head any longer.

A man recently retrieved information on where to track you down. If you showed up at Mehaffey's, you would have been killed.

This letter is in good hands. Your kidnappers are your friends. Trust them!

Sincerely,
Robert Rhodes

When Preston finished reading, Matt turned and stared at Gary. Mr. O'Neil didn't believe the letter.

"You're stupid if you think I'm fooled by a letter you wrote. Preston said he doesn't know anything about the briefcase and what I know, I'm not telling you."

"You will," Matt said as he headed for the door. "Enjoy the music."

Gary was prepared to be defiant as long as necessary. Matt hoped the storage house scenery helped him make up his mind to rat out everyone, but that wasn't the main objective. If Preston thought about it long enough, he would realize Matt and his crew already knew all they needed to know about the briefcase. They wanted Gary to talk about the briefcase, but bigger plans were in the works.

THE SOUNDS SIGNALED WHAT was going to take place. Kurt wiped the crust from his eyes and noticed the barn was no longer blanketed with darkness.

Jim was the first to peek his head around the stall.

"How's everything going?"

"I managed to sleep for a while. Preston slept like, well, a baby. Sharon is still asleep."

"It's going to get noisy in here. We still have Chelsea's play pen so we cleaned it and set it up in the living room. You can take him to the house if you want."

"I'll take you up on that offer."

Kurt handed Preston to Jim so he could pull himself up. The rustling of the hay beside Sharon startled her. She opened her eyes and saw the men exchanging Preston.

"Where are you going?" she asked Kurt.

"Jim and Elaine have a spot for Preston inside. I'm taking him to the house because they're ready to milk. Jim said it's loud and I don't want Preston startled by the commotion."

They had not shown affection in front of the Alexanders, but Kurt bent down and kissed Sharon on the forehead.

"I'll come back after daybreak and they're done milking."

Kurt went to the house and wondered if the Alexanders went by Eastern Standard Time. It was 4:40 in the morning and the rest of the Alexander clan was stirring. The scent of Maxwell House and raspberry muffins was evidence Elaine had been up for a while. The smell of straw, dust, and dung were replaced by the aromas coming from Elaine's kitchen.

He helped himself to a cup of coffee and peeled the muffin out of a pink baking cup.

Colt joined his father, as did Elaine, but the younger Alexander children were still in the house. They finally appeared and were ready to head outside.

"Mornin'" Tyler said to Kurt.

"I think they started without you."

"Nah, they're always a little antsy to get started," Chelsea noted. "As long as we're in the barn at a quarter 'til five, we're all right. We'll put in two hours and then go back to bed."

The one hundred twenty minutes flew by. It seemed like Kurt had just placed Preston in his new resting spot before the creaky front door opened.

"Doc Badnarik will be here shortly," a smiling Elaine said to Kurt, who was resting on the couch.

It must have been the thought of having someone else in the house who could keep an eye on Preston because Kurt nearly went into a comatose state. Jim spoke to Kurt after finishing his morning duties around the farm, but Kurt didn't respond.

Doc Badnarik visited the barn and reported to the Alexanders that Sharon was doing well, considering the circumstances. She needed to remain in the barn for another twenty-four hours, but could move to the house sometime Monday morning. He also checked on Preston and stated he was fine.

Elaine whipped up a small breakfast and wouldn't take no for an answer. Doc Badnarik gave in and joined them for a quick bite. Upon finishing their meal, the Alexanders thanked Doc Badnarik for his services and said they would see him later that morning.

The Alexanders hadn't missed a Sunday morning service in at least three years. The last time they missed, they felt badly, but God understood. However, townsfolk didn't.

There were many rumors why the Alexanders weren't in attendance that fateful Sunday. They were losing their farm. They were getting a divorce. Colt got drunk the night before and wrecked his car. The last one was a bit understandable as Colt had a little James Dean in him, but the reason they weren't at Calvary was they had to pick up Elaine's mother from the airport, who was visiting from Lubbock. After being the area's focus of weeklong gossip, Jim decided they wouldn't miss church again unless they were out of town.

Elaine poked her head in Chelsea's bedroom, which was to the left of the kitchen, and went to the back of the house to wake the boys.

"Breakfast is on the table. Get something to eat before you clean up."

Jim and Elaine discussed leaving Kurt alone, but they didn't know much about their visitors. They were pleasant and didn't seem to pose a threat, but the Alexanders were concerned about the situation. A stranger wearing a wedding ring had a baby in their barn and her husband wasn't Kurt, yet he kissed her on the forehead before he walked to the house earlier that morning.

They agreed Kurt should go to church, but one of them needed to stay behind. Elaine volunteered. Chelsea could watch Preston, but Elaine felt more comfortable providing daycare services that morning.

Kurt was started by the gentle shaking of his left arm. He opened his eyes and Jim was hovering over his body.

"If you're hungry, there's food on the table. As you know, I'm a God fearing man. My family attends services every Sunday and we're heading to church within the hour. I would like you to be my guest."

It took a few seconds for Kurt to come to his senses. Once he was aware of his surroundings, he asked Jim to repeat himself.

"Breakfast is served. It's Sunday so we're going to church. Elaine is staying here to keep an eye on Sharon and Preston. I have a shirt and tie that will fit you and your blue jeans will be fine. Most men will have on their Sunday best, but visitors get a free pass, especially if they're wearing a tie."

"I'm not sure you want to sit beside me in church. You have lost one church to a disaster in these parts and could lose another if I step foot inside the place. I would rather stay here and leave the worshiping to you."

"That's where I have a problem. I have one rule around here," he said while drawing serious doubts from his family. "OK, maybe a few. Let's put it this way...I have a major rule. If you stay under this roof, you will go to church. I'm not saying I'll kick you out of my house, but don't leave me that option."

The thought of wearing a tie nauseated Kurt. He hadn't worn one since his wife's funeral. He lost her and a daughter during childbirth, but it was something he never talked about. Sharon was the only person he had opened up to about his tragic losses.

"If you insist, I guess I'll attend my first church service today."

While Kurt took a shower, Elaine pressed a shirt and selected one of Jim's favorite ties. Kurt attempted to put the tie on in the bathroom, but his experiment didn't turn out well. Elaine gave him a helping hand and he looked almost as snazzy as Jim or the boys, who were dressed to impress from head to toe.

Kurt felt uncomfortable wearing Levis while the rest of the fellows had slacks on, but kept telling himself, "At least I'm going."

Jim walked out the front door and headed to the barn. He swung the left door open and backed the station wagon into the driveway. They piled in and began their drive to Calvary.

Mr. Alexander was a slow driver. It gave him more time to draw out his already lengthy stories. After the Amish-like trip to church, he wheeled the station wagon into the graveled side parking lot. The church wasn't very big. It looked like a typical country church. Most are either built with white planks or red bricks. Calvary Baptist was white, but had lost a few shades of its original color and could have used a fresh coat of paint. A tiny car port was built on the side for elderly people or husbands to prove their chivalry.

The sign in the front yard welcomed guests and visitors alike. It had the times of Sunday school, worship, and Wednesday evening service. The sign also had the name of Pastor John Parker Browne on it. The message the church was trying to parlay took up most of the space. "The wages of sin is death. Repent before payday!"

When he saw the billboard's warning, Kurt thought about asking the Alexanders if he could stay in the station wagon.

They got out of the vehicle and started across the parking lot. It was a beautiful morning and a few members congregated near the front entrance. Most of the women wore hats and neatly ironed dresses while the men were as advertised.

A row of perfectly manicured hedges ran along the side of the church away from the carport. The two-sided entrance had four brick steps and was covered by a small roof, which was held up by three white pillars.

As Jim and his kids exchanged hellos with other members, Kurt stood at the base of the entranceway admiring the big steeple. A large cross sat on top of what appeared to be a tiny lookout chamber. The ensemble was the newest addition to the church. Several large oak trees surrounded the church and Kurt received an unexpected lesson about the addition.

"Hello. I'm Ellie Mae Hendershot."

Kurt reached out and shook the feeble hand of the eighty-two-year-old lady. Someone had wheeled her up the ramp and stopped near Kurt.

"I see you're admiring our steeple and bell house. That was built seven years ago. We used to have a few more oak trees, but a bad lightning storm knocked a few of them over. A large peel of lightning hit the tree closest to the church and sent a big branch on top of our old steeple. It knocked the steeple off the church, but had that branch hit the roof, it would have caused more damage. Some say it happened because of Brother Radke's affair and that's still up for debate. Cy Harper donated the money for the new addition. He owns the area's largest feed mill."

She finally took a breath. Her old lungs proved to be rather windy. Kurt realized jabbering was an art form in Texas.

"I'm Kurt Carson. It's nice to meet you Mrs. Hendershot."

The bell rang at ten minutes 'til and everyone started bustling into the church. Deacon Frye manned the doorway and gave Kurt an account about Calvary Baptist. Had the Alexanders not interrupted, Kurt could keep the claim of never attending a church service.

The Alexanders walked to the fourth pew on the right side of the church. It was their spot. The windows looked well-crafted from the outside, but an inside look at the stained glass gave one a greater appreciation of the hands that designed them.

Two small pews, one on each side of the pulpit, were on the stage. A man stood up and walked to the stand. He thanked everyone for coming and read Psalm 23. He returned to his seat and another man walked over to the microphone and led three songs—*The Old Rugged Cross, I Stand in Awe, and How Great Thou Art.*

After the third song, twelve men passed out crackers and grape juice. Kurt was confused, but could tell people what was on the menu when it came to the Lord's Supper.

Pastor Browne took charge of the service and was animated. He hooted and hollered, sweat and stomped, and whispered and wowed. His sermon on the most important choice you will ever make cut to Kurt's heart, and many others for that matter. He talked about the three crosses people can choose—rebellion, repentance, or redemption. He finished by asking, "At what cross do you find yourself today?"

Kurt wasn't sure about his answer, but he found the pastor interesting.

Two people responded to the invitation song and asked for prayers. Once again, Kurt didn't understand the principle, but knew his current situation called for prayers. His first attempt at praying to God instantly relieved some stress. Money baskets were passed out and Deacon Frye followed with another prayer. The congregation sang *There's Not A Friend* to close the service.

Kurt met more members after the service and slotted another visit in his mental calendar. The Alexanders and Pastor Browne's family were the last to leave. The Alexanders stopped at Polk's Family Restaurant. It was a tradition. Elaine was not allowed to cook on Sunday. It was another of Jim's rules. Usually, the family dined inside the establishment, but they ordered food to go so they could eat with Elaine and get something for Sharon.

They returned to the farm and everyone enjoyed the afternoon meal. Colt and Tyler left to land a monster out of the Parson's pond and Chelsea went to a neighbor's house. Elaine retired to her bedroom for a weekly Sunday afternoon nap.

Jim asked Kurt to take a walk with him through one of their fields. They talked about the church service, the barnyard delivery, and Kurt's thoughts on Texas. They walked for a while before Jim popped the question.

"Whose child is Preston and how are you and Sharon connected?"

The question took Kurt by surprise, but he figured it was coming.

"I didn't think we would leave without you asking. Preston is my son and I'm in love with Sharon. She is married to a man named Gary and he is gone all the time. He travels the world and she doesn't know what he does. They have a young son named Trevor, whom Gary never takes time to do anything with. He's a rotten man. Sharon has thought about leaving him for the last year or two, but is afraid of what he might do to her."

"So the two of you are involved in an affair?"

"I'm not proud, but it's true. She left Mesa for Fresno a month or so ago because she needed someone with her. Her mother welcomed her with open arms. We planned on avoiding one another until after Preston was born, but something changed our plans."

"What are your new plans?"

"I hated lying to you on the trip to Fresno. I'm from Mesa. The reason I traveled to Fresno was to keep an eye on Sharon and my unborn child, who Gary thinks is his. I was also in danger. The house that went up in smithereens was mine. Someone was sending me a message. Since that happened, I keep looking over my shoulder. Your lesson from Corinthians...I didn't need it because I never stayed at a random woman's house. I know it doesn't make what I'm doing with Sharon any better. Sharon and my wife were acquaintances and we met after my wife died. We talked about her death and became close, too close."

Jim wasn't sure how to respond. According to his morals, he should run him off his property. Mr. Alexander was a good judge of character and believed Kurt was a good person.

"I didn't let on, but I thought you were involved in the Mesa explosion. I don't condone what you're doing with Sharon, but I'll let God decide your sentence at the appropriate time. Tell me, is my family safe?"

"I made sure we didn't leave a trail in Fresno. I wouldn't be here if there was a possibility of your family being harmed. I'm sure the people after me believe I died in that explosion. I know I haven't said it, but I'm appreciative of the hospitality you have extended to us. I desire a fresh start. Austin would be a great place for a new beginning. I have been down on life the past few years. I was a trader and made a lot of money before I lost my wife."

Jim wasn't happy, although he didn't show it, but the last part of Kurt's words pierced his heart.

"How did you lose her?"

"She was pregnant and had difficulty throughout the pregnancy. She went into labor five weeks early and gave birth to a baby girl.

However, neither of them made it through the day," Kurt said as he turned his back to Jim.

Mr. Alexander let Kurt stand there painfully reminiscing. After three or four minutes, he put his hand on Kurt's shoulder.

"I can't imagine losing a child. I don't know how I could survive if anything happened to one of my children. Elaine and the kids are my life. You're a strong man. I'm sorry to hear you experienced it."

Kurt used a handkerchief Jim handed him to wipe away the tears.

"Thanks. I lost one child and won't let it happen again. I love Sharon and want to have a family with her. Again, I'm not proud of what I have done, but I know it's going to work out for the best."

"What are your plans after you leave Austin?"

"I haven't thought that far ahead. I know I can't go back to Mesa, which is where Sharon will have to go. It tears me apart that I will be away from Preston for a while, but I'll figure something out."

"Would you like to stay here for a while?"

The invitation was unexpected, but it didn't take long for Kurt to formulate a plan.

"I'll think about it," he said as thoughts were springing to mind.

They finished talking and made their way to the house. Jim went inside to take a nap in his La-Z-Boy while Kurt went to the barn to see Sharon, who was resting.

"Sharon, are you awake?"

Her eyes opened and she smiled.

"Yes. How was church?"

"It was different, but I liked it. It's strange, but I can see us living here and starting a life together."

"That's impossible. We don't know anyone and I can't leave my life back home."

"I have a surprise for you. Mr. Alexander and I took a walk in the field behind his storage barn and he asked if I would like to stay for a while. I told him about my house in Mesa and your situation with Gary. I assured him we weren't being followed. I have an idea and think it solves everything. I'm going to ask if they will set up a room for me in their basement and I'll work on the farm for free. I can keep Preston with me. When you get back to Mesa, tell your mother and

Gary you had a miscarriage due to the stress of being kidnapped in Fresno. I know it will be hard, but it's best for now."

Kurt's plan wasn't what Sharon had in mind, but it would accomplish two things. It kept Kurt in a place where no one would find him and it solved the problem of keeping Preston out of harm's way, in case Gary found out he wasn't his child.

"I wasn't sold on your idea of leaving Fresno the way we did, but it seems to be working out. I like the first part of your plan. Leaving you behind would be hard enough, but leaving Preston would kill me. Then again, Gary will kill me if he discovers either of my secrets. If the Alexanders are willing to let you stay, it's probably best. We need to find a way for me to see both of you as often as I can."

Kurt made a spot beside Sharon. He nestled next to her and they laid there in the barn like they were staying in a luxurious suite in one of the best hotels in the world.

The fact they were in the barn was lost in the peacefulness of the moment. It seemed as if the luck of the secret lovers was changing.

IT HAD BEEN HOURS since the door closed behind the masked trio. Preston and Gary listened to "Tall Paul" nearly ninety times since their visitors departed. It was taking a toll on them.

Not only was the music driving them mad, but their muscles were aching. Their lower backs burned and their buttocks tingled. Their legs were also stiff. At one point, Preston extended his right leg, but the chair wobbled and he gently eased it back into place. They sat atop a card house and had to deal with pain.

Preston hadn't spoke since he and Gary were left alone, despite the fact they didn't put the gag back in his mouth. He finally broke the silence.

"I don't deserve this. Mr. Stenson sent me to Mehaffey's Pub to meet a guy named Phil Seevers. I was supposed to get information on a campaign Stenson & Rhodes was slated to conduct for Buckeye Health. I received a phone call telling me to meet him at Goodale Park. A few minutes after I got there, guys jumped out of a vehicle and chased a man who supposedly worked for Seevers. I heard gunfire and raced to my car."

Preston slowed down to catch his breath.

"Once I got back to Stenson & Rhodes, I received a letter from the guy who was chased at the park and a phone call from the men who pursued him. Later that night, I was roughed up by the pursuers in the parking garage near Goodale and kidnapped. Fast forward a bit and now I'm in this situation, not sure if you or I will be killed. This is where I woke up after they kidnapped me. They have used scare tactics and are out of options. I'm scared."

Matt, Dane, and Lauren enjoyed the show from the first storage house. A buck's head was mounted on the wall behind Gary and its eyes watched everything. They were impressed with Preston. Instead of worrying about a life in Myrtle Beach, maybe he should think about Hollywood.

Preston waited for Gary to respond, but he was an expert. He knew they were watching and wasn't speaking. The room was quiet for fifteen minutes and the door opened once again. Both men perked up. Although it was muffled, Gary screamed at the top of his lungs through the rag.

Lauren walked over to Preston and slipped a horse bridle over his face. He tried to resist, but the tiny dose of electricity sent through his body made it easy to give up the fight. Behind him, two hooks were firmly embedded into the wall about the width of the stage. Lauren hooked the end of the bridle straps into the wall and tightened them so Preston couldn't talk.

She walked over to Gary and began questioning him after taking the rag out of his mouth. Lauren's voice-over was startling to Preston. It reminded him of a guy he saw at Four Corners. A gentleman sat at the bar and put something up to his throat each time he talked. Apparently he had a hole in his trachea, either from years of heavy smoking or shrapnel to the neck in 'Nam.

"You saw what happened to Preston. You're going to talk on your own or I'll help you," she said with a distorted laugh. "What do you know about the briefcase?"

"I told that other freak I wasn't talking. You can question me all you want, but you're not getting..."

The voltage interrupted his words and sent pain throughout his body. Lauren barely touched Preston, but she gave a hard shove into the side of Mr. O'Neil. PETA could cry all they wanted about animal cruelty, but there weren't demonstrations about using cattle prods on humans.

"Now, where was I? Tell us about the briefcase!"

Gary wasn't talking. He knew he would have to withstand torture, but he wasn't giving in. His defiance made Lauren mad. She never imagined doing something like that to a person, but each time she used the prod, picana, hotshot, or whatever term someone used to dub the device, she felt she was getting vindication for her father. She didn't understand at first, but she was starting to comprehend how Matt, Dane, and a deceased Brock felt about Rhodes, Stenson, and anyone else involved with them.

She slowly walked behind Gary, letting him think about where she would jolt him next. Lauren rammed it into the left side of his rib cage and the shock made Gary's body twitch quickly. His movement caused the unstable chair to teeter and nearly collapse underneath him.

"What do you know about the briefcase?"

Again, Gary didn't say a word. She knew she could send enough electricity through his body to light up a Christmas tree. He wasn't talking.

Lauren gave up and left them alone. Although a bridle was available for Gary, they wanted to see if he would talk to Preston after his first torture treatment.

After the pain subsided somewhat, he began to talk.

"I'm sorry. They won't get away with this. Stenson and Rhodes are looking for all of you. They think you are involved in this operation. You were cornered at Lauren's apartment. This might make matters worse, but I have to tell you. There is a $5 million bounty on your head. The same goes for the rest of the people involved in stealing the briefcase. I can vouch for you. I don't want anything to happen to you, but the rest will be killed."

Listening to Gary's rationale and sorry excuses made Preston sick to his stomach, which was in sad shape from a lack of food. He let his words go in one ear and out the other, but Matt knew Gary was starting to crack.

"We'll get to him," he said to Dane and Lauren. "I didn't know if it was possible, but we have him set up. Wait until you see my surprise."

Lauren and Dane looked at each other.

"That's not a surprise," she said.

"I love surprises," Dane joked.

The surprise Matt had in store would certainly stun all of them.

Chapter
Twelve

THE EXCITEMENT BUILT FOR several days. Stenson dialed Gary's number with great anticipation.

"Hello."

"It's me," Stenson said while trying to contain his enthusiasm. "What about this weather today?"

"It's typical for Ohio. How did your stocks do today?"

"Up and down like a stripper on a greased pole. I want to let you know about a cookout this weekend. It starts at noon and lasts until everyone is good and ready to leave."

There was a get together at Stenson's house, but it was the first time Gary heard about it. Stenson planned the party so he would have enough to talk about during the first experiment over the phone.

"I guess I'll see you then."

As soon as Stenson laid the receiver on the hook, he rushed out the door and headed to the post office and rented apartment. He proudly carried the materials he and Robert put together. Big Boy was more than happy to always be the one delivering them to the apartment. Stenson enjoyed the adrenaline rush. He wished he could receive an assignment from Gary.

He stopped by the post office and retrieved the keys to the briefcase. He also sent out pieces of mail for his wife.

Stenson arrived at the apartment after sunset. He strutted to the front door and walked in. Rhodes had told him about his interior design skills and Big Boy liked what he did with the place. If a television was set up in the living room, it could serve as Stenson's man cave. Getting away from June would be a welcome retreat.

Stenson walked into the kitchen and grabbed the screwdriver off the table. He went to the bedroom and unscrewed the register face. Big Boy reached for the briefcase until he felt the handle. He pulled out the briefcase and took it to the kitchen table. Stenson unlocked their cherished item and laid a map in it. He opened the compartment and placed a folder inside the pocket.

Harry locked the briefcase and returned it to its resting spot. He put the screwdriver on the table and flipped off the lights as he left.

Gary carefully instituted his plan. Each of his recruits could be dropped at a moment's notice. When they received their walking papers, each hit man was given fifty thousand in cash and the relationship ended. That rule helped him keep a ten-man roster at all times.

Every day, the recruits drove by Gary's house. Each assassin was assigned a number and they knew when their number was called. Gary had a shed outside his home that he turned into a mini-bar. It was a great place to watch games and play poker with the few friends he had.

A small billboard, one like McDonald's or other fast food restaurants use to announce specials and messages, was placed outside the shed. A zero was usually the only thing on the sign. When a case was assigned, Gary changed the zero to the number corresponding with the hit man receiving the job.

Several times, visitors asked him what the board meant. He adopted the McDonald's idea and claimed it was the number of people his shed was serving. It sounded ridiculous, but it made people laugh.

Gary walked to his shed and pulled out lucky number seven. He figured it was the best number to use for their test run.

Henrik was number seven. Last names were unknown and Gary didn't want to know them. Zero was on the sign since Stenson and

Rhodes hatched the plan. When Henrik drove by and saw seven on the board, he sprung into action.

At 5:00 a.m. sharp, he walked into the post office and retrieved the keys. His next stop was the apartment. His first visit, one of three he made while in the program, to the apartment was euphoric. The job paid handsomely, but the thrill of the kill motivated each of Gary's hit men.

It didn't take long to open the briefcase. He jotted numbers from the map and opened the compartment in the other half of the briefcase. He removed the folder and took out the photo. Henrik studied every square inch of Melvin Clarke's face. He didn't skip one detail...the beauty mark on his right jaw line, the tiny scar just below his hairline, or the way his goatee grew differently on the left side. If Henrik was an artist, he could draw or paint a perfect image of Mr. Clarke.

He tore the photo's bottom right corner off before placing the rest of the picture in the sink. Henrik burnt the map first and the photo was next to go. He washed the ashes down the drain and left the apartment in the same condition it was in before he arrived.

When Henrik walked to his car, he sensed he was being watched. The money being paid to the neighborhood watchdogs wasn't a waste. They reported suspicious activities around the apartment to Stenson and Rhodes. They knew when someone should be there and when someone should not.

Number seven drove to the library and waited a few minutes before it opened. He was the first visitor that morning. He walked around the library, picking up a book here or there to look interested. A college-aged guy asked if he could assist him, but Henrik rejected his offer.

Henrik made his way to the back corner and pulled out the book. He tucked it under his arm with other books he grabbed while venturing down the aisles. If Harry, Robert, or Gary saw number seven, they would be proud.

He ducked into a private study booth, laid out the series of numbers, and began looking them up. The code was 19-12-9-11-11-8-16-1-17-2. He began turning through the pages and deciphering the numbers. G-R-O-V were the first four letters. He reached 11, which was circled, and looked in the index. It was written beside the United

States. His hand shook due to the nervousness of the moment. E-C-I-T-Y were the final five letters. Grove City is where the target lived.

He peeked around before shoving the book back into its hiding spot. He left the other books in the room.

"Thanks a lot," he said to the library worker in his Swedish accent as he disappeared through the exit.

Henrik returned to his apartment and flipped on a black lamp resting on a TV dinner tray. He held the small piece from the photograph underneath it and the name Melvin Clarke appeared. He had two weeks to eliminate the target.

Finding a person in a random city is nearly impossible without a little extra information. Asking around for Melvin would make Henrik a suspect once he came up missing.

The phone book was the best place to start. There were several Clarkes in the book, but Melvin and Victoria were unlisted. Without inside information, he had to do a lot of leg work. It took him several days, but he finally discovered where Melvin worked. He used a pay phone outside a supermarket and dialed the Rhodes Tire and Rubber Company.

"How may I direct your call?" the secretary asked.

"I need to speak with Mr. Clarke."

"He's on the clock. Is this an emergency?"

"Yes. I believe his home is on fire."

"I'll get him."

The secretary paged Mr. Clarke and explained the situation when he stepped into the office. She transferred the call to another small office room and he answered the phone in a panic.

"This is Melvin. Is my family safe? Is my home all right?"

"Mr. Clarke, I'm new to the area. I'm not sure if it is your home," Henrik stated as his thick Swedish accent threw Melvin off. "Do you live on...?"

"308 Toltec Circle. That is where I live," Melvin nearly shouted.

"I'm sorry to bother you. You are the wrong Mr. Clarke. I live on Meadowgreene Lane and the Clarke's house was on fire. I knocked on the door, but no one was home. I thought this might be your work number."

"How did you know I worked here?"

The dial tone signaled he wasn't getting an answer. As soon as Henrik hung up, he scoped out Meadowgreene Lane. He went back to his apartment and waited for sundown.

Henrik parked his car about one hundred yards from the Clarke residence. Barking dogs and three or four passing cars were the only sounds in the neighborhood. He found a gas can on a back porch near a lawn mower, two houses to the right of where the Clarkes lived.

He snatched the can and ran to the backside of where M. and Cindy Clarke lived. Henrik poured gas on the ground in the back and down the left side of their house. He lit the match and the inferno began. Henrik ran to his car.

He could see smoke billowing above the street lamp in front of their home. The neighborhood mutts woke up everyone and several neighbors checked on the situation. Someone called the fire department and the family managed to safely make it out. Feeling sorry for someone wasn't part of his job, but at least the innocent family wasn't harmed.

When Melvin Clarke read through *The Dispatch* the next morning, he found the story on A-3. The headline—*Fire destroys home, family safely escapes*—explained it all.

The phone call from the accented man wasn't a farce. Melvin looked around the breakfast table at his wife and kids. He was thankful they were safe and didn't have to go through an ordeal like the one on Meadowgreene Lane. Yes, his family was safe, but something was in store for Melvin. It was only a matter of time before number seven got to him.

AVA HADN'T HEARD FROM Sharon for a week. She contacted the police without knowledge they already talked to Stenson. The police knew something wasn't right, but couldn't connect the dots. Things worsened once they discovered Jackson and Ryule were dead.

Visitors stopped by Ava's house that day, but they couldn't find evidence linked to Sharon's whereabouts. It was like she vanished into thin air.

Kurt purchased a typewriter at a local mart in Austin. He finished his handiwork and mailed the letters from the hotel. As the officers were leaving, the mailman arrived.

Dear Ava,

Sharon didn't die in the explosion. She is alive and doing quite well. She is very beautiful, but don't worry, we're not going to lay a finger on her. There is one problem. We need money! We have a family in Europe who contacted us about the baby. Once it arrives, he or she is going to France for $200,000. However, that can be avoided by sending double to Harry "Big Boy" Stenson in Columbus, Ohio. He will let us know he has the money and Sharon and her newborn will be released.

We hope you make the right decision.

P.S. Sharon hopes Trevor is doing well and says he is to remain with Ava until she returns to Fresno.

An identical letter arrived at the O'Neil residence in Mesa. Gary read his letter and was immediately on the phone with Stenson.

"Hello."

"You're a dead man."

"What are you talking about?"

Gary read the letter to Big Boy. The correspondence further cemented Stenson's feelings that he was being set up.

"Listen to me. Why would I be involved in kidnapping your wife? Sharon is a dear person to me as well," he dishonestly said. "Here is what happened. I sent Jackson and Ryule to keep an eye on Sharon in Fresno. I know I should have told you, but I didn't and you'll have to get over that. They were conned by a kid and ended up being chased by cops. After a serious high-speed chase, they were thrown in jail."

Stenson paused until Gary said, "Continue."

"That night, there was an explosion at a local motel. The room where the explosion occurred was rented by a fake name. However, the investigators found a briefcase a few doors down. When they opened it, they found a picture of Sharon inside. One of my business cards was also inside. The investigators called me and I flew to Fresno last week. Police in Columbus questioned my family. I was cleared of wrongdoing, but someone is causing problems for us. I didn't play a part in this. If someone sends money, I'm turning it in to the police."

The only part of the story he left out was the fact Sharon was accompanied by a naked man in the photograph, the same man who lost his house to a "gas leak" in Mesa.

Gary was upset he didn't know about the situation.

"It appears you're telling the truth, but where is Sharon?"

"That's a good question. I have people looking for her in Fresno and Ava's house is back under surveillance. Your house is also being watched. The best thing to do is to stay clear of your home."

It was one of the few times in Gary's life he didn't respond as expected. Stenson had that effect on him.

They agreed they would work together to remedy the situation, but Gary was uneasy. Although Sharon was safe in the back country of Texas, the men swore they were going to find her and who was responsible for sending the letter.

Back in Fresno, Ava was ready to have a breakdown. She couldn't believe someone kidnapped her daughter and blamed herself for allowing Sharon to stay with her.

"If I wouldn't have let her stay with me, none of this would have happened. I'm finished with this town."

It was the first time Ava talked about Fresno that way. Maybe there was a glimmer of hope she would pack up what little belongings she had and leave the place for good.

The phone startled Ava. The cops wanted to listen in on the call, so they picked up the receiver in the living room when Ava answered the one in the kitchen.

"This is Ava."

"Hi Ava, it's Gary. I know a little bit about Sharon's disappearance."

"So do I."

"I received a letter in the mail today and..."

"So did I."

Gary started reading the letter and before he reached the eighth word, Ava read along with him.

"I'll stop since it's obvious someone sent us the same letter. I don't know who is behind this, but I will find out. I talked to Harry Stenson and he said he doesn't know who's behind it either. He informed me he doesn't have a deal in place with anyone and if money arrives at his house, in his bank account, or by any other means...he will inform the proper authorities."

Gary was interrupted by a much deeper voice than Ava's and figured it was the police.

"We spoke to Mr. Stenson and I'm sure we'll be in contact with him again," Shields said. "Do you trust him?"

"We have been friends for several years. He can lie with the best of them, but I don't think he would lie to me. I'm pissed! Harry is also angry. My wife is missing and she's carrying my child. Stenson wouldn't lay a finger on Sharon even though they have their differences."

"We need to take possession of the letters sent to you and Ava. I'll send someone to Mesa this afternoon and we'll get in contact with you. We'll do our best to locate Sharon."

Shields stayed with Ava in case the kidnappers came back for Trevor, who slept through the morning's ordeal.

Reynolds, the same investigator who questioned Stenson at the Fresno Police Department the prior week, visited Gary.

While Gary was going over information with Reynolds, Captain Luango and Shields visited Columbus. It was the second meeting with Harry Stenson and the third would be later that week.

The visit didn't last long. Stenson wiggled his way off the hook once again. Although neither incident was his fault, he was guilty of crimes and should have been behind bars long before the motel explosion or Sharon's fake kidnapping. It would be ironic if he went to the big house for something he was innocent of doing.

Stenson became more paranoid after the second meeting with the law. They no sooner pulled out of his driveway when he decided he was going to get the briefcase and give the police $400,000 from a mysterious donor.

He drove to see Rhodes and discuss the matter. Rhodes gave him the money and called the Fresno pests two days later.

"The money arrived today in a manila folder that wasn't postmarked," Stenson explained to Luango. "What should I do with it?"

Luango thought about ways he could spend it, but he wasn't a dirty cop. He received various awards throughout his distinguished career and was regarded as a humanitarian among his peers.

"I'm opening an account with Fresno First National and I want you to deposit the money into it. You're doing the right thing with the money and it eliminates you as a suspect in the kidnapping, but you are still linked to the explosion. I'll get in touch with you if we need anything else."

Kurt accomplished his goal. He had Stenson on the ropes and was going to eventually land a haymaker to put him on the canvas. He felt badly for Ava, but Sharon would return home in a few weeks, so he knew she could survive a little longer.

HENRIK PAID CLOSE ATTENTION to 308 Toltec Circle. For five days, he watched when the lights came on in the morning and what time they were turned off at night.

He knew Melvin opened the front door at 6:20, about the time Columbus' birds started chirping in unison, and retrieved the morning paper from the front porch. The bus stopped at the end of Toltec each morning at 7:38 and picked up nine kids, including the Clarke children. His wife exercised on the treadmill in the front window each afternoon. Melvin's wife left their house at 2:45 and drove to the elementary school, picking their kids up at 3:03 each day. Henrik knew what time Melvin pulled in the driveway after his shift at Rhodes and that the family ate dinner soon thereafter.

He discovered Victoria started her menstrual cycle before his five-day watch ended. Discarded mail, coffee grinds, a pizza box, soggy paper towels, and white plastic sacks mostly filled the trash bags at the end of their driveway. Henrik opened them on Tuesday evening after Melvin took them to the curb. He was halfway through the second bag when he found what he needed.

A letter from a local men's club was addressed to Melvin. The club was inviting men who played softball in the fall league for a get-together on Saturday. Heavy cocktails and finger foods would be provided and they would discuss the upcoming winter basketball league. A few hands of poker were also in the realm of possibility.

Mr. Clarke owned a small pickup truck. He drove it everywhere, including work, the grocery store, and to play golf the third afternoon Henrik followed him everywhere. His wife drove a Cadillac, but Melvin didn't use it once in five days and didn't drive it that Saturday evening.

The social gathering was slated to start at 7:00 p.m. Melvin went shopping with his wife during the afternoon, which was done so he could attend the party with his over-the-hill jock friends.

At 5:40, one of the garage doors opened and Melvin backed his pickup truck onto Toltec. Henrik thought he had been spotted a time or two and was right. Melvin sensed he was being followed, but thought it was his imagination getting the best of him.

Melvin Clarke's stalker posed as many things—a jogger, a pizza delivery guy, a sweeper salesman, and even a Jehovah's Witness. Each day, Henrik wore a different disguise. Gary's hit men used that trick to perfection, but the Swedish assassin was arguably the best.

He waited patiently until Melvin drove past the corner where he stood. He took one of the barking dogs from Melvin's neighborhood and appeared to be a gentleman taking his pet for a nightly stroll.

Mr. Clarke was in a hurry to arrive at the get-together. The event was supposed to be over around 11:00 p.m., but he and a few buddies planned on leaving by nine-thirty so they could surround the main stage at Club Fantasy for an hour or two.

The pickup eased through the stop sign and Melvin managed a half-hearted wave. Henrik, who nodded as Melvin drove by, had parked his car just before the stop sign. He dropped the leash and quickly hopped in his vehicle.

It took a few minutes, but Henrik managed to get behind Melvin, who wasn't paying attention. He had drinks, socializing, and naked women on his brain.

He pulled into the men's club, but Henrik kept driving. Melvin got out of his truck. Hoot and Jimmy Boy had already lit up a couple of stogies in the parking lot and Melvin joined in on the fun.

Henrik parked his car facing the main drag in front of Movies Unlimited two blocks away from the men's club. He sat in his vehicle for nearly an hour, waiting on the sun's last rays to dip over the horizon. When the street lamps flickered, he popped his door open and grabbed the duffel bag he brought along for the ride.

Traffic was fairly busy, so the Swede waited until the coast was clear. He didn't take advantage of the sidewalk that led straight to the lot where Melvin's truck was parked. Instead, he walked between two businesses and used an alleyway leading to the back trash bins at the club.

He didn't see anyone at the back of the club, but Henrik noticed a door cracked. The hit man walked quietly to the door and carefully peered in. The kitchen area was temporarily deserted. Empty bottles of bourbon and rum were on the counter and a keg was on ice. He figured the refrigerator was stocked with brewskis and he was right.

"I'll grab you one," one of the men attending the party shouted.

Henrik was nearly discovered, but he ducked out of sight before the gentleman lumbered into the kitchen.

He crept along the backside of the building and looked down the side. He heard guys talking, but the noise came from inside. The raucous gathering of married men—a wedding ring was in the bylaws and a few had no doubt said "I do" just to join the club— would be an embarrassment for any wife, thus the reason it was a men's only club. The fact scantily clad cocktail girls and gentlemen magazines circulated around the establishment would end nearly every membership, save for a few of the men that had freaks for wives.

Henrik looked into the parking lot after he made his way down the side of the building. There wasn't a sound coming from the lot. As he was ready to dart between cars, a stranger called out behind him.

"May I help you?"

The uninvited guest turned around and met one of the club's lookouts.

"I'm new to the area. I'm looking for a good time and it sounds like this is the place."

"Are you married?"

"Yes, but I don't wear a ring."

"Are you over thirty?"

"Yes. I'm thirty-eight."

"Where are you from?"

"I am from Sweden, but came back to America. I graduated from Cincinnati and returned to my homeland for several years. I missed the United States and decided to return. I have an uncle who lives in this neighborhood. I'm living with him until I get accustomed to things here in Central Ohio."

"Where is your wife?"

"She's in Sweden. Once I get a job and find a place for us, she will join me."

The burly security guard explained the club and extended an invitation.

"We have induction meetings at 7:00 p.m. on the first Monday every month. Stop by and see if it's for you. I have to get back to my post. By the way, what's in the duffel bag?"

Henrik didn't answer.

"I don't want to cause trouble, but I need to look inside the bag. There are some crazy people and you never know what someone's capable of doing."

"I'm a private person and I refuse to let someone rummage through my things."

"Well then, we have a problem," the lookout said as he shook his head. "One way or another, you have to let me see the contents of the duffel bag. Make this easier and open the bag!"

Henrik dropped the bag on the sidewalk and backed away.

"Fine. Take a look."

The man kept eye contact with Henrik as he crouched down. Before he could unzip the bag, he lost three of his teeth. A swift kick in the mouth jarred his head back and he saw stars, the kind that crackle around from a dizzy spell.

Despite dizziness and blood spilling everywhere, the man got up.

He rushed Henrik, but the Swede's arms moved so rapidly it was like fast-forwarding a Bruce Lee action scene. Several short jabs and karate chops put the man on his knees. He latched his arms around the foreigner's waist and tried to wrestle him down. However, in one crushing blow, Henrik slammed the fleshy part of his palm near the wrist into the man's nose. The downward blow rendered the man motionless.

Had the event happened six months later, Henrik would have been caught on film. The bouncer's death is what motivated the club to install a surveillance system on the premises.

He picked up the duffel bag and hustled to the parking lot. The tussle left him little time. He meticulously maneuvered around the parking lot until he reached the back of Melvin's truck.

Five days of watching for any chink in Mr. Clarke's armor was about to pay off. Henrik knew how he was going to eliminate Melvin. He waited for the opportune time, a moment that had arrived.

A toneau cover enclosed the bed of Melvin's truck. Henrik eased the tailgate down and placed his duffel bag in the bed. He unlatched both sides of the cover and slithered into the back of the truck. He reached for the tailgate and pulled it toward himself. He lifted the cover a bit so he could shut the tailgate.

A few men discovered the body left behind by Henrik. The noise from the tailgate drew their attention. They investigated by going up and down the spaces in the lot, looking for anything suspicious.

Two snaps, one on each side, made things simple. A slight pull upwards lifted the cover at a 45-degree angle. Henrik snapped both sides in place and waited for a lift back to Toltec.

Melvin and his buddies didn't get the opportunity to leave early for Club Fantasy. The police shut down the gathering. The body was placed in a black bag and several members decided their wives were right. A club like Charlie Hustle's wasn't for them.

Mrs. Clarke found out what happened and drove to the club, as did several other wives. Many tried to use the severity of the moment to their advantage. They tried to get inside to see if their husbands were all right, but bylaws were bylaws. A murder wouldn't change them. Wives were to wait outside. If the building had windows, many of the ladies would cup their hands to the window and firmly press their face against their hands, hoping to catch a glimpse of what went on inside.

Melvin walked out of the club after midnight as authorities finished their work.

"This is the last time you'll visit Charlie Hustle's. As of now, your membership is canceled," Victoria declared. "You have been coming here for six years and I despised every minute of it. Hopefully, they'll shut this place down. Let's go home."

Charlie Hustle's wasn't closed until nine years after the incident. Ownership erred and let an undercover cop become a member. The cocktail girls were still there, as was the booze and cards. However, some of the cocktail girls graduated to better tips. A back room was built and turned into a show palace. The owner of Club Fantasy heard the rumors and informed police about the illegal activities.

The undercover cop received a few lap dances and perfumed boob slaps to the face during his private work. He secretly wanted to remain a member, but duty prevented him from a lifetime membership. The dancers would have been a slap on the wrist, but the money the girls and the club made on the side wasn't reported. The IRS swooped in and shut the doors.

Victoria eventually got her wish, but was unaware of her innocent prediction. Melvin loved going to Charlie Hustle's, but he had made his last visit. Within hours, his membership to life would be revoked.

Chapter Thirteen

THE NIGHT SEEMED TO drag on for Preston and Gary. They knew the words to "Tall Paul" and sang along to keep from going crazy. The music was working to perfection. The cattle prod wasn't successful with Gary. Had Preston been withholding information, the hotshot would cause him to spill his guts.

They knew most of the information Gary thought he was keeping from them, but to move their plan along, Matt's regime needed the elder O'Neil to talk.

Lauren opened the door a little after midnight and proudly carried the cattle prod. Preston's body cowered at the sight of the handheld device. If he could get his hands on it, he thought of a few places on Lauren he would stick it, especially if she zapped him again.

The prod wasn't going to be in action. Lauren was sent to the storage house to give them something to think about. She paced back and forth in the center of the room before speaking.

"Who's going to tell us what we want to know?" she asked as she walked over and unhooked the leather bridle straps attached to the wall behind Preston.

Preston was agitated with everything. The voice effect made his frustration worse. He used his tongue to push the bridle out of his mouth.

"Why don't you let us hear your voice? You have us tied up and in extremely bad predicaments, yet you hide behind a voice that isn't yours."

Matt didn't want Lauren engaging in much conversation with their captives. He entered the room and took charge.

"You want to talk about hiding Preston? You're withholding information from us about the briefcase we know you have, so don't give us a line about hiding," Matt said while wondering if he was acting or starting to go mad.

He walked over and whispered to Lauren, and she followed his instructions.

"If you are going to remain silent, we'll move to phase three. It seems you're enjoying the music and the shock treatment must have been therapeutic."

Lauren started running the water in the bathtub. Matt stood behind Gary while she waited for the water to reach the top. He pulled out a syringe and walked next to Gary. He flicked it twice and prepared to shove it into the side of Gary's neck.

"If you stick me, it will be the last thing you do."

Considering Gary's situation, Matt and Lauren got a good laugh from his threat. Humor aside, they knew what Gary was capable of doing.

Disregarding Gary's warning of impending doom, Matt jabbed him in the neck with the needle. Gary was in a drunken state within sixty seconds.

"The water is ready," Lauren said.

Matt ripped the duct tape off Gary and instructed Lauren to grab the gun from the milk crate.

"If he grabs me or tries anything, shoot him! I don't care if I'm in the way, keep firing."

Matt knew the drugs in Gary's system wouldn't allow him to lift his head, but he wanted Lauren to stay focused. Gary was aware what was going on, but couldn't put up a fight.

Matt placed shoes on Gary's feet and carefully lifted him off the stage. He handcuffed Gary's hands and shackled his feet before dragging his limp body to the bathtub. Matt hoisted Gary and leaned him over the edge of the tub. Matt grabbed the back of his neck and shoved his head under the freezing water. After ten seconds, he pulled him out.

"What do you know about the briefcase?"

Matt knew he wouldn't get a quick answer, so the dunking continued until he got a response. He asked Gary the same question each time he yanked his head from the water.

"What do you know about the briefcase?"

Gary finally responded. Matt wished his response was the one he was looking for because his hands felt like hypothermia was setting in.

"I'm not talking about the briefcase. You can drown me."

Matt pushed Gary's head under the water. Lauren thought Matt was going to drown him, but he pulled him out of the water again.

"I'll keep this up all night. You were under the water thirty-five seconds and I'll add a second each time I pull your head from the water. What do you know about the briefcase?"

The tortuous dunking reached sixty-six seconds and it was all Gary could do to breathe. Matt knew he would eventually drown if he continued. He also knew his hands would have to be amputated if he didn't stop.

"What do you know about the briefcase? Tell me and this can stop."

He hadn't said a word since they reached thirty-five seconds. The session was wearing them out. Gary suddenly spoke.

"I told you, I'm not talking about the briefcase. You can ask anything about me," he said while wheezing and gasping for air.

Matt kicked Gary in his right side and let him slump to the floor.

"If you don't tell me what I want to know, whether it's about the briefcase or yourself, you will visit 'The aquatic center' on a daily basis."

Matt grabbed Gary by his arms and pulled him to his stage. He lifted him and let him plop too hard in the old chair. It squeaked and swayed back and forth. It nearly collapsed, but Matt was able to tape Gary's arms, head, and torso back in place. He knew he couldn't take him out of the chair again because it would cave in the next time.

Lauren and Matt left the room. Matt was exhausted from the tortuous session and needed to sleep. He couldn't imagine how Gary felt. They woke Dane once they got back to the warehouse. It was his turn to keep watch. He walked over to the first storage house and took a seat near the surveillance equipment.

Gary and Preston were sleeping. Their shut eye would serve them well. Matt was going to set the morning off with a bang and it would surprise everyone.

ON MONDAY, KURT AND Sharon woke to the thunderous marching of hooves click-clacking along the rubber mats in the milking portion of the barn. Kurt smiled at Sharon and kissed her.

He took off Mr. Alexander's shirt and tie and hung them from a nail in the barn before he went to sleep. He slept in an undershirt and wished he hadn't done so. The itching from the straw scratches lasted several days. He got up and put his shirt on.

"I'll be back in a while."

Jim wasn't surprised to see Kurt.

"Howdy," Kurt said as he attempted a Southern drawl.

Jim laughed and shook his head.

"You'll have to try harder than that. Breakfast is on the table if you're hungry."

"That can wait. I would like to help you."

Jim never refused help, especially on Mondays. He needed to finish as quickly as possible because he had to hit the road. He was scheduled to drive a shipment of goods to Pittsburgh. The drive was easy, but he wished he was going west.

Jim had shuttled two groups through the barn and was ready to march in a third. Kurt was quickly thrown into the fire. Elaine joined them a few minutes later. Hooking hoses to cows' udders was strange, but it didn't take long for Kurt to understand the milking process.

Things ran smoothly until one of the Bessies was defiant. No matter how much Kurt pushed and shoved, she wouldn't go in her stall. He nearly took a hoof to the privates, but tumbled out of the way.

His fall brought Jim and Elaine to tears. Kurt wanted to give them a piece of his mind, but thought of Pastor Browne's words about forgiveness and decided to laugh with them.

He brushed himself off and went back to work. Kurt reached into a sack of sugar cubes and pulled out a handful. The peace offering made her cooperate. He hooked the hosed contraption to her udders and wiped sweat off his forehead.

"She's a tough one," Jim said.

"Now you tell me."

"The sugar cubes are something we try to avoid, but there are two or three we occasionally have to bribe. She's one of them."

The Alexander children joined them later than usual and Kurt thought they would be in trouble. He found out their shift started an hour later on Mondays. They partially got ready for school and took over for their dad so he could leave town.

"I have to get on the road. Get started Tyler and Chelsea. I need to talk with Mr. Carson."

They walked outside the barn and Jim asked about the proposition he made on Sunday.

"What did you decide?"

"I talked to Sharon and would like to stay."

"I'm happy to hear that. I'm always worried about Elaine and the kids when I'm on the road. I would like to have someone here to keep an eye on them. It would make me feel better."

"Are you asking me to stay longer than we discussed?"

"That's up to you. We have talked about hiring someone the past few years. We held off because we knew the younger kids would eventually be old enough to help. However, you never know about Colt. He's a good boy, but he's always chasing the girls. Also, I don't trust anyone. The Parsons hired a farmhand to help them two summers ago and he stole from them. This morning is the first time I have seen you in action, but I know you're a good worker. I'll make sure you're paid well and find you a place nearby."

"I have a few ideas. You said your basement is used for storage. I don't know how much room is down there, but I would like to stay here. As for the pay, I'll work for free in exchange for Elaine's good eats and a spot in the basement."

"We can make room for you, but I wouldn't stay in the basement. If you don't mind, I won't argue. We'll feed you for free regardless. Most of the food we eat is what we grow and harvest. I still want to pay you."

"Sharon and I talked. She is going back to Fresno to pick up Trevor and see her mom. She'll also figure out what to do about her situation with Gary."

"Do we have an agreement?" Jim asked as he extended his hand.

"There is one final detail. I want Preston to stay with me. I know it might cause problems for a while, but it's for the best. Sharon will send money for Preston and I, so you won't need to pay me."

Jim pulled back his hand and ran it through his thinning hair.

"Elaine adores children and would love to have Preston stay with us. She always wanted more children, but I didn't think it was fair with me on the road all the time. You are both welcome additions."

They shook hands and Kurt returned to the doorway of the barn. Jim started his rig, which made every two-by-four in the barn rumble. The Alexanders stepped behind Kurt and waved in unison. It was a family tradition to wave as Jim pulled out of the driveway.

Colt closed his eyes and prayed.

"Lord, be with our daddy as he travels to the land of the Yankees," he said as Elaine nudged him and smirked. "Give him good driving conditions and return him to us safely. Help him be a light for you as he drives his truck and comes in contact with other people along the way. Amen."

The family turned and walked back into the barn to finish the morning's milking. Kurt was amazed he was thinking about religion. He didn't know much about it, but he learned it was more peaceful thinking about God.

He said a prayer for Sharon and Preston. Kurt then walked to the back entrance of the barn to filter in one of the morning's final groups.

A few weeks passed and Kurt exceeded the Alexander's expectations. He learned his way around the farm and did things without asking. He was an extension of Jim and helped make their farm more prosperous.

Doc Badnarik gave Sharon a clean bill of health. She was up and moving around remarkably well. Sharon spent every minute of the day with Preston.

Chelsea had grown fond of Sharon and spent less time at the neighbor's house and more time at home. Elaine loved having Sharon there and thought she was a positive influence on Chelsea. The weekend arrived and the mood in the house changed. Sharon's time in Austin was drawing to an end, but like Kurt, she had fallen in love with the Alexander way of life. She even went to church with them and found it uplifting.

After church on the second Sunday following Kurt and Jim's agreement, it was time to take Sharon to the bus depot. Kurt stayed behind at the farm for precautionary reasons. Colt drove Sharon to the depot and she found it twice as beautiful the second time through. The agony she was in on the way to the farm kept her from truly enjoying Austin's scenery. She looked out the window to hide tears from Colt.

Sharon didn't want to return to Fresno or Mesa, but she missed Trevor and her mother. If she could move the two of them to Austin, she wouldn't cross the state line again.

Colt pulled next to the curb two blocks from the depot and dropped off Sharon. They felt it was best if she walked the rest of the way in case someone was watching. They had to be certain no harm could be brought upon the Alexanders or Kurt.

She opened her door and they said parting words. As Sharon was slowly shutting the door, she opened it, put one of her knees on the seat, leaned over, and kissed Colt on his right cheek. He blushed.

"You're a fine young man. I know you are mischievous at times, but continue being yourself. Your father loves you very much and is a worried parent. You're his oldest boy and getting closer to being on your own. I'm sure that's difficult for him to handle."

"Thanks Mrs. O'Neil. I hope you come back."

Colt turned his head because he was about to let a woman outside his family see him cry for the first time. Sharon sensed he was ready to let his emotions get the best of him, so she closed the door and started down the sidewalk.

She safely made it to the depot. She had her belongings tagged and was on her way to Fresno. She cried as the bus passed under the "Leaving Texas" sign. She couldn't stop thinking about Preston, Kurt, or the Alexanders. She hoped to talk her mother into moving to Texas. Selling her on the vegetables and farm life would be the angle. She could attend Calvary and meet several friends there. Sharon planned things in her head and hoped they would change.

BEFORE DAYBREAK, PRESTON DECIDED to stop acting. Neither of them could see an inch in front of their face. The bulbs, which produced red colored glares, were off.

"Are you awake?" Preston whispered through the darkness.

"Yes."

"Why don't you tell them about the briefcase or whatever they want to know?"

"I'm not telling them anything. If I tell them about the briefcase, they will kill me. If they let me go, Rhodes and Stenson will have me killed. I would rather keep my mouth shut and die with dignity."

"Do you think being treated like we are is respectful?"

"If I could get my hands on them, I would teach them a lesson about respect. I have done things that are wrong. That is why we are here. If I talk, it's only going to make things worse. They know you don't have anything to do with this. They're going to keep you locked up and do more bad things to you, but they have you in front of me to get me to talk. It's not going to work."

It was strange for Gary to talk the way he was. He never talked to his family from the heart, if he even had one. After all, he participated in a meeting that placed a lottery-like price tag on his son's head.

"Does the briefcase have anything to do with your job?"

"I know what I do for a living has always been a secret. Your mother tried to get it out of me. I won't tell you what I do, but yes, the briefcase is part of my job."

"Then why don't you tell them it's your job and let this end?"

"It's not that easy. You can't fill out an application for my job. There's somewhat of an interview, but it's not a job you'll find in the classified section."

"I think you should tell me what you have done all these years?"

"You have had a good life. When your mother died, I tried to support you. I didn't work nearly as much once we moved to Columbus. I paid for your college and helped you land a great job at Stenson & Rhodes. You're twenty-eight now and I don't owe you a thing."

"One way or another, they will get it out of you."

Matt felt refreshed after getting four hours of sleep. He almost walked into the room on a couple occasions, but thought Preston was performing admirably. Preston wasn't acting.

He listened as Preston's pleas continued for fifteen minutes. Gary reached his breaking point.

"You sound like one of them. I'm not telling you what I do, nor will I tell them. I know you have different reasons, but you should give it a rest."

Gary's words signaled it was time for Matt's big surprise. He walked out of the first storage house and made a phone call. He left the door open and the moonlight reflected around him. Lauren and Dane could see him talking on his phone.

The neighborhood around the warehouse was sparsely populated. Country houses were sprinkled up and down Route 23. Once traffic reached Johnson Road, the road in front of the warehouse, there was only one house until the top of the hill. It was the same hill they drove up the night the pair of teenage lovers were going at it near the entrance to the warehouse.

Real estate was cheap around the warehouse and some of it was off limits. There were empty lots across the road and a condemned shack that made the warehouse look like a Hilton.

The neighborhood on top of the hill was a hidden gem. There were seventeen houses and each had a price tag of at least half a million. If they were in ritzy areas around Columbus, they would double in price.

The phone call was made to 59114 Johnson Road. A man answered the phone and Matt greeted him.

"It's time."

"I'll be there in an hour," he said to throw off anyone who might be listening.

He drove past the warehouse and turned onto Route 23. The sun was stretching its arms and working out the kinks, but still had a few minutes before it was fully awake. He unlatched the chain and pulled onto the access road. He quickly reattached the chain and drove down the trail.

He maneuvered through the opening in the fence and eased next to Lauren's car.

"Stay here!" Matt said as he peeked into the first storage house.

He shut the door and crossed the road to greet their visitor. They shook hands and read each others eyes. Both men were uneasy.

"Are you ready?"

"I told you I was when you asked me to do this."

Matt walked in first and turned on the red lights.

"Good morning Gary. Good morning Preston. Are you ready to talk?"

Their silence said it best.

He left the room and returned with a ladder. He reached above Preston's head and barely turned on a spigot. The dripping water landing on his forehead annoyed him. Preston tried to move his head, but the duct tape only gave him an inch or two of leeway.

"The water will drip on your head until you tell us what we want to know. I bet Hippolytus de Marsiliis would tell you that Chinese water torture drove several people insane in the 16th century. It's your decision...the dripping water or tell us what we want to know."

Matt had something different in store for Gary. His arms and hands were tightly wrapped to the chair. Gary could wiggle his fingers, but had about the same leeway as Preston.

"For some reason, I have always loved the xylophone. I enjoy its sounds. I haven't played one before, so I guess this will have to do."

Talbot reached into his pocket and pulled out a crescent wrench.

"I'm giving you another chance to speak. What do you know about the briefcase?"

Gary looked straight ahead, ignoring Matt's words.

"All right. Have it your way."

Matt swung the wrench like a tomahawk chop, cracking the knuckle on Gary's left ring finger. He let out an awful scream. The room was supposed to be sound proof, but the man standing against the door heard Gary.

His broken knuckle ballooned to the size of a ripe grape. Gary knew he couldn't withstand all ten knuckles being broken, but was adamant about not talking.

"Tell me about the briefcase!"

Gary looked at Matt like he wanted to say something, but scowled before looking ahead again.

"I have already heard do, so it's time to hear re. I'll continue with mi, fa, so, la, ti, do, and when I hit that eighth note…once I'm out of notes, I'll make up two more. You can avoid that by telling me what I want to know."

Matt used the wrench again, snapping Gary's pinky on his right hand. Like his ring finger, the knuckle on his pinky was broken and looked like a camel's back. His second scream might have been louder than the first.

"Do I hear information about the briefcase? Going once. Going twice. Sold!" Matt said as he smashed Gary's left thumb.

His screams were replaced on the third blow by intense wailing.

"You can avoid this Gary. Tell me what I want to know and you can go home or wherever you want."

"You sonofabitch. I'm not telling you anything. Go ahead and break my hands. Break my legs. Break my ribs. You won't break me."

Gary was living up to his reputation. His crying didn't alter Matt's perception of him. The tortuous sessions could continue for years. Matt knew they wouldn't get information from him. He withstood enough electricity to keep a home warm for a northeastern winter and was efficient enough under water to make a Navy Seal envious. Broken knuckles and intense pain made him stronger.

It was time to unveil the wild card.

Matt walked to the door and looked back at Gary.

"Since you won't tell me what I want to know, maybe you will tell him."

Heath A. Dawson

Rhodes walked into the room and Gary was stunned. Preston was equally shocked. The last time he saw the man's face was in the parking garage. All of a sudden, Preston's ribs hurt.

"Hello gentlemen. I see your gracious host is treating you well. Preston, I want you to tell me what you know about the briefcase."

Preston wanted to cuss Matt and wished he could get his hands on Lauren's prod. It would make a great murder weapon. He thought he had everything figured out. Now, he wondered if Matt was in on the scam and if his father was innocent.

Lauren and Dane watched with great interest. Lauren didn't know who Rhodes was, but Dane filled her in. He was commanded to shoot Rhodes on sight, but Matt had apparently befriended him. Everyone was confused.

"Why should I tell you about the briefcase? You know everything about it."

"You're right. I do, but I need to know what you know."

Preston felt like Gary. If he told them what they wanted to know, he could be killed. If he didn't tell them, he could be killed.

Rhodes pulled out a gun and pointed it at Preston.

"Robert, what are you doing? He doesn't have anything to do with this. He is in the dark. Leave him alone."

Rhodes turned around and stared at Gary.

"You screwed up Gary and now we're all in a mess. Thankfully, these people are going to clean it up for us."

"What are you talking about?"

"Here's the deal. We have been screwed by your ole' pal Stenson, my business partner and the man you tell everything. Stenson planned to have your son killed. He set up a meeting with Seevers so one of the assassins could take him out. If I hadn't told Matt about the meeting, Preston might be walking streets of gold as we speak. Stenson's next mark was going to be you. If you think back several years, it's clear that Stenson isn't your friend. Do you remember when those letters were sent to you and Ava?"

"How could I forget?"

"Stenson was behind the whole thing. He had the motel blown up because Sharon was staying there with another man. She never told

184

you the truth because she was afraid. He lied to you, he lied to the cops, and he lied to me. It's time that rat gets what he deserves."

"If you're involved with these people, why do I need to tell them about the briefcase? Why are Preston and I tied up? Why are we being tortured? Do you see my hands?"

His questions were understandable. The reason Preston was tied up was obvious to everyone except Gary. Preston was in the room to get his father to talk, but they didn't need Gary to tell them about the briefcase's dark secrets. They already knew what they needed to know. Matt's main objective was to get Gary to talk about the briefcase so they could tape it and send it to Stenson, who would think Gary had double-crossed him.

Rhodes was brought in on the plan to get Gary comfortable enough to believe Stenson was double-crossing everyone else. It was an ingenious plan. They hoped Gary would help eliminate Big Boy. As for Rhodes, he would be taken care of later.

"I know you don't understand how Sharon died. I'll tell you how it happened. Stenson had her killed. He swore his innocence, but masterminded her death. You were sent to Indianapolis on business so you would be away. He needed Sharon out of the way because he didn't want you to find out her dark secret. He was also sending someone a message."

"What secret and what message?"

"You and Sharon raised Preston like he was your own, but for Sharon, it was natural. The reason she did so is because he is her son. Sharon had an affair with a man named Kurt Carson, the same man Preston said he saw mommy kissing years ago."

"You're lying."

"When you asked Stenson to keep an eye on Sharon, he never stopped watching her. He had men spying on Sharon in California, but they lost track of her. Sharon eventually went back to Fresno before resurfacing in Mesa several days later. The surveillance started again. Stenson lost her trail a few times and couldn't figure out how she was giving them the slip. She finally made a mistake, or so it seemed."

Rhodes had Gary's full attention.

"Two years had passed when Kurt Carson visited Sharon in Mesa. The visit took place on a weekend you were out of town. One night after he dropped Sharon off at your house, Stenson's men followed him to a gas station and staged a robbery. Kurt was shot and killed during the fake heist. Sharon immediately traveled to get Preston and placed him in an orphanage. All that time, you thought she had a miscarriage. Preston is her child and that is why she was adamant about adopting. She knew someone at the orphanage and they helped her stage the adoption. They claimed the state placed him in the home because his father had been killed."

Rhodes paused for a minute to see if Gary had anything to say. Gary had looks of anger, disgust, shock, hate, and revenge.

"Stenson put two and two together and found out Preston was her son. He didn't want you knowing the truth because it could have put our operation in jeopardy. You know I wanted Stenson to keep a close eye on everyone in the loop. With Kurt apparently out of the picture, we thought the saga had ended."

"It didn't?"

"Stenson had your house phone wired. After a few months, Sharon began talking frequently to another man. We couldn't figure out who it was or where the man lived. It took time to find out who he was, but when Stenson made the startling discovery, he knew we were in trouble. We spent a year trying to find the man, but couldn't locate him. He sent a message to Stenson and me saying we were going to be exposed, so Harry sent him a message by killing Sharon the night of the summer party at the golf club."

"Who was the man?"

"It was Kurt Carson."

"I thought he was murdered," Preston chimed in.

"We all did," Rhodes answered.

"If he wasn't murdered, who was and where is Kurt now?"

"After escaping from death's grip once, and seemingly twice, Kurt knew they wouldn't fail a third time. The note that read 'You're next' at Sharon's crime scene was enough to keep him away for good. He wanted revenge, but had to steer clear of what was going on."

"How do you know all of this?" Preston asked.

"That's not important."

"Who was the man they killed?" Gary asked.

"His name was Kurt Carson. It seems unbelievable, but it's the truth."

Rhodes stretched the truth while talking to Gary and Preston in the storage house, but most of it was accurate.

"Kurt knew we were after him. He searched phone books and couldn't find anyone with the name Kurt Carson. The local newspaper landed on Kurt's doorstep and it was almost as if God had sent him a gift. He read a story about a man's release from prison after a two-year stint. Had he been a hardcore criminal, the trip would have been out of the question. The man had been in jail because he embezzled money at the bank where he was employed and marijuana was found at his residence. Kurt Carson was a risky choice, but Kurt contacted him anyway. Kurt asked him to travel to Mesa to see Sharon. He warned there could be trouble because a dangerous group of men had been trying to find him."

Preston was having trouble envisioning his mother associating with criminals.

"The man took Kurt's $3,000 offer without hesitation. Kurt told him to watch for anything suspicious. He drove the rental car to Mesa and met Sharon on a Friday night. She didn't allow the man to stay with her, but put him up in the fanciest hotel in town. The second night, they went to dinner. Kurt had the visitor give Sharon home videos, several pictures, and all of Preston's information in case Stenson's men eventually found him. She kept touching his hands during dinner and thanking him. When he stopped in front of the O'Neil residence to drop her off, Sharon hugged him, thanked him again, and said good-bye."

Gary and Preston were stunned. Lauren didn't know half the things Rhodes was telling them. She had trouble believing it. Lauren couldn't imagine what Preston was thinking.

"Stenson's hired hands followed him to the gas station. As he was paying, two men barged into the store. One robber forced the clerk to hand over the contents of the cash register and lie face down behind the desk. Kurt was ordered to his knees. The clerk heard the gun blast and human remains splatter all over the walk-in cooler. He grabbed a rifle from underneath the counter. As both men exited the store, he filled their backs with buckshot."

"Please stop! I have heard enough," Lauren said.

"Cops were called to the scene and it seemed obvious what had happened. The next day, the robbery was the lead story in every newspaper within one-hundred miles. The name Kurt Carson appeared throughout the story. Stenson assumed the problem was solved."

"Why are we here?" Gary asked.

"You need to tell them about the briefcase. They know my part of the story, but they need details from you. One way or another, we're going to get Stenson."

In a move that took them by surprise, Gary began talking. He told them the entire story of the briefcase and how he, Stenson, and Rhodes were involved. He didn't skip one detail. Under the mask, Matt smiled from ear to ear. Stenson was going to explode when he listened to the tape. Someone else would also be irate.

Matt had what he needed. The tapes were already being duplicated. That night, two were put in the mail. Stenson received a special delivery and a second person also signed his name on the dotted line for a postal worker the next day.

The tapes were the beginning of the end for those involved with the briefcase.

Chapter Fourteen

THE RIDE TO TOLTEC wasn't the most comfortable journey Henrik had ever been on, but it beat those long flights across the Atlantic.

Victoria pulled into the driveway first and opened both garage doors. She eased her Cadillac into the garage and Melvin pulled his truck beside her. Victoria shut the doors. Melvin turned off the ignition and as he hopped out of his truck, the arguing began. His wife didn't believe in fighting in front of the kids, who were inside with a sitter, so they let their words reverberate throughout the garage. Their verbal bout entertained Henrik. Listening to Melvin try to limp his way out of Victoria's doghouse was amusing.

The fighting escalated and continued for nearly twenty minutes. The babysitter finally opened the garage door to see if everything was all right. They assured her they were fine.

They walked into the house. Melvin turned off the garage light as he pulled the door shut behind him. Henrik heard him turn the deadbolt and press the lock on the door knob.

Things settled until Henrik heard a car pull into the driveway.

"Thanks Mrs. Clarke," the sitter said.

"Hello Mrs. Colvin," Victoria hollered out to the driveway. "Take care, Tiffany. We'll call if we need you to come over next week."

The Clarke's babysitter and her mother pulled out of the driveway and Victoria closed the front door. An hour passed and everything was silent. Henrik unsnapped both sides of the cover and lifted the left corner. He created enough space to look into the house. He could see through their laundry room and into the kitchen. A light on the stove had been left on and appeared to be the only watts generating inside the residence.

Henrik eased the cover up and hoisted his left leg over the tailgate and onto the bumper. After placing his right foot on the bumper, he stepped down to the garage floor. Henrik closed the toneau cover and grabbed his duffel bag.

The Cadillac had a security alarm, so he walked down the right side of Gary's truck. There wasn't a lot of space between a workstation that sat to the right of the steps and in front of the Cadillac. Henrik pushed his body as close to the workstation as possible and slid his way to the steps.

The alarm didn't sound and Henrik was ready to make his next move. He sat his bag on the steps and pulled out a glass cutter. The door leading from the laundry room to the garage was white and had a Solar Shield Frame. The glass in the door was double-paned and diamond cut. The lifetime warranty sticker was about to be voided by Henrik.

He took out a water bottle and squirted the glass. The Swede shoved a suction cup against the wet glass. He used the glass cutter to score a circle big enough for his arm to fit through. On the verge of breaking the first layer of glass, he tugged the suction cup. Henrik repeated the same steps before locating the deadbolt and unlocking it. He then twisted the lock on the door knob.

The door had a slight squeak to it, but not enough to be heard throughout the house. He crept into the kitchen and hit the jackpot. He saw Melvin hunched over in a recliner in the family room. Henrik crouched beside the island in the middle of the kitchen and worked his way around it. The kitchen had two entryways. One was from a living room in the front part of the house and the other from the family room where Melvin was snoozing. The family and living rooms were basically one, so he snuck into the living room.

He walked against the wall and peered around the corner. Melvin's head was slumped into his left shoulder. Henrik didn't waste time. He stabbed him in the right quad with an arsenic-laced syringe. Melvin instantly woke up, but Henrik ducked into the kitchen and was at the back sliding glass door when a light from the main bedroom came on.

Melvin reached for his leg, but poison was setting in. Victoria turned on a hallway light and rushed in to investigate the commotion. The noise from the glass door made her look into the kitchen. All she could see was a blur of black.

As she dialed 9-1-1, Melvin's body began shaking violently. Her husband was dead before an emergency crew arrived.

The police found the holes in the laundry room door, but both glass circles were missing. Henrik had snapped both sides of Melvin's toneau cover, leaving behind no trace as to how the killer got into the garage. Number seven was a master at what he did. There weren't fingerprints because of the gloves Henrik wore and he didn't leave anything at the scene. It was like a ghost had been in their home. They tried to lift prints off the back porch, but Henrik had pulled his shoes off and slipped them into his duffel bag after cutting holes in the glass.

Rhodes received the news on Monday that Melvin Clarke had been murdered, bringing a smile to his face. It was one less person he had to deal with and one less buyout to worry about paying.

Melvin Clarke was a guinea pig and the field experiment worked. He was the first headache Robert and Harry got rid of, but not the last. They were all pleased with Gary's recruit. He did a magnificent job.

Steve Birch was next on their list. He agreed to take a one-year buyout, but was back in Rhodes' office two weeks later with an attorney. He wanted more money. Things could have gone badly if the lawyer moved quickly on the case and a hearing had been set.

Gary replaced the zero on his shed's billboard to a two. When Jacques, who was from Montreal, drove by and saw his number on the board, he envisioned how he would take out his target.

He visited the post office, apartment, and library. He followed the instructions like it was an exact science. When he returned to his apartment, Steve Birch's name appeared under the black light.

It had been weeks since the zero had been changed to a different number. Jacques knew the last number was seven. He had circled the date on a calendar in his apartment and wrote a fake appointment on it.

Once he saw the date, he looked for murders that occurred over the previous weeks. He spent the first day doing enough investigative work to land him a job with a crime scene unit.

There had been five murders in the span of twenty-two days. Melvin Clarke was the most intriguing. He was poisoned by an arsenic-laced syringe after an intruder broke into his home. It signaled the work of an assassin.

Jacques read the clippings about Melvin's death and found out where he worked. He wondered if Mr. Birch worked there as well. It didn't hurt to investigate. Number two parked his car at the juncture of Route 23 and Johnson Road fifteen minutes before the midnight and morning shifts were set to end. He lifted the hood on his car, pretending to be a stranded traveler.

The midnight shift ended at 7:00 a.m. and he watched each car slowly drive by. A few workers stopped, asking if he needed help while others rolled down their windows to see if he wanted assistance.

"A friend will be here shortly," Jacques responded.

He didn't see Steve that morning, but found him later when traffic hit the roadways a little after 3 o'clock. Birch was behind the wheel of the third car that passed by. Jacques slammed the hood and hustled to the driver's seat. He started his car and followed at a distance.

Steve Birch was single and lived near Buckeye Lake. He made the lengthy trip to work every day. Steve didn't have children, but had two cats to keep him company.

Two days later, Jacques watched Steve leave his home for work a little before 6:00 a.m. The darkness served number two well. He found a spot on the wooded hillside behind Steve's house. Jacques aimed the high-powered rifle at a window above Steve's kitchen sink.

Around 4:00 p.m., Steve returned from work and relaxed for a while. Nightfall was approaching as he made himself something to eat. Jacques watched through the scope, waiting for an opportunity.

After Mr. Birch finished his dinner, he walked to the sink to put his plate and silverware in it. The bullet zipped through the woods, piercing a small hole in the window and crashing into Steve's chest. He slumped to the floor where he remained for two days before deputies found his swollen body.

Jacques made his way up the hillside around nine-thirty. He crossed a road and jogged down a dirt path with the rifle case strapped over his left shoulder. He reached the parked car he had hidden in deep weeds behind a combine near a corn field. He caught his breath and started the engine. The second mark had been successfully removed.

Over the next several months, more targets were eliminated. Cops visited the Rhodes Tire and Rubber Company on a weekly basis. Six employees who worked there had been murdered. The common link between them is they worked at Rhodes.

Stenson and Rhodes felt like they were above the law. Despite visits from authorities, they would continue the program until they saw fit to shut it down.

A MAILMAN SHOWED UP at Stenson's house asking for a signature. Big Boy wasn't expecting anything so it piqued his interest. He scribbled his name on the yellow slip and the mailman handed him a copy.

Harry closed the door and walked into his private study. He sat the postal envelope on his desk and noticed there wasn't a return address. Big Boy shook it and heard something inside the oversized envelope. He opened it and a tape was inside.

He popped it into a stereo/cassette player sitting on his desk. The voice startled him. Gary hadn't contacted Stenson for days and wasn't returning phone calls. Big Boy visited Gary's house, but there weren't any signs of him. Rhodes also hadn't heard from Gary in days.

Gary talked openly on the tape about the briefcase and their operation. He named Rhodes and talked about his own involvement. Stenson wasn't happy about Robert or Gary being mentioned, but he would have killed Gary right there in his study once he heard his name.

Stenson did this and Stenson did that. The tape linked Big Boy to the entire operation and there was no way he could get out of it. Gary had double-crossed him. He thought about taking the gun out of the top drawer and swallowing a bullet. Stenson was too big of a coward to do that.

Stenson didn't know who Gary was talking to on the tape. The other voice he heard was distorted. They obviously didn't want Stenson to hear their real voice. Gary did most of the talking, but the other person asked questions from time to time.

The conversation lasted nearly an hour. Stenson, Rhodes, Gary, and every person ever involved in his program had taken vows to never speak about the briefcase or the activities they were conducting.

Gary didn't omit any facts. Stenson was tied to the post office box, Rhodes to the apartment, and Gary's shed linked him to all of the crimes. Forget about a creek. They were in a leaky row boat on the ocean without oars. Stenson didn't know how long he could tread water, but he had to contact Rhodes. They needed to get rid of Gary. He had talked and it couldn't be overlooked.

Harry picked up the phone and dialed his partner, who was at the new plant in Cincinnati. He still maintained a residence in Columbus, but his family also had a house on the east side of Cincinnati. Rhodes' back and forth travel made him happy the tires were free.

Robert didn't need to look at the caller ID. He knew it was Stenson.

The mail was usually delivered before noon at the new Rhodes Tire and Rubber Company in Cincinnati. The postman dropped off the mail at the service desk and the in-house delivery person carted it to the respective departments.

Usually, there weren't many pieces of mail needing a signature, especially Rhodes' John Doe. The front receptionist signed for incoming mail needing signatures, but occasionally a piece of mail couldn't switch hands without an autograph from Rhodes.

It was mandatory that Rhodes signed his name to receive the envelope. Rhodes' office was the size of three or four large living rooms, a definite upgrade from the one he had at the warehouse in

Columbus. His office, located on the second floor, was the centerpiece of the rotunda and overlooked the entrance on the first floor.

He didn't like to be bothered when his door was shut so the page from the receptionist put him in a foul mood. Robert had fired more than a handful of receptionists who had paged him when his door was closed. He forgot about his aggravation after opening the piece of mail.

"Mr. Rhodes, pick up line three. Mr. Rhodes, pick up line three."

"This is Robert Rhodes."

"Sir, there is a piece of mail here at the front desk that needs your signature."

"How many times do I have to tell incompetent people it is imperative I'm not bothered while my door is shut? That is the first thing you were told when you interviewed for the job. I'll be there in a minute, but you might not want to be there when I come down."

Although it would have taken him a minute to walk out of his office and make his way down the curving staircase, he took the elevator, the only one in the building. It made him feel more important. He was the only one who was allowed to step foot in it, unless he gave someone permission. The receptionist had only used it once in the seven weeks she worked there. She remembered thinking she could have gone up and down the Sears Tower by the time she reached the second floor on Rhodes' prestigious climber. The thing had a mind of its own and seemed to work sporadically.

The doors opened and Robert walked out. He signed for the mailman and gave him and the receptionist, who hadn't disappeared long enough, scowling looks.

Once he had the envelope in his hand, he shook it and heard something inside. The bubble wrap kept it in place, but the heads on the tape is what he heard rattling.

Rhodes was so interested in opening the envelope he took the stairs. His choice of travel was a topic of conversation in the cafeteria the rest of the day. The receptionist had never seen him use the stairs. Robert had done so on two occasions and both times were due to repairmen servicing the out-of-order elevator.

As Rhodes reached his door, he turned around and walked over to the railing.

"Susan, I'm shutting my door."

The comment was unnecessary, but proved a point. He was a jerk.

He closed the door and sat on a leather sofa in the center of his office. Robert often received comments from visitors that his office looked more like a Major League Baseball locker room. There were five high-definition televisions that usually had CNBC, ESPN, the Deuce, The History Channel, or Hugh Hefner's network airing.

Sports memorabilia, items from safaris, expensive handcrafted furniture, and a fireplace plated with Algerian marble made his office even more extravagant.

He ripped the perforated seam along the back of the envelope and tipped it upside down. The tape fell in his lap and Rhodes thought he was living in the 80s again.

"Who listens to tapes anymore?" he thought to himself.

Rhodes had even upgraded his Elvis collection to CDs.

He didn't have a tape player in his office so he buzzed the receptionist.

"Do you know if we have a tape player in the building?"

"I only have a radio on my desk. I'll ask around."

"Don't waste my time! Tell someone in shipping and receiving to go buy one. Use your company card. I need it within ten minutes."

It was impossible for her to have it in his hands in that amount of time, but Susan knew she better try. She gave Merle, one of the old-timers in the shipping and receiving department, her card and told him what she needed.

Rhodes was angry when it arrived thirty-nine minutes after he called the receptionist. He called her three times while he impatiently waited.

Susan carried the box to his office and sat it on the floor outside his door as she was instructed.

Rhodes opened the box and plugged the cord in the outlet. He popped the tape in the deck and pressed play.

He listened to the tape as Stenson had—in total disbelief. Harry was furious about Gary's confession, but Robert burned with rage. He immediately called the receptionist.

"I need you in my office. Take the elevator," he said as if it were a privilege.

Susan rode the elevator for the second time. Claustrophobia nearly got the best of her.

The slight knock drew yet another rude comment from Rhodes.

"Knock on my door like you mean it," he grumbled.

It had only been seven weeks, but it didn't take long for those working under Rhodes to despise him. With all her built up emotion, she beat on his door, which actually impressed Rhodes.

"Come in."

The receptionist walked into the room and Rhodes asked her to close the door. She was the only one in the building who knew the tape arrived. If he could get away with it, he would shoot her, wrap her in the Persian rug spread in the center of his office, lug her to the trunk of his car, and launch her off a bridge over the Ohio River.

Although she didn't know what was inside the envelope, it wasn't hard to figure out since he wanted a stereo/cassette player.

"We need to talk about the envelope. Do you know where it came from?"

"The first I knew about it was when the mailman brought it into the building."

"I'm going to find out who did it and I will fire them!"

Rhodes was trying to instill fear into the young receptionist. She was hands down the best looking employee who had worked for him and that was enough to keep her around.

"How much do you make per hour?"

"Ten dollars."

"You now make fifteen as long as you don't say a word about the envelope."

"I don't care who walks in and asks questions. I have seen envelopes, but not that one."

Although she was young and naïve, Rhodes felt comfortable entrusting her with the secret. It was probably naïve of him to think she wouldn't say anything, but he knew she wouldn't mention it to anyone she worked with.

"I guess we have a deal."

"It's a deal, sir."

"There is one last thing. I need you to come over here and turn around."

Susan, wearing a tight yellow sundress that amplified every beautiful curve of her body, hesitated for a moment before walking over to Rhodes.

He flipped her spiraled blonde hair away from her right ear and whispered, "This is our secret." She was frightened by his creepiness and disgusted when he patted her on the butt and said, "You may leave now."

She wasn't sure if fifteen per hour was worth having his disgusting hands touch any part of her body. Quitting crossed her mind, as did filing sexual harassment charges, but she was making more money at twenty-two than her parents. She could deal with riding the elevator every so often and visiting Rhodes in his office. Los Angeles had been calling her name for a while and the pay raise would help her eventually make the move. She could handle a pat from time to time.

As she left his office, the phone rang.

"Let me guess, you received one, too?"

Stenson was panicking on the other end of the line.

"What are we going to do about our surprise packages?"

"First, you need to calm down. We're going to get Gary for what he's done. However, we need to be careful because he's in charge of the hit men and could turn them on us. He's in a better position than we are at the moment."

"I'm nervous. Talbot and his crew are messing with us and now Gary is blowing off at the mouth. If we don't come up with a plan soon, I think you know how this is going to end."

"The Talbot kid is more than likely the one who sent the tape. We know they snatched Preston. Lauren's apartment is being watched and Gary was on his way there the last time I talked to him. We managed to take one of them out near her apartment, so that says to me the rest of them were close by. Gary was supposed to visit Lauren and I bet they got to him."

"It doesn't matter. He talked."

"They might have forced Gary to talk because he's the last person I expected to converse about the operation. However, we can't be sure of what's going on. You're right. Whether or not he was forced to talk, he threw us under the bus and has to pay for it."

They talked for another five minutes and decided Rhodes needed to go to Columbus. He grabbed his things and locked his office. He surprisingly took the stairs once again. When he reached the bottom, he gave Susan a provocative look that made her want to vomit.

"I'll be out of the office for the next day or two. Key appointments need to be pushed back to next week. Take care," Rhodes said with a wink as he left the building.

IT HAD BEEN NEARLY two months, but a seventh target needed eliminated. There were two firsts about the mark—it was a female and was going to take place outside the United States.

Her name was Rhonda Beckman. She was one of the most popular employees at Rhodes Tire and Rubber Plant. She and her husband hosted parties that were talked about for the next year. Nearly every employee was invited and half of those lucky enough to receive an invitation attended.

They were involved in charity work and got Rhodes to donate money and items from time to time. She organized fun outings for the employees to attend. If a popularity contest would have been conducted at the facility, she would have won.

She was part of the group that didn't want to move to Cincinnati and frowned at a buyout. She desired more money than was being offered. She and Rhodes went round and round for weeks over the issue. He didn't like very many people, but he had a soft spot for Rhonda. Her persistence got the best of him. There wasn't a way around it. She had to go.

Stenson and Rhodes met at a downtown eatery to discuss the matter. Rhodes knew Rhonda and her husband were taking a western Caribbean cruise. She had talked for months about the places they were going to visit and the excursions they were going to take.

They wanted one of their hit men in the program on the cruise ship, preferably someone familiar with one of the four areas—Belize, Roatan, Grand Cayman, and Cozumel—the lovebirds would be visiting.

It was against their rules to exchange materials in public, but the case was unusual. Rhodes slid the folder across the table and Stenson looked inside. There was a photograph of Rhonda and a map with 12-9-4-43-17-4-25 written on it. Forty-three was circled. The Island of Roatan is where they decided it needed to happen. A plane ticket to Miami, which is the cruise capital of the world, and information from AAA Travel Agency were also inside the folder.

Big Boy called Gary and asked him to stop by his house. He dropped by to visit Stenson the next day and was informed of the plan. Gary was put in charge of the folder.

Once Gary had the folder, he said parting words to Stenson. He went home and put ten on the board. However, the message "C Me" was underneath the number. It was the only time the letters didn't signal the end of a hit man's time in the program. Number ten wasn't being dismissed from the program, although it was his lone assignment. Gary needed to give him additional information. The assassin was on Gary's porch long enough to see the door open and grab a folder. That was the extent of the visit.

Angel, who was from Guatemala, was familiar with Honduras. He had several family members there and visited at least once a year. He was to keep an eye out for Rhonda and her husband as soon as he boarded the ship. When he found the pair of tourists, he was to befriend them and eliminate Rhonda when the opportunity presented itself in Honduras. When he finished the task, he would take a single-engine plane back to his country and disappear forever.

Number ten went through the ritual of visiting the post office, the apartment, and library. The travel agency was his last stop. He had read through the information in the folder and booked his spot on the ship. He also had his cousin arrange to have a plane waiting for him in Honduras and informed his family he would be returning home. One of his uncles would be waiting on him when the plane touched down in Guatemala. After he returned to his apartment, he put everything together and was prepared to fly to Miami.

When Angel gathered his luggage, an economy-sized suitcase and a backpack, at the Miami Airport, he wheeled it to a bus waiting outside. He hoped to see the vacationing couple, but would have to wait.

The bus made its way through Miami. Vacationers took in sites along the way, including the Orange Bowl. They reached cruise ship row within minutes. Angel could already smell tropical smoothies and Avon perfume elderly women had doused on their Hawaiian blouses.

It was an impressive site. There was an entire fleet of cruise ships waiting for vacationers. Spanish conquistadors would have been jealous.

After passing what seemed like an armada, the bus pulled into a giant lot next to their cruise ship—Royal Seas *Pristine*. Angel was amazed at the size of the cruise ship. He went around the side of the bus to get his luggage, but quickly realized the pampering had begun. Several employees worked at break-neck speed. They were carrying luggage, directing people where to go, and making sure no one got off on the wrong foot.

Angel walked to a line that had formed next to a building and waited. The ship was set to leave port at 4:00 p.m., but it was only pushing noon. He waited patiently in the crowded line as it slowly moved. Thirty-five minutes later, he was inside the building next to the ship.

He escaped the muggy Miami weather and was seated inside an air-conditioned paradise, but the registration process was a pain. Besides more waiting, vacationers were starting to annoy him. Nearly 75 percent of the people wore bright colors or Hawaiian prints and were overly chatty. The men wore straw hats while the ladies wore oversized pink or white sun hats that nearly took someone out every time they swiveled their heads. Angel had to tilt his head away on several occasions while he waited for his number to be called.

The perfume the bingo lovers wore gave him a headache. Despite his agitation, Angel didn't show it. He had a stone cold expression and looked like he could be a leader of a drug cartel. He was there for business, not pleasure.

His number was called and he handed the woman his papers and a fake ID. She stamped his papers and handed him a Royal Seas sail and sign card.

"This is how you pay for things aboard the ship and your room will be billed accordingly. Thank you and enjoy your cruise aboard *Pristine*."

He ambled to a set of escalators that ascended to the entrance of the cruise ship. Each passenger was asked to pose for a photograph underneath a welcome sign. Once he completed the annoying task, Angel handed an employee his sail and sign card. She scanned the card and politely said in an Australian accent, "Enjoy your cruise!"

The Guatemalan had never been to Las Vegas, but he imagined *Pristine* was as close as he would get. The only boat he had been aboard was one of his family's fishing boats and it certainly wasn't an impressive vessel like *Pristine*. The glitz and glam was unbelievable. The rotunda was magnificent. Every floor surrounded the rotunda, which was lit with millions of white lights. A piano player displayed his talent on the ivory at a bar near guest services. A few thirsty passengers were on their way to their first hangovers of the week.

The elevator was also fantastic. The glass sides allowed riders to see into the rotunda, which had a well-crafted double-sided staircase that stopped above where the piano player sat.

Angel got off the elevator on the first floor. He walked past the rotunda bar and made his way to the Excursion Center. The Beckmans had booked a horseback riding adventure in Roatan and Angel picked up more information on the shore excursion.

The Caracol Package was what the Beckmans booked. A school bus would be waiting for them once they docked in Roatan and take those who selected the package to El Rancho Barrio Corpus. The horseback tour made its way down a beautiful hillside, traveled along the ocean for a while, wrapped through part of a fertile area that was heavily blanketed with trees and plant life, and ended at a hotel and restaurant on the beach in West Bay.

It didn't take Angel long to figure out how he would carry out his mission. The biggest problem he faced was finding Rhonda Beckman before Wednesday's port of call in Honduras. He took his bags to his cabin and the search for Rhonda began.

Chapter
Fifteen

THE RELATIONSHIP BETWEEN SHARON and Kurt was a major headache for Stenson. Many resources were exhausted trying to locate Kurt, but Big Boy couldn't track him down. Sharon was also elusive at times. She knew people were following her, but gave them the slip every time.

There was an old movie theatre near the O'Neil's home in Mesa. Sharon had three or four friends waiting behind it in different cars each time. Sharon exchanged rides and would wait a few minutes after a friend drove off in her vehicle before leaving. That was how she eluded them.

The men eventually caught on that Sharon knew she was being followed. Stenson increased the surveillance and had two groups follow her. When Sharon noticed their new trick, she added a friend or two behind the movie theatre. Big Boy tried to one-up Mrs. O'Neil. He had cars parked at different spots and was going to follow every car pulling out of the theatre.

Sharon had a different plan that afternoon. All of her friends pulled out and each car was followed. Meanwhile, Sharon slipped into the theatre and watched a late matinee with her boys.

Sharon had never taken Trevor or Preston to Austin, but decided it was time to take them to the Alexander farm. She peered into the back parking lot after the movie ended. She had each boy grab one of her hands and they hustled to a vehicle left behind by one of her friends. They got in the car and drove straight to the bus depot. The rearview mirror was void of followers, but it ended up being her last trip to Austin.

She only left town every few months, but Stenson was tired of her antics. He couldn't designate an army of men to follow her. Her lifestyle wouldn't be tolerated any longer. Stenson made the decision to eliminate Sharon because of her trips and his startling discovery.

Sharon arrived in Austin and grabbed her suitcase. Her routine was always the same. She sat outside the depot and watched each passenger go their separate ways. After an hour or two, she got up and walked to the same spot Colt dropped her off the first time she left Austin.

Colt saw her come around the corner with Trevor and Preston in tow. As always, Sharon had a giant smile, one that could light up Austin. Colt got out of his vehicle and walked around to open the door. She sat her suitcase down and embraced him.

"Get in the truck boys."

"Who's that man, mommy?" Preston asked.

"I'm your cousin Colt."

"That's a weird name," he said.

Sharon and Colt chuckled at her youngest son's sense of humor.

Preston did most of the talking on the way to the farm, but Trevor added his two cents. The boys seemed to ask a million questions.

Colt steered the pick-up onto the unpaved road. He pointed at the big field on the left and told the boys that was part of where he lived. They reached the T and Colt talked about the corn in the silos behind the barn and the chicken houses on the hill.

"Can you see that pond down there?"

Both replied, "Yes."

"There are fish in there bigger than sharks."

The comment drew a look from Sharon.

"Is Shamu or Jaws in there?" Preston asked.

"See what you started," Sharon said.

"The tour guide will keep quiet."

Colt turned left and drove past the cemetery. The eldest Alexander offspring made good on his promise. He didn't give the history of the cemetery and it pleased Sharon.

They pulled in the driveway and the family was excited to see Sharon. As soon as Kurt saw a head lean past Sharon, his eyes welled up with tears. It had been nearly three years since he had seen Preston. He had pictures and home videos, but seeing his son in person was an emotional high.

Kurt ran out the door and scooped Preston into his arms. He was overcome with joy and didn't think about what he was doing. Preston began crying and Kurt realized what he had done. He handed him to Sharon, who was trying to get Trevor off her leg. He was also frightened and ducked behind his mother, latching on for dear life to her left leg.

"It's all right boys. They won't hurt you. Do you want to see the animals?"

The boys weren't sure about Kurt, but they took to Jim. He bought two toy rifles at a truck stop in one of the small towns he drove through earlier in the week. Sharon wasn't happy with the choice, but the boys ran around making noises with their mouths while aiming at everything in sight. Their fun changed Sharon's mind.

They walked across the road and into the barn. They loved going to the zoo, but neither had visited a farm or seen animals roaming in a field. A newborn calf was in a stall and the boys instantly forgot about their guns.

Jim opened the gate and carefully walked them into the stall. They caressed the calf and giggled at the way it kept trying to suck their little fingers. Elaine handed Trevor a bottle and the calf began drinking the milk. Preston was mad because he wanted to feed it, so Sharon told Trevor to let Preston help him hold the bottle.

When they finished, Jim led them to a pasture. Several cows responded to his cattle call and the boys touched some of them near one of the troughs. Preston and Trevor were fascinated. Mr. Alexander had new friends.

Jim kept outdoing himself that day. After they left the pasture, he started a tractor and took the boys through one of the giant hay fields.

"I even got to steer," Trevor said when he got back. "Mr. ummm..."

The adults looked at each other inquisitively. Sharon told Kurt before her visit that no one should say their real names. After the episode at the dinner table with Preston, she knew they were liable to blurt anything. Kurt informed everyone except Jim. He whispered to Jim and explained not to tell his real name. Sharon scolded Colt about his slip, but it was imperative for Jim and Elaine to keep their identities secret.

"Mr. McDonald," Jim said as he winked at Sharon and Kurt.

"You mean like Old McDonald?" Trevor asked.

"I'm that guy people sing about."

It was as if the boys met Santa Claus. Jim introduced Elaine as Mrs. McDonald.

"Who's the scary man?" Trevor inquired.

"That's Uncle Bob," Jim replied.

Kurt didn't want to be referred to as the boys' uncle, but didn't have a choice.

Jim interrupted the questioning and declared it was Preston's turn to hop aboard the John Deere. They drove into the field and Kurt patted Sharon on the back, which drew a "get your hands off my mom" look from Trevor. Kurt knew the visit would be tough, but was happy to see them. Preston was equally as excited when he returned with Jim from the field.

While Jim and Preston were in the field, Elaine returned to the kitchen to finish dinner. The menu included homemade macaroni and cheese along with hot dogs Colt grilled while they surveyed the farm. She also made a batch of chocolate chip cookies from scratch and had different flavored Kool-Aid on the table as well.

Elaine opened the door and called everyone in for dinner. The boys acted like most kids when it's time to eat.

"We're not hungry," they said in whiny voices.

Sharon told them they needed to get plenty of energy to play on the farm. The boys couldn't wait to get back outside so they hurried into the kitchen.

When they gazed at the spread on the table, Elaine had equaled Jim's status with the boys. Macaroni and cheese, hot dogs, cookies, and Kool-Aid was like a prisoner's last meal to children.

Neither of the boys said a word at dinner. After nearly licking his plate clean, Preston asked if they could go back outside. Before everyone sat down, Elaine placed a dish towel over the cookies to keep them warm and keep the boys focused on the main course. When she pulled the towel off the cookies, their eyes became as wide as the state they were visiting.

One was all Sharon normally allowed, but it was a special occasion. The boys washed down the morsels with another glass of Kool-Aid and the sugar high began to kick in. It was time to introduce the boys to something else they had never done.

Dusk was approaching, but there was time for a few casts. Jim and Colt gathered their poles and grabbed a tub of worms from the refrigerator.

Jim hopped in the driver's seat while Colt got in the bed with the boys, who were having the time of their lives.

They reached the Parson's pond and Preston was frightened to get out.

"What's wrong?" Jim asked.

"Will those sharks eat us?"

"Seriously, what line were you in when God was giving out smarts?"

It wasn't often Jim said things like that to his kids.

"I didn't think about it. Sorry."

The foursome fished until they could barely see the bobbers. The boys reeled in a bluegill or two, with some help from the older fellows. Colt wasn't a cast and wait fisherman. He was in search of bass. After a couple of guppies, as he called them, he finally landed a largemouth that weighed about four pounds. Trevor and Preston thought they had seen one of the great whites Colt told them about on the ride to the farm.

He took the hook out of its mouth and envisioned how good it would taste. However, the Alexanders never kept a fish from the pond unless they were fishing with the Parsons and had their blessing to take it home. Colt knelt down, put it under the water, and let it go.

Once the semi-paralysis wore off, the fish cut through the water like a mariner. It jumped out of the water in the center of the pond like a porpoise at Sea World, mesmerizing the boys.

They loaded the gear and headed back to the farm. It was past their bed time, but the boys kept everyone up with their exciting fishing stories.

Trevor and Preston finally wore down and fell asleep on the couch. Shuffling feet woke them the next morning. Jim wanted the boys help him milk the cows. Like normal kids, they were cranky and wanted to lie back down. Sharon finally got them up.

After a quick breakfast, the entire household went to the barn. Trevor and Preston were quite the helpers. They were glued to Jim's hip. They helped him bring in each group and argued about who would pull the lever that dropped the grain into the feeding troughs.

After they finished milking, everyone except Jim and Kurt returned to the house and went back to bed. The boys needed all the sleep they could get because more fishing and tractor rides were in store. While everyone slept, Kurt talked about seeing Preston again. Jim missed him as well.

"It's good to have him back on the farm," Jim said.

"Yes, it is. I wish it was permanent."

"As you know, God works in mysterious ways. We never know what is in store for us."

If they knew what was in store for Sharon when she returned to Mesa, they would have made sure she never left Austin.

IT HAD BEEN NEARLY a day since the door to the second storage house opened. Preston and Gary barely spoke to one another during that time. They were tired and ready for the ordeal to end. Then, something happened that was music to their ears. "Tall Paul" finally stopped playing. They heard it hundreds of times and it would forever be embedded in their minds. The silence was exhilarating.

The door flung open and Matt walked in first. He was followed by Rhodes.

"Good morning gentlemen. Preston, we no longer need you."

Matt placed shoes on his feet and freed him from the duct tape.

"Where am I supposed to go? You know I can't go back to my old life."

"We created a new one for you."

Matt, who was still robed and masked, walked to the door and opened it.

"You're free to go."

Preston didn't know whether to run or beg to stay. The malnourishment and not using his legs for several days dropped him to the floor as soon as he tried to take a step.

"I can't walk."

Matt and Rhodes helped him to his feet. Preston put an arm around each man. He tried taking steps, but they basically dragged him out. Lauren was waiting for him outside the storage house. She was in regular clothes and helped Rhodes take him into the first storage house.

It wasn't a four-star hotel, but they had gone to great lengths to make sure Preston would recuperate quickly. When he saw the bathtub, Preston hoped it wasn't his turn to test his breath holding skills. The steam rising from it made Preston wonder if they were going to scald him.

"Don't be frightened. The bath is warm and we're going to place you in it," Lauren said.

They took off his shoes and boxers, easing him into the tub. The warm water instantly soothed his joints and bones. It had been over a week since clean water touched his skin, excluding the dripping water on his forehead in the second storage house.

Rhodes left the first storage house once Preston was comfortable. Lauren pulled up a chair and sat beside him. She began washing Preston's body and the experience had them reminiscing about taking baths together in college.

She washed his hair and rinsed him off. Dane, who closely watched the monitor, came over and helped lift him out of the tub. Lauren wrapped a towel around him and set him on the edge of a couch. Even though she had seen him naked on numerous occasions, she tried to be respectful.

"I have a fresh set of clothes for you."

Lauren wrapped a towel around his waist and pulled a clean pair of boxers to the top of his thighs. Preston managed to yank them up the rest of the way.

"I have some comfortable clothes for you."

She put a pair of jogging pants on him, along with a T-shirt and hooded sweatshirt.

"I can't explain how good this feels. Once I eat, I'll feel like a new person."

Lauren left the storage house and returned with enough food to feed a small army. Lauren placed the food on the table. She put Preston in a roll chair and wheeled him to the table. He was having trouble with his arms, but managed more than enough strength to stuff himself.

When he finished eating, Lauren wheeled him back to the couch. Preston quickly fell asleep and didn't wake up until late afternoon.

Rhodes walked into the second storage house and was besieged.

"Robert, I don't know what is going on, but I want you to get me out of here."

"Gary, I want to help you, but you have to help yourself. We already explained that Stenson is who we have a problem with."

"After what you told me, I want to get my hands on him. You know I was unfaithful to Sharon throughout the years and was not a good husband, but deep down, I loved Sharon. She mothered my only child. Robert, the note the masked man had Preston read earlier seemed to be fabricated. However, I believe we are friends. I don't know why you let them torture us the way they did, but we're on the same side."

The more Gary talked, the more Matt knew he was sold.

"I know you were put through a lot the past few days. I didn't have anything to do with what happened. I was contacted by your kidnappers to help them get rid of Stenson. When I found out Stenson was doing things behind my back, I was willing to help them. If I find the man, he'll be sorry he ever did business with me."

"I want to be the one to get rid of Stenson," Gary said as his words cut through the storage house like an aborigine's machete.

Gary was a crafty poker player because he was a master at bluffing. It was one occasion where he was not bluffing. He had lost his wife and only child and was left to raise an adopted son by himself. In his mind, Stenson cost him his entire life. His thinking was pathetic because Gary's crooked ways was the reason he was sitting in the storage house, but Matt and Rhodes had him believing differently. Stenson had also been fooled by Matt as had Rhodes—The Robert Rhodes.

SATURDAY WAS ANOTHER EVENTFUL day for the boys. Jim burned through a tank of diesel fuel in his tractor giving the little Mesa visitors rides throughout the day. The boys were thrilled Mr. Parson let them fish in his pond again. Jim and Kurt, who took Colt's place, tried to get them to put worms on their hooks and take the fish off, but Preston and Trevor didn't want anything to do with that part of fishing. The men just smiled and continued baiting and removing fish from their hooks. They enjoyed watching the boys and wished they were staying longer. After fishing, Mr. Parson gave the boys a tour of the chicken houses, which reeked of an ammonia-like smell that left everyone but Mr. Parson in tears.

The day came to an early conclusion as Preston and Trevor ran out of gas around eight-thirty. They slept soundly throughout the night. The next morning, Elaine had another feast waiting on the table after the milking was completed. Everyone ate and started getting ready for church.

Sharon had purchased cute outfits for the boys. They wore matching khakis and oxford shirts, with the first button undone. She slicked their hair to the sides and both could have passed as true southern gentlemen.

Neither had been to church before and the only time the boys dressed up was when they attended a large scale social gathering in Mesa.

"Where are we going mommy?" Preston asked.

"We're going to church today."

Sharon was embarrassed she had never taken the boys to church. She had told them about God, but Trevor had never stepped foot in his house and Preston was too little to remember. Kurt became accustomed to his Sunday visits to Calvary and looked forward to it. Although he wasn't a true local, he accomplished what many outsiders had difficulty doing—he was treated like one.

Jim pulled the station wagon out of the barn and the adults, along with Tyler and Chelsea, got in the vehicle. Sharon agreed to let the boys ride with "cousin" Colt, whom they attached themselves to over the weekend.

Colt was ordered to lead the procession so Jim could keep a close eye on his driving. They made their way past several small farms and Cy Harper's feed mill. Colt turned into Calvary Baptist's graveled lot and parked in the family's usual spot. It was the first time Jim hadn't parked the station wagon there since the last time they missed church. He parked two spots down from Colt's pickup and everyone straightened their outfits, while Sharon attended to the boys.

She combed their hair once again and brushed the lint off their shoulders. The Alexander clan, including Kurt, and their visitors barely made it halfway across the parking lot before Ellie Mae Hendershot, who was eighty-five and still going strong, spotted the boys.

"And who do we have here?"

"These are my boys," Sharon responded. "This is Trevor, who is seven, and this is Preston, who is five."

"Is this the one you had in the barn?"

The question could have only come from someone as wise as Mrs. Hendershot. Sharon and Kurt didn't think anyone would bring it up. Ellie Mae was a walking memory bank and didn't forget anything that happened in the Texas Hill Country. Sharon took a moment to think of a solid response before answering.

"We're supposed to be like Jesus, so I guess we should all be born in a barn," Sharon said as she gently nudged her boys away from Mrs. Hendershot. "Good to see you again Ellie Mae."

Ellie Mae wanted to continue their conversation, but Sharon quickly engaged in a conversation with Deacon Frye's wife. She was known as the "candy lady" to the children who attended Calvary. Every church has someone who keeps the dentists busy and Margaret Frye was that person. Against parental wishes, she gave the children a couple pieces each and every Sunday. It wasn't that the parents were against Margaret's generosity, it just wound the kids up. Calvary almost needed someone walking the aisles on child patrol once services started.

They ventured to the steps and Kurt noticed the sign had been changed. He remembered the first warning he read. It had only changed eight or nine times. When the board was changed, it was a big deal.

The new warning read, "God's making a list, but he'll only check it once."

It obviously was a correlation to Christmas and the message made its point.

After a few songs, the Lord's Supper was passed around. The boys were inquisitive. It reminded Kurt of the first time he witnessed it. Sharon couldn't keep their hands away, so she let the boys partake, which didn't set well with a few members, but she knew they would get over it.

Pastor Browne was up to his usual antics. He roamed around the stage and pulpit like a caged lion at the zoo. He certainly made more noise than any animal. As he made his closing remarks, he called the boys to the stage.

"We have a few visitors today. He asked their names and they responded into the microphone."

Nearly every woman smiled from ear to ear and forgot about their participation in the Lord's Supper. The congregation had around ninety members and found it to be a blessing when they had visitors, especially little children.

"God bless you both," Pastor Browne said as he patted them on the head and helped them return to their seats.

The service ended and, as usual, the Alexanders were among the last to leave. Polk's Family Restaurant was pretty full that day, but the Alexanders had called ahead to reserve a spot. The party of nine shared plenty of laughs and thoroughly enjoyed their meals.

They sauntered to their vehicles and drove back to the farm. The household was somber each time Sharon left and sadness was setting in again. However, it was more difficult because they also had to say goodbye to Preston and Trevor.

Sharon packed their belongings and it was time for them to leave. She hugged everyone before she and Kurt walked around the side of the house. During her visit, Sharon decided it was time to end things with Gary and start a new life in Austin with Kurt. They discussed the matter before giving each other a warm embrace.

They returned to the driveway and Sharon hopped into Colt's truck with Trevor and Preston. The boys contorted their necks as long as they could to wave at the people they were leaving behind.

As usual, Colt was talkative on the way to drop them off. Preston and Trevor engaged in the conversation, but Sharon was quiet. It was the most difficulty she had leaving the farm. The ride to their drop-off spot and on the way back to Mesa was spent thinking about moving to Austin. She was depressed, but the vision of living in Texas near the Alexander farm was enough to change the way she felt.

Colt dropped them off and they exchanged hugs while gathered on the street. He handed Sharon the suitcase and got back in the truck. The trio began their walk down the sidewalk and Colt drove away.

They safely reached the bus depot and were on their way back to Mesa, where tragedy awaited.

Chapter
Sixteen

THE FIRST DAY AT sea signaled it was time for Angel to clock in. He walked to the fun deck to look around the pool area for single women. Several ladies were either catching rays, sipping mixed drinks, listening to music, sharing stories, or reading. Angel didn't spot what he was looking for, so he ventured to another part of the ship.

He ascended a flight of stairs and spotted what he had in mind. Two peroxide blonds with bosoms big enough to nurse everyone aboard the cruise ship were soaking up rays on the sun deck. Their bikinis nearly qualified for sun bathing on the nude deck. If the younger boys on the ship weren't occupied by the water slides and pool, every little Johnny would have been checking out the busty friends. It was obvious why they were bordered by several men, those of the married and single variety.

Although Angel resembled a cartel man, he was blessed with good looks and charm he used to his advantage.

He walked past the Barbies, who were in their early thirties, and looked down at their fingers through his sunglasses. Neither girl sported a ring. In his mind, they were open territory. Angel didn't stop, but the friends noticed the tan Guatemalan and talked about him as he passed.

Angel laid a towel on a chair about a dozen spots down from the girls. He watched as several men clumsily conjured up conversations with the bombshells. They were unimpressed with what the men had to say. It was apparent the guys surrounding the girls like sharks circling chum were not their boyfriends.

A man's wife walked across the sun deck and her look said it all. It was time for him to retreat to their cabin and receive a private tongue lashing. The man reluctantly gave up his spot and Angel didn't pass up the opportunity. He gathered his things and walked to the vacant spot without looking at the girls or saying a word. He spread his towel, put his hands behind his head, and leaned back in the sunshine.

The girls wanted to speak to Angel, but thought he might be like the rest of the lame pickup artists loitering around their spot.

Ten minutes passed. One of the girls broke the silence.

"Was the other spot not good enough?"

"The sun seems to be shining a little brighter over here," he said with an accent that gave both women goose bumps.

Their puzzled looks said it best. The girls weren't sure if he understood what they were asking. He could be casting a pickup line, hoping one of them would bite.

"The sun is shining brightly no matter where you sit today," the other girl snapped.

"Then sit in my old spot and give us a report on what you think."

The girls laughed. His comments still didn't convey what he was up to.

"My name is Blair," said the girl who Angel challenged.

"My name is spelled A-N-G-E-L, but it is pronounced Aun-hell. It is nice to meet you. And who might your mystery partner be?"

"I'm Laney."

"It's nice to meet you. Blair, when are you going to march down to my old spot and bring us back a report?"

Angel obviously understood English and was messing with them. Blair played along and sat in his empty chair. She continuously looked at Angel and Laney, who were engaged in a discussion about why they were on vacation. Blair felt left out and returned to her spot.

"What did you find out?"

"I think it's just as sunny, but it was boring."

"That's my point. The two of you were over here and I was bored. It seemed like the sun was shining more brightly on you. I'm here by myself and thought you looked like you would be fun to hang out with this week."

"We're here together, but we're not together," Laney said. "Where are you from?"

"I live in Venezuela."

"We're from Asheville, North Carolina."

The trio spent the next few hours talking, relaxing, and drinking more Mai Tais than they should have. Angel accomplished his goal. He found two single ladies to pal around and blend in with while searching for Rhonda. He would use the girls to help him introduce himself to the Beckmans. And if he got lucky, he'd bed one or both of the Carolina dolls.

The breeze picked up late in the afternoon, so they went to their cabins. They were slated for early dinner and decided to sit together each evening. While Angel was hanging out with the women, he saw Rhonda and her husband walking along the fun deck. He wanted to follow the couple, but figured they would be easy to find.

Angel told the girls he would meet them for dinner a little before 6:00 p.m. in the rotunda. He showered and was seated in the rotunda at 5:20. He wanted to keep an eye on people as they walked to dinner. His early arrival paid dividends.

At 5:50, he watched closely as Geoff and Rhonda Beckman exited a hallway and strolled into the rotunda. They were dressed like country club snobs, signaling they were on their way to eat. The dining area required guests to be dressed appropriately. On the last night of the cruise, passengers were invited to attend a formal, which required a suit and tie for gentlemen and a cocktail dress for women. Khakis and button ups were fine for men while most ladies wore sun dresses each night leading up to Saturday.

Angel erased a day of fun from his memory after spotting the Beckmans. He enjoyed his time with the Carolina beauties, but seeing the Columbus couple reminded him not to get off course.

The biggest nuisance on the cruise was the continual picture taking done by the ship's staff. They were everywhere. At every turn, someone snapped a photograph. People on the cruise were being taken advantage of because photographic memories were important to nearly every passenger. Cruises cost a pretty penny and Royal Seas knew if people were willing to spend money to voyage Caribbean waters, they were willing to shell out more on souvenirs, items in gift shops, and photographs.

Angel stood up and grabbed a wondering ship photographer who was capturing everything that moved.

"Will you take a picture of me and the couple approaching us?"

The photographer placed Angel near a scenic backdrop and stopped Geoff and Rhonda.

"It's picture time."

The irritated couple hesitated, but stood next to Angel and the photographer took two shots.

"Thank you," the photographer said as he turned to annoy the next passing group.

Angel seized the opportunity as the Beckmans were set to walk away.

"My name is Angel," he said, extending a hand to Mr. Beckman.

Friendliness was a quality that permeated throughout the week. Everyone was friends within minutes and Geoff wasn't going to be rude, despite the photographer interrupting their stroll through the rotunda.

"It's nice to meet you. I'm Geoff and this is my wife Rhonda."

Angel tried to keep the couple preoccupied with small talk, but could tell they were ready to continue their route to the dining area.

"I'm here alone. Would you mind if I joined you for dinner?"

Rhonda agreed.

"You are more than welcome to join us."

"I forgot something in my room. If you get our table, I'll join you in a few minutes."

They momentarily parted ways. The couple disappeared down the hallway that led to the dining area and Angel walked along the wall in the rotunda. He made a complete circle and returned to the spot where he said he would meet the girls.

Laney and Blair, who looked like dolled up pageant queens, were seven minutes late. Laney had on a green sun dress that was begging Angel to lift the bottom and go to town. Angel also gave Blair a dose of head to toe stares. She had on a pair of white see-through pants with a low-cut navy blouse. He nearly announced his sudden desire to skip dinner and go straight to dessert. Earlier in the day, he favored Laney, but Blair looked equally amazing.

"Shall we?" he asked, extending an arm to each lady.

The threesome, which Angel envisioned happening before duty called in Honduras, walked arm-in-arm to the dining area. A maître d' stopped them at the entrance.

"Are you with another party?"

"We're with the Beckmans," Angel responded.

The man looked down at his list and smiled.

"Right this way."

He seated the trio at the table with the Beckmans.

"This is Blair and this is Laney. I met them earlier."

The girls hit it off with Rhonda and they planned the rest of their week. Angel carefully selected the girls and they were serving him well. Angel and Geoff didn't talk as much. Mr. Beckman was focused on the chests of the women talking with his wife.

Angel caught him looking, as did Blair and Laney. Rhonda never caught him in the act, but she noticed the girls were well endowed. She knew they could have any man on the ship, but Rhonda could hold her own in the looks department.

Dinner was served and they enjoyed each other's company. Geoff ordered a bottle of pear flavored wine and it went down so smoothly he purchased a second bottle. Following dessert, they went to the theatre and watched a Las Vegas-style show. The longer Angel was aboard the ship, the more he felt like he had been to Vegas.

The show ended and they stood up. Although the ship wasn't rocking, they were a little inebriated and felt like they were swaying.

"Let's go sing," Rhonda suggested.

She saw a karaoke bar earlier in the day and placed it in her memory bank. The five passengers made their way to the bar and Angel ordered a round of drinks.

The piano player took requests and Rhonda's list kept them there until last call. They belted songs off key, but had a grand time doing so. For the first time, Angel had second thoughts about killing Rhonda. It was past 2:00 a.m. and he was ready to retire to his room.

Angel shook Geoff's hand and hugged Rhonda.

"I'm calling it a night."

"We'll see you tomorrow at dinner and do it all again," Rhonda said as she and her husband said good-night to the girls and disappeared around a corner.

Blair called out to Angel as he was walking away.

"The moon seems to be shining a little brighter over there than it does over here."

Angel smiled. He turned around and looked at Blair.

"Would you like a report?"

"That would be nice."

Angel walked over to Blair and Laney, who was holding herself up against a wall.

"I would have to disagree. I think the moon is pretty bright over here as well."

Blair leaned into Angel's right ear.

"I'm tipsy, but Laney is wasted. I need to get her to our room. Once I get her to bed, would you like to come to our room?"

"I'll help you get her to your cabin and then you can come to my room. I'm on C deck. I have a balcony and we could really see the moon from there."

They each put an arm under Laney and slowly walked her down the flight of stairs to J deck. They reached room 159 and went inside. Although Angel was a cold-blooded assassin, he was still a gentleman. He helped Blair place Laney on the bed and stepped outside.

Five minutes later, Blair opened the door and they walked to Angel's room. Angel had brought a small bottle of rum with him on the cruise and poured two drinks.

They toasted and took a sip. The ensuing silence made things a little awkward.

"Let's check out the moonlight," Blair proposed.

They stepped out to the private balcony and the full moon accented the crashing waves below.

Blair and Angel were leaning over the rail when he put his arm around her. She had been anticipating his touch since his pickup line earlier in the day. Blair wasn't a slut, but had been with a handful of partners in her time. She took Angel's arm and moved it to her waist as she moved closer to him.

She was inches away from Angel's face when he kissed her. The kiss melted her soul. It was the most passionate kiss she had ever received. There weren't enough nets to catch the butterflies fluttering inside her.

They continued kissing for approximately fifteen minutes. She reached for the door and pulled it open, trying to tug Angel inside. He pulled her back onto the balcony and quietly shut the door.

"I'm sorry. I'm not usually like this."

Angel didn't respond to her comments with words. He reached down and unsnapped her white pants, which slowly slid to the floor. He unbuttoned his shirt and took it off, unveiling a twelve-pack and pecs that made her want to touch every square inch of his skin.

He was ready to take off her shirt, but she didn't give him a chance. Her shirt hit the floor and his pants quickly followed. He slipped off his shoes and kicked his legs free of his pants.

Angel unsnapped her bra, revealing natural breasts a plastic surgeon would admire. She slipped out of her thong and took off his boxers. The erotic moment reached its breaking point.

Blair grabbed the rail on the balcony and Angel got behind her. She asked him to stop after three or four minutes of heated action.

"Hand me my shirt!"

Angel followed orders and Blair stuffed the shirt in her mouth. The thirty-minute session was breathtaking. Had the shirt not been in her mouth, her parents would have heard her moans in Carolina.

They gathered their clothes and went inside. Blair was going to return to her room, but Angel invited her to stay. They climbed into bed and snuggled before falling asleep. When she woke the next morning, Angel had breakfast waiting on the balcony.

The sunrise was just as romantic as their encounter a few hours earlier. They ate in peace, taking in the views. Blair had forgotten about Laney, but realized she needed to return to their room.

She promised to find Angel around lunch time. Blair kissed him before closing the door behind her. Angel sat on the corner of his bed and thought about ignoring the mission. He would finish out the week and move to Carolina when he returned to the states. However, he had family in Guatemala and was intent on completing the assignment before calling it a career. He didn't have a romantic link at home, but knew he couldn't let a romantic encounter distort his view.

Later that morning, a soft knock interrupted Angel's nap. It was Laney and Blair.

"We're going to ancient Mayan ruins when we dock in Belize. We'd like you to go with us," Blair said.

Angel politely declined, but agreed to meet the girls later. The afternoon passed and they met for dinner. Following their meals, they took in a show and visited the karaoke bar with the Beckmans.

The clock struck 2:00 a.m. and the bar closed. Laney was more coherent after a second night of drinking and singing. Blair told her she was going to Angel's room again, but Laney wanted to join her. Blair had filled her in about the previous night and Laney also wanted to experience the passion.

After noticing Laney wasn't going to leave, Angel invited both ladies to his room. Blair declined, but Laney clutched Angel's arm.

"I think I'm going to bed," he said while winking at Blair.

Laney tried to talk Angel into taking the party to his room, but didn't have any luck. Angel went to his room and began getting ready for his mission.

He ripped off the tags from his small suitcase, lit them on fire in the sink, and washed down the ashes. He laid an outfit on a chair by the bed and got undressed. Angel put a few belongings in his backpack and stuffed the rest in a garbage bag. He launched the bag and his open suitcase over the balcony.

Number ten flipped on a light by the bed and read for thirty minutes. As he reached to turn off the light, something startled him.

He opened the door to find Blair in a bath robe.

"I told you I wasn't a slut, but Laney is the opposite. I shouldn't have told her about our encounter last night. May I come in?"

Angel shut the door and her robe dropped to the floor as soon as he turned around. A second night of passion ensued. She had fallen in love with the Guatemalan. If he spent more time with the lovely lady, he would be next.

Blair, who once again slept like a baby, awoke to another breakfast on the balcony. Angel didn't have much to say and she thought something was bothering him.

"Did I do something wrong?"

"No. I have a lot on my mind today."

"What's on your agenda?"

"I'm going to wander around. What about you?"

"We're going to snorkel the barrier reef. I better get going. I'll see you tonight."

"Sounds good."

Blair closed the door. Angel knew it was the last time he would see her.

The captain announced over the intercom that the ship was pulling into Coxen Hole. Angel knew he couldn't turn back. Rhonda Beckman was the target and no one was going to stop Angel from accomplishing his goal.

PRESTON RECOVERED AFTER A few days in Lauren's care. Gary, who was locked up in the second storage house, also felt better, despite a few broken knuckles. They put a plan together and Gary would be the star of the show.

The door opened and Rhodes walked in.

"We have a plan and think you'll like what we have to say," Rhodes said. "Before we let you go, we want you to do something for us. I'm taking you to your house and I want you to contact each hit man."

"I don't call them and they don't call me."

"I know that. Each day, I want you to put a different number on the board until they've all been assigned."

"But they'll go to the apartment looking for a briefcase that's not there. Also, there isn't an assignment."

"You don't need to worry about those issues. All you need to do is change the board and we'll return safely to this spot."

The apartment was being closely watched, although Robert and Harry had steered clear of the place. It was going to be nearly impossible for anyone to sneak in and out of the apartment. Since the briefcase was stolen, Matt had carefully planned everything and getting the briefcase inside the apartment with a new assignment was also well thought out.

The new case was Harry "Big Boy" Stenson. Since they had eliminated three of the hit men, seven maps with the same code were in the first storage house. There were seven lighters and seven pictures of Stenson with his name in the right corner. The first trip to the apartment would take place as soon as Gary changed his board.

"Are you ready to go?" Rhodes asked.

"I guess."

They handcuffed and blindfolded Gary so he didn't know the location of the warehouse.

Dane and Preston stayed behind to keep an eye on things, but Matt, Lauren, Rhodes, and Gary got into Rhodes' vehicle.

They drove to Gary's neighborhood and stopped several houses down. They sat in the car for thirty minutes observing the scene. It didn't look like anyone was watching his house. Rhodes and Gary got out of the car and walked toward Mr. O'Neil's residence.

Gary punched in the code at his entrance gate. It opened and he led Rhodes down the cobblestone driveway to the side of his house. They reached the shed and Gary unlocked it. They went inside and Gary didn't think about who would receive the first assignment. He didn't know they were all going to receive the same assignment—Stenson.

He pulled out the number four and placed it on the billboard. Gary locked the shed and returned to the car. They drove back to the warehouse and led Gary into the second storage house, which is where Preston was when he returned.

"We're not going to torture you anymore, but you have to stay here for your safety," Rhodes said.

They closed the door. Rhodes and Matt then drove to the apartment. As they pulled onto the street, several eyes watched. Rhodes got out of the car and those watching eased their guard, although they were used to seeing Stenson more frequently.

Rhodes entered the apartment and placed the briefcase in its usual spot. He was in and out within five minutes. One of the spies waved to him as he left and Rhodes waved in return.

The first day went smoothly. They would repeat it six times. Things were going well until the fourth day when a visitor dropped by Gary's house. The encounter changed everything.

PRISTINE DOCKED AT COXEN Hole and passengers were free to leave the ship. Angel admired the view from his balcony.

An enormous range of rolling wooded hills served as the backdrop at Coxen Hole. Several houses lined the water's edge, which was built up with large boulders around the dock's hub and shoreline. The aqua-colored water sparkled like diamonds. It was more inviting to guests than Belize, especially since boat rides weren't required to reach the dock.

The cove was buzzing with activity. It seemed like a hundred school buses and vans were waiting in a graveled parking lot for tourists. Although Angel was a hundred feet or so above the organized chaos, noises echoed throughout Coxen Hole.

A native committee—each member wore multi-colored robes and masks—welcomed visitors with a ritualistic dance. The sight wasn't unusual to Angel, but visitors were fascinated. As the lot began to clear, Angel bid the ship farewell. It took him several minutes, but he finally stepped off the balcony and went through his room. He shut the door and made his way to the exit area.

A worker scanned his identification card and he stepped off the ship. The Miami weather was frigid compared to Roatan. It was well over a hundred degrees with humidity. Angel's shirt was soaked by the time he walked from the pier to the security gate. A guard looked at his Royal Seas card and fake driver's license. Pablo Hernandez from Venezuela was given clearance to pass through the gate and into the parking lot.

His cousin was waiting nearby in a rundown mini-van. Those living where his family resided in Roatan were barely above the poverty line. The ten thousand he paid his cousin to arrange everything amounted to a year's wages.

"Is everything prepared?" Angel asked.

"The plane is waiting and I'll take you wherever you need to go."

His cousin didn't know what Angel's intentions were in Roatan. He and Angel's family thought he wanted to return home and it was the easiest way for him to do so. If illegal activities short of murder were necessary to survive, many wouldn't frown upon it. But neither they nor Christo would forgive him for murder.

"The horseback riding adventure at El Rancho Barrio Corpus is my first destination."

The van pulled left out of the lot onto a bumpy road. At several points, the van barely had enough space to drive past the houses sitting on the edge of the road. The houses were crumbling and covered with rusty tin roofs. Villagers sat near the road and watched as each vehicle drove by.

"A man who owns one of the biggest mansions in Roatan helped raise funds to fix a lot of the roadways on the island. Unfortunately, this roadway isn't scheduled for repair until midway next year."

They exited the neighborhood of homes and drove for a while before reaching the highway. Sandy Bay and an old church were landmarks on the way to El Rancho Barrio Corpus. They followed the meandering roadway and eventually reached the top of a hillside. They nearly came to a stop at a hairpin turn in the road before traveling the last half mile. A sign on the right side of the road welcomed them.

When Carlos dropped Angel off at the ranch, those who signed up for the Caracol Package were there, including the Beckmans.

"Welcome Senior to El Rancho Barrio Corpus."

Angel responded in Spanish and they had a lengthy conversation, which included a few pats on the back and several laughs. The longer the mission lasted, the more Angel wished he could abort the assignment.

When Rhonda and Geoff saw Angel, they hustled over to him.

"How are you feeling today?" Rhonda asked with a devilish grin.

"I'm fine."

Tito, the ranch leader, broke up the circle and placed the Beckmans on their horses. Angel then mounted his horse.

The tour started and snaked through the top of a hillside. They finally reached a clearing and the only thing in Angel's view was palm trees, lush jungle, and glistening Caribbean waters. The tour continued past the man's house Carlos had told him about. The white mansion was beautiful. The Mediterranean-style home had steps leading in all directions. Each stairway was accompanied by white railings and hundreds of white spindles. The main stairway started at the driveway, eventually stopping at the front door, which hid behind several Roman-like pillars. A drug lord would be more than happy to call the place home.

After an hour or so, the tour ended and everyone scattered. Angel saw Carlos watching from the van. The hit man kept his eyes on Rhonda once they were at the private resort in West Bay.

Geoff disappeared inside the hotel for a happy hour or two while Rhonda walked around outside. Geoff wasn't a sunbather, as his pale skin clearly displayed, and didn't enjoy frolicking in the ocean. Rhonda would be alone for a while and didn't mind. As she walked toward the restroom area, she spotted Angel sitting on a bench in a shaded area.

"Hello. Are you going to enjoy the ocean waters?"

"I'm not sure. Where did Geoff run off to?"

"He's not an ocean person. He likes to hang out on the ship's deck, with his shirt on of course, but he'll drive me nuts if he's forced to lie in the sand. We go through this every year when we go to Myrtle Beach. He went to the bar inside the hotel. You should join me on the beach."

"I might accept your offer."

"I'm going to change. I'll see you in a few minutes."

Rhonda entered the restroom and Angel walked to the van. He grabbed his backpack and told Carlos to wait fifty feet from the entrance.

Angel returned and went inside the men's restroom. He dashed into a stall, unzipping his backpack and pulling out a small blow dart about the size of the round prong on a utility plug. He quickly dissembled a Bic pen and discarded the tip and cap down the toilet. Angel carefully put the dart into the pen's tube. He threw the ink cartridge in the trash can and pulled the door slightly open. Angel made sure no one was wandering around.

He walked past the women's room, which was on the right-hand side, and moved some thick brush along the building. He quietly waited until the women's restroom door opened and slammed behind her. Rhonda looked for Angel, noticing his spot had been vacated. Number ten remained hidden in the brush, waiting for her. As she strolled by, Angel blew the poisoned-tip dart into the side of Rhonda's neck. He turned around and fought his way through the brush until reaching the roadway where Carlos awaited.

Rhonda felt the stinging in her neck and thought she had been bitten by a horsefly or mosquito. Dizziness was rapidly taking over her body as she sat down in Angel's empty spot. The world around her kept spinning faster and faster and the poison finally stopped her heart. She slumped over on the bench. Stenson and Rhodes' latest target was eliminated.

Angel jumped in the van and Carlos drove off.

"Why are you out of breath and why did you cut through the woods?"

"Don't ask questions. Get me to the airport as fast as you can."

Carlos didn't hesitate. He followed his cousin's orders and quickly got him to the landing strip. The plane was waiting. Angel embraced his cousin and got out of the van. After jogging approximately one hundred yards to the plane, he handed the pilot a thick envelope full of money and the plane was airborne in seconds.

Geoff was notified his wife had been found dead outside. He rushed out to see her surrounded by a crowd of people. The local police were on the scene and witnesses gave accounts of a local man sitting on the bench. Gary had chosen the right assassin because Angel blended in perfectly.

All passengers except Geoff and Rhonda Beckman, and Pablo Hernandez were accounted for. Geoff was staying on the island and there weren't any signs of Pablo. The ship was searched from top to bottom. Pablo had vanished. Authorities in Roatan were alerted that the man was wanted for questioning. They wouldn't obtain answers.

The case of Rhonda Beckman was never solved. The news of her death was a shock to everyone at the tire and rubber plant, but Rhodes didn't lose sleep upon hearing one of his favorite employees had been murdered.

His wallet continued getting heavier as targets were eliminated. An accidental drowning, a house fire, a busted brake line...the list went on and on. Although an end didn't seem to be in sight, a pair of enemies loomed and the operation would come to a screeching halt.

Chapter
Seventeen

SHARON SPENT SEVERAL YEARS trying to figure out what Gary did for a living. Her friends were also inquisitive. Sharon was a lady of leisure and the women in Mesa admired her. Most would have ignored Gary's wrongdoings to experience Sharon's luxurious lifestyle.

As one of the wealthiest couples in the area, Sharon wanted to know how Gary supported their standard of living. Gary spent more time away from home the more he talked to Stenson. Robert Rhodes entered the picture and Gary started disappearing at odd times. Gary's increasing absence improved their material life. Sharon decided it was time to find out what Gary did.

Although Stenson didn't become obscenely wealthy until pairing up with Rhodes in the late 80s, Big Boy had his hand in numerous illegal activities. He and Rhodes were friends before becoming business partners and were as corrupt and crooked as any of the local mafia groups.

Stenson urged Gary to move to Columbus for years. Rhodes and Gary met when Robert asked Stenson to provide him with a little muscle. The unions were gaining power and several of Robert's employees were becoming troublesome well before the crisis began in 1987.

Rhodes didn't like unions and despised union leaders. In 1980, a strike at the plant helped Rhodes decide to take matters into his own hands. He asked Stenson, who had ruffians track down gambling bets and IOUs from time to time, to orchestrate a problem solving unit. At the time, Gary was his top thug.

Gary flew to Columbus and met Rhodes. They hit it off. Robert named Gary his new "Secretary of Defense."

The strike started because employees at the Rhodes Tire and Rubber Company wanted better benefits, namely health insurance. The sickness, one that came to full light in 1987, was forcing workers to use sick time like never before. Each employee was given two week's worth of sick, vacation, and personal time. Most used their time by early summer.

Workers lost money because they were forced to take unpaid days off. The union took a stand, stating things needed to change. They asked for two weeks of vacation time, five sick days, and three personal days. Rhodes balked at their demands and a long fight ensued.

When second shift workers walked out late Friday evening, a handful of employees showed up for third shift. Rhodes was blindsided. He heard rumblings that people were unsatisfied, but never imagined people would follow through with their threats. He shut the plant for the weekend, leaving a notice on a fence.

The plant will be closed over the weekend. The facility will reopen Sunday at 11:00 p.m. and any worker who doesn't show up for their ensuing shift will be terminated. Participating in a strike is the same as quitting. You wanted a couple of extra days and this weekend grants your wishes.

When *The Dispatch* hit newsstands on Sunday, the weekend shutdown and ensuing strike was splattered on the front page. The story had Central Ohio talking, but the classified section created a bigger buzz. The ad took up an entire page. It was hard to miss due to the large print and fancy colors.

Wanted: Hard-working laborers for local tire and rubber plant. Starting pay is $9.50 per hour with solid benefits. All shifts available. Contact Robert Rhodes at 614-231-8654.

The union delivered the first blow, but Rhodes struck back. The advertisement was a message from Rhodes to anyone who thought about striking. Scabs were being openly recruited and the pay was better. Workers at the plant started at $7.60 per hour and received a quarter raise every nine months. They also received a $100 Christmas bonus. The plant was open seven days per week, including holidays, but employees worked four eight-hour days and then were off two. Only the office staff had the same days off every week. Rhodes always did things differently.

Calculators crunched numbers as soon as employees and union reps read $9.50. The scabs would be paid $15.20 more per day, $76 more per five days of work, and $3,952 more per year. Phones were also busy that day and the news spread like wildfire.

The Rhodes Tire and Rubber Company was one of the better paying factory jobs, but $9.50 an hour was better than a lot of business professionals were making.

Those who had decided to strike gave it a second thought. They knew they were going to be replaced and jobless. If they crossed the line, they would work alongside fresh faces making more money in their first day and it didn't sit well with them.

Rhodes had outsmarted the strikers. He was trying to end the strike as soon as it started. When Sunday night rolled around, his efforts to avoid a strike didn't pan out.

He never visited the plant on Sundays and didn't usually start until 9:00 a.m. on Monday. Rhodes stopped by the plant early Sunday evening and there was a stack of resumes waiting with a security guard at the check-in station. The phone was ringing off the hook when he stepped inside his office. His answering machine was full of messages from people wanting a job. Stenson's ad created a circus, but the show was just beginning.

It was past seven-thirty and the security officer was at Rhodes' door.

"Sir, I think you need to come outside."

The men went outside and hustled to the entrance of the facility. New tenants were moving into one of the houses on Johnson Road. Several trucks with furniture and food were being unloaded. The abode had seen better days, but the union bought the old house and strikers would be there twenty-four/seven.

"Do you want me to call the police?"

"No. We can't do anything. They outsmarted me."

Third shift workers arrived anywhere from ten to ten-thirty. Several workers got there early, turning the break room into a smoky canteen. Those who arrived early didn't have much to do except hang out with other prompt hillbillies, as Rhodes liked to say.

Rhodes started watching the clock at 10:00 p.m. It seemed like he checked his watch every thirty seconds. Not one car had pulled into the entranceway and it was 10:45.

Finally, at five 'til, a caravan of eight cars pulled into the entrance. Each car was filled with four workers. Rhodes watched the strikers across the street. They waved banners and picket signs and booed loudly. Tomatoes and eggs filled the air. Rhodes and the security guard took cover in the gate house.

"Get the swine on the phone," Rhodes said.

The security guard dialed police and two cruisers were in the middle of things at 11:15. The cops split up and interviewed both groups. Those who arrived for work said they didn't want to press charges. They rode to work with half of their friends and the other half was across the street.

Strikers were encouraged to leave the premises, but there wasn't anything that could be done if they didn't. They promised not to throw anything else at the cars, but it didn't mean they would leave them alone. Officers were satisfied nothing further would happen.

Rhodes didn't open the entire plant because only thirty-two workers showed up that night. Two were foremen in other areas of the facility, so Rhodes put them in charge of the sections that were open. They worked their shift and went home.

No one dared drive to work alone. That morning, the eight cars left the parking lot at the same time. Strikers yelled insults and obscenities as each car turned out of the driveway. The nineteen first shift employees and twenty-seven afternoon workers received the same treatment.

Seventy-eight plant employees crossed the line while five office workers decided they needed paychecks. The eighty-three workers made up nearly a fourth of Rhodes' workforce. Over half stayed out of the battle and found work elsewhere while the other fourth turned the place across the street into a fraternity/sorority house.

By Wednesday of the first week, Rhodes hired two hundred replacement workers. The non-picketers were treated badly, but the scabs were despised. It was almost as if they arrived in a bus adorned with Michigan tags and everyone got out wearing maize and blue.

The eighty-three original workers dwindled to sixty-seven by Wednesday. Some had a change of heart about striking or finding different work. The sixty-seven remaining employees detested the new workers just as much as the strikers.

Those who crossed the picket line were ridiculed, but the scabs were under immense pressure. Media outlets were on the scene night and day. Some of the new employees were careless and granted interviews or made statements. When they did, their names were made public and strikers used intimidation tactics.

Threatening phone calls were made throughout the day. A few worked because some quit. Most calls were ignored and the disregard was a mistake. Driveways were sprinkled with nails. Mailboxes were destroyed. Bricks were thrown through windows. Animals were stolen. Vulgarities were painted on houses and vehicles. Nearly every method of destruction was executed.

The strike entered its second month and things continued to worsen. Rhodes continually replaced employees and the total of original workers dwindled to forty-one. Although the strikers were seemingly controlling the situation, Rhodes wasn't giving in. He ignored profanities they shouted and found their threats amusing.

Things finally came to a head during the seventh week of the strike. A small crowd huddled in front of a burn barrel in the yard across the road. A few people sat on a couch on the porch. Rhodes was late leaving the facility and it was well after dark.

Rhodes had hired two more security guards to walk the grounds at the plant and each night one stood at the entrance to keep an eye on the strikers. As Rhodes pulled out, it was the first time he didn't hear obscenities or insults. As he started down the road, one of the men huddled around the barrel pulled out a rifle and fired at Robert's vehicle.

The car screeched to a halt and the strikers scattered. They were unsure how their former check signer would react. The security guard ducked for cover near the gate house and yanked his gun from the holster.

Rhodes looked at his dashboard. Smoke seeped from a hole the size of a tangerine above his glove compartment. He felt something slowly trickling down his neck. He flipped on the overhead light and looked in his rearview mirror. The streak of blood caused him to check his body. The only wound was from a piece of glass that had pierced the side of his neck. Rhodes used a handkerchief to pull out the glass fragment and wipe away the blood.

Strikers watched from the windows inside the dark house. They noticed he turned the inside light off. Reverse lights signaled Rhodes was ready for a confrontation.

He backed up until reaching the front of the house. Rhodes sat inside the idling vehicle watching the house for nearly an hour. All but one of his ex-employees peeked out blinds or curtains. He surveyed things from a deer stand hidden in a pine tree near the house.

All Rhodes wanted was an explanation. He would ignore what happened if someone confessed they were the shooter. The front door never opened. Rhodes was fed up with the cowards inside. It was time to put an end to the strike.

THE APARTMENT WAS PROTECTED by watchful eyes. When Rhodes dropped the briefcase off with the new assignment, those watching didn't think anything about it, although Stenson usually spent more time at the apartment. Each visit by Rhodes thereafter was ignored.

There were always strange faces dropping by, but visitors were never there more than fifteen minutes. After the briefcase was stolen, Stenson and Rhodes told their neighborhood informants people were no longer welcome. Stenson wanted notified each time a stranger entered the apartment.

When Mathias (number four) dropped by the apartment, Stenson was alerted. Visits by Luc (number six) and Zeek (number eight) were also reported to Harry. Big Boy was going to remain mum about the visits, but informed Rhodes about the activity at the apartment.

Rhodes returned to Columbus after he and Stenson received their tapes. He wasn't ready for more bad news. Had the lookout told Harry that Rhodes also stopped by a few times, Stenson might have pieced things together.

"It's obvious Gary is in control of things. He needs eliminated," Stenson said.

His words were harsh. Rhodes didn't like the idea of getting rid of Gary.

"I think we should visit him. We thought he was kidnapped, but it's apparent he's up to something. Our informants know what Matt and Preston look like and it wasn't them."

"We shouldn't be seen together," Rhodes said. "You need to check on him."

Stenson agreed. The dial tone signaled their conversation was over.

One of his friends owned a carpet business and Stenson paid him to borrow a van. When Stenson pulled into Mr. O'Neil's neighborhood, he parked the van near the top of the gradually inclining road so he could keep an eye on everything happening below.

Stenson watched and waited several hours. It was mid-afternoon when he saw a vehicle start up the hill. It passed the first two mansions on the right and slowed down in front of the third one. Two men got out. Stenson couldn't recognize them from where he was sitting. He looked through binoculars and was astounded. It was Gary O'Neil and another man. The mystery man had a scarf around his face and wore a long coat, despite a temperature in the high fifties. The vehicle that dropped them off turned down the first lane on the right. Stenson saw it turn around and park about thirty yards away from a stop sign.

Matt saw the carpet cleaner making his rounds, but didn't think twice about it. The man got out of the van and approached one of the gates. He pressed a buzzer and didn't get a response. He walked to two or three more houses.

Stenson got back in the van and drove down the hill. He started slowly down the lane where Matt was parked. Stenson suddenly made a sharp turn, blocking the road. He jumped out of the van pointing a sawed-off shotgun at Matt.

"Get out of the vehicle!"

Matt's first instinct was to stick the vehicle in reverse and drive as fast as he could. The problem he faced was the lane didn't have an outlet. He could back up another one hundred fifty yards, but wouldn't have anywhere to go. He knew as soon as he touched the gearshift Stenson would unload buckshot into the vehicle.

"Don't shoot! I'll do whatever you want. They hired me to drive them here and take them back."

"Where is back?"

"I pick them up and drop them off at a different location each time."

"Listen Talbot! You think you're smart. I know who you are and why you're here. Put your hands on your head!"

Matt did as instructed.

"We're walking to the gate and you're going to get them to open it. Is that clear?"

"Yes."

Matt walked in front of Stenson until they reached the gate. Big Boy crouched beside an entrance pillar while Matt pressed the buzzer. Gary answered the call from inside the shed.

"We have a major problem. Two cars drove by and I think Stenson was in one of them."

"Go back to the car and we'll be out."

"You have to open this gate now. Two of the men are walking down the hill and one of the cars drove by again. I'm trapped. You have to let me in."

The gate opened. Stenson grabbed Matt and shoved the barrel of the shotgun to his throat. They walked briskly down the driveway and reached the front lawn. Gary threw a fit if anyone walked across it. Stenson ignored the rule, crunching Gary's perfectly manicured grass with his heavy steps and Matt's shuffling feet.

Gary was exiting the shed with a number in his hand when he saw Stenson.

"If you run, the blood from his head will stain the revered ground we're walking on. Why did you double-cross me?"

"Do you really want to point the finger at me? I know you were behind Sharon's death. You knew she was having an affair with Kurt Carson, whom you tried to kill, but it was the wrong Kurt Carson. You knew Preston was Sharon's child. I know you were going to have Preston killed at Mehaffey's Pub. I could go on and on."

"Some of those things might be true, but it was for your own good."

"You did it for my own good? I think you did those things to help yourself."

"Gary, doing what's best for me is also best for you and Robert. I don't understand why you told them about the briefcase. You laid everything out on the table and we could be facing life behind bars or even death. Those options aren't appealing."

"Tell me how we're in that kind of trouble!"

"The tape is how we're going to go down. You gave every last detail."

"I don't know anything about a tape."

"I received one in the mail a few days ago. I wasn't the only person that..."

"I did as well," Rhodes said as he walked out of the shed.

Stenson was speechless.

"Yes, it's me Harry. Gary didn't double-cross us. The man you're holding hostage is responsible. He was the one who sent the tapes. I know Gary has a lot of hard feelings toward you because of the things he found out, but we can resolve our issues."

"When I talked to you about coming here, you told me I needed to be the one to make the visit. Why are you here? Why is Matt Talbot driving you around? He's the person we're supposed to be after."

The questions made sense. The four men were either confused or didn't know what to say. Matt was also frightened.

"I did say you needed to come here, but thought I needed to be here also. I was afraid there could be trouble if I wasn't around. I was the one who kidnapped Gary."

Gary thought Rhodes had lost his mind. He was either lying to keep Stenson off guard or something else was going on. Matt and his group was who kidnapped him, but maybe they worked for Rhodes. Gary and Stenson were certainly confused. Matt and Rhodes were the only two who knew what was going on.

"Explain why the tapes were made. Gary was talking, but if you had him under your control, why would you let them make a tape and send it in the mail? You're lying! Put your hands up or I will blow your heads off!"

Four arms quickly reached for the sky.

"You're putting a different number on the board each day. I want to know who you're sending the recruits after. Is it me?"

Harry's question didn't get answered. He asked again.

"You're sending them after me, aren't you?"

Matt knew they were at a disadvantage because Stenson had talked with Rhodes—the real Robert Rhodes. The good news was Stenson thought he had been double-crossed by Rhodes. The biggest problem they faced was Stenson was the only person in contact with Robert.

"I want all three of you to walk in front of me. You're taking me to where you're staying. We're taking the van I drove here and if you try anything funny, your life will end with one squeeze of my finger."

The gate opened and the foursome walked to the van. A few housewives stared out their windows. They saw the shotgun in Stenson's right hand and dialed 9-1-1. The van disappeared around the corner before the panicking women could recite anything to the operator.

Matt was behind the wheel and Gary sat in the passenger seat. Stenson was behind Matt with the shotgun shoved into the back of his seat. They knew Matt would die if they tried anything foolish. They were left with one alternative.

After a lengthy drive, the van pulled onto Route 23. Stenson hadn't been in that part of Central Ohio since the late 80s. Things hadn't changed, but he wondered where they were going. As they pulled up to the pathway, Matt told Gary to get out and unhook the chain. Stenson approved. The van drove through and Gary rejoined them after he reattached the chain.

Matt drove the vehicle past the circular party spot and continued down the tree-lined trail. After driving through the bushes and hanging branches that had invaded the path, they reached the railroad tracks. Stenson was bowled over as soon as he saw the warehouse. Gary was equally knocked for six.

"Is that the old Rhodes Tire and Rubber Company?" Big Boy asked without needing an answer.

Stenson looked at Rhodes, who nodded.

They drove over the tracks and pulled into the back section of the warehouse. They got out and Harry started having flashbacks to when the place was a thriving business. He couldn't believe what an eyesore the place had become. Several people who worked for Rhodes had been murdered and Stenson could feel several presences ready to pounce on him when he stepped out of the van.

They walked across the small road that ventured through the facility. Lauren, Preston, and Dane heard shuffling feet and opened the door. They didn't expect to see Stenson, especially Preston, who wondered what kind of change-up they were throwing him.

"If it isn't Preston O'Neil...Stenson & Rhodes' finest," Harry said with sarcasm.

Stenson forced them into the first storage house. Big Boy asked several questions, but every answer conflicted with what he and Rhodes talked about over the course of the ordeal.

"Robert, I want to know what's going on."

He looked at Matt as if he needed approval. Matt shrugged as if to say the secret didn't matter any longer.

"We have been screwed by Rhodes. I haven't talked to him since the late 70s. Robert tricked our dying father on his death bed into signing papers that left everything to him. The Rhodes Tire and Rubber Company was supposed to be left to both of us. Our father wanted us to be equal partners, but Robert had a taste for money. He did everything he could to keep every penny for himself. The case went to court and I lost. It dragged on for years and I couldn't keep up with the big-time lawyers he had. We haven't talked since."

"You're lying."

"I received a card from my sister-in-law when I got cancer saying they were praying for me, but I knew God wouldn't answer their prayers. Robert doesn't know I live in Columbus. In fact, I don't live far from here."

"Then who are you?"

"I'm Ronald Rhodes, obviously Robert's identical twin brother. I'm the only other child of Raymond and Margaret Rhodes."

The news silenced the room. Dane didn't know it was Ronald. Preston and Gary were confused. Matt sat in his seat and couldn't help but smile.

"What are you smiling about?" Stenson asked. "Do you think I believe these lies?"

"It doesn't matter what you believe. Your ways have finally caught up to you."

"What do you mean?"

"You should ask Gary about those numbers on his board again."

"Gary, am I the next case?"

"Yes, but I thought he was Rhodes all along. They tricked me into talking and doing other things."

The unbelievable situation got worse. The lights in the first storage house flickered before going black. Matt had another wild card up his sleeve. The female EMT had been in the warehouse since Gary was kidnapped. Matt wanted her to stay at the ambulance when they pulled out of the lot, but she insisted on going with them. Matt gave her a secret signal to let her know of danger when they walked across the road.

Savannah knew Stenson was wielding a gun as they walked into the first storage house. She walked around the backside of the storage houses and pulled the lever on the electric box.

The darkness startled everyone. Stenson was in the middle of the room and had everyone against a wall.

"If I hear anyone move, I'll shoot."

Everyone sat still, but Gary moved behind Stenson. Gary grabbed him and three shots went off as they wrestled. Matt raced for the door and made it safely outside.

"Stop or I'll fill you full of lead," Gary said.

Matt turned around and they looked intently at each other.

"I don't think you want to do that dad."

THE PHONE AT STENSON'S residence rang as soon as Rhodes walked through his front door.

"Harry, I want that house burned to the ground. I don't care if every person dies. Those bastards just shot out the back window on my Cadillac and a piece of glass lodged in my neck. I'm lucky they didn't kill me. I want every striker to get what they deserve."

Gary was in Mesa, but Harry decided business needed to be conducted in person rather than over the phone. He asked him to visit Columbus, but Gary had Trevor for the weekend. It was a rare occasion, but Sharon was out of town on business. The urgency in Harry's voice meant business couldn't wait.

"Fly out here and you can stay the weekend."

"I'll be on the first flight out of town," Harry replied.

Gary and Trevor drove to the airport and were waiting on Stenson when his plane landed. Stenson always had a gift for Trevor, which is why he loved to see him.

When they returned to the O'Neil residence, it didn't take long to get down to business. Harry explained the strike and shooting incident.

"That house needs to be a bonfire. Robert doesn't care how it happens. If people have to die, so be it."

As Harry continued talking, Gary took a small notepad off the side of the refrigerator. He tore off a piece of paper and scribbled notes. He wanted to know every detail. They spent the evening discussing things and developed a plan.

They spent the next day enjoying their time together. They snuck in eighteen holes, which wasn't easy because Trevor was running around the links.

Day turned to night and they cracked open a few brews. Gary put Trevor to bed and their drinking increased. The two buddies were on the verge of being drunk. They sobered when the front door opened.

Sharon wasn't supposed to be home until Sunday evening, but the event she attended was poorly planned. It would have been a waste of time to spend another day in Portland, so she flew home early.

The men sat up straight, looking as if they had seen a ghost. Sharon was a creature of habit. Her schedule was like clock work.

The fact she was home early surprised Gary. Despite guzzling a twelve-pack, Gary's mind was focused on how to explain why Big Boy was in Mesa.

Sharon's look said it all. Gary needed to clarify things, but stayed in his spot longer than he should have.

Sharon walked to the kitchen and sat her things down. When she cleaned or organized the house, she was meticulous. She knew if something was moved. If a finger print was left on the toilet handle in the spare bathroom—no one in her household was supposed to use it—Sharon could tell.

She noticed the notepad on the fridge was crooked. The pen attached to it was also missing. Instead of hearing "I didn't touch it" from Gary, Sharon did a three-sixty around the kitchen. She saw the pen on top of the counter and noticed a piece of paper folded and tucked under the pen cap.

Gary and Stenson watched every move she made. Sharon decided to get their minds off what she was doing.

"Do you drunks need another one?"

They were shocked she didn't ask Gary to go to another room so she could grill him about Stenson's visit.

"I'll take one."

Mrs. O'Neil reached inside the fridge, grabbing two cold ones. She didn't need an answer from Gary because there was always a reason for him to drink. She handed them their beers. After Sharon walked back into the kitchen, she moved her things to the counter. Sharon flipped open her small suitcase and the men couldn't see her hands. She snatched the pen and paper, tucking them into some clothes.

Gary needed to see what Sharon was up to. He stumbled to the counter, noticing the pen was gone.

"What happened to the pen that was sitting on this counter?"

"What pen?"

"The one from the notepad on the fridge. There was a piece of paper wedged under the pen cap that has important information on it."

"I just walked in the door."

Gary thought he left it on the counter, but maybe his drunkenness caused him to forget what he did with it. He became testy with Sharon, but didn't want to make a big deal about it. He failed. The hushed arguing turned into Gary grabbing Sharon and shaking her. The episode got to Stenson.

"Gary, you need to relax. Let's sit down. You need to cool off a little."

He nudged Gary toward the living room and gave Sharon a look of support. His kindness threw her off guard, but was appreciated. Gary had a tendency to get physical with Sharon when he consumed alcohol.

She gathered her things and went to their bedroom. She took the piece of paper from the cap, placed the pen in her pocket, and put the paper into one of her magazines. Sharon was putting her things away when Gary barged into the room.

"You have that piece of paper and I want it."

Sharon was afraid things were going to get physical again, so she called for Stenson. He entered the room, stopping a second incident from occurring. Stenson pulled Gary into the hallway and calmed him.

"You have to stop. We know she has the piece of paper, but what does it prove?"

"I wrote down things about the house and..."

"It doesn't matter. The house is in Central Ohio. She won't read or hear about it out here. You're always careful about everything and I like that about you, but you need to relax. You messed up this time, but it's just a piece of paper. Don't worry about it."

Stenson's words did the trick. Gary went downstairs and passed out on the couch. Stenson retired to the guest room and Sharon waited in the darkness for an hour. When things were silent, she turned on a lamp by her side of the bed.

She opened the magazine and laid the piece of paper out. Sharon read about a house that was going to be torched and the number of people staying at the house during each shift. She was unsure if the house was home to a business.

Every detail of the house—how many windows and the location of each one, where the doors were located, how many rooms were in the place, etc.—was scribbled down. She continued reading and there was an outline detailing how the plan would be implemented.

Sharon was disgusted. She needed to do something to stop innocent people from possibly being killed. She couldn't let Gary or Stenson know what she had discovered.

If Sharon wasn't linked to Gary, she would have been killed by Stenson. Neither Big Boy nor Gary suspected anything because Sharon outfoxed them. She had breakfast waiting on them when they entered the kitchen the next morning. The pen and paper were on the counter.

"You owe me an apology."

Gary saw his missing information sitting almost exactly where he thought he left it.

"I was straightening the living room and it was stuck in the arm of the chair where you were sitting. It goes to show you had too much to drink."

Gary grabbed the pen and paper and shoved the items in his pocket. Sharon had eased his mind and he quietly ate breakfast after his apology.

Stenson showered after finishing breakfast and Gary drove him to the airport. Gary was going to Columbus three days later. It said that on the piece of paper Sharon read.

"I'll see you in three days," Gary said as he dropped Stenson off at the terminal.

Neither knew Sharon would also be traveling in three days.

Chapter Eighteen

GARY PUT HIS SUITCASE by the front door. He hugged Sharon, grabbed his things, and walked out the door. Sharon watched as he placed his things in the trunk, got into his car, and pulled out of the driveway. His horn signaled goodbye. It was safe for Sharon to run upstairs and pack a few days worth of clothes in an overnight bag.

Sharon's flight schedule included a two-hour layover in St. Louis before catching a plane to Columbus. Gary had a direct flight from Phoenix to Columbus so his misdeeds would more than likely be under way before Sharon arrived in the Buckeye State.

Her plane landed in Missouri without any problems. Sharon sat in an uncomfortable chair at the airport for two hours reading a magazine she bought in Arizona. The boarding call blared over the intercom. It was time for the second leg of her cross-country trip. They ran into turbulence, but the plane landed safely at the Columbus Airport. She waited in a crowded line, watching for her luggage on one of the numerous conveyor belts. Sharon saw her royal blue overnight bag and squeezed through a small opening in the throng of waiting travelers. She booked a room at a nearby hotel and paid a cabbie to take her there.

Memories flashed through her mind as she walked into the room. The last time she stayed in a hotel was in Austin when she was pregnant with Preston. Sharon recalled the beautiful scenery Texas had to offer. It also made her think how much she missed Kurt and the Alexander family. She grimaced when she thought about Fresno.

"Hopefully, this room won't be blown to smithereens," she thought.

She experienced an amazing night of sleep. The hotel bed was like a sponge and nearly swallowed her body. When she woke up, she felt like a new person. She opened the curtains, inviting the bright Columbus sunshine to join her, ordered room service, and grabbed the complimentary paper in front of her door.

Sharon skimmed through the rag, but since she didn't know much about Ohio, the news wasn't interesting. However, a small story on 7A about the strike caught her attention. She read the article and her stomach turned every time Rhodes was mentioned. The most useful information to Sharon was the paragraph about a house purchased by the union for strikers. It didn't take long for Sharon to figure out what was going on.

Although she would love to visit as many shopping centers as possible, take a stroll along the Olentangy River, and check out the hallowed grounds at *The Horseshoe*, she knew she didn't have time.

She rented a car at the airport and the first place she went was Stenson's small PR firm on the outskirts of downtown. Mrs. O'Neil veered onto 315 and eventually found herself in the rat race known as 270.

She was careful when she reached the road leading to Stenson's firm. Sharon figured every corner of the building was being watched. A hat and sunglasses provided a disguise. She eased to the stoplight, looked into the business, and saw a woman sitting behind a counter. It appeared everyone else had gone home for the day.

Sharon couldn't go in because it would blow her cover and let her husband know she was in town. She decided to find out where the Rhodes Tire and Rubber Company was located.

Mrs. O'Neil drove for a while before stopping to ask for directions. Although the plant was one of the biggest in Columbus, it took three stops before she found a gas station attendant who knew the location of the facility.

The drive to the plant took her to the middle of nowhere. She couldn't believe one of Columbus' up and coming businesses was located in the land of hilljacks. She reached the end of Route 23 and turned right onto Johnson Road. It didn't take long to spot the house across from the plant. She knew it was the house Gary had written about.

It was a brave move because the house was under constant surveillance. Sharon flipped the hood on her windbreaker and was met at her car by one of the strikers.

"May I help you?"

"Who is in charge? I'd like to speak to them."

"We're in the union and we have representatives who advise us. Would you like to speak to someone on our committee?"

"Yes."

"What can I help you with?"

"Can we go inside?"

"That's not possible. The only people allowed to step foot inside the place are strikers and union reps."

"I understand. All of you are in danger."

"Sorry to be rude, but we know that ma'am."

"I'm not talking about the strike. Someone is planning to burn this house to the ground."

"How do you know?"

"I saw something I wasn't supposed to see. They are unaware I know what they're up to."

"What are their names? Is Rhodes behind it?"

"Rhodes wasn't around when I found out. Two people he is involved with plotted the whole thing. It's supposed to happen in the next few days."

The surveillance crew reported to Rhodes. They didn't know who it was, but they knew it was a woman. They thought it could possibly be the man's wife. Rhodes looked and dismissed the unidentifiable woman as a non-threat, but ordered someone to follow her when she left the house.

Sharon finished her conversation with the man and strikers were on high alert. Strikers watched every car that drove by, convinced Rhodes was behind the wheel.

Sunset was less than two hours away. Traffic on Johnson Road was typically slow at that time of day. A second visitor shook things up.

Gary wasn't a procrastinator. Mr. O'Neil wanted to see a pile of rubble by the time the moon lit the night sky.

Gary called about a water break at the house on Johnson Road. The water company sent someone to the address. When the man pulled his truck in the driveway, he was met by the same striker who talked to Sharon.

"May I help you?"

"Someone called about a water break. I'm here to check it out."

"I'm sorry, sir, but there isn't a water break. No one called your company from this address."

The men stood in the driveway arguing about the phone call for several minutes.

"All right, so no one called from this residence. At least let me come in and check things out and we can go on about our business."

"I can't let you in. Only strikers and reps are allowed in the house."

More arguing ensued and the visitor finally understood he was not getting inside the house.

"You can keep me from going inside the house, but I'm checking the water meter."

Checking the meter wouldn't solve a water break problem, but the unexpected visitor was doing it to annoy the man he was arguing with. Strikers were very tentative after Sharon's visit.

"Scare 'em," he said over a walkie-talkie.

As the man approached the meter in the front yard, a shot was fired from the deer stand. The bullet kicked up dirt ten feet from where the man was standing. He ran to his truck, got in, and left a trail of dust. He called the police when he got back to the office and they visited the house once again.

They asked questions and everyone said they heard a shot fired. The water man pointed to where he thought the bullet came from. Police checked the premises and surrounding property, but couldn't find anything. They gave them the same good behavior warning that had already been issued and left.

Gary was standing at the warehouse with the surveillance team when the bullet zipped through the trees. They knew the location of the shooter.

With dusk rapidly approaching, Gary went into action. He began walking down Gilbert Road. When Gary reached the dead end, he entered the woods. He circled around until reaching a massive open field, which is where the development was built later. Mr. O'Neil walked through the field and reached the left side of Johnson Road. It ended at Gilbert Road, but was later extended up the hill and throughout the housing development.

He walked down the hill, getting closer to the deer stand. It was nearly impossible to walk silently across the pine tree section of land, but Gary avoided cracking large limbs or pine cones.

Darkness had set in, but Gary crept next to the tree where the deer stand was located. The man in the stand heard rustling and quickly turned his head. He peered down through the branches, but it was too dark to see anything. He thought it was a squirrel or chipmunk.

His next thoughts were about death. Gary climbed to a point high enough in the tree and fired three shots. The silencer muffled the trio of blasts. The man fell off the stand and crashed through branches. His body was losing blood by the second. Gary hurried to the ground and looked a few feet above his head. The man's body hung motionless in the thick branches. He was gasping for air. Gary knew he would be dead by the time he reached the opening near the house.

Gary moved to the edge of the property line on the right side of the house and crouched down. He could see people on the porch and most of the lights were off in the house.

The yard on the backside of the house met a large alfalfa field that attracted some of the state's best bucks. He worked his way through a portion of the woods so he could get into the field. Gary reached the edge of the alfalfa field and looked at the pair of windows on the top floor. Neither was emitting light, but the window on the bottom floor was well lit. Gary could see the heads of a few people. If people were watching, it would be harder to see him on the backside of the house because it was darker.

Dressed in camouflage, Gary blended in with the ground he was crawling across. Gary slithered to the house and sat against it. He reached into one of his cargo pockets and pulled out a small bottle of lighter fluid. Gary sprayed as many of the old boards as he could and saturated a patch of grass about five feet from the house. He lit the match and laid it on the grass. The flame worked its way to the house. A fire started when it reached the house.

Gary ran and dove into the alfalfa field. He watched as the little fire turned into a full blaze. The smoke alarms in the house weren't up to par. The fire reached the roof and started down both sides of the house.

Strikers called the fire department. By the time fire fighters reached the old place, 75 percent of it was gone. Tragedy had struck.

Gary passed the fire truck as he pulled out of Rhodes' parking lot. Mission accomplished.

Sharon woke the next morning and couldn't wait to see if there was news on the strike. Unfortunately, her anticipation was met with disbelief. The story was the centerpiece on 1A. It detailed the blaze, recapped the strike, and memorialized the two victims. She cut out the story and placed it in her suitcase. Sharon, who managed to lose her trailers the previous day, had planned to stay another day, but it was time to leave Columbus behind.

Stenson was convinced he needed to eliminate Sharon due to her affair with Kurt. If any doubt remained in Stenson's mind, Sharon's knowledge of the house fire cemented her fate.

THE ALEXANDERS DIDN'T RECEIVE many special deliveries. The package didn't specify who it was for and was void of a return address. Elaine opened it and couldn't understand why they received a newspaper from Columbus, Ohio.

Mrs. Alexander removed the trash can lid, but Kurt stopped her, asking if he could see the newspaper. Sharon had told him about her visit to Columbus a few years earlier.

It was 1984. The newspaper was dated 1980. Kurt read the paper front to back, including the advertisements and classifieds. He knew it was sent for a reason, but missed it the first time through.

Kurt unfolded 1A again and reread the house fire story. When he read the fourteenth paragraph, it finally hit him.

"She notified us something was going to happen. She never said her name, trying to keep her identity hidden. If she hadn't warned us, we might have lost more than Warren and Jack."

Kurt wondered if the story had something to do with Sharon or perhaps Gary was a fireman, so to speak. He wanted to call Sharon, but knew what could happen. He put the paper in a shoebox in his makeshift room downstairs.

Another package arrived the next morning. Elaine handed it to Kurt when he came in for lunch. He sat at the kitchen table and opened it. The only thing in it was a business card from Stenson's PR firm. Kurt feared someone was on to him. He couldn't imagine leaving Austin.

When the brown truck pulled in the next day, everyone wondered if they should move the country post office to the farm. Kurt stopped the tractor in the field where he was working and jogged to the driveway. Elaine signed for the arrival and handed the package to Kurt. He settled in the front porch swing and opened it like a kid ripping off wrapping paper at Christmas.

It was a photograph of a professional golfer. An autograph was scribbled at the bottom, but Kurt and Elaine couldn't make it out. Kurt took it inside and laid it on the counter. Later that night, Colt was washing up for supper when he saw the picture.

"That's cool. Who sent the autographed photo of Gary Player?"

Elaine looked at Kurt, who understood what was going on. He picked up the photo and walked downstairs. Someone wasn't on to his whereabouts. Sharon was sending the mail. The photograph of Player came from the O'Neil residence in Mesa. The photo was taken from the gallery. Sharon was telling Kurt that Stenson and Gary, not Mr. Player, had something to do with the house fire.

He went upstairs and ate another masterpiece prepared by Elaine. He assured her they were safe, but explained Sharon had discovered something terrible.

The truck showed up a fourth and final day. It was a pamphlet with a scenic picture of the state's capital city. *Home, sweet home* was written in the center of the brochure. Sharon's handwriting made him feel better about the special deliveries.

Kurt was positive she was telling him about Gary and Stenson's involvement in the house fire, but the last piece of mail had him puzzled. He didn't tell anyone in the Alexander house about the meaning of the deliveries from the first three days, but Kurt asked Elaine what she thought about the fourth arrival.

"I think she's telling you she misses Austin and wants to be here."

Kurt couldn't get Elaine's words out of his head the rest of the day. He knew what he needed to do. He was going to Mesa and bringing Sharon back with him, one way or another.

Jim arrived home from a run later that day and tried to talk Kurt out of going.

"You had two close calls and won't be so lucky the next time."

"I have to bring her here."

"Kurt, if Sharon moves here, you know they'll track her down. She's been lucky to have visited as many times as she has. I've stood behind you, but if you go to Mesa, you'll need to find another place to live when you return."

Kurt was hurt by Jim's words, but knew what he had to do. He was going to Mesa no matter who issued ultimatums. When Kurt returned to Austin, Mr. Alexander's ultimatum would be the last thing on their minds.

WORD REACHED STENSON THAT Sharon was in Mesa. She had been in Austin, but it was her last visit. Gary had informed Stenson she was becoming more and more inquisitive about where he was going and what he was involved in. Sharon wanted a reason to leave him. Stenson knew it was time to get rid of Sharon O'Neil.

Stenson told Gary to fly to Indianapolis to track down someone who claimed they knew who started the fire at "The Rhodes House", as it was dubbed by strikers.

No one in Indianapolis, at least to the knowledge of Stenson or Rhodes, knew about the fire. The person was fictitious and Gary spent a frustrating weekend trying to chase a ghost.

The person who knew about the house fire was in Mesa. Sharon was fed up with Gary constantly leaving her and the boys behind. Her feelings regarding the issue and trip to Austin gave her the courage to finally leave Gary. It was time to play her trump card.

Sharon copied the article from *The Dispatch* and sent it to Stenson. A typed note accompanied the story.

Stay away from me and my boys or I'll let everyone, including the police, know how despicable you are.

Stenson knew who it was from. Gary was right. She found the scribbled notes a few years prior and it was coming back to haunt them. He couldn't tell Gary because he didn't want him knowing there was a motive to get rid of Sharon.

Gary left for Indiana on the eve of the golf club party. Ava, who was almost on her last leg, but stubbornly living in Fresno, was in town visiting the family. She was old-fashioned and didn't believe in divorce, but had set aside her moral beliefs and was encouraging Sharon to start a new life. Ava labeled Gary's absence as marital unfaithfulness.

Sharon planned on leaving her boys with their grandmother, but Trevor was being clingy. He didn't want to stay with Ava and was throwing a fit. Sharon decided to take him with her so it would give her a reason to leave the party early and an excuse not to drink.

The teal designer dress Sharon slipped into accentuated every curve on her frame. It went well with the silver stilettos and sparkling diamonds in the necklace, bracelet, and earrings she was wearing. She looked absolutely stunning. Sharon was the most whispered about person every year at the party.

The valet took over for Sharon when she pulled to the front of the club. An attendant met her at the end of the red carpet. He walked her to the door and Sharon notified him that Trevor, dressed in a black suit, would escort her into the ballroom.

As usual, all eyes were on Sharon. The jealous women who usually sneered couldn't help but smile. Trevor looked like a gentleman as he escorted his mother to their seats.

Every year, the party was the same. There was lots of drinking, socializing, gossiping, dancing, and eating, in no particular order. Sharon usually took part in three of the things. She wasn't much of a gossiper. Mrs. O'Neil left that to the catty women who didn't have anything better to do with their time. She also didn't drink, despite constant badgering from many of Mesa's well-known lushes.

Sharon enjoyed the fine meal and dancing with Trevor. Other ladies tried to cut in, but shyness kept him wrapped tightly around his mother's waist.

Mingling was also something Sharon enjoyed, but most of her socializing eventually led to questions about Gary. "What is he up to?" "Where is he?" Once his name started leaking into her conversations, it was time to leave the shindig.

She was the fourth or fifth woman to leave the party. The other women left because they were better suited for an ice cream social at the library. The valet pulled her vehicle to the front entrance and helped Sharon and Trevor get in.

Sharon thanked the gentleman and pulled away from the club. The men were waiting in the parking lot for Sharon. The pursuit began as she pulled through the front gate. Sharon noticed they were being followed within a hundred yards after leaving the club.

Mrs. O'Neil tried not to panic. She didn't want to frighten Trevor. When a second car pulled behind her, she knew they were in trouble. Sharon pulled off the main road because she was deft at handling the area's back roads. It was a costly mistake.

The chase intensified and both cars following Sharon's vehicle were making brazen moves. Trevor screamed uncontrollably as his mother's car was thrust forward from the back bumper being smashed into by their pursuers. Sharon did an admirable job of keeping control of the vehicle, even though they were rammed from behind again and again.

Although the road was winding, the back car sped up past the vehicle directly behind Sharon. It pulled next to Sharon's car and tried forcing her to the side of the road. She held her ground and swerved hard into the side of the car. The demolition derby was interrupted by an oncoming car.

An accident was narrowly avoided. The drivers behind Sharon weren't as bold after the near miss. They waited for a straight stretch and pounced on the opportunity. The second vehicle in the three-car line pulled up to the left side of Sharon's car and the third car used the shoulder on the right to squeeze beside Sharon. She slammed into the right car, but her attempt to send it off the side of the road failed.

Both cars wedged Sharon's vehicle, bringing it to a halt after the straightaway turned into a curve on the top of a hill. The men in the car on the left got out and drew their guns. They surrounded Sharon and Trevor. The car on the right eased past Mrs. O'Neil's vehicle and disappeared. It stopped nearly a mile ahead, blocking the road.

One of the men walked around the car and pulled Trevor out. He pressed the gun against his right temple. Trevor's body shook and almost caused the man to squeeze the trigger.

"Calm down, honey. It will be all right," Sharon said to Trevor.

The back door of the car on the left opened and Stenson stepped onto the pavement. He shook his head. Sharon shrieked in horror.

"Did you really think this was going to end any other way? Get out of the car!"

Sharon unfastened her seat belt and stepped out of the vehicle.

"I didn't mean to threaten you. I want to be left alone and get my children in a safe environment. You know what Gary does and I'm sure that house fire isn't the only crime he's committed for you."

"Your sob story is falling on deaf ears. If you want to know what Gary does, I'll tell you. He takes care of situations...or problems as we call them. He might do things that are wrong, but the good book says a sin is a sin. Let's talk about your sin. You've been running around with Kurt Carson for several years and I know you're still spending time with him. That doesn't qualify you as a Good Samaritan. I know Preston is your son. I know all your dirty little secrets, but I've kept them to myself."

"What about your secrets?"

"I know you were involved in a motel being blown up in Fresno a few years ago and you tried to pin it on me. They found the photo of you and Kurt in a briefcase and you had stuck one of my cards in it to put me at the scene. I'm not above the law, but I passed that test with flying colors."

"Harry…"

"Save your words."

Stenson handed her a bottle of whiskey.

"Drink this until I'm satisfied."

She refused at first, but the gun jammed into the side of Trevor's head made her begin chugging. Sharon drank nearly a fourth of the bottle. Stenson opened the passenger door and put a baggie in the glove box.

"Turn the car so it faces the embankment," Big Boy said to his driver.

"Please don't do this."

"We're not going to hurt Trevor. We'll make sure he's OK."

Stenson put her car in neutral and forced Sharon to get in. She wanted to hug Trevor, but Stenson wouldn't let her. She avoided crying, trying to stay strong for Trevor so he wouldn't be afraid. Stenson backed away from the car and grabbed Trevor. The men pushed the car and as it started moving forward, Sharon stuck her head out the window and looked back.

"His name is Harry Stenson. I love you."

The car teetered over the ledge and raced down the steep incline. Its momentum stopped when it smashed into a tree. Sharon was thrown into the steering column and front window. She was killed on impact.

Trevor yelled "mommy" over and over. Stenson's men got into their vehicle. Big Boy reached into his pocket and placed a note under a rock near the edge of the embankment that read, "You're Next!" He looked down the hill and couldn't see any movement. Flames engulfed the vehicle.

Stenson walked to the car and looked at Trevor's back. Tears streamed down Trevor's face as he looked down at the fiery crash.

"Be a good boy," Stenson said as he got into the car.

They drove from the scene and those in the car ahead saw it was Big Boy and his entourage.

"Did we run into any problems?"

"Not one, sir."

Both cars drove off and a spine-chilling quietness hovered around the area. The only thing that could be heard was the burning car. The faint noise of the crackling fire was interrupted by a speeding vehicle.

Trevor squinted and tilted his head to the right when the headlights hit his face. The man who stepped out of the vehicle was someone he saw a few weeks earlier.

He was afraid of him at the farm, but Trevor's legs couldn't move quickly enough to get to him. Kurt scooped Trevor up and tried comforting him.

Kurt had been in Mesa for a couple hours. He drove to the party and parked in the lot. When he saw Sharon walk out of the club, he exited his car and hoped to reach her before she drove off. She reached the front gate as he waited for cars to pass. He noticed a car tailgating her as they drove down the road that entered the club. Kurt hustled to his car, but lost track of Sharon.

He drove around the vicinity and didn't see Sharon. He backtracked and saw a small county road that branched off the main route. Unfortunately, he was twenty minutes too late.

"Mommy said Harry Stenson and she loved me."

"Your mom does love you and Preston. We'll keep that man's name to ourselves. You can't tell anyone. Do you understand?"

Trevor nodded and said, "Uh-huh."

Kurt put him in the back seat. He buckled him in and they drove all night until reaching Austin.

The Alexander family was shocked when they saw the visitor Kurt had with him. Trevor ran to Jim, but the smiles didn't last long. Overtaken by sorrow, Kurt fell to his knees.

It took nearly an hour for Kurt to calm down. The entire family shed many tears when Kurt told them the details of what happened. Jim Alexander didn't believe in revenge. He was a "turn your other cheek" kind of fellow. The first ounce of hatred he ever felt filled his heart that night and it didn't leave.

Revenge would take place, but it had to wait.

Chapter
Nineteen

GARY WAS SO STARTLED by Trevor's words that he nearly pulled the trigger. Gary shook his head in disbelief while Trevor nodded to let him know he was telling the truth.

"I'm Trevor. Stenson left me at the side of the road the night my mother was murdered."

"You're lying. Why should I believe anything you say?"

"We could go to a hospital and take a blood test or you could ask Kurt Carson."

"He's still alive?"

"Kurt has been in the same place since he left Mesa. He lives on a secluded farm in God's backcountry. He raised me, with helping hands from others. To me, he's my father. I didn't like doing the things I did to you, but revenge has been on my mind for almost twenty-three years. As soon as I saw Stenson jump out of the van near your house...it is the same face I've had nightmares about since my mom's death. I would like nothing more than to see him suffer."

The rustling in the first storage house made Gary temporarily forget about the family reunion, although things discussed throughout the day flashed through his mind. As he lowered the gun to his side, the lights came on. Lauren, Dane, and Ronald were pleased to see the electricity working in the storage house. Preston had become accustomed to living in the dark so it didn't bother him.

Stenson was the only one not standing. One of the three gunshots had struck him in the left side. He was lying on the floor writhing in pain and begging for help. He covered the wound with his right hand as blood trickled between his fingers. Matt called for Savannah and she attended to Stenson while Gary held him at gunpoint.

She had brought a small medical kit with her from the ambulance and used items from it to patch Stenson's wound. Savannah finished bandaging him and Gary forced Big Boy to sit on a chair.

"How was killing Sharon for my own good? Why did you let me think Trevor also died in the crash? He's been alive all these years and was raised by the man Sharon had an affair with. The boy I raised has a brother. Did you know Trevor was alive?"

"I've told you several times, none of us are saints. Each time the briefcase was used, all three of us were involved. Every time a family grieved because of the briefcase, we were the reason that family was destroyed. I kept things from you over the years that I'm not happy about. Rhodes has done things to me as well, but it's benefited us in the best way possible."

"How can you think losing my wife and son is for the best? I know I was an unfaithful husband and a rotten father, but that doesn't mean I didn't love my family. I know some would say, 'that's not love,' but I loved Sharon, Trevor, and Preston."

"If you found out what Sharon was doing, it could have caused major problems. She was ready to leave you and I know how that situation would have played out. Sharon disappeared every few months and took both of the boys with her the last time. I knew she was leaving town to see Kurt. We failed in our attempts to get rid of him. He was going to eventually bring us down, which is what's happening. Our past is catching up to us."

"We're getting what we deserve, but you ruined the lives of my sons. You're going to pay for what you've done," Gary said as he pointed the gun at Stenson. "Everybody get out of here!"

Preston was the only one to disobey Gary's command. His body was frozen. He tried to take a step, but his muscles refused to work.

"Preston, I want everyone to leave this room."

The youngest O'Neil boy stared at the wall in front of him. "Now!"

Everyone standing outside the first storage house jumped. Stenson's body also flinched, but Preston stood like a statue.

Gary walked over to Preston. He latched onto his right arm and tried to nudge him toward the door. Preston wouldn't budge. Gary was irritated, but the tears streaming from Preston's eyes made him relax. His youngest son wasn't making the slightest sound. The tears were quiet and painful. One dropped from his left cheek to the floor, followed by one from his right cheek. A small puddle formed after five minutes.

"Please leave the room," Gary whispered as he put his arm around Preston.

He wanted to grab the gun from his father and put a bullet between Stenson's eyes. His dad would be next. Preston also felt like popping one into his head. Gary's arm around his backside made Preston slightly regain his sanity. For some strange reason, he followed Gary's wishes.

The door closed behind Preston and no one knew what was going to happen inside. Things were very quiet. No one said a word outside the storage house. Mother Nature had waved her wand over the area. The birds weren't chirping and the early evening crickets had fallen silent.

The first gunshot in the storage house interrupted the silence and didn't provide music to anyone's ears. Trevor started to run into the storage house, but Preston grabbed him. A second gunshot caused more uneasiness.

"You know how this needs to end," Gary said, sitting the gun on a chair and sliding it in front of Big Boy. "I'm ending the program. As for Rhodes, I don't know what will happen to him. I have to do the right thing. I'll see you in hell Harry."

The sentiment outside was Stenson took the first bullet and Gary then turned the gun on himself. Everyone wanted to open the door after thirty minutes of inactivity. Trevor kept going back and forth on whether to open the door. He breathed a sigh of relief when the door opened and Gary walked out.

Gary turned and shut the door. He hugged Preston and took a long look at Trevor before handing him the surveillance tapes from inside the room.

"I have to go. All of you could still be in danger, but it's going to end soon. I want everyone to stay out of the storage house."

"Where are you going?" Preston asked.

"I have to take care of business."

Gary walked across the road and started the van. He turned the vehicle around and drove over the railroad tracks, disappearing as he moved further down the trail.

Inside the storage house, Stenson looked at the gun Gary had placed in front of him. Gary had fired two bullets into the couch, leaving Stenson to believe one was in the chamber.

Stenson sat on the couch contemplating what to do. He could save the last bullet and shoot the first person who walked through the door. Big Boy knew assassins were ready to take him out and was scared of what was going to happen. He couldn't stomach the thought of being murdered. Turning himself in was an option, but he didn't want any part of living behind bars.

The option in front of him was the best solution to his problems. Stenson thought about taking his life in his private study when he received the tape, but loved himself too much. However, things had changed. Stenson knew what was in store for him in the after world. Taking his life wouldn't change his fate.

He reached for the gun and ran his fingers up and down the barrel. He began sobbing uncontrollably as he placed the barrel in his mouth. The taste of the weapon made him think of the lives he helped ruin. Gary was right. The three of them were rotten people and would burn in Hades' most evil section.

Stenson's hand trembled as he gained enough courage to flex his index finger. He finally calmed down and closed his eyes. He inhaled as deeply as he could and pulled the trigger.

IT TOOK SOME TIME for Kurt and the Alexander family to become accustomed to having Trevor stay with them. They were nervous about having unexpected visitors dropping by the farm and Trevor's presence made it worse.

They figured Gary would show up in the driveway someday. Jim often thought he would take a bullet from a sniper while plowing or mowing one of the fields. He looked over his shoulder every time he was on the road. Things nearly got the best of him on several occasions. He and Elaine discussed the idea of dismissing Kurt and Trevor from the farm. Thoughts of Sharon kept them from doing it. They loved Sharon and missed her as much as Kurt did.

They decided Trevor needed to remain on the farm as long as possible. It meant keeping him at the house on Sunday mornings. Jim asked for forgiveness each time he stepped foot in Calvary, but knew God understood. Kurt rarely left the farm, except to visit Cy Harper's store and to attend Sunday morning service every few weeks. Kurt became more of a hermit once Trevor lived with him in Austin.

Members of the congregation frowned at his frequent absences, but Kurt fabricated a story about a sickness that had the area's best doctors puzzled. Kurt eventually told Doc Badnarik the truth and he fibbed when necessary.

Elaine wouldn't allow Trevor to stay with them unless he was home schooled. She taught him most of what he knew. The Parson family knew Trevor was staying with the Alexanders. They tried to keep his stay as quiet as they could. Word eventually leaked, but not for a couple years.

Jim, who had retired from driving across the country, took the same rifle from the Halloween scare off his gun rack when children services showed up in his driveway.

"Get off my property," he said, pointing the gun at case workers.

"We're here to talk to you about the boy."

"You'll have to bring Sheriff Mulvaney and a few deputies with you. That boy isn't going anywhere until I see papers. I'm giving you fifteen seconds to vanish. If you're not gone before I open my eyes, I'm decorating the side of your car."

Arguing wouldn't get the case workers anywhere. They buckled up and the man driving spun gravel as he sped off. Jim actually reached fifteen and could see the backend of the vehicle, but had made his point.

The next day, the gentlemen returned to Mr. Alexander's driveway. They were escorted by a pair of cruisers, including one driven by Sheriff Mulvaney. Jim walked onto his front porch with a shotgun in hand.

Sheriff Mulvaney got out of his cruiser and tried defusing the situation. He looked at his deputies and shook his head as if to say, "Keep your guns in your holsters."

"Jim, we don't want trouble. They're here to find out about the boy. Let them in to discuss the matter. I know you're not going to use that weapon, so put it on the porch railing and we'll be on our way."

Jim and the sheriff had known each other for years. In fact, Colt had settled down and married Mr. Mulvaney's middle daughter. They lived on a farm a few miles down the road.

"With all due respect, I'll use this weapon if I have to. I want them to leave us alone."

"Once they get answers, this will be over."

Jim swung open the front door and held his hand out, inviting everyone to step inside. The case workers had a stack of folders and nervously sat them on the kitchen table. Kurt and Elaine joined Jim. Sheriff Mulvaney, who shook Jim's hand and gave Elaine a hug when he walked in the house, told his deputies to stay outside. He leaned against the wall in the kitchen to keep an eye on things.

"Where is the boy?"

"He's not here," Jim answered.

"That's obvious. Where is he?"

"He's staying with relatives."

"We need to know the location of the boy, where his parents are, and who he is."

"I'm his father," Kurt said. "He's twelve and smarter than the five of us sitting here. I moved to Austin several years ago when my first wife died. She and our daughter didn't make it through child birth. The boy was staying with my fiancé back west. She was like his real mother and he needed that presence in his life. When the opportunity presented itself to work here on the Alexander farm, I left Matt with her. They visited every other month."

The case workers looked at each other with disbelief.

"You can ask anyone around these parts. Go and interview every member at Calvary Baptist. They've seen him before. When my fiancé and I split, I brought Matt here with me. I didn't want him in schools down here, so I have him home schooled by Mrs. Alexander. I hope that clears everything up and you'll leave us alone."

"We'd like to speak with Matt and run some tests on him."

"What kind of tests?" Elaine asked.

"It's nothing against you or the people in this house, but we have standard procedures we have to follow. When are you expecting him to return?"

"He'll be back early next week."

"Then we'll plan on meeting you here a week from today at 10:00 a.m. Please have the boy here so we can resolve this situation."

The case workers left paperwork with Kurt and the Alexanders to fill out before their next engagement. The men left the house when the impromptu meeting adjourned. Sheriff Mulvaney waved his two deputies to go on about their business and he stayed behind.

"We need your help," Jim said to the sheriff.

"I don't know what I can do. I understand Trevor is part of this family. Jolene and Colt look at him as their boy. You have been careful about where Trevor is allowed to go and where you take him. Kurt, I've told everyone who asks about him that he is your son. I'm not sure I can keep children services out of this."

"Do you think they'll go to Colt's farm looking for Trevor?" Jim asked.

"They could. The only way I've been involved in something like this is escorting children services to take a child out of a home. Had he been here today, that is what would have happened. I could lose everything I've worked so hard to achieve if they find out I know Trevor is staying with Colt and Jolene."

"Would you take him to your house for a while?" Elaine asked Sheriff Mulvaney.

"Maybe for a couple of your homemade pies," he joked to ease the tension. "You know I can't do that. My advice is to let them take Trevor or you have to go on the run Kurt."

Although Mr. Carson was accustomed to farm life, he still caught himself staring at motorists who moved slowly down the road.

Gunshots from area hunters or from farmers shooting at varmints still caused him to duck for cover. He had resided in Austin with the Alexanders for nearly ten years and never ran into trouble from his past. No matter how secure Kurt was on the farm, he always felt like he was on the run.

"Taking Trevor elsewhere isn't an option. I've been running for almost ten years, so why would I want to leave here and do the same thing I've been doing? This is my home. The Alexanders are my family and I'm not going anywhere. I believe God wants me here."

Kurt got up from the table, walked to the kitchen window, and stared outside for several minutes before finishing what he had to say.

"They're not taking Trevor from me. I'll figure something out. I can't let him go back to his father in Mesa or wherever he lives. At least Trevor has a fighting chance at making something of his life. I'm not so sure about Preston. It's difficult knowing another man is raising my son while I'm raising his boy. You try waking up to that thought each morning. I pray every day that Preston is all right, but I know Sharon is looking over him and I have to do the same for Trevor. She'd want me to do my best to keep him from growing up around Gary, who didn't do much with the boys anyway."

When Kurt finished, Jim and Elaine were wiping away tears. Sheriff Mulvaney, as tough as he could be at times, was also moved.

"I understand your position, but you have to understand mine. You have to let them take Trevor if you don't want to run. I'm not trying to be heartless, but it's as simple as that."

Kurt took a seat at the kitchen table and stared at the carvings in it. Jim stood up after several minutes of waiting for Kurt to say something. Jim walked Sheriff Mulvaney to the front door while Elaine grabbed Kurt's hands.

"It's going to be OK. We're going to figure out a way to keep Trevor here."

Kurt heard Sheriff Mulvaney pull out of the driveway, but continued staring at the table as a million thoughts ran through his mind. Elaine was drained after trying to get Kurt to say something for two hours. She excused herself from the table and left Kurt alone.

As dinnertime rolled around, Kurt was still in the same spot. Although the old pizza shop had changed hands a few times since Kurt's first visit to Austin, it was still open. Elaine decided to order pizza.

Jim returned with a couple pies and sat them on the kitchen table. Tyler and Chelsea, who was the last Alexander child left in high school, strolled into the house.

"What's up foreigner?" Tyler said while slapping Kurt on the back.

Tyler and Kurt often traded playful barbs, but Kurt wasn't in a joking mood.

Everyone loaded their plates and left Kurt alone at the table. After Elaine finished, she tried to get Kurt to eat. He gently shook his head no and continued burning a hole through the table.

Throughout the evening, Jim and Elaine tried to talk to Kurt. Tyler attempted a few more jokes, but their permanent visitor was about to go AWOL. A little before midnight, Elaine turned off all the lights in the house except for a small one above the kitchen sink.

"Good night," she said as she patted Kurt on the back.

He waited for another hour and got up from the table. He packed a small suitcase for Trevor and gathered some of his things from the basement. He wrote a short note to the family. He placed it on the table and walked out to the vehicle he used at the farm.

Kurt drove to Colt and Jolene's farm and knocked on their door. Colt grabbed his .45 out of the nightstand and peered through the blinds in the bathroom. His nervousness passed once he saw Kurt.

"What are you doing here at this time of night?"

"Children services will be here looking for Trevor soon. They visited the farm again today. We were able to hide him here for a few days, but our luck is about to run out."

"Where are you taking him?"

"Somewhere he hasn't been for a long time."

Colt helped Kurt rustle a cranky Trevor out of bed.

"We have to go. The case workers were back again today and they want to send you to your father."

"I'm not going," Trevor said as he closed his eyes.

Colt picked Trevor up and slung him over his shoulder like a bag of feed. He put him in the car and gave Kurt a lengthy embrace.

"Keep in touch."

"I left a note at the house."

"Take care."

Kurt hopped in the truck and drove off.

NO ONE WANTED TO step inside the first storage house. The group standing outside knew what kind of scene waited inside. They didn't want to stay at the warehouse, so they locked the door and drove up the hill to Ronald's house.

Preston couldn't believe how close Ronald lived to the warehouse.

"Have you always lived up here?"

"After Robert moved everything to Cincinnati, this is where I belonged. The ground that once housed the Rhodes Tire and Rubber Company is cursed. I've always felt vindicated because Robert got exactly what he deserved after conning our father into giving him everything. Once this development was under construction, I was compelled to move here. Every time I drive by the old warehouse, I hear my father's voice telling me my brother will pay for what he's done. It took me a long time to drive past it without thinking about the people who died because of Robert or thinking about how differently things would have been if I had been involved. I can finally drive by it knowing the end is near for my brother."

"You knew what was going on before Trevor contacted you?" Lauren asked.

"I've known all along. Just like everyone else, I heard rumors, but I knew what kind of person my brother was. I'm certain the whispers around town were more than gossip. A chance encounter solidified my opinion. A man stopped me on the street one day and told me, 'You're gonna rot in hell.' I told the man I was Robert's twin and he apologized after realizing I wasn't the wretched man he thought. We ended up going into a small eatery and discussed things for several hours. The man's name was Steve Birch."

They pulled into his driveway and Ronald finished the story.

"While we were talking, I saw a man taking pictures of the eatery from across the street. He looked like a run of the mill tourist and I didn't think twice about it. Four days later, I read Mr. Birch's obituary in *The Dispatch*. I received a letter at our old house and the gist of it told me to stay out of my brother's affairs. I became a recluse after the letter. All I thought about was what my brother was doing to people and how God could let him do those things."

Ronald opened his door, got out, and peered into the car.

"I quit my job and spent most of my days looking out the windows of our home. When the announcement was made about the move to Cincinnati, we purchased a lot and have lived here since. I've never felt safe up here and I only go out when I have to, but surviving cancer makes you appreciate being alive. I'm not sure why God dealt me bad cards, but I know I'll have a lot more than my brother does when it's all said and done."

Ronald's words captivated his four visitors. Trevor was impressed. He couldn't sense an ounce of bitterness in Ronald's voice. Revenge had been in Trevor's heart for years. "Let God dish out the punishment" is the stance he should have taken.

They entered Ronald's home and his wife greeted their visitors. They walked into the living room and began talking about the situation. Each of them was tied to the story in different ways, but hoped it would soon be over.

If Gary had anything to do with it, the situation would be resolved soon.

Gary reached his home, drove down the cobblestone drive, and got out of the van. Mr. O'Neil had assigned Mathias (four), Zeek (eight), and Luc (six) to Stenson, but needed to route them to the warehouse. He put all three numbers back on the board and drove to the apartment. Gary sat at the kitchen table waiting for each man to arrive.

Mathias passed Zeek coming out of the post office and they gave each other a strange look. When Mathias brushed past Luc outside, he knew they were the other assassins. He recalled seeing them at the meeting at Stenson & Rhodes.

Zeek wasn't surprised to find the post office box empty. Luc walked in and noticed Zeek peering into an empty box. He gave the man a puzzled look and Zeek nodded. They both knew where they had seen the other man before. They didn't know whether to draw weapons or race to the apartment. An incident was avoided as both went their separate ways.

Mathias opened the front door to the apartment. He was startled when he saw Gary smoking at the table.

"Relax! I'm not here to hurt you. We have some business to discuss. Have a seat on the couch. We'll wait for our other visitors."

Luc arrived next. He noticed a light on in the apartment and knew it must be the man he passed on the sidewalk outside the post office. The assassin darted down the side of another house and crept up to the kitchen window. He looked through the curtains and saw a man sitting at the table and another seated on the couch. He gently tapped the window and Gary ordered Mathias to open the front door.

Number six walked around to the porch and joined the twosome. They waited nearly twenty minutes before Zeek showed up. He wasn't as cautious as Luc. Zeek strutted to the front door. Mr. O'Neil was waiting for him. Gary opened it and invited him in.

"As you know, the last assignment you received was Harry Stenson," he said to the three men sitting on the couch. "He was and still is your assignment. You know where he works and what he does. The problem is you're not going to find him. He is at the old Rhodes Tire and Rubber Company. If you go there, he'll be in the first storage house. The first to find the place and bring me back Stenson's head is the winner."

They were bewildered and looked at Gary while waiting for further instructions. Gary was done talking. Mathias jumped up and raced out the door. Zeek and Luc remained on the couch, but quickly realized Mathias had a head start.

Gary watched the last two pull out of their spaces on the street. He went to the bedroom and took the briefcase out of the register. Gary placed a map in it and hid what would be the last folder in the compartment. He tucked the briefcase back into its spot and turned off the lights.

Gary sped off for Route 23. He had left the chain unhooked so he could drive through the entrance quickly when he arrived. He got out of the van, walked across the muddy path, and reattached the chain.

Mr. O'Neil drove to the back of the ancient facility and parked on the right side of the warehouse. He didn't want his vehicle to be seen. He went inside, hustled up a flight of half-missing stairs, and took a spot where he could see the storage houses. The show was about to begin.

Matthias' head start seemed to pay off as he was the first to pull up to the warehouse. He parked his car near the gate and looked around for several minutes. He scanned every building, deciding the place was a dump while doing so, but couldn't see the barrel pointed at him through one of many small openings in the side of the warehouse. Gary was watching every move he made through the scope on the rifle aimed at his chest.

Matthias walked out of Gary's sight and found the opening in the fence near the railroad tracks. He cautiously went into the warehouse and glanced around. Number four walked past the room where Preston had been locked up and saw the bed. Matthias took mental notes. Every few seconds, he checked his backside, as if expecting a sneak attack. He snooped around in the old break room and didn't see anything that concerned him.

The old creaky stairs were tempting, but Matthias decided to pass. He wasn't interested in what the second floor had to offer. He walked outside and started across the road to the first storage house. The bullet ripped through his right shoulder blade. Mathias did a one-eighty and fell to his back in pain. He reached for his gun, but a second and third bullet ended his movements. Gary rushed down to his body. He checked his pulse to verify his work. Gary struggled to drag the heavy corpse into the second storage house. Once he got him inside, Gary laid Mathias near the makeshift stage he sat on a few days earlier.

As he opened the door, he heard an approaching car. Gary wanted to get rid of the car parked at the entrance, but it was too late. Luc had found the warehouse and noticed the car sitting near the security check-in building. As he attempted to turn around, Zeek slammed his vehicle into the side of Luc's car. The pile up would have wowed any county fair audience.

Luc was nearly unconscious. His head had crashed through the window on the driver's side and his face was carved like a turkey.

He also had multiple broken ribs. He was in serious pain, but Zeek was about to end his misery. The impact broke Zeek's collarbone, but he unbuckled his seat belt and gingerly opened the door. He limped to the driver's side and looked in. Luc's head was against the head rest and his mouth was wide open. He barely rolled his eyes at Zeek before the bullet entered the center of his forehead.

Zeek walked along the fence line behind the storage houses and climbed to the top. The old razor wire had deteriorated and was easy to cut. He made his way over the top and hobbled to the first storage house. The lock presented a small problem, but a bullet could take care of that. He drew his gun, but Gary was in his spot on the second floor. He took aim at number eight and put the bullet in the back of Zeek's right leg. He instantly fell to the ground in agony.

Zeek pulled himself against the building. He tightly held his gun, but it wasn't a match for Gary's rifle. Mr. O'Neil put a second bullet just above Zeek's heart. The third assassin was dead. Gary gathered the shells from the gun and ran down the stairs, which caved in as he neared the bottom. He lay choking in the dust and splintered two-by-fours. He felt like he had been in a train wreck. Gary picked himself up from the rubble and limped to the first storage house.

Gary laid the rifle next to number eight and grabbed the gun from Zeek's hand. He shot off the lock and carefully opened the door. Stenson looked at Gary as he stepped into the storage house.

"You have to help me. I'm not going to make it."

Gary noticed blood seeping through the bandages. Stenson had lost a lot of blood and the couch was soaked.

"I tried to shoot myself with the gun you left, but there weren't any bullets in the chamber."

"I know. I took the last one out before I handed you the gun. I wanted you to suffer as much as possible. I've done your dirty work all these years and it's over now. I'll let you do the job this time. This bullet has your name on it."

Gary laid the gun on the floor and kicked it toward Stenson before he walked out. He surveyed the scene and hurried back to the van. He nearly ramped over the railroad tracks and heard sirens in the distance. O'Neil saw three cruisers race by on Route 23 and waited until it was clear. He sped to the entrance and took down the chain. He turned left onto Route 23 and drove to his home in Upper Arlington.

The paper arrived at Ronald Rhodes' mailbox the next morning. He was an early riser and had read the article three or four times before his guests meandered into the kitchen.

"Check this out."

They took turns reading the story. Three men had been shot and killed in an apparent shootout. The identities of the men were not known at press time, but the name of a fourth victim was well received news from many who read *The Dispatch* that morning. All of Ronald's guests read the sixth paragraph of the story and smiled.

A fifty-six-year-old man identified as Harry Stenson apparently died from a self-inflicted wound.

They didn't know Gary killed the assassins, but they had their suspicions. They also wondered if Gary shot Stenson before he exited the storage house, but vowed not to say a word about what happened. All agreed Gary was a worthless soul, but he was trying to put a stop to the briefcase program and the wrong they had caused, despite using murderous ways to do so.

The story was also read at another Rhodes' household, but the news wasn't as pleasing. The article brought up a lot of old haunts. It talked about the strike in the early 80s and the house fire. The journalist's narrative also provided details about the contaminated water samples, buyouts, and mysterious deaths of several employees that had worked at the Rhodes Tire and Rubber Company. The Hayes Carlson Company, aluminum factory, and Vandervort Tire Industries were also mentioned in the history section of the story. The piece of writing was rubbish in Robert's opinion. He wanted to barge into the newsroom at *The Dispatch* and strangle the journalist. Maybe the briefcase could be used one final time.

Robert couldn't believe what had happened. Stenson was dead and he hadn't heard from Gary in days. He wanted to ignore everything, but felt something strange was going on. Robert knew he would face a slew of questions from cops and would be under the microscope for several weeks or even months.

Rhodes needed to let things die down, but couldn't forget about what happened at the warehouse. He knew O'Neil was involved and that he was probably Gary's next target. Robert needed to eliminate him. The only problem was Gary still had four more assassins at his disposal. Robert thought about things the rest of the morning and came up with a game plan he hoped would serve him well.

Chapter Twenty

THEY ONLY STOPPED TO fill up on gas and get food. Kurt wanted to get to Fresno as soon as possible. Ava hadn't seen Trevor in a few years and thought he died in the crash that killed Sharon. Ava wasn't in the best condition when Sharon was alive and Kurt knew she would be worse.

Her health nosedived after receiving the news about her daughter and grandson. Ava suffered a severe stroke and the left side of her face was paralyzed. She also walked with a limp and kept her left arm tucked closely against her body.

After taking Trevor to Austin, Kurt avoided contact with Ava for nearly three years. He ended his silence a year earlier when he sent her a postcard. He didn't put a return address on it because he knew he was taking a risk. Stenson had her house under observation for eighteen months, but declared, "No one is in contact with the old hag."

Ava was too feeble to get out much. She stopped her weekly visits to the senior center and wasn't able to go to church, due to the large steps in front she couldn't navigate. Her trips to the beauty parlor were also cut back. There wasn't a reason to get her blue hair hived up every week, so she went every third week.

She didn't have many visitors. One of the widowed church deacons stopped by the first few months after Ava became a shut-in, but she felt the old pervert wasn't as concerned about spreading the gospel as he was with trying to get a little loving from her. The postman was her only regular contact with the outside world.

Sharon's mother had become a loner. The crops in her back yard kept her alive. She wanted to give up her fight for life after the stroke. Ava saw visions of Sharon waving her onward to heaven, but who would take care of her vegetables? Seeing her crops grow and blossom each spring through the early autumn was keeping her going. Her doctor recommended she quit gardening, but Ava merely downsized and figured that was obeying his orders.

Kurt pulled onto South Poppy Avenue and thought of the little boy he employed a few years earlier. Reminiscing brought a smile to his face, but he couldn't help but wonder if someone was staking out Ava's house, which was still yellow with a green porch. The paint on the house was peeled back and the porch had turned into a mint shade of green. Kurt was sure she was in violation of a city ordinance, but so was half of South Fresno.

He parked the car and told Trevor to stay put.

"I know where we are."

"I figured you would when we pulled up to the house."

"I'll be back in a minute or two."

Kurt walked to the porch and opened the front screen door. He knocked loudly because he figured Ava's hearing wasn't good. He heard rustling inside, but wasn't sure if Sharon's mother was coming to the door. Kurt waited two minutes and knocked again.

"I'm coming. Be patient."

The door opened and Ava squinted at Kurt.

"Wait while I put on my glasses."

Her bifocals didn't help Ava recognize Kurt. They had spoken on the phone, but never in person.

"Hello, Ava. I'm Kurt."

She wanted to throw open the door as quickly as she could, but wasn't a spring chicken. Ava unlatched the hook on the screen door. Kurt stepped inside and she put her arm around him while weeping. Kurt tried containing his tears, but all he could think about was

Sharon and Preston. Ava used her cane to slowly walk to the coffee table and grab a small box of tissues.

"I'm all right."

"It's OK. I own stock in Kleenex and don't tell me you're fine. I can see through that lie. I know you hurt as much as I do. This pain will last until I die. Have a seat on the couch. I have something to show you."

"I also have something to show you."

Kurt hurried to the car to get Trevor. They walked across Poppy and strolled up to Ava's front door.

"Wait a second," Kurt said to Trevor.

Ava had disappeared to retrieve the item she wanted to show Kurt and wasn't in the living room. Kurt opened the door and told Trevor to sit on the couch.

Trevor's grandmother exited her bedroom carrying a small urn. Kurt knew what it was. He watched Ava struggle to get down the hallway. Kurt walked back and took the urn from underneath her right arm, which she was also using to maneuver the cane.

Kurt clutched Ava's left arm and helped her get to the living room. Ava turned the corner and saw a boy sitting on her couch. Ava had lost most of her vision from the stroke and could only make things out clearly up to five feet in front of her.

"Stand up and say hello to your grandmother."

"Is that you, Preston?"

"No."

"Then who is it?"

"It's me grandma. It's Trevor."

Ava started trembling. A second stroke was minutes away unless Kurt could calm her. He and Trevor put her arms around their necks and helped her to the couch. Kurt second guessed whether he should have made the trip.

It took nearly an hour before Ava relaxed. Kurt gave Trevor's grandmother her medication and propped her comfortably on the couch. Trevor knelt down on the floor beside Ava, holding her hand.

"I thought he was dead. How did he make it through the crash?"

Kurt described what happened to Sharon and how Trevor survived the ordeal. He explained Sharon warned him about what was going on and that was why he was in Mesa the night she was killed. He told Ava about Stenson and how her house was being watched because of the affair. Kurt apologized. He showed her articles detailing his house explosion and the house fire in Columbus. He told her about Gary and the things he was caught up in. Kurt could have gone on and on—his time with Jim and Colt Alexander had turned him into a yapper—but Ava eventually stopped him.

"Preston is doing OK. I see him once a year and Gary calls the first Saturday of every month. That's a picture of him on the mantle."

Kurt looked at the picture and was joined by an inquisitive Trevor.

"I'd like to see him again," Kurt said.

"Not here. Gary brings him to South Fresno every year for a weekend as soon as school lets out. He won't let Preston stay with me. They stay in a hotel, despite my pleas. Someone should tell Gary that Trevor is alive. He should be raising him and you should be raising Preston."

"I know things are messed up. Ask Trevor what he wants to do."

"Would you like to see your father?"

"I'm sitting beside him. I may call him Kurt, but he's my dad."

His words were convincing. Ava wanted to argue, but knew Trevor and Preston should both be raised by Kurt.

"Ava, I have a proposition for you. I want you to live with us."

"I can't do that."

"And what good reason can you give me?"

"I have a house to take care of and I won't leave my crops behind."

"Your house is paid off and, where we're going, you'll have a garden."

"Sharon continually encouraged me to leave South Fresno. If I wouldn't do it for her, do you think I'll do it for you?"

"I'm not asking you to do it for me. I'm asking you to do it for him," Kurt said as he tousled Trevor's hair.

"What about my visits with Preston? Gary will find me and then you'll be in danger again."

"If you come with us, contact with Gary and Preston will have to end."

"I can't do that."

"Then the State of Texas will place Trevor in a home until he can be reunited with Gary."

"How do you know that will happen?"

"That's the reason we're here. Children services showed up at the farm looking for Trevor. Mr. Alexander pointed a shotgun at them and they left without incident. They showed up the next day with the sheriff and two deputies. Fortunately, Trevor was staying with Mr. Alexander's son when they showed up or they would have taken him. You have a choice. You can stay here and Trevor will be turned over to Gary or you can go with us and help raise him."

"If I stay here, Gary will get custody of Trevor and I'll get to see both of my grandsons every year. That sounds like a better option."

"It does if you want a ruthless hit man raising your grandsons. He's not only an assassin, but he's also best friends with the man who had your daughter murdered. What's to say he wasn't part of it? I think having him raise one of your grandsons is bad enough."

"If I do come with you, where are we going?"

"I won't tell you until I'm certain you're going with us. I have to protect the family we live with. If I told you, you could tell Gary. I won't take that risk."

"What will we do with my house?"

"We'll take care of that. Do you want to come with us or not?"

"Sharon would never tell me where she was visiting, but told me I would love it there. I'm not going to live much more than a few years. Maybe it's time to get out and see the country."

Kurt thought it would take more convincing, but Ava was already trying to get to her feet. She wanted to pack her things before she changed her mind.

Kurt drove to a local grocery store to get boxes. He then stopped by a rental company and leased a small U-Haul trailer to pull behind his vehicle.

They spent the rest of the day boxing Ava's belongings—there weren't many because she had donated most to charitable organizations—and packing the trailer. Kurt also called the utility companies and canceled services to the property on South Poppy.

Kurt was dressed and waiting for Ava, who was also an early riser. Kurt's internal alarm clock was based on shuffling cows in and out of a milk barn. He had been sitting on the couch since 5:00 a.m. and it was six-thirty when Ava got up. Kurt woke Trevor and they pulled out of South Fresno an hour later.

Before her stroke, it would have taken captivity to get Ava out of South Fresno. She wasn't kicking and screaming, but Kurt knew she wasn't thrilled about leaving the only place she had ever known.

"Are you ready to find out where we're going?"

"Just wake me when we get there."

Ava laid her head back. It didn't take long before she was dreaming of the land she left behind.

Kurt smiled as he looked in the rearview mirror and saw her sleeping. He thought of Sharon on the Greyhound when they traveled to Austin the first time.

THE MAILMAN BARELY HAD enough time to pull away each morning before Helen Rhodes opened the mailbox to see what was inside. She sifted through a few pieces of junk mail and a bill or two before discovering the mysterious correspondence. She eagerly ripped open the envelope in the driveway, braving the brisk morning air.

The check fell out as she opened the letter and somersaulted through the air before landing on the ground. Helen picked it up. She was astonished at the amount. She wanted to know why her brother-in-law sent them $250,000.

Dear Ronald,

I know I've been a terrible brother over the years. I always tried to steal the spotlight from you when we were growing up and my intentions usually worked. You did things the right way while I cut corners and used as many people as I could to get where I wanted to go in life. My wickedness was never more evident than the day I took what was rightfully yours from our father. I think about him every day. I don't expect you to forgive me. I wouldn't forgive you if the same thing happened to me.

I'm in deep trouble. I'm afraid I'm not going to be around much longer. I want to apologize to the man who is supposed to be my equal, but is twice the man I am. I would have sent more money, but as I said, trouble is lurking. I hope you can accept the gift and my sincere apology. I would like to talk to you in person, but I know that's asking a lot. Take care, Ronald. Despite what you think, I love you.

Robert

Helen bent over a second time after reading the letter, but it wasn't to pick something up. She was overtaken by emotions. Ronald and their guests were eating breakfast when he realized it had taken Helen longer than usual to get the mail.

He excused himself from the table and walked to the bay window in the front room. Ronald saw Helen crouched over and thought something was wrong. He barged out the front door and ran to his wife's side.

"What's wrong? Are you all right?"

She slowly lifted her hand and softly shook the letter. Ronald took it from her and read it. Their house was the first one on the left in the development. When he finished the letter, Ronald walked down the driveway and took a right.

"Where are you going?"

Ronald didn't answer her. He walked nearly fifty yards until he could see the warehouse. Tears began to flow when he looked at the decomposing place. He thought of his father and what he'd want him to do. The way Ronald handled the situation proved his character. He never once thought about the figures his brother scribbled on the check. Had the roles been reversed, Robert would have been sitting across from a banker.

The youngest twin—Ronald was born seventeen minutes after Robert—wasn't worried about money. His resentment toward his brother throughout the years wasn't due to missing out on his share of the family fortune. He wanted to be part of keeping their father's legacy intact. In many ways, his brother ruined their surname.

Ronald was startled by Helen's touch.

"What are you thinking about?"

"I know we've talked about the situation a million times, but it's hard to look down this hill and not think about my dad. I know he'd want me to talk to Robert. He always told me, 'Ronald, family is all you have.' He was right, but Robert isn't family. He claims to be a Rhodes, but he isn't. He proved that the day he backstabbed me and our father. He decided he was better than us and would do anything to make a name for himself. He did that, but look where he's at now."

"You say you don't want to see him, but deep down, you want your brother back."

"I do. I want it to be the way it was when we were kids. Things changed during our junior year in high school. He replaced me with other friends and replaced them with best friends. He looked up the ladder and did anything to get to the top. He always looked for attention while I sat in the shadows. We are identical twins, but there's nothing identical about our personalities. I didn't mind that. I was good with numbers and schoolwork came first. Robert was good at football and having a good time came first. I don't know if the first sixteen years of our lives means anything to him or not. I know the last forty haven't."

"I don't think you should see him. Even though you have a lot of questions you'd like answered, I think it's best to keep him out of your life."

"I do have things I want answered. You know the biggest question I have for him. Maybe he'll answer it and maybe he won't. I'd like to ask him...why?"

"We've lived here in peacefulness and you've been a lot better since we made the move. What will happen if you don't get the answers you're looking for?"

"I know I won't hear what I want to hear. He won't call himself a coward, a cheat, a liar...that he ruined his twin brother's life by his own greediness."

"Let's go inside and think things over."

"There's nothing to think about. I'm going to see Robert."

Helen and Ronald walked back to their house. He stopped his wife before they opened the front door.

"How much did he send?"

"Two hundred fifty thousand," Helen said with wide eyes.

"Take it to the bank and open an account in your name."

"Why? I can't do that."

"Don't ask questions. I don't mean this disrespectfully, but do as you're told. I want you to go there right now."

"You sound like your brother."

"It's not the money I'm worried about. I'm concerned about you."

"Is something going to happen to you?"

"That's a question. Do you remember what I said a few seconds ago?"

"Please tell me you're going to be all right."

"I'm going to be all right."

He pulled his wife close and kissed her on the cheek.

"Everything is going to be OK."

THEY DIDN'T HAVE LEIS, but everyone gathered to give hugs and handshakes as Kurt turned the car off in the driveway. Ava was amazed at their excitement.

She slept three-fourths of the trip, but was awake when they reached the road between the Alexander's land and Mr. Parson's property.

"Where are we?"

"Officially, you're in Texas Hill Country. Unofficially, you're in Austin, Texas. There's actually a city name, but I've never heard anyone call it that. I only hear it called Austin and that's where I proudly say I'm from."

"Is this where Sharon used to visit when she left Mesa?"

"Yes. She loved it here just as much as I do, if not more."

Ava's vision was distorted. Picasso would have painted some interesting pictures of the farm looking through her eyes. She could see outlines of the house and the barn in front of their vehicle. She imagined expansive fields behind the barn and noticed the shimmering of what appeared to be a small pond down a bank at the side of their house. Kurt couldn't wait for her to see Elaine's garden and rose bushes.

Kurt got out and walked around the back of the vehicle. Jim met Kurt and helped him get Ava out of the back seat.

"Welcome to our farm Mrs. Talbot. I'm Jim Alexander."

"Thank you," Ava said while leaning forward to study the features of Jim's face. "I'm not trying to be rude. My vision isn't all that good. I can only see about five feet in front of me. Everything past that point is basically a blur."

Elaine and Chelsea walked closer so Ava could see them as well. Tyler, who was wrestling with Trevor in the yard, wasn't as worried about an introduction.

"I'm Elaine, Jim's wife, and this is our daughter Chelsea."

"I hear Trevor roughhousing with someone. Who is it?"

"That's our middle child. His name is Tyler. We also have an older son. His name is Colt. He'll be over with his wife Jolene later tonight."

"I hear you have a garden for me to tend. May I see it?"

"I'd be glad to show it to you."

Elaine helped Ava saunter to the side of the house. Ava saw blurred outlines of where the past season's crops had grown. A smile radiated from her face as she walked closer.

"I can't wait to help you."

"I know you'd like to help, but I have different ideas."

"Kurt told me I was going to be able to help. Are you telling me because I need a cane to get around...you think I won't be able to help?"

"I didn't mean it that way Mrs. Talbot."

"Please, call me Ava."

"I'll do that, but the children will call you Miss Ava. That's old-fashioned southern manners."

"That will be fine."

"I have eight rows of crops and they stretch about forty feet. My idea is that I'd like to give you the last two rows to grow whatever you'd like. I also raise rose bushes and want you to have a section to take care of and distribute however you'd like."

Ava's feistiness quickly turned to humility.

"I'd like that Mrs. Alexander."

"Well, let's get you inside. I'm sure y'all are ready to eat. I cooked up a little something for you. And please, call me Elaine."

Kurt and Jim walked behind the ladies. Kurt shook his head laughing at Elaine's comment. Elaine's a little something was enough to feed the entire population in the Texas Hill Country.

They went inside and ate Elaine's "a little something." Like Sharon, Ava was fond of Elaine and she felt the same about Mrs. Talbot. They talked about gardening until the men got bored and went to the barn.

Colt and Jolene eventually showed up. Ava was like her daughter because she also made Colt blush.

"You're a very handsome man and you're a pretty girl."

They sat at the kitchen table telling stories about Trevor and Preston. For the first time, Ava wished she would have left Fresno years ago. She was on her last leg in Fresno, but being in Austin made her feel alive again. In Fresno, besides her gardening, all she did was watch TV and feel sorry for herself. She was more active since her move to Austin. The strength in her left side was improving daily and her cane was becoming a fashion accessory.

Elaine and Ava were outside in the garden getting ready for the rapidly approaching planting season. While Kurt was in Fresno, children services made a surprise visit. They discovered Kurt and the boy left town, thus nullifying the scheduled visit they were supposed to have.

Jim and Elaine thought the issue had been dropped since Kurt wasn't around, but word spread that he and Trevor were back in town.

"I'll be right back," Elaine said to Ava.

"I'd like you to leave our property."

"We know the boy is here and we're taking him with us."

"That's not going to happen."

"We'll pull out of your driveway if you'd like, but the sheriff will be here shortly."

Elaine didn't argue. No one said a word until Sheriff Mulvaney pulled in behind the first vehicle.

"I want this issue resolved today," Sheriff Mulvaney said as he stepped out of his cruiser. "This has gone on long enough. If the boy is Kurt's, we'll prove it and they'll leave you alone. If he's not Kurt's boy, then he's leaving this farm."

"We're not here to cause problems. We just need the situation resolved," one of the men said.

"Take the men inside sheriff and I'll get Jim and Kurt."

Elaine hopped in the truck and drove into one of their fields. Jim and Kurt rode back with Elaine and the trio went in the house.

"Where is the boy? We need to talk to him."

Elaine called Jolene. She explained what was going on.

"He'll be here in a few minutes."

The front door slowly opened as the men from children services discussed issues concerning the case. Everyone sitting at the table thought it was Trevor, but it was Ava. Kurt felt comfortable because he had explained everything to her. Sheriff Mulvaney was inquisitive about the elderly woman, as were the two visitors.

"We don't need another person involved," one of the men said.

"She is a big part of this," Kurt said.

"We need to interview parents or relatives first. We'd like others, except for Sheriff Mulvaney, to excuse themselves from the room."

The only person they thought would remain in the room was Kurt. When he stood up and walked out of the room with Jim and Elaine, the men watched with curiosity. Ava was the only person remaining at the table.

"Who are you?"

"Ava Talbot. I'm Trevor's grandmother."

"Was he staying with you the last time we were here?"

"Yes. I lived in South Fresno and Trevor was visiting me. I couldn't stand the thought of going another year without seeing him, so I decided to leave Fresno for good. I live in Austin now. I'm going to raise him."

"Where are his parents?"

"His mother...Sharon O'Neil...was my daughter."

"Was?"

"She died in a tragic car accident in Mesa, Arizona. I have the articles and obituaries to prove it. I'm also Trevor's godmother. His father is a worthless human being. I know Kurt said the boy was his, but he's as close to a dad as he'll ever have. I want Kurt to raise him here on the farm because it's an ideal situation."

"We'll have to determine if that's true."

"What is Trevor's full name?"

"Trevor Matthew Talbot."

Trevor walked into the kitchen and answered a slew of questions. His answers proved he wasn't being held against his will and hadn't suffered physical or mental abuse. They determined he was living a healthy and happy life. After talking with Trevor, the men interviewed Jim and Elaine, and then questioned Colt and Jolene.

"Trevor has a wonderful support system," one of the workers whispered. "We can let him stay here for the time being, but we have to locate his father. The grandmother is technically his legal guardian, but if the father wants him, we have to remove him from this home."

"Let's explain things and we can be on our way," the other man said.

As Sheriff Mulvaney listened to the men, an idea sprouted in his mind. He refused to help the Alexanders hide the boy at his ranch, but didn't say he wouldn't help them.

The men asked everyone to gather in the kitchen and delivered the news. Everyone patted each other on the back and Trevor ran outside. The "woo hoo" he let out could be heard at every surrounding farm. The children services workers told the family they would stay in touch.

Mr. Alexander escorted the men to their vehicle. Their departure was much smoother than the first day their wheels hit Jim's driveway.

Sheriff Mulvaney began explaining his plan as Jim joined them in the kitchen. No one thought it would work, but it was worth a try.

The sheriff arrived at the jailhouse early the next morning. Butch Warden was a local criminal who spent his life in and out of the county jail. He spent a six-month stint at the state penitentiary, but was a small time criminal. Punching any man who looked at him wrong, inciting riots at the local tonks, public drunkenness, cattle swiping, and other mischievous acts were his specialties.

Warden was in the county jail for an eleventh stay. He had been there for seventy-six days and had another forty-four to go when Sheriff Mulvaney surprised him with breakfast in bed.

"Get up Butch. I need to talk to you."

"What did I do now? I suppose the long arm of the law is here to rough me up and then enjoy a hearty breakfast while I sit in the corner licking my wounds."

"I'm here to offer you a deal. Get out of bed and enjoy breakfast before I toss it in the trash. I want you to listen closely while your woofing that down. I'm prepared to let you out forty-four days early, but there are a few conditions. You have to stay inside your trailer on Fox Trot Road all forty-four days. The second condition is you have to stay out of trouble. I know raising hell is in the blood of the Warden clan, but you have to straighten up. When the forty-four days are up, I'll try to get you a county job as long as you keep your record clean."

"I think I can adhere to those rules," he said with a devilish smirk. "What are the other conditions?"

"There is only one more."

The sheriff provided Butch with the details surrounding Trevor. Butch was to claim he was Trevor's father, but complain heavily about child support. A blood sample was out of the question. Mulvaney knew the court wouldn't order one because he and Judge Newsome looked out for each other.

Warden agreed to the stipulations.

Children services showed up at the county jail a little after lunch. Sheriff Mulvaney walked the men back and left them alone in the cell.

"If he threatens to hurt you, just holler."

The men glanced at each other with fear in their eyes. Butch didn't need to tell anyone he was from the wrong side of the tracks. He didn't need obligatory institutional artwork or burning eyes to scare anyone, although he had both. Two-hundred fifty-five pounds chiseled on a six-four frame earned respect.

They spent less than ten minutes with Butch. He admitted he was Trevor's father, but didn't want custody. He told the men Ava was to raise him. He said he'd send money as often as he could, but didn't want to be forced to pay child support. The men were satisfied with the information Warden supplied, but wanted a blood sample. They wondered how he had a tryst with a woman from Arizona, but didn't want details.

They left the jail and spent a few months trying to get a sample from Butch, but Judge Newsome wouldn't rule in their favor. Eventually, the case was dropped. Trevor was free to mix with society. Ava enrolled him in the same school district the Alexander children attended and began taking him to Calvary each Sunday. Ava and the Alexander household had to deal with whispers that Trevor was Butch Warden's son, but they dealt with it considering the circumstances.

Sheriff Mulvaney didn't like releasing the man townsfolk dubbed "Barabbas" after word leaked of his pardon, but Butch held true to his promises and began working for the county in the water and sewer department. He didn't cause many problems and Sheriff Mulvaney began bragging after several months that his jail changed people.

People in the community rolled their eyes when Mulvaney exalted Butch because they knew he hadn't changed. Everyone was waiting for Butch to show his true colors. He was still visiting tonks, although he wasn't throwing haymakers at innocent citizens, and walked a few crooked lines here or there. He might not have been in the news as much, but people knew an incident was around the corner. They were right.

The Warden clan was the most infamous band of wrongdoers in the Texas Hill Country. They bred like rabbits and a new group of trouble makers hit the streets every few years. Butch was always going to be Butch and it was a good thing for those living on the Alexander farm.

Chapter
Twenty-One

GARY WASN'T SURE IF it was safe at his house. He envisioned dying in a mishap or being executed in his sleep, so he rented a room at a small motel in the bad part of town. If Rhodes had people looking for him, they couldn't track him down there.

Mr. O'Neil had eliminated three of seven assassins left and was ready to eliminate three more.

He drove to the apartment of assassin number ten. On the way, Gary thought about another assassin who was previously number ten. Angel was used to eliminate Rhonda Beckman and his talents should have been further utilized, at least in Gary's opinion. Gary wished his bosses would have kept Angel in the program. He opposed Angel's single assignment, but always followed orders. Maybe he'd track down the Guatemalan someday.

Gary waited for Tomas to leave the apartment. Rhodes couldn't contact the hit men and they were still driving past Gary's house every day. Tomas walked out the front door and looked around before getting in his sports car provided by Robert and Big Boy.

The car whipped around the corner and Gary went into action. He used his spare key to get inside. Like all of the assassins, Tomas kept his place neat and orderly. To the naked eye, it looked like the place was ready for a walk through, but Gary wasn't a landlord ready to show prospective renters the place.

Gary didn't touch anything. Each assassin knew if something was out of order or if an uninvited guest was present. Gary snooped around before nestling into his spot.

Tomas returned thirty minutes later. He closed the door and put his keys on the counter. He sat on the sofa and turned on his laptop. Gary couldn't see what Tomas was doing, but heard him pecking on a keyboard. Gary waited patiently as hours passed.

Around seven-thirty, the smell of food made Gary hungry. Tomas, who couldn't hear Gary's roaring stomach, finished eating and watched TV before taking a shower. The light flipped on in the bedroom and Gary heard Tomas rustling through dresser drawers. Tomas walked back to the light switch and flipped it off. He sat on the bed and suddenly felt sharp pains. He tried to stand, reaching for his gun on the nightstand. Tomas crashed to the floor. The deep gashes in his Achilles tendons were squirting out what seemed like pints of blood with every heartbeat.

Gary rolled out from underneath the bed and swung his left arm with full force at the side of Tomas' neck. Number ten yanked the screwdriver out, but Tomas was dead in seconds. Gary gently closed the door behind him and was ready to leave the apartment when he noticed Tomas had left part of a sandwich on the coffee table. Gary shoved it in his mouth, stopping hunger pains for the time being.

He peered through the blinds and didn't see anything. He grabbed a small trash bag from underneath the kitchen sink and hustled out of the apartment. Gary took off his gloves and shoes. He placed them in the trash bag before getting in his car. After slipping on loafers, he drove to one of the sites where he and Stenson often disposed of things. Gary dumped the bag in a small pit and struck a match. The bag burned quickly and the gloves turned into a pile of ashes. The soles were all that was recognizable. He shoveled a few scoops of dirt over the pit and returned to his motel room.

Gary left the door to his room open. He checked under the bed before looking in the closet and shower. No one was there. He pulled the door shut. He slipped into comfortable clothes and tried to sleep.

Gary woke up every time he heard a noise, clutching the gun he had tucked under the pillow beside him.

He only got an hour or two of sleep, but was ready to take out his second target. Evgeni was perhaps the deadliest of any assassin to participate in the program. It would take more than a Philips flathead to eliminate him.

Gary drove to the Russian's apartment and slipped an envelope in Evgeni's door while on his daily venture to Upper Arlington. When Evgeni returned, he pulled the envelope from the door. He was extremely suspicious of everything. He dropped it on the ground and stepped on it. Evgeni used a knife to open the envelope and turned it upside down. Nothing fell out. He looked inside and saw a piece of paper.

The note took Evgeni by surprise.

It's Gary. Meet me at Four Corners on High Street tonight at seven-thirty.

Evgeni and the other assassins were recruited by Gary, but their contact ended once they landed on American soil, unless they were being removed from the program. They were given an apartment key, along with directions, a fake passport, and $25,000 when the handshake took place. When an assassin reached the airport in Columbus, a high-end sports car was waiting in the overnight parking lot. The hit man picked up his vehicle and drove to an apartment provided by Rhodes.

Each assassin was to retrieve a small package from the glove box when arriving at the apartment. A key to the post office box, another $25,000, and instructions were inside the package. The main rule was driving by Gary's house at their appointed time each day. The only time they were to contact Gary was if "C Me" accompanied their number on the board.

The Russian thought it could be a setup and was prepared for a confrontation. He gathered some things and stuffed them in a satchel. He grabbed magazines for his gun and put them in a blazer he had slung over a kitchen chair. He tucked the gun in his waistband and sat in a recliner for five hours watching the apartment door.

It was a little before 7:00 p.m. when Evgeni stood up and put on his blazer. He walked into the bathroom and opened the window. He eased himself to the ground and was on the sidewalk between his apartment and the adjacent building. Evgeni looked across the parking lot to see if anyone was watching his apartment.

There were shrubs on a hillside near the road that led into the area where his apartment complex and the abandoned furniture store was located. Landscapers were trimming the shrubs, but Evgeni felt they were looking around a little too much. He noticed a truck parked approximately one hundred feet or so down the road.

Evgeni slipped behind the building and walked to a small stream. It wrapped around to a large culvert that went underneath the road where the truck was parked. He quietly moved through the watered passageway to reach the other side of the road.

He climbed the small bank and peered over the hillside. The workers trimmed away, but were still taking their eyes off their work a little too much. Evgeni darted down the hill and moved behind their truck. He reached in his satchel and took out an old T-shirt. The assassin pulled down the back license plate and unscrewed the gas cap.

The shirt was dry, but number seven was making sure that wasn't the case much longer. Evgeni ripped the shirt and used a tire iron to stuff it into the tank, leaving a foot or so hanging out. He poured lighter fluid on the shirt and lit it. He ran up the hill, but one of the men saw him.

The men dropped their hedgers and ran toward the truck. They thought the man was stealing tools out of the bed. Evgeni safely made it into the culvert and plugged his ears. The explosion sounded like a tank. Fortunately, the men didn't get to the truck in time, but the blast gave them a ride neither wanted. It was as if they had triggered a claymore mine. The explosion lifted them from the asphalt and launched them several feet through the air. They landed on the side of the hill with major headaches and minor abrasions.

Evgeni ran along the ditch line and made it safely between the building and his apartment. He climbed through the bathroom window and went to the front room to peer into the parking lot. The men were lying on the ground. He didn't have time to watch them.

He ran to the bedroom and quickly changed. Evgeni used the front door the second time he left and got in his sports car.

He pulled onto the street and passed an ambulance and police car a mile down the road. If he would have read the paper the next day, Evgeni would have discovered the men weren't interested in espionage. They were legitimate workers and the reason they were looking around so much is because they were taking their good ole' time. The longer they worked, the more they got paid. Their boss often checked on them and they were making sure he wasn't around. Evgeni was always careful and on the defense. Gary knew it wouldn't be easy to get rid of him.

HER OBITUARY RAN IN the *American-Statesman* and the *Chronicle.* Kurt also had it appear in the *Fresno Bee*, which was against his better judgment. Ava beat the odds and lived longer than anyone expected.

She suffered a second stroke four years after arriving at the Alexander farm. It robbed Ava of her sight, but she continued to garden, with some help.

Elaine begged her time and time again to take it easy, but Ava Talbot was from the old school. If she could have had it her way, she would have died working in her garden.

Kurt didn't expect Ava to last long after her second stroke. She collapsed at the kitchen sink while washing a light load of dishes. The Alexanders had driven to town, which was a Saturday afternoon tradition, and Kurt was plowing the field farthest from the house. Tyler and Chelsea were away at their respective universities. Trevor had just passed his driver's exam and was the one who found Ava.

Trevor didn't have time to call for help. He picked up his frail grandmother and carried her to his car. He drove up the road past the cemetery and turned right at the Parson's farm. Kurt saw him driving down the road. When Trevor jumped out of the car, Kurt knew something was wrong. He heard Trevor's pleas for help when he turned off the tractor.

"It's grandma. I found her at the sink when I walked into the kitchen."

Kurt tried to calm Trevor, but his heart was racing as well. Trevor jumped in the back seat and propped his grandmother's head on his lap. Kurt weaved through traffic, trying to get to the hospital as quickly as possible.

They rushed Ava into the Emergency Room. Jim and Elaine joined them at the hospital, as did Pastor Browne. The doctor explained she had suffered a second stroke and it robbed Ava of her remaining vision.

Ava was nursed back to health and left the hospital after a three-week stay. She made several friends during her time in the hospital. Even though she couldn't see, they offered her a volunteer position, which she politely declined.

After a few weeks, Ava was back to her antics. Mrs. Talbot had counted the steps it took to get from the front door to the garden and often tried to sneak out to it. She didn't want to be relegated to sitting on a couch waiting to die.

Elaine took her to the garden when Ava's constant badgering got the best of her, but Mrs. Alexander tried to keep her inside as much as possible. Those close to Ava thought she wouldn't last much longer than a year. Ava proved them wrong.

Miss Ava was there when Tyler and Chelsea walked the stage on their graduation days. She also attended Trevor's graduation from UT, even though she did so in a wheelchair. She had withered away to about one hundred pounds, but remained as positive and upbeat as the first day she set foot on Texas soil.

There were a few scares along the way, but Ava kept fending off death. She told Kurt each time that she was staying alive until she could see Preston again. Kurt regretted lying to her, but always told her he was working on a reunion.

After watching Ava battle for so long, Kurt thought she might be around to celebrate a century of life. However, he knew she wouldn't make it another twelve years, but Ava was just a few weeks away from turning eighty-eight and he didn't think that was possible seven or eight years prior.

Elaine planned a big birthday bash. She knew eighty-nine wasn't realistic. It was going to be Ava's last birthday. An open invitation was sent to the congregation at Calvary Baptist. Cy Harper donated a few hogs and word quickly spread that the event of the summer would take place at the Alexander farm.

Tents were set up in the field closest to the house and rumors circulated that a big-top circus was coming to town. No, there wouldn't be elephants, although a few of the men would have disagreed, nor would there be lions, tigers, or bears. There would be a popcorn stand, pony riding for children, cotton candy, and a few slightly bearded ladies.

Anticipation built for nearly six weeks and when late July finally rolled around, everyone was ready for the Alexander shindig.

Ava didn't know what was going on. She heard people working outside Wednesday and it lasted until Saturday morning. Cars started lining both sides of the road around noon at the Alexander farm. They nearly stretched from the state route to the cemetery.

Miss Ava heard familiar voices. She asked Elaine what was going on, but the cat would have to let itself out of the bag.

The sounds from activities outside piqued Ava's interest. Elaine helped her to the front porch and Ava smelled barbecued hogs and various pies. They walked into the tent where various foods were spread out on lengthy tables and Ava smiled as additional scents blended with ones she had already smelled.

"Is this for my birthday?"

"Do you think we would go to all this trouble for you?"

Ava started crying and everyone knew the cat had escaped. Everyone stopped what they were doing and began singing Happy Birthday. Their words rumbled across the Texas Hill Country. People swear that you can still faintly hear the words echoing throughout the area.

The day was filled with laughter, good eats, a little Warden moonshine that someone snuck in—even Sheriff Mulvaney took a few swigs—celebrating one of the area's most beloved foreigners and, of course, tons of story telling.

Ava was presented with enough birthday gifts to keep her old shaky hands busy for the next six months, if she made it that long. Kurt had the best birthday gift, but waited until most guests left. He discussed his plan with the Alexanders and they frowned upon it at first, especially the man of the house.

Jim could recite scripture with the best of them. Kurt often told him he had missed his calling. Every time Mr. Alexander delivered a spur of the moment sermon, Kurt thought about the one he received when they first met.

"Leviticus 19:11 says, 'Do not steal. Do not lie. Do not deceive one another.' I guess one out of three is pretty good."

Trevor had been a Sig at UT and stayed in contact with several fraternity brothers. Kurt explained the plan to Trevor and he thought it was a good idea, albeit a dishonest one. Trevor made the phone call and his "brother" arrived at the farm around 6:00 p.m.

Elaine took Ava in the house and told everyone she was getting tired. She sat her on the couch and left her alone with Kurt.

"I have a surprise for you Ava."

Trevor and his fellow Sig walked into the living room and sat beside Ava.

"Hi grandma," Trevor said. "What's it like to be sitting on the couch with your grandsons?"

"Preston, is that really you?" Ava asked while reaching for the young man's left knee.

"It's me grandma. It's Preston," the imposter said as he gave Mrs. Talbot a hug.

A succession of sloppy pecks on his cheeks wasn't part of the deal, but Trevor's friend understood. He felt badly about betraying the old woman's trust, but knew it was a white lie worth telling.

"Is this really Preston?" Ava asked Kurt again.

"It's your youngest grandson."

"Kurt, would you please excuse yourself from the room while I visit with the boys."

Ava usually went to bed at 9 o'clock sharp, but could have outlasted the boys that night. She unintentionally ignored Trevor most of the evening and kept apologizing. He assured her it was all right.

She was a little disappointed that Preston didn't want to talk about his trips to Fresno. He mentioned the scenery and the fact his grandma's house was yellow with a green porch. Although it was a small detail, his memory of her house made Ava proud. Ava stayed up visiting until 1:00 a.m. Her head kept nodding, so they decided to call it a night. The boys stretched her out on the couch and she was asleep before they stepped out of the room.

Trevor asked his friend for forgiveness.

"I'm sorry for keeping you here this late. I still don't feel right doing that to her, but she'll talk about it for the next month. I know you didn't agree to what I'm about to say. If you can, say hi to her when you call me. Even if it's two or three minutes, I'd appreciate it."

His "brother" didn't have a problem with Trevor's new request. His friend had a ninety-minute drive and needed to get on the road. As the two embraced, Trevor slid something into his pocket. It was a $100 bill with a thank you note from Kurt wrapped around it.

"What's that?"

"Gratitude. Take care. Call me in a few days."

Trevor went in the house and Kurt was sitting at the kitchen table with a cup of coffee. He also had one waiting for Trevor.

"I'd like to get your grandmother into bed, but she looks so peaceful. I don't want to disturb her."

"It's been a long day for her. She might have an extra ache or two in the morning, but she'll be fine."

Trevor and Kurt drank their coffee, which was a mistake because it kept them up for another hour or two. Trevor, who had an apartment in downtown Austin, slept in his grandmother's room, which was Chelsea's old room.

Kurt flipped off the kitchen light and headed downstairs. He laid in bed thinking about the previous day's events and eventually dozed off. He, along with everyone else, woke up to Elaine's horrifying shrieking.

Ava had kept her word. Kurt raced upstairs and knew what had happened as soon as he turned the corner in the kitchen. Ava's blue hair was matched by blue skin. She had put off death until she and Preston were reunited. Kurt instantly blamed himself. Everyone in the house tried easing his mind.

"She told you she was going to keep breathing until she saw Preston and she held up her end of the bargain," Elaine said through tears. "She went to bed last night as happy as she's been since Sharon was alive. I know it was deceitful, but she died in peace and you're the reason. Don't beat yourself up. We all agreed it was the right thing to do."

Each member of the household took time kneeling beside Ava. Trevor spent the longest time beside her and it was fitting. Although they perceived Ava as family, she was to Trevor.

After Trevor kissed his grandmother on the forehead, EMTs and the county coroner took Ava from the house.

Pastor Browne shocked everyone at Calvary that Sunday morning. His foot stomping and roof raising antics were put aside. It was the first time in nearly five years that he didn't deliver a hell, fire, and brimstone sermon. He taught his flock about loving your family and recited several scriptures. He talked about Jim and Elaine and how they loved their family and gave generously to others outside their family. He centered most of his lesson around Acts 10:2.

Had Jim and Elaine been able to attend, they would have been moved to tears. At the end of the love offering, Pastor Browne led a closing prayer that thanked God for sending them Ava Talbot. Most eyes were wet well before he said amen.

That Wednesday, Ava Talbot's funeral service took place at Calvary Baptist and she was laid to rest in the old cemetery. It took a week or so before life returned to normal. Her obituary was read by a pair of eyes in Fresno that Kurt had hoped to avoid. The man had met Gary several years earlier and they stayed in contact. He notified Gary as soon as he finished reading the obit.

Gary was stunned. He knew Ava vanished from Fresno without a hint of where she was going. Her house had been sold a few months after she left town and Gary hadn't heard from her since. He figured she had already died. The fact she made it to her eighty-eighth birthday surprised him.

Later that day, Gary met with Stenson. He told Big Boy Ava passed away. When Gary told him she died near Austin, Stenson knew Kurt couldn't be too far away. Gary thought Kurt had been killed, but Stenson knew differently. He hadn't forgotten about the man and knew he'd finally make a mistake.

Stenson's next meeting that day was with Rhodes. The two met near Dayton at an Olive Garden.

"I think I've found Kurt Carson," Stenson said.

"Where is he?"

"I believe he's living near Austin, Texas. Preston's grandmother passed away and her obituary ran in the Fresno Bee. One of Gary's buddies alerted him. It was a stroke of luck for us. I checked the Austin papers and her obit ran in the *Chronicle* and *American-Statesman*. Her service was at a small church called Calvary Baptist. After all these years, I think we have him Robert."

"Well, let's get the ball rolling. It's time for Kurt Carson to pay the piper."

They wrapped up their conversation and dug into their meals. They ate enough to feed four or five men. They agreed to meet a week later at the same spot.

Stenson and Rhodes agreed it wouldn't be a typical assignment. Big Boy called Calvary Baptist and talked to Pastor Browne. He said he was a friend of Ava's from Fresno and even produced fake tears. Pastor Browne shared too much information. Stenson found out she had lived with the Alexanders and her grandson Trevor. He also told Big Boy about Kurt. He had hit the jackpot.

Big Boy conducted research online and found pictures of Calvary Baptist. He wasn't interested in the dimensions of the church. The landscape and scenery surrounding the church is what drew his attention. He also found useful information about the Alexander farm. He drove to Dayton again and met with Rhodes, who had also dug up information. Rhodes had somehow found a picture of Kurt through the Austin Bureau of Motor Vehicles. He had blown it up and gave Stenson the photo. The two gluttons again filled themselves to capacity and winked at one another as they departed.

Stenson asked Gary to swing by his office so he could give him the materials. It was the second and last time he would ever be given information.

"The briefcase is ready to go. We need you to give this to your selected man."

The meeting was short and to the point. Gary drove home and put a new number on the board. Filip drove by the next morning and saw his number. However, "C Me" meant he had to drive by a second time.

He stopped by Gary's Upper Arlington home around six-thirty that night. He buzzed Gary and announced who he was in his thick French accent.

Filip walked across the cobblestone driveway and reached the front porch. The door opened and a hand holding a folder was all Filip could see. He took it and was on his way. He drove by the post office and the apartment. He retrieved the briefcase and took out the map. He wrote down the series of numbers and studied the photo, before tearing off the corner. He finished at the apartment and visited the library.

The next mark was assigned and the French assassin was leaving for Austin at 8:00 a.m.

GARY WAS WAITING ON Evgeni at Four Corners because he didn't want him to suspect anything. Evgeni pulled up to the curb across from the establishment. He was supposed to meet Gary at seven-thirty. Number seven was fifteen minutes early and sat outside for twenty-five minutes. He watched every person that walked into Four Corners, including Gary, and everyone that walked along the street. The assassin also carefully watched each vehicle.

He scribbled notes about everything imaginable. Evgeni probably could have recited what each of the one hundred fifty or so people were wearing and the make and model of each vehicle that passed by. He also knew how many buildings were on each side of the street and where possible escape routes were located. Yes, Evgeni was going to be hard to take down.

Feeling comfortable, Evgeni walked into the bar/restaurant at 7:42.

"First, let me tell you why we're here so it can ease your mind. We have a special assignment that needs careful attention. This is the second time I've had to meet with one of my recruits and it's only out of necessity."

"Fair enough," Evgeni replied with a lie of his own.

Gary not only wanted Evgeni to feel relaxed because he was waiting on him, he also wanted to finish him off as quickly as possible. Gary had ordered two drafts when he sat down. Right before Evgeni walked into the establishment, Mr. O'Neil put rohypnol in his own draft. It was a risky move, but he knew Evgeni was smart.

"I took the liberty of ordering drafts. Enjoy."

"Take a drink of mine first!"

"It's safe."

Evgeni switched the drafts.

"That's strike one Mr. O'Neil. Take a drink or I'll shoot you under this table right now."

Gary cocked his head to the right and leaned over. A nine-millimeter Beretta was pointed at his stomach.

"All right, I'll take a drink to satisfy your paranoia."

He grabbed the stein and chugged down about a third of the twenty-four ounce draft. Evgeni told him to stop when he was satisfied. Gary thought he had outsmarted him, but the Russian was too good. He pushed the rohypnol-laced draft to the edge of the table and ordered a new one.

Evgeni called it correctly. Gary had taken a huge hack and missed. Strike one. Gary readjusted himself and stepped back into the batter's box.

The men ordered and didn't have a lot to say. Gary finally broke the silence by pulling out a file from a briefcase, not the hailed item from the apartment, and slid it across the table to Evgeni. He had come up with a fake mark. He found a man's picture in a magazine and said it would take place in the Wisconsin Dells. Gary told the Russian that the family would be vacationing there in two weeks and were staying at the Great Wolf Lodge. Gary had a room reserved for Evgeni.

The assassin was starting to feel more comfortable. Their talk was interrupted by a waitress delivering their meals. They finished eating and a second interruption took place. Two ladies sitting nearby got up and walked over to Gary and Evgeni.

"Are these seats taken?"

Evgeni didn't give Gary a chance to reply.

"If we wanted company, we would have brought women with us. Now, please turn around and go back where you came from."

The women were disgusted by the Russian's lack of courtesy. Gary knew it was strike two. He had paid the women $250 each to show up and stage the encounter. He wanted them to help him get Evgeni drunk, but like an old car, that plan backfired.

"It could have been the best night of your life you vodka guzzling pig."

Evgeni mustered a slight smile and was turned on by her hatefulness. It seemed as if hate oozed from his pores and he enjoyed people who dealt with him in the same manner.

Gary had hoped phase three of the plan wouldn't have to be executed, but it was a last resort. The men finished eating and said their good-byes. Evgeni forced Gary to walk out first. He watched him walk to his car through the front window of Four Corners. Mr. O'Neil pulled away and Evgeni walked to the bar and sat down in front of where Clint Harbor was standing.

"What can I get ya?"

"I need a cab."

"I'll have one pick you up right away."

The Russian didn't trust driving the car Stenson and Rhodes had provided. Gary didn't leave the table once during their meeting, so he couldn't have rigged a bomb to his vehicle, but someone else could have.

Clint got a phone call from a cabbie and he told Evgeni his ride was outside. The assassin quickly rushed out the door and got in the cab. He handed the driver directions to his apartment.

Gary didn't have a bomb attached to Evgeni's vehicle, but there were enough explosives strapped to the car at the entrance of the apartment complex to rival any senseless bombing in the Middle East. Mr. O'Neil called in a favor from one of the goons he had dealt with in the past. Gary paid the man $15,000 and he did the rest.

The Ford Ranger was parked at the entrance. The back left tire had been slashed so it looked like it was an emergency stop. The bed was filled with explosives. The cap on the back shielded the evidence.

As the cab turned left into the entrance, Evgeni noticed the broken down truck.

"Stop!"

The goon hiding in the well-manicured shrubs had already pressed the button. The truck was launched into the air and took the cab along for the ride. The cabbie was dead on impact, but Evgeni had opened his door as the blast erupted. He was on the pavement in a bloody pulp.

The man in the shrubs was long gone before the cops arrived for a second time that day. Gary received a text from the goon that read, "To Russia with love." Mr. O'Neil knew the deed had been accomplished.

Gary picked up the morning paper with great anticipation. The pair of explosions dominated the front page. O'Neil didn't know the first one had taken place. The names of the victims were being withheld, but Gary knew Evgeni had successfully been eliminated.

Eight recruits in the program were gone and Gary had one more to go before assigning the final mark. Gary walked into the motel room and sat on the bed. He was envisioning himself on a tropical island in the middle of the Caribbean. His son had almost brought him down, but Gary was two hit men away from becoming a free man.

Chapter
Twenty-Two

FILIP LANDED IN AUSTIN the day after receiving his assignment. He paid for a rental car at the airport and drove straight to Calvary Baptist. He was born and raised in Paris and had grown accustomed to Columbus. Filip was used to big city life and the rural backwoods was a bit uncomfortable.

Although he had never driven in the Texas Hill Country, the directions to Calvary were spot on. He pulled into the lot and surveyed the surroundings. Two cars, one belonging to Pastor Browne and the other leased to the church's secretary, were parked in the lot. There were enough spots for a clear shot, but getting away would be the problem. Option one was put on the backburner until other alternatives could be researched.

The Frenchman drove around the small burg a couple times over the next few hours. Farms dominated the area. However, the street which led to Calvary Baptist was the central hub of the town. Polk's Family Restaurant was the centerpiece. The post office and Cy Harper's feed mill were also main attractions. There was an assortment of other shops scattered downtown, but it certainly didn't stand out as a desired destination for shopping fanatics.

Filip was hungry so he stopped at the family restaurant, a place the Alexander family and Kurt frequented regularly. It was option two.

When he walked through the front door, everyone stopped what they were doing. Strangers rarely dropped by, unless it was for directions. Filip graciously obeyed the sign displaying the day's specials, one that kindly told patrons, "Please seat yourself." When he took a seat, the regulars knew their Mapquest skills weren't necessary, as if most had the internet anyway.

The restaurant hadn't changed since the mid-60s. Mr. Polk's father started the business in the late 30s. When he was too ill to run the restaurant, he passed it down to his oldest son. Mrs. Polk talked her husband into redecorating the place. The décor made visitors feel like they were transported in time when they passed through the door. Regulars enjoyed it and so did out-of-towners.

An announcement was made each time a patron walked through the door, thanks to the jingling bells Mrs. Polk had hanging on the back of the door knob. The left side of the restaurant had eight booths, which is where Filip took a seat. The center of the room was dominated by five circular tables for large gatherings and the bar was on the right side of the room. Several coffee drinkers and gossipers staked ownership in particular swivel stools at the bar, which didn't serve liquor.

"What would you like to drink?" a waitress asked.

"Coke."

"What kind of Coke, sir?"

"Coke," Filip said with a confused look.

She walked to the counter and poured his Coke from the fountain. She returned with his drink and took his order. He asked for two eggs over easy, with bacon, sausage, and toast. The place was silent as he ordered. His French accent was easily detectable.

Four of the "stool owners" divided themselves and sat in the booths on each side of Filip. The locals sat with their backs against the wall, constantly staring at the unwanted guest.

"Where ya from, boy?" one of the farmers asked.

Filip was reading a *Chronicle* he purchased from the rack outside and didn't move a muscle. He continued as if he didn't hear a word.

"Do ya have a hearing problem, boy?" another farmer asked.

Again, the visitor kept his eyes glued to the pages. The farmers weren't happy about being shunned, especially by a foreigner, which is what every person who visited or moved to their town was called. Filip, in fact, was more of a foreigner than everyone except the German family that moved to town about a dozen years earlier. They were still foreigners, but became town regulars once they placed membership at Calvary.

Two of the men got up and sat down across from Filip.

"I didn't invite you to sit with me," he said, breaking his lengthy silence.

"We don't have to ask if we can sit with ya. We've been coming to this restaurant every day since we were kids. I think we have a right as loyal patrons to sit wherever we'd like, Frenchy."

The nickname Old Man Cater gave the visitor drew several rounds of laughter. It was unoriginal, but the point was well made. They wanted him to leave their town. Filip would leave as soon as possible, but he was going to kill one of their converted foreigners.

"If you'd like to remain alive, you will never call me that again."

"Oh, did I hurt little Frenchy's feelings?"

Filip let out a sigh of disappointment and slid out of the booth. As he stood up, Old Man Cater jumped up and blocked his path to the doorway.

"You don't want to disrespect me a third time. I let you get away with calling me Frenchy twice. You ruined my meal and it's best if I leave. Get out of my way!"

"If you'd like to leave, you'll have to go around me...Frenchy."

Those were the last words Mr. Cater spoke for a month. Filip delivered a pair of rib-rattling shots to both of Mr. Cater's sides before grabbing his neck and slamming his head so hard off the table that he bit the end of his tongue off.

The other good 'ole boys tried intervening. Filip jumped in the air and landed a roundhouse kick to the other man that had been seated across from him. He then flipped Buster Pate, who had jumped on his back, onto the floor and nearly crushed his larynx with a forearm shiver to the esophagus.

Dump Milligan, his fourth assailant, grabbed a steak knife from the table. He danced back and fourth with the knife in his right hand and eventually swung it at Filip's left side. He quickly blocked the attempt and grabbed the pressure point on Dump's right wrist all in one move. The farmer dropped the knife and "Frenchy" grabbed it with his right hand out of midair and jammed it into the man's right thigh.

Filip didn't wait for cops to arrive or anyone else to attack him. He calmly reached into his wallet, pulled out a twenty, and placed it on the end of the table. He looked at the waitress and thanked her.

As he walked out the door, no one moved. They were mesmerized, as if they had just watched one of Hollywood's finest action stars. Sheriff Mulvaney had been contacted, but it was too late. The visitor vanished as quickly as he had appeared. The second option was a no go.

Mr. Milligan was rushed to the hospital and the knife was safely removed. It would take several weeks of rehab to walk freely of pain, but he'd survive.

Sheriff Mulvaney asked if they wanted to press charges, which was a wasted question. They knew the incident was their fault. If charges were pressed, Filip would take his assailants down with him.

Polk's Family Restaurant was buzzing the next morning. The *Chronicle* mentioned the fracas in Section A. As usual, eyewitnesses in those parts had a way of distorting the truth, especially if someone had wronged a member of their good 'ole boy club.

For the second time in as many days, the restaurant fell to a hush. Butch Warden had been permanently banned from Polk's after an incident eight years earlier. Warden's six-month stay in the Big House stemmed from a fight in the restaurant. His cousin Denny was jumped one night in a local tonk after he made a pass at another man's fiancé. The pass would have given most women the willies, but John Proffit's old lady loved sex and she had pulled down her panties more than once for Denny Warden.

She loved teasing men. She usually wore the tightest get-ups in the Texas Hill Country. Showing off her perfectly proportioned double Ds while bending over pool tables gave her great satisfaction.

She didn't discriminate either. Denny Warden didn't need to show her his credentials. As long as he could please her, she'd oblige.

If Jim Alexander knew Colt took a turn with her when he was a senior in high school, he would have thrown him out of the house and never let him set foot on his property again.

Denny spent most of the night having eye sex with Crystal Wyatt. Her fiancé got redder with each Budweiser he chugged. When Crystal "accidentally" brushed Denny's groin area as he walked past the pool table, John Proffit had seen enough. He forced Crystal to leave the bar and told her he'd be home soon. Actually, she was fine with it because she knew Denny wouldn't be far behind and they could get a quickie in at their secret spot.

She jumped into John's Dodge pickup and roared out of the lot. John also knew Denny wouldn't stay much longer. He waited five minutes, sat his half empty bottle on the counter, and paid his tab.

Butch's cousin didn't make it around the corner. Two men grabbed him from each side. The Wardens were ferocious fighters, but John Proffit's buddies were equally skilled. They forced him to the ground and beat him to a pulp. John waited in the bar several minutes so it didn't look obvious. After paying his tab, he darted around the corner and joined in on the beat down.

Denny was barely recognizable. John keyed Denny's Trans-Am and tossed his bloody body in the back of a friend's truck. They stopped in front of Denny's house and dumped him in the ditch, which is where Butch and Denny's brother found him the next morning.

Word spread and everyone in town knew who the culprits were. The Wardens could have landed Proffit and his crew in the pokey, but the Warden clan didn't believe in involving the law. They believed in settling matters on their own.

Butch Warden heard through the grapevine that John Proffit was eating breakfast alone at Polk's early one morning. Butch parked a block away from the restaurant and his steps could be heard all the way down Main Street.

"Don't do it Butch," yelled a man who was hanging outside of Cy Harper's mill.

He ignored the plea and marched into the restaurant. Mr. Polk saw him and knew what was about to take place. No one could have stopped it. John Proffit caught the first haymaker on his right earlobe. The buzzing in his ear lasted the better part of a year.

Butch yanked John off the bar stool and gave him a steady diet of right and left jabs. Sheriff Mulvaney was en route with deputies and it was a good thing. When the door flung open, Butch had John Proffit on the floor annihilating him. It took seven men, including Sheriff Mulvaney and three deputies, to pull Butch off.

Butch put his hands behind his back and went silently. It took eight surgeries to fix John Proffit's battered face. Crystal Wyatt dumped him and is still making her way through the local tonks and beds in the area. The incident landed Butch Warden a six-month stint in prison for assault. He would have faced twenty-five to life had he not been interrupted.

The stool at the bar had never been used since that day. Every time an out of towner started to sit on the stool, someone in the restaurant hollered, "It's broken."

"Butch, you need to leave," Mr. Polk politely said.

The morning coffee hadn't begun to work its magic, but Butch Warden's appearance at 6:35 did the trick.

"It's OK," Sheriff Mulvaney bellowed from the back booth.

"With all due respect, I know you call the shots around these parts, but I decide who dines in my establishment."

"Relax!" the sheriff said. "Everyone dig in. Butch, I believe there's a seat that has your name on it."

For the first time in over eight years, the stool was about to be used, with disapproval from Mr. Polk. Butch sat down and swiveled left and then right.

"It's a little squeaky," Butch said as he grinned.

The tension subsided as everyone roared with laughter. Some were sold Butch Warden was doing his best to fit back into society. It appeared he was there to eat breakfast before he started his day with the water and sewer department, but a few people knew why Butch was there, including Sheriff Mulvaney.

Most of the early morning crowd was talking about Old Man Cater and Dump Milligan. They were in the hospital and, depending on who was telling the story, were doing fine or being examined by the county coroner as they spoke.

Buster Pate was a little sore from his ride through the air, but the fourth man—Sunny Warden—was set to have his jaw wired shut later that morning due to the kick he took to the chops.

Butch wanted to hear the gossip. He wasn't going to pound the stranger quite like he beat John Proffit, but Butch wanted to let him know he wasn't welcome and no one messed with the Warden clan, especially one of his brothers.

Butch quietly ate breakfast while soaking in conversations around him while Sheriff Mulvaney watched. When Butch finished, his eyes fixated on his coffee mug. It was time to have a talk.

The sheriff patted Butch on the back and told him it was time to leave. Butch didn't argue. He paid his bill and left an $8 tip. Mr. Polk wanted to warn him not to return, but instead thanked him for his patronage.

When they went outside, Sheriff Mulvaney told Butch to forget about retaliation.

"You've done well for yourself and stayed out of trouble for a while now. Don't screw everything up by finding that Frenchman and landing a second stint up the river."

"I'm not out for revenge. I was hungry and missed Mr. Polk's fine cuisine."

"You can BS everyone else, but I know how your mind operates. You have to let yesterday go. I checked the motels and no one has a Frenchman staying. If he pops back up, he'll be escorted out of town. You let me handle things."

Butch listened to Sheriff Mulvaney, but didn't store an ounce of the gibberish. He was going to get revenge no matter the cost.

STENSON AND RHODES SENT a high-end call girl every other week to each of the assassin's apartments. They thought their assassins needed to have a little fun due to their confinement while in the program. Gary strongly objected, but it was a losing cause.

Gary argued that it left a trail. Rhodes took care of that problem. He sent instructions to Madam Gigi's, along with $10,000 as a thank-you gift. An unmarked envelope arrived every Friday at Gigi's with $15,000 in it and necessary changes. Madam Gigi questioned things at first, but as time went by, the arrangement was beneficial to both parties. It kept the illegal business booming and the assassins from straying.

The girls were not allowed to ask the gentlemen work-related questions and had to arrive and leave promptly. Madam Gigi never found out who was sending the money or why the men were being serviced in kind. Gary didn't know who the girls worked for, but the arrangement was about to end.

The five girls arrived every other Saturday at 9:00 p.m. and stayed until eleven-thirty. The same five were used—two blondes, a pair of brunettes, and a red head. They visited one through five the first Saturday and six through ten the following Saturday. One of the instructions Rhodes included was the five girls had to draw cards. He sent the ten apartment locations and each address was labeled with a number between one and ten. The two numbers each girl drew was where they were sent.

Gary drove to the apartment of his next target during his crescendo tour. He lived in a trendy area. The girls melted when they drew number five. André was physically striking and knew his way around the bedroom. They also loved his studio apartment. They weren't allowed to ask questions, but the five girls thought he was an artist. Yes, he was an artist, but his easel was only dotted with different shades of red.

The drawing took place and Skylar, the red head, drew the five of hearts. She envisioned a night of passion with André. Most assignments were shady investment bankers, mendacious mortgage brokers, or corporate scoundrels. André was different than them and was the best of the Saturday group.

Skylar arrived at 8:58. She was escorted by some of Madam Gigi's finest muscle. The escort service, brothel, or whatever one wanted to call it was frowned upon by the conservative part of society. Rumors that Madam Gigi's was basically a prostitution ring were in fact true. However, she silenced the opposition.

"They're not paying for sex. We're a legitimate dating service providing lonely or shy men with companions for the evening."

Sting operations were organized to bust Madam Gigi's on occasion, but she knew about the operations before some members of the task force. She took care of the right people and always had inside information as soon as it was available.

Gigi didn't employ tramps, druggies, or con-artists. She ran it like a classy, sophisticated business, one that was open Friday and Saturday only. Sex for money was illegal, but it was the most respected business of its kind in Columbus, excluding the stiff part of society. One of the girls that worked for her three years earlier was discovered by a talent scout. Since her departure from the service, she had graced the covers of several fashion magazines. Madam Gigi always said each time she picked up one of the magazines, "Great girl and I miss her, but we have ten or so right now who are even better looking." No one argued that fact. The girls in her service looked like *Sports Illustrated* swimsuit models. They were beautiful women looking for a big break. A couple moved to L.A. and appeared in B movies, but most of the defectors found rich sugar daddies, most being the same corrupt clients they met on a "date".

The list of clientele was lengthy. Besides bankers and brokers, the list included cops, lawyers, doctors, dentists, pharmacists, therapists, psychiatrists, and any other reputable working professional that sprung to mind.

The driver walked Skylar to the door and André opened it at 9:00 p.m. She thanked the man and he returned to the black Navigator. One of Madam Gigi's main rules was each girl had to be accompanied by company muscle. It let the client know not to step over the boundary line.

The driver delivered the girl to the desired destination and accompanied her to the door. Once she went inside, he retreated to the vehicle and waited for a phone call. He would drive them anywhere they wanted to go, but a customer was never allowed to drive one of Gigi's girls. It was a safety precaution.

Gary didn't know how the escort service operated and was surprised to see the large man, one that was six-five and 300 pounds. It definitely threw a wrench into his plan. He couldn't walk up to the window, fire bullets into the Navigator, and go on his way. The night air was a little brisk, but it was Saturday night and sidewalks were bustling.

He walked into a nearby night deli and asked to use a phone.

"My car broke down and I'm a hundred miles from home. I can't get a signal on my cell phone."

"Is it a local call?" the man behind the counter asked.

"Yes."

The sandwich artist couldn't decide if Gary posed a threat. Mr. O'Neil picked up on his skepticism and pulled out $500 from his wallet and sat it on the counter.

"This should ease your mind."

He led Gary into a small office area and told him to make it quick.

Within thirty seconds, Gary brushed by the employee and thanked him.

All Gary needed was a diversion. The tow truck definitely served as one. The man in the Navigator argued with the truck driver for several minutes. He finally got tired of arguing and called the cops.

When the police arrived, Gary knew he had hit a home run. The man who resembled an NFL lineman was fighting a losing battle. He got in the Navigator and slammed the door shut. The cops got in their cruiser and pulled into the spot the Navigator vacated. They let the man know he wasn't hanging around that night.

Thirty minutes passed and the cops eventually moved on. Gary didn't waste time. He pulled the bouquet of flowers from the trunk and walked to André's door. Mr. O'Neil sat it on the mat outside the door and rang the bell. Gary hid in the shadows, watching and waiting. The door opened and André looked around. He wanted to kick the flowers over. In his line of work, everything was suspicious. Skylar saw the flowers from where she was sitting and tried to slide past André at the doorway.

"Don't touch them," he said, putting his arm out to stop her.

"Why?"

"Don't touch that bouquet!"

Gary heard them arguing. André couldn't give her a reason not to touch them. It wasn't as if he could tell her he was an assassin and someone might be trying to kill them.

He knelt down and pulled the flowers out of the dark vase. A bomb wasn't planted in the bottom. Apparently, the flowers were safe. He shoved them back in the vase and took them inside. Skylar was beaming. The note on the tag said the flowers were from the night's lover.

André was upset about the interruption. Dinner had already been digested and he was ready for dessert. Skylar was preoccupied by the flowers. The aromas coming from the orchids, lilies, tulips, roses, and other flowers were amazing. It was an odd assortment, but Gary had the florist stuff as many scents as she could get into the vase.

André's wish for dessert was about to come true. After smelling the flowers, Skylar was ready for action. The fragrances had made her euphoric, almost as if she was on an ecstasy high. Her brown skirt hit the floor first. Her cream collared shirt was next to go, followed by a Victoria's Secret bra. André was ready to pounce on her lightly freckled body. He stood up and Skylar began undressing him.

As she bent over to untie his shoes, the first sign of dizziness hit. She reached up for his belt and zipper and started to fade. She slowly made it to her feet and told André she wasn't feeling well. He assured her she'd be fine and that he'd do the work.

With his shirt halfway over his head, André heard Skylar fall to the floor. He pulled his shirt back down and noticed she had passed out. Number five couldn't figure out what was wrong with her. He was lightheaded as well, but not to the point of losing consciousness. André thought something could have been wrong with the food. Then it hit him. The flowers!

Chloroform was usually best utilized on a rag, but Gary had soaked the flowers enough to do the trick. André quickly peered through the blinds and didn't see anyone. The Navigator was gone and he knew what happened. It was around ten-thirty, but time for Skylar to leave. André put Skylar's skirt and shirt on her and threw her over his shoulder. He took her to his vehicle and raced to Goodale Park. He sat her on a park bench and drove home.

Gary thought about waiting for him in the apartment, but knew André would check the place inside and out, which he did. The Navigator pulled up to the curb at 11:25.

André cocked his firearm and waited for the driver to walk up to his door. At 11:35, the ringing startled him. He had forgotten to grab Skylar's small clutch when they left. Two minutes later, the man beat on his door. André cautiously opened it, leaving the chain attached.

"The girl's not here. She left about an hour ago."

"That's not how things work. Where is she?"

"I told you, she's not here. Someone sent her flowers and the small card claimed they were from me. I never sent them. Also, you have never left before. I want to know what's going on."

"I'd like to know as well. The cops claimed I called a tow truck. I never called, but they made me leave the area. I think you're playing me. Where is she?"

The man kicked in the door before André answered.

He immediately saw André was a squeeze away from ending his life.

"Man, you don't want to do that. All I want is the girl. I didn't send flowers and the tow truck story isn't bogus. Tell me where Skylar is and I'll be on my way."

Rapid pops sent the driver face first to the concrete. He was gasping for air as Gary walked through the doorway.

"No, you won't be on your way," he said while firing a bullet into the man's head.

Gary checked the man's pulse and pulled the gun from his waistband.

"We need to vacate the premises."

André froze. He tried to make sense of everything, but things had happened too fast. Like Ryule many years before, he didn't have time to organize things in his mind. Gary played the situation to perfection.

As number five turned, Gary fired four shots into his back with the driver's gun. He didn't wait to see the outcome. He slid his nine next to André's crumpled body and rushed out the door into the shadows.

The police were on the scene four minutes after Gary disappeared. The cops walked in and thought the usual—another robbery gone badly. The crime scene unit agreed that it looked like an attempted robbery, but thought a third party was involved. When they discovered Skylar's clutch, she was an immediate suspect.

Sunday morning, she was taken in for questioning. Skylar explained why she was there. She told the cops about the flowers and how she woke up at Goodale Park at 5:00 a.m. They knew she had been drugged. The flowers tested positive for chloroform and the card with André's name pinpointed him.

The cops knew about the tow truck incident and that the call came from the deli shop, which didn't have cameras. Witnesses from the shop described an older man with gray hair and black framed glasses. His double XL black jogging suit added nearly thirty pounds and the boots he wore made him appear two inches taller. Gary threw the glasses in one of those fancy street trash cans when he walked out of the deli and washed the coloring out of his hair as soon as he got home. The jogging suit was also beneficial in the shadows, as were the boots, which left size thirteen footprints at the crime scene. Gary wore size eleven.

All the evidence was pieced together, but didn't add up. The driver had broken into the house looking for Skylar, who had been drugged by André. He was shot twice in the back and once in the head. André took four shots to the back. The last severed his spine. They knew another person was involved, but Skylar was cleared of wrong doing.

The case was never solved, but the uptight part of society got their wish. Madam Gigi's was shut down following the murders. Most of the girls branched into other escort services, but the twenty-three-year-old Skylar enrolled at State and never had another "date" again.

Gary had accomplished his goal. Victor, Marco, and Pavel had been taken out by his son's crew. He had taken care of Mathias, Zeek, Luc, Tomas, Evgeni, and André. Jensen was the lone assassin left in the program and Gary had a special assignment for him. The crescendo was over. It was time for the finale.

IT HAD BEEN FOUR days since the incident at Polk's. Nearly two-thirds of townsfolk avoided dealing with the Warden clan, but they still had plenty of people who gave them scoop. If something happened in the area, the Warden clan knew about it, particularly when it came to corruption.

Sheriff Mulvaney and his boys were looking high and low for the Frenchman. No one had heard or seen a thing since the live action flick took place in the restaurant, except the Warden clan.

There were too many Wardens to count and nearly everyone in the area was somehow related to a Warden. As Denny often proved, the Warden men liked their women and they in turn liked them, despite their oft crooked ways and lack of respect for those outside their clan. Each male over eighteen from the Warden clan had at least two kids and most of them had five to eleven spread out over the Texas Hill Country.

The Wardens were one of the most powerful families in their part of the Texas Hill Country. Their power didn't stem from money, although several within the clan were fairly affluent. The Warden's strength was due to numbers.

J.B. Warden was ninety-seven and should have been dead at thirty. His bar fights were legendary. He'd been stabbed more times than all of the Warden men combined, or so he liked to claim. However, scars proved he had been punctured more times than a woman at a deranged spa treatment. He also was a chain smoker and heavy drinker, but looked healthier than most farmers cultivating their hallowed grounds.

He and his wife Earlene had eight children. Their second oldest son, Chet, was Butch's father. Chet and Dixie Warden had three boys—Butch, Sunny, and Randy Lee—and two girls—Jo-Dee and Patty.

Chet's brother, Pete, was far more promiscuous and was the one with eleven children. Denny was Pete's boy. True to Warden form, Denny's siblings produced legions of children. It was his nephew Hank who stumbled across the Frenchman.

Hank and some scalawags he hung around decided to go swimming on Mr. Posey's land. The property was adorned with "No Swimming" and "No Trespassing" signs. Everyone knew Mr. Posey didn't hunt so shotgun blasts startled his neighbors even during hunting seasons. When a rifle interrupted the peacefulness around his neck of the woods, people guaranteed he was chasing intruders from the strip pit.

The pit had long been abandoned, but was one of the finest swimming holes in Texas. Four people had drowned over the years and Mr. Posey fought hard to get the county to fill it in. After constant rejection, he took matters into his own hands. Some claimed he shot the rifle to scare off people, but others said Mr. Posey was just a bad aim.

Colt and Jolene went skinny dipping once while they were dating and had their clothes hanging on a tree. One of Mr. Posey's "warning shots" blew Jolene's panties off a branch. She and Colt always disputed the "bad aim" theory.

Although the strip pit was close to the Alexander farmland, Colt and Jolene decided it was off limits.

Mr. Posey's land butted against the strip pit. The land used to be owned by a natural resource company. Mr. Posey bought the land so he and his family could fish, which was another no-no for violators. The Alexander's property line formed the last part of the triangle. The strip pit was located through twelve acres of woods beside the Alexander's biggest field.

An old dirt road led to the strip pit. Mr. Posey constructed gates, fences, and other contraptions to keep people away, but they always destroyed them. He figured buckshot was the last resort.

Hank Warden and his lackeys hopped the partially erected fence and almost made it to the clearing when Hank noticed someone had beaten them to their spot. Hank told his friends to be still. They were lucky the stranger didn't spot them first.

"Y'all wait here. I'm getting a closer look at that fella."

Hank made his way around one of the paths and reached the top of the strip pit. He looked down at the man and thought it was the stranger he had heard his uncle Denny and Butch talk about. He didn't waste time getting back to his buddies.

"We have to get out of here. I have to tell my uncle Denny that the mysterious man is still in town."

They hopped the fence again, nervously looking around for Mr. Posey and his Remington rifle. They safely reached the car and drove to Denny's house.

Hank explained the situation to his uncle and Denny dialed Butch. He picked up Randy Lee and raced to his cousin's house. The Warden trio sped over to Mr. Posey's land.

When they reached the strip pit, they could faintly hear a tractor in the distance. Kurt was wrapping up late night duties on the farm.

Butch sent Hank and his friends to pester Mr. Posey about swimming at the pit. They needed to occupy him so the others didn't have to dodge warning shots.

Hank had explained where the man was stationed. Butch, Randy Lee, and Denny stood above the pit looking down, but the man was gone. Butch instructed his brother and cousin to stay at the top of the pit and keep an eye on things. The woods served as a getaway on a few occasions and no one knew the landscape better than Butch.

He used an old hunting path to make his way to the edge of the field Kurt was mowing. Butch could see Kurt in the distance, so he ducked back into the trees and pushed through the thicket until reaching another open path. After another fifty yards, the man Buster Pate and Dump Milligan described to him was crouched down over a fallen tree. The rifle was carefully aimed at the Alexander's field and the scope proved what was about to take place.

Butch pulled out his .45 and quietly crept twenty yards behind the man. He picked up a heavy rock and threw it down the trail. The loud thud caused Filip to lose his focus and pull his head away from the rifle. It gave Butch enough time to run toward the assassin. The first blast entered Filip's right shoulder blade and the second took out his left shoulder. Butch knew exactly what he was doing.

With Filip's strength to lift a rifle taken away from him, Butch stopped and took cover behind a tree.

"Why are you here?"

Filip didn't answer. Butch had heard the man let his actions speak louder than words. He peeked around the tree and a bullet from a small .22 caliber pistol went zinging by.

"Were ya going to kill Kurt or were ya after an Alexander?"

He received more silent treatment. They were at a stalemate until Randy Lee and Denny walked up the trail.

"Stop! He has a gun. Denny, walk back around the strip pit and come out on the high side of where we're standing. Randy Lee, tell Kurt what's going on and then secure the man from the left side."

Neither could carry out Butch's orders. Filip turned the .22 on himself and died instantly. The Wardens stood over his body, rummaging through his clothes. They couldn't find "Frenchy's" identification. The man was a mystery.

Suddenly, Butch began to panic. His gun was registered at Old Man Cater's collectible shop and it was against state law for a felon to own a gun. How could he prove the man was going to shoot Kurt? It sounded like another farfetched Warden tale.

They immediately ran through the woods and around the strip pit to Denny's Trans-Am. They disobeyed speed limit signs on the way to the sheriff's house. Denny slammed on the brakes in the sheriff's driveway, kicking gravel and dust everywhere. The Wardens piled out of the Trans-Am. It was only a small part of the Warden clan, but Sheriff Mulvaney was instantly alarmed.

"Sheriff, you need to come quickly. I did something and need your help."

Butch explained what happened and Sheriff Mulvaney took them in his Ram to Mr. Posey's land. They guided the sheriff to the Frenchman's body.

Butch surged into his blackmail plot before Sheriff Mulvaney could refuse to help him.

"You know Trevor isn't my boy and yet you had me lie to the state workers. I complained about child support and refused to let them prick my finger for blood. Everybody knows you and Judge Newsome are tight. Why didn't he order a hooligan like me to give a blood sample? The court records will prove that Judge Newsome didn't rule in their favor. I know the names of the men who stopped by the jail to visit me and have them on speed dial."

"You can't prove anything!"

"People were curious why you let me out of jail early and how I got the job with the water and sewer department. The story adds up. If that's not enough evidence, you know Jim and Elaine Alexander won't lie. Oh, and one last thing. For the first time since 1978, you're opposed on the November ballot. Do you think people will vote for you with a scandal like this over your head?"

Sheriff Mulvaney thought about mowing down the three Wardens standing with him in the woods. He knew Butch Warden had him by the balls.

"I guess it was a case of self protection," he said as he bent over and put the gun in Filip's hand. "Butch, this is gonna hurt, but it has to be done."

The bullet entered Butch's left leg and he screamed in anguish.

"Wait five minutes, run to the Alexanders, and report the shootings to the station," Sheriff Mulvaney instructed. "I'll come back as quickly as I can."

Twenty minutes passed and the sheriff returned with deputies and investigators.

Butch was taken to the hospital. He and the sheriff had words about his limp over the next several years, but it sure beat going to prison, even though Butch had protected an innocent civilian from being hurt. His rap sheet would have been enough for a prosecutor to get him locked up for a long time.

A month after the Frenchman's death, a knock interrupted dinner at the Alexanders. Butch Warden was there to talk to Kurt.

They went outside and Butch swore Mr. Carson to secrecy. After they shook hands, Butch spilled his guts about what had happened. He wanted Kurt to know someone had tried to kill him. Kurt had a newfound respect for Butch Warden and they became friends after his visit.

"I have some things to tell you as well," Kurt said as he explained why the man was in Austin.

Butch couldn't believe the things Kurt told him about the motel explosion, the affair with Sharon, and years on the lam. The profile fit a Warden, but certainly not Kurt. Mr. Carson begged Butch to allow him to let Jim and Trevor in on their secret. Butch agreed.

The next day, Kurt told Mr. Alexander and Trevor the truth about Filip's death. They thanked Butch Warden for saving Kurt's life. They had waited years to avenge Sharon's death. The Frenchman's appearance and subsequent death proved it was time.

Chapter
Twenty-Three

KURT, TREVOR, AND JIM started formulating a plan to get Preston to Austin, but they didn't know much about him so it made it difficult. They knew his father's name was Gary and he and Preston lived in Columbus, Ohio. Sheriff Mulvaney agreed to help them after they explained Trevor wanted to find Preston.

Mr. Carson never told anyone about the items stored in his shoebox in the basement. Elaine saw the paper, but didn't know the meaning behind it. Kurt knew it was time to take action after Filip had tried to kill him. Jim and Trevor knew about Sharon's death, Kurt's house explosion, and his attempted murder, but it was time to show them what the shoebox materials meant.

He pulled out the newspaper detailing the house fire. After they finished reading it, Kurt stated Gary was involved. The story talked at length about the feud between striking employees and Robert Rhodes. Kurt showed them Stenson's business card. It was similar to the card he attached to the briefcase in Fresno years earlier.

"This man is a friend of Gary's. They were college roommates. Sharon talked about him on several occasions. I know that Frenchman was sent here to kill me. I think they're involved with Rhodes as well. They haven't forgotten the things I know about them, the house fire and Sharon's death in particular. I'm still upset about Ava's death, but her obituary gave them information they were looking for. It's the worst thing that could have happened."

Trevor pulled out his laptop and the four men began searching for information about Gary O'Neil. His name was linked to a company in Columbus. Stenson & Rhodes had a Web site, but it didn't have an employee bio section. It listed Harry Stenson, Robert Rhodes, and Gary O'Neil as the three ranking employees. Kurt was right. The trio was in a crooked alliance. Stenson was also a partner in the Rhodes Tire and Rubber Company. Kurt knew the public relations firm was the key to finding Preston.

The last item he pulled out was the picture of Gary Player.

"This picture may not mean much, but the golfer's name is Gary and it was sent to me by Sharon. She was trying to tell me that Gary was a 'Player' in the house fire. Stenson was involved and I'm sure Rhodes also had a hand in it."

After a lengthy discussion about the PR firm and the three men, Trevor knew it was time to head to Columbus. He watched every move Stenson made in the Buckeye State's capital. He thought he had been busted a few times, but Trevor's wardrobe always made him look like a student at State.

It took Trevor a few days, but he finally saw Harry "Big Boy" Stenson meeting with Robert Rhodes. He looked into Rhodes' background and most of the Web hits linked him to a warehouse that had since been abandoned. The rest of the hits were links to stories on www.rhodestirerubberco.com.

Trevor decided to check out the warehouse. He discovered the old path on his way there. When he pulled into the lot at the warehouse, he knew he would have to jump the fence. He opted to drive back to the path and check out where it led. He stopped his car near the chain and unhooked it. He drove down the rutty path and it stopped at the railroad tracks. He parked his vehicle, got out, and crossed the tracks. The fence near the tracks had a small hole in it, so he wiggled through and crept to the back of the old facility. He noticed the rotted house across the street and instantly knew it was where the fire had taken place.

He snooped around the warehouse for an hour or so before going back to his hotel. The oldest O'Neil boy nearly pulled an all-nighter as he researched more about Rhodes. All the stories he read talked about numerous deaths and claims of cover up. He also found out about several murders of ex-employees. A lot of the articles talked about Rhodes being a possible suspect, but nothing could be linked to him.

Trevor was staying in constant contact with Kurt and Jim in Austin. Sheriff Mulvaney passed along new information he dug up to Jim or Kurt and they relayed it to Trevor. They all felt like each day brought them closer to Preston.

Stenson stopped by the apartment when he needed to drop off materials. Trevor followed him there one night. Looking out the curtains to make sure he wasn't being watched was a ritual for Big Boy, but a small piece of fabric stuck to the window sill that evening. Trevor had parked a block away and quietly dodged between houses without being spotted by some neighborhood watch dogs.

He peered through the window and saw Stenson at the table with the briefcase. He couldn't make out what he was doing, but Trevor figured it was corrupt. Trevor walked back to his car and a group of guys yelled out to him, but before they could stop him, he peeled out of the parking space and sped down the street.

Shortly after 4:00 a.m., Trevor returned and broke into the apartment. It was a trick one of the Warden boys had taught him at a party. He had watched Stenson go into the only bedroom before he split earlier. Trevor walked into the empty room, using a small pocket flashlight to look around. The room was empty. He walked into the kitchen and saw the screwdriver sitting on the table where Stenson had the briefcase.

Trevor grabbed the screwdriver and went to the bedroom. The Phillips was only needed for the light switch cover on the wall and the register on the floor. He unscrewed four screws, popped the register face off, and looked into the register. He didn't see anything, but felt around and found the case.

He didn't have a key to open it, but had a small bag of tools and used another Warden trick to get inside. Trevor found the map with numbers written on it. The only compartment in the briefcase was also locked and he was unable to pick the lock. He at least had a series of numbers.

Trevor tucked the briefcase into its hiding spot, put the screws back into place, and returned the screwdriver where he found it. He watched the apartment for a few days and saw a man walk in on the third day of his stakeout. He waited for the man to exit and followed at a safe distance.

The library was the man's next stop. Trevor saw a worker's badge sitting on the counter at the welcome station. He flirted with the girl at the desk and swiped it while she was preoccupied in la-la-land. The foreigner declined his assistance so Trevor switched to a different plan.

He went back to the desk for a second round of flirtation. Trevor convinced her that a man was stealing books. She said she would inform her supervisor so they could look at video surveillance. Trevor again used his charm and talked her into quickly reviewing the tape. They discovered the man wasn't stealing books, but was hiding them. Trevor apologized for his mistake and told the girl he'd be back every day as long as she was working.

The man left the library and Trevor, who had waited patiently at a table, went back to the section where the man hid the book. He found it and saw letters next to the first twenty-six page numbers. He pulled out the series of numbers he found in the briefcase and began writing the corresponding letters.

It took Trevor nearly an hour to figure out what the circled number meant, but he found the answer in the index. Dublin, Ohio. He was confused, but four days later, a woman was gunned down in Dublin, which was unheard of in the ritzy suburb of Columbus. She was an ex-employee of the tire and rubber plant. Mrs. Dobbins was the thirty-eighth to either be murdered or die in some sort of mishap.

Trevor called Austin that night and explained something bigger was going on than they had imagined. He had discovered who was behind the murders of the employees.

"It's Stenson. It's Stenson."

"Calm down," Kurt said.

"To make a long story short…Stenson went to an apartment and put some information in a briefcase. Another man stopped by and retrieved a series of numbers and something else out of a locked compartment. He went to the library to decipher the code from a hidden book. A woman was killed four days later. I translated the code as well and Dublin, Ohio, is what the series of numbers spelled. Guess where the woman died?"

Kurt wasn't in the mood for guessing games.

"Stenson is behind the killings of employees who worked at the old warehouse. He's helping Rhodes get rid of people for some reason or other. Claims of a cover up are not claims. Their accusations are true. I don't have proof Gary is involved, but I'm sure he is."

"I'll talk to Sheriff Mulvaney so he can alert…"

"I don't want the law involved anymore. These are the people that killed my mother and the woman you loved. We have dreamed of getting even. We'd like to see them rot in jail for the rest of their lives, but I don't think it's going to be that simple. They have taken more than just one person away from their family and friends. I may have to face consequences, but they're going to pay."

"Don't do anything stupid," Kurt replied as the phone went dead.

Trevor had to get in the compartment, but didn't know how. He put it on the backburner and continued his research.

He compiled notes on the thirty-eight victims, memorizing the names of each one. Trevor started visiting the families who lost loved ones, either by contaminated drinking water that led to cancer or by a tragic mishap, including murder.

Some shut the door in his face as he began explaining why he was there. Others hung up on him. He eventually found partners in Dane and Brock. Dane was a high-tech wizard while Brock was beneficial because of his risky personality. Trevor broke into the apartment again and they set up the video cameras in the attic's crawl space.

Dane set up a feed to a wireless laptop and they decided it was best to stay at the warehouse. Brock was in charge of getting into Stenson & Rhodes. He was also appointed as lead detective and his primary goal was to dig up information about Preston.

The receptionist at the front desk was more than willing to give Brock information about Preston, especially since Brock claimed he was one of Preston's good friends from college. Brock used the guise they had lost touch and wanted to catch up with his old pal.

She was ready to page Preston, but Brock said he wanted it to be a surprise when they "bumped" into each other. They chatted three or four minutes and Brock discovered Preston was still not over an ex-girlfriend. The receptionist wanted to hang out with Preston when she first started, but he declined because of a girl named Lauren.

Once Brock had Lauren's name, Dane started looking into her past. Trevor visited the Residents of Everett Wren. He explained the situation to Lauren. She said Preston was always troubled about his mother's death. She also indicated Gary was a dangerous man. Trevor told her about his plan and that he needed help. Lauren agreed, but said they would always need to look over their shoulders.

Trevor checked in with Austin later that night. He wanted the shoebox materials sent to Columbus. The items arrived two days later.

"It's time to warn Preston. We need to tell him who he's working for and the danger he's in. One of the men is our dad. I want him out of Stenson & Rhodes as soon as possible."

They wired the VCR in the attic to scare Stenson, Rhodes, and Gary. Trevor wanted them to believe several tapes were floating around. There weren't any tapes, but there were plenty of CDs. Dane had recorded everything at the apartment since he set up the surveillance. All they were waiting for was another man to pop in.

While Trevor and his crew were sneaking around Columbus, things were dicey with Stenson and Rhodes. When one of the assassins completed an assignment, they wrote an X on a sheet of paper and placed it in an envelope. The assassin slipped the envelope in Gary's mailbox, which was located at the front entrance, and Gary then relayed the message to Robert and Big Boy.

Each assassin had a two-week period to complete an assignment. It had been over three weeks since Filip left for Austin. They wondered if he had fled the country. It was time to send someone else to Austin.

Each morning, Dane reviewed the action from the previous night. He'd fast forward through each recording in about ninety minutes. Dane was enjoying a morning cup of coffee while watching the CD from the night before. Dane's scream woke Trevor and Brock and they huddled over the laptop. Shortly after they went to bed, someone visited the apartment. Trevor immediately recognized Stenson.

"This is the last piece of evidence we need. We'll drop it off at Stenson & Rhodes later this morning and then I'll contact Preston. Once we've reunited, we'll send duplicates of our materials to the police. They are finished ruining people's lives."

ROBERT DIDN'T EXPECT TO hear from his brother, but had been waiting for a phone call from his long lost twin since he sent the insincere correspondence. He didn't like giving away $250,000, but felt a slight bit of remorse for what he had done to his flesh and blood.

Each day, Robert asked the secretary, who had grown tired of his increasingly aggressive advances, if he had any messages from Ronald. His phone was busy with the usual stream of business traffic, but Robert needed to hear from him.

A letter showed up in the mail the next day and the waiting was over.

Robert,

Against better judgment, I've decided to see if we can bury the past. Let's meet this Saturday in Columbus at Four Corners. See you at 6:45. I'll pick up the tab.

Ronald

Robert Rhodes smiled the rest of the week. He wanted to temporarily return to his brother's good graces. He had crafted a detailed scheme to pin all the blame on Stenson, Gary, and his brother. With Stenson dead, it made things easier. The extortion payment to his brother was the start of things.

While Robert's plan was in motion, Gary was working on his final assignment. He was going to use Jensen to take out Robert, but needed help from Trevor.

Preston's phone rang as he and Lauren were getting ready to leave Columbus. They were going to give Austin a try. Lauren and Preston stopped by her apartment the previous day and moved everything out.

"Hello."

"It's Gary."

"I see you've been a busy man and still haven't changed."

"I can truthfully say that I'm not proud of the way things have played out. Preston, I'm a crooked man, but I love you. I thought Trevor was dead all these years. I also love him. I wanted to get out years ago, but I loved the lifestyle more than I did my family. I'm truly sorry."

"It's a little late for that. Why are you calling me?"

"I need to talk to Trevor."

Preston handed the phone to Trevor, who was having breakfast with Ronald and Helen.

"Make it quick."

"I need everything you stole from us, including the briefcase."

"I can't do that."

"I'm finishing what I started. After that, I'm leaving Columbus for good."

"If I give you the briefcase, book, and other items, what's going to stop you from eventually using it against us?"

"This blockbuster won't have a sequel."

"Where are you going?"

"I'll drop you a postcard."

"I guess it's safe to assume your wreckage from the last few days serves notice that you're getting out of the business."

"You've made the correct assumption, son."

Gary was scheduled to show up at the Rhodes' residence in an hour. After Trevor rid himself of the briefcase and book, he was going to Austin.

Ronald and Helen were disappointed to see their guests leaving. The couple never had children so company was welcome. The first of the five visitors to leave was Dane. He was going to Denver to work for a high-tech software company. He was leaving Columbus in a couple of weeks.

Savannah was the next to go. She had been free to leave for days, but had taken a liking to Trevor. Savannah and her fiancé were on the ropes and had pushed their wedding date back a few times. He had called over three hundred times since her "kidnapping" and her place of employment left a message announcing she no longer had a job.

Savannah hugged Mr. and Mrs. Rhodes while thanking them for their generosity and hospitality. Lauren and Preston were next on the good-bye list, but they were all getting together in Austin in a few days. Trevor walked Savannah to the cab and gave her a hug and kiss good-bye.

"I'll see you in a few days," she yelled out the window as the cab drove away.

Everyone settled into their seats and chatted a while longer, but the sound of a running engine in the driveway signaled Gary had arrived.

He waited at the car and Trevor and Preston went outside to meet him.

"I never thought I'd see my boys together again."

"Spare us the emotional fireworks," Preston said with approval from Trevor.

"Before I hand you these items, I want you to know I still think you're a rotten individual."

"You're words are truthful, but also painful. As I said on the phone, I'm sorry for the pain I've caused the two of you. I'll never face the families who have suffered because of Harry, Robert, and me, but I regret all of that as well. We were ready to kill anyone who was involved in taking the briefcase, but I'm glad things turned out the way they did. Knowing you're alive has changed me."

"What a confessional and repentance," Trevor said.

"I don't blame you for the hatred you have. I want you to know I love you both and I'll try to stay in touch."

Gary embraced his boys before Trevor handed him the stolen goods. He backed out of the driveway and it was the last time either of them saw Gary.

THE PACKAGE ARRIVED A little before noon. Preston was running one of his crummy errands for Big Boy when it was delivered to his office. Following his errand, he chatted with Clint Harbor while getting a bite to eat.

When Preston returned from Four Corners, he sat his small briefcase on the floor and examined the package. He shook the cardboard box and heard items moving inside.

Preston anxiously opened it and was vastly disappointed. He flipped through the newspaper first. He had heard about the house fire and the cover up claims more times than he would have liked. The paper didn't mean a thing to him. Then he pulled out Stenson's card and immediately wanted to vomit. Thoughts of Stenson always made him sick.

The third item wrapped in tissue paper really caught Preston's attention. It was a photo he recalled from his youth. He had known every golfer's name since he was old enough to talk, but didn't understand why Gary Player had been sent to him. The most intriguing thing about the photo was it had once hung in one of his father's rooms. Preston was confused.

He reached in the box and pulled out a folder. It contained four graphic pictures of a dead man lying in the woods. He didn't know the man, although it would have been hard for anyone to identify him through the gore. Preston sat the photos aside and pulled out the last item.

A white sleeve contained two discs. He popped the first disc in his computer and it was blank. Preston inserted the second disc and watched the five-minute clip. He saw Stenson walk into an empty room and pull a briefcase out of a register. The scene switched to the kitchen and Preston saw him put a few things inside the briefcase. Again, the scene shifted. Stenson was back in the bedroom hiding the briefcase. The lights were turned off and the video ended.

Preston didn't know what he had just watched. He looked inside the box to make sure nothing else was in it. "Beware of S&R and your father" was on the bottom of the box in small print.

He rested his head against his $2,500 black leather chair and suddenly needed a drink. Preston put all of the materials in a manila folder, except the second disc, and threw the box away in the cafeteria. He didn't know who sent it, but someone was warning him. O'Neil put the folder on his piled desk and locked his office.

"I'll be back in the morning," Preston said to a secretary on his floor. If he drank too much, he might not be in until the afternoon.

Stenson was irritated when he found out Preston left for the day. He wanted to go over some things with him, but Preston's absence canceled that idea. Stenson had the secretary unlock Preston's door and went inside.

As he began to put the folder on top of Preston's large pile, curiosity got the best of him. Big Boy opened the first folder on Preston's pile and his mouth nearly hit the floor. The newspaper article proved Preston had seen too much. His business card and the photo of Gary Player confirmed Stenson knew exactly what someone was saying.

Then he saw the pictures of Filip. Stenson didn't know who the man was, but someone had written Austin, Texas, and the date on the back of each photo. Big Boy knew their assassin was dead.

Each computer needed a secret passcode to log on. Stenson had one that worked for every computer in the building. He placed the disc in the drive, but it was blank. Someone knew too much. He gathered the materials and put them back in the folder. Stenson called Rhodes and they met in Dayton for dinner.

Big Boy showed Robert the items Preston had lying on his desk. They talked about the materials, but the disc was the most perplexing. They wondered what could have been on the disc. There wasn't a way around it. The second Austin trip had to be canceled. They knew someone in Austin was on to them and someone in Columbus was causing problems. Preston was the only person linked to the information. In Stenson's mind, Preston had to be the next mark.

Stenson drove back to Columbus and dropped by Phil's house. Buckeye Health and Stenson's firm had been working on a deal for quite some time. Stenson told Seevers he'd like him to meet with one of his associates at Mehaffey's Pub in three days. Phil agreed and Stenson moved to the next part of his plan.

Big Boy called Gary and told him to hold off on the Austin assignment.

"We have a change of plans. We'll get to that, but we have to be patient."

Gary was kept in the dark.

Stenson dropped by the apartment and put Preston's photo in the folder. Mehaffey's Pub was the code in the series of numbers, but 11:00 a.m. and the date were also written on the map. He left the apartment and went to phase two.

Robert was also into real estate and all the apartments where the assassins stayed were owned by Rhodes, although he never met them. Stenson sat outside one of the apartments until the man returned from his daily trip past Gary's house. He told the man who he was. Victor didn't believe Big Boy, but he knew too much about the operation. He could have been a cop, but the $75,000 bonus eased those concerns.

The assassin got up the next morning and stopped by the post office before heading to the apartment. He grabbed the screwdriver and took off the register plate. The snap nearly broke two of his fingers. A rat trap had replaced the briefcase. Victor was ready to assign himself to Stenson. The briefcase was missing and someone had some explaining to do.

Victor visited Big Boy at Stenson & Rhodes later that day. Harry wasn't happy to see number nine at his business, but was more than happy to get him behind closed doors. As soon as Stenson shut the door, Victor was one squeeze away from painting Stenson's office walls a new color.

"What was that about?" Victor asked as he showed Stenson his fingers.

"I don't understand."

Victor pinned Stenson by his throat against one of the walls.

"The briefcase wasn't there and my fingers were nearly chopped off."

"They must have stolen it," Big Boy said.

"Who?"

"The same people who sent Preston O'Neil incriminating information about us and our program. They're on to us and we need to figure out who they are. I highly doubt Preston is behind this, but he was your assignment. He's Gary O'Neil's son."

Harry received permission to reach inside one of his cabinets as Victor put the gun to his head. A secret compartment contained a thin carrying case. Stenson entered the code on the dials and opened the case. He grabbed an envelope from the case and closed it.

"This is to show you that you weren't being set up today. Here is $100,000. If you agree to a new plan and complete the job, I'll give you another $900,000."

"What is your plan?"

"I'm postponing the meeting where the hit was supposed to take place. I want you to follow Preston O'Neil's every move. I'm instructing Gary to assign three assassins to work with you. I know each of you work alone and that is how we prefer things to be done, but this problem calls for drastic measures."

Victor agreed and a new deal was in place. The assassin left Stenson's office and Big Boy called Seevers. The meeting was pushed back. Big Boy's next call was to Gary. After they hung up, Gary put Marco, Pavel, and Jensen's numbers on the board with "C Me" underneath their numbers. Each hit man dropped by Stenson & Rhodes the next three days. Victor was there the first day with Big Boy when Marco visited. Pavel was next to go through introductions. They met with Jensen the last day.

The four hit men began watching the apartment and Preston's every move. They didn't know Trevor, Dane, and Brock were also doing the same thing each day. Stenson and Rhodes wanted to find the "thieves and blackmailers" and were using their resources to find them. Trevor and his crew were also digging up as much information as they could.

Trevor knew they didn't have much time when he was followed one day. Trevor watched the black Expedition in his rearview mirror for several miles. He was on his way to the warehouse, but had to abort his trip. Trevor jumped onto 270 and drove around the giant loop twice. Wasting gas at $2.44 per gallon wasn't enjoyable, but he had to lose the Expedition.

He whipped onto 315, making his way to High Street. As the chase intensified, Stenson's thugs knew they were following one of the people involved in stealing the briefcase. Trevor lost them after he turned onto Russell. He darted down a small alley where a garbage truck was picking up trash. He should have waited at the end of the alley, but Trevor squeezed past the truck and the house on the other side of the alley. The trash collectors yelled profanities at the daredevil, but Trevor kept driving. There wasn't enough room for the

Expedition to squeeze through. Trevor succeeded in losing the thugs, but things had changed.

Days passed and the meeting day arrived. Stenson decided Mehaffey's Pub was where the hit would still take place. The only change was he wanted Preston and Phil both gunned down. Trevor and his crew also knew what was supposed to take place.

The phone rang at 8:15 and the young PR associate answered. It was supposed to be the beginning of the end for Preston O'Neil. Stenson had plans for Preston that morning, but so did someone else.

Chapter Twenty-Four

GARY MOVED EVERYTHING HE owned to storage units. His house wasn't on the market, but Gary didn't plan on living there in the foreseeable future. Gary paid for the maid and grounds crew to drop by once a week, but canceled other services, including internet, television, and things of that nature.

Number two was the last man standing in the program and was about to receive the final assignment. Gary didn't know about Robert's plan and that became a problem.

After the warehouse shootout, Robert knew things would get worse. The police showed up at his Cincinnati house and took him in for questioning. They felt he had something to do with the murders and mishaps over the years, but couldn't prove anything. On three separate occasions, lawyers looking to make names for themselves tried to land Robert in prison. He wiggled off the hook each time because juries weren't presented with substantial evidence. Payoffs didn't hurt either.

Three men were murdered in a bloody shootout on grounds where his company was formerly located and his partner also died at the scene. The police thought it was suspicious that the men lived in different apartments owned by Rhodes. Again, they couldn't prove anything. Rhodes attempted to serve eviction notices to the remaining assassins to cover his trail, but Gary knocked off two of them before they could be served.

Policemen visited Rhodes' house in Cincinnati again to take him in for more interrogation, but he wasn't there. They located him at his Columbus home. Rhodes' attorney wouldn't let him say much and the police were at yet another dead end with Robert Rhodes.

Jensen was notified that he was to be out of his apartment by the end of the week. He didn't take the news well. Rhodes attempted to serve the other man, but discovered he already moved out.

After Jensen received his notice, Gary coincidentally showed up. Jensen was prepared to kill Gary, but carefully watched him as he sat something next to his door.

Jensen opened the door and the briefcase was tucked under the shrubs below a window. A small note was taped to the briefcase and number two was written on it in black Sharpie ink.

The hit man didn't know what to think, but decided it was moving day. He packed his things and headed to the library. Although it was two in the afternoon, he carried the briefcase, which was already unlocked, in with him and rushed to the hidden book. Jensen took a seat in one of the small sitting rooms and opened the briefcase.

Gary had written a short note explaining Rhodes had eliminated the other assassins and Jensen was next on his list. He claimed it was the only way to safely communicate. Jensen wondered if Gary was lying, but believed the part of his note that stated Rhodes had also murdered Stenson.

He deciphered the series of numbers. He unlocked the compartment and took the picture out. He folded it in half and stuck it in his pocket. Jensen threw the keys, lighter, and map in the trash. He took the book, briefcase, and Gary's note with him.

Jensen checked into a room Gary had reserved at the Embassy Suites and waited. Gary would call when the time was right.

It had been weeks since Gary talked to Rhodes, but he was going to use the "hiding out" excuse. He knew Rhodes wouldn't buy it, but wanted him to think he desperately needed his help.

Robert had a good inkling Gary was still alive and behind all the assassins' deaths, but didn't expect to hear from him. Rhodes' phone rang and Mr. O'Neil was on the other end.

Each carefully selected his words. Gary began with the kidnapping story. He explained he and Preston had been tied up in one of the storage houses at the old warehouse and their kidnappers interrogated them for several days.

"I hadn't seen anyone for days when I heard gunshots. A man opened the door and it was Stenson. He untied me, but looked like he was ready to kill me. Fortunately, someone intervened and I managed to get away. I have been looking over my shoulder ever since. I read the story about what happened and knew Stenson was dead. The only conclusion I came up with is that you're behind it."

"I've been dealing with this mess for days, but I'm not at fault. The cops have either visited me at one of my homes or contacted me by phone every day since the warehouse ordeal. I thought you were to blame and still do."

Gary was a better poker player than Rhodes and alleged he wasn't in contact because he was following Stenson's orders.

"I thought I might be next. It's obvious someone's trying to eliminate the program. Sure, the assassins drive by my house every day, but I haven't put a number on that board since receiving orders from Stenson to put four, six, and eight up at the same time."

"Those were Stenson's orders?"

"Yes. He dropped by my house two days before the shootout and I placed all three numbers on the board the next morning. Do you think Stenson was trying to stop the program and eliminate us as well?"

"He would have killed you instead of untying you. Did you see bodies when you left?"

"We had company in the second storage house. Mathias walked in and asked what was going on. His visit was unexpected. I think Stenson would have killed me if not for number four's arrival. Big Boy made up a story about saving me from the people who stole the briefcase. Mathias and Stenson drew guns and I didn't wait around to see what happened. I hobbled across the road and heard a gunshot. The next thing I heard was Stenson yelling for me as the screeching car stopped at the front gate."

Rhodes chuckled as if Gary had delivered a punch line.

"Luc had arrived and I heard another shot. I saw Zeek walk around and climb over a fence. He went straight for the second storage house because the door was open. He saw Mathias' body and cautiously walked out the door. Stenson dropped him on the spot. Zeek fell against the wall. I made it across the railroad tracks and looked through some pine trees. Stenson again called out for me, but sirens were getting closer. Someone had called the police. I ventured through the woods to a junk pile and nestled into a spot. I heard another gunshot and that was the last of the shooting. I heard cops combing the area and footsteps in the distance, but they never got close. I waited approximately thirty hours before I left and have been hiding since."

"Do you expect me to believe all of that?"

"That is what happened."

"I think we need to meet."

"Name the time and place."

"Four Corners at 6:45 on Saturday."

"I'll be there."

They hung up and began hatching their plans.

Robert immediately got on the phone and switched his meeting with Ronald to Mehaffey's Pub and moved the time to 8:00 p.m. He told him he was going to be running a little late because of a meeting, thus the reason for the time change.

Saturday rolled around and Ronald was at Mehaffey's Pub at 7:50. He looked at the front door every time it opened. After waiting an hour, Ronald left. He attempted to contact his brother, but his calls went straight to voice mail.

Across town, Robert was waiting on Gary at Four Corners at 6:45. Rhodes planned to take out two targets in one night. Gary had a feeling that Robert was up to something so he skipped the meeting. His gut feeling served him well.

Rhodes dropped by one of the apartments after discovering an eviction notice wasn't necessary. He let a painting crew in and was having new carpet put down.

The man watched the work crews for days. He wanted to know who had screwed him over. He thought it was Gary, but wasn't sure. The stranger finally tracked down Rhodes. Robert had only seen him once. They met in the meeting held at Stenson & Rhodes.

Robert was terrified when the man grabbed him. He thought he had discovered who was behind the warehouse and subsequent killings. The hit man told Rhodes he was going to kill him and would make sure it was a slow and painful death.

The former Stenson and Rhodes gun-for-hire used ketamine to sedate Rhodes. His car was parked in the alleyway where he nabbed him. He stuffed Rhodes into his vehicle and drove to a boarded abandoned house near Children's Hospital. The tortuous sessions and extensive questioning lasted for days.

He couldn't break Rhodes down and knew why. Robert wasn't who betrayed him, nor had he eliminated any of the assassins in the program. They finally struck a deal. Robert would pay him $750,000 to get rid of their common problem—Gary O'Neil.

Gary had a scheme of his own. Jensen followed Rhodes for a few days. When Rhodes walked out of the restaurant after being stood up, the shot from across the street sent him to the pavement. The target had been hit. Jensen quickly packed his gear and exited the parking garage in a car painted like a pizza delivery vehicle. No one noticed because of the panic on the street. Several people tended to Rhodes, but it was too late. The damage was done.

Jensen and Gary met in a dimly lit parking lot near *The Horseshoe*. They turned off their parking lights and Gary walked up to Jensen's window.

"The deed has been accomplished."

Gary handed Jensen a duffel bag with ten envelopes. Each contained $5,000. He also handed him the number to an offshore account in the Cayman Islands. Mr. O'Neil informed Jensen he was satisfied with his work. Number two was pleased with what awaited in the Western Caribbean financial institution.

They shook hands and as number two flipped his lights on and began to inch away, Gary fired a bullet into Jensen's head. The car swerved to the right and crashed into a concrete barricade that protected a towering lightpole.

Gary calmly walked over to Jensen's car and put a second bullet into number two. Blood immediately gushed from his chest. The Indian giver reclaimed his cash, but left the fake account number with

Jensen. He also grabbed the briefcase and the book. Gary got in his car and drove to the Columbus Airport.

Flight No. 4177 took off from the runway and Gary felt a calmness overtake his body. It was the first time since Gary met Stenson that he felt like he could have a regular life. He had told Preston and Trevor that he was going to enjoy life—Caribbean style!

Their dad went to sleep envisioning piña coladas and white sand.

THINGS IN AUSTIN HAD somewhat settled down. Ava's death and the Frenchman's visit still had everyone talking, but town whispers were mostly centered on one man.

Butch Warden was still a hot topic of conversation. A few people thought they knew what happened, but the full details would never be known. If he had in fact shot the Texas Hill Country intruder, many would have forgiven him.

Nearly six weeks after the shooting, Pastor Browne had just started hooting and hollering when the doors at Calvary Baptist swung open. Many in the congregation began squirming in their seats. Some fidgeted because they felt uncomfortable. Others shifted to get a better view of their visitor.

A small percentage moved to make room for the man while other seat scooters were signaling he wasn't welcome to sit with their family. An armchair weather forecaster on the left side blurted, "They must be calling for lightning today."

The Alexanders and Kurt were aware he might show up. After the incident in the woods, he stopped by their farm every day after work. He and Kurt were best friends, which also had the town gossiping.

The race for sheriff between Mr. Mulvaney and Boone Atkinson was the only topic discussed more than Butch Warden.

Jim nudged Elaine and she asked everyone in their row to scrunch together. Mr. Alexander stood up and motioned Butch to join them in their pew.

He slowly walked down the aisle, not knowing if the church would become a fiery furnace or if a mass exodus would take place. The smoke detectors remained silent and no one moved toward the exit. Butch Warden visiting Calvary Baptist was certainly enough to put the race for sheriff on the backburner for the next week.

Pastor Browne was speechless for the first time in his career. He tried spewing out a few words, but stuttered through each syllable. He walked over to Deacon Frye in the second row on the left, whispered in his ear, and then took a seat on the stage.

Deacon Frye walked to the podium and led the church in a lengthy prayer. He rambled on for nearly ten minutes about judging. Butch didn't understand why the deacon was talking about two-by-fours in people's eyes and a son who had the hideous name of Prodigal. The congregation understood Deacon Frye's prayer.

Butch had his left eye closed, but squinted to keep his right eye open. Pastor Browne always held his hands up to the sky and kept his eyes tightly closed during prayer, except that Sunday. He clasped his hands and cupped them around his eyes. He peeked over his left hand and made eye contact with Butch. A smile assured Butch it was OK for him to be at Calvary Baptist.

Pastor Browne walked to the podium and thanked Deacon Frye for a lovely prayer. He also thanked him internally because it gave him time to collect his thoughts.

He delivered his flock a curveball. The bulletin informed members and guests alike that Pastor Browne would conclude his series on "A life in Hades." Instead, he preached about loving others. Butch Warden changed the landscape that morning and forever at Calvary.

Following a wonderful service, several people, some who had ignored Butch for decades, made their way over to greet him. Some members were truly happy to have him there, but others wanted to dig up a little dirt. Regardless of their logic, invitations to Polk's Family Restaurant were aplenty. Butch politely declined because he was going with the Alexander family.

The crowd dispersed and everyone rushed to Polk's to get a good spot. The secretary's husband got a speeding ticket on the way there, which was also talked about for the next week or two.

Pastor Browne was the last to shake Butch Warden's hand.

"Thank you for being part of our worship today. You're welcome anytime. God loves us all and I hope you could feel that this morning."

"I appreciate the open invitation. And yes, I feel different today."

"We hope to see you next Sunday."

The gossip had already reached town. Mr. Polk couldn't believe the news. He hadn't seen Butch since the day he was searching for the Frenchman.

When Butch walked through the door with the Alexander family, Mr. Polk greeted him.

"Your seat's open," he said to a circle of grins. "I'm sorry for the way I treated you the last time you were here. All of us have room for change. Today's meal is on the house."

The tension that hovered throughout the eatery the last time Butch visited was nowhere to be found. He ate his meal and shared several laughs. Butch joined Mr. Alexander, who was a pipe smoker, on the street following their meals.

"This ought to give everyone plenty to talk about for the next month. What do you have up your sleeve next?" Jim questioned with a smile.

Butch Warden seemed to outdo himself the following week. He was back at Calvary and placed his membership. Each passing week, another Warden showed up with him.

"God and Calvary Baptist are changing lives," Pastor Browne proudly proclaimed. He even put the words on the sign outside the church.

Once Butch's presence at Calvary was commonplace, the talk shifted to another subject. Late September began the stretch run for the sheriff race. Boone Atkinson was leading in the polls. The Atkinsons were referred to as "blue bloods" in the Texas Hill Country. They had old oil money and were spending it on their campaign. Sheriff Mulvaney had painfully thrown in the towel and was ready to spend his last full month on the job.

The first Sunday of October rolled around and Butch Warden asked if he could say a few words before the service started. Pastor Browne agreed, but wished he hadn't.

Favoring candidates from the pulpit was strictly prohibited.

Butch only talked for seconds, but it was the end of Boone Atkinson's run.

"I'm asking for forgiveness. Five years ago, I had an affair with Madeline Atkinson. I've done a lot of bad things and I'm trying to put the ways of the devil behind me. Please pray for me and vote for sheriff next month."

Boone Atkinson and his camp held a press conference denying Butch Warden's claims. They filed a lawsuit as well, but Judge Newsome turned his nose at it. The church was fined, but Preston and Trevor took care of it with one of the envelopes Gary had shipped from his tropical paradise.

Sheriff Mulvaney received the victory phone call after 11:00 p.m. and dialed Butch Warden first.

"I'm still the sheriff. I took 68 percent of the votes. I'm not happy about what you did, but thanks!"

"God forgives us of our sins. I'll get up this Sunday and have people pray about my penchant for white lies."

They laughed for several minutes.

Three months passed and a new topic circulated throughout town. Preston O'Neil and Lauren Emory were getting married. Everyone was excited, as was the man in Cincinnati. He had kept close tabs on the happenings in Austin. The only correspondence between Gary and Austin was a package with several envelopes and the real number to the offshore account in it. They were waiting for Mr. O'Neil to make a mistake and he did.

The wedding date drew closer, but Preston and Trevor hadn't heard from Gary. The post office worker finally called Cincinnati. Rhodes paid the man twenty-five hundred per month to keep a close eye on mail that went to the Alexander farm.

"A postcard arrived from Gary O'Neil."

"Read it."

"Hello. I'm at the Raffles Resort on Canouan Island. I couldn't imagine a place this beautiful. If you squint hard enough, you can almost see Jesus walking across the turquoise sea. The five-star services are amazing. I couldn't survive now

without a daily spa treatment. The views are breathtaking and the white sand bleeds into the water, creating a perfect union. The vegetation is as green as a rain forest. I'm taken aback every day by each glorious encounter with the best of God's nature. By the way, Preston, the golf is magnificent. I love you both and drop me a note when you can. Just send it to the resort and I'll get it."

The voice on the other end of the line thanked the man for his services and said a $5,000 bonus was on its way.

Three days later, a private plane landed on the fifty-nine hundred-foot runway. Gary O'Neil had company. His days of drinking piña coladas in a private cabana on the beach were over.

Each night, Gary enjoyed the sunset from the same spot on the island. Evgeni watched him for five days and knew his routine. Gary wouldn't have recognized Evgeni if the Russian told him who he was. The assassin had been through four plastic surgeries during his time as a hit man. He was cold hearted and didn't care what he looked like.

Gary was stretched out in his spot when Evgeni walked up to him.

"Is this spot taken?"

His face was unrecognizable, but the voice certainly was not. Gary knew what was about to happen.

"Have a seat if you'd like."

"Do you know why I'm here?"

"That's a stupid question."

"Did you think you could get rid of me that easily? I have been waiting for this day since the night you tried to kill me. You're probably wondering how I survived that explosion."

"I read the paper and it said two people died."

"That is correct. The cab driver went up with the car, but I managed to open the door before the blast and was halfway out when the bomb went off. I have some scars, but I've used them as a daily reminder."

"So who was the other person?"

"A man was jogging past when the bomb went off and he was launched into a ditch. I pulled myself up and reached my apartment before the police arrived. They knocked and knocked at my door for two days, but I didn't answer. I tracked down Rhodes after he tried to evict me and we knew you were behind everything. He had conned you into meeting him, but you made the right decision to not show up. However, the postcard to Austin wasn't a wise choice."

"So that's how you tracked me down?"

"Yes."

"Just get it over with."

"I'd love to see you suffer before I end your life, but that's not an option. So long Mr. O'Neil."

Evgeni shot Gary once in the head with a silenced Beretta. He waited for the sun to set and then placed the gun in Gary's hand. The Russian walked back to his room and waited for his private flight the next morning.

Number seven reached St. Petersburg two days later and called Cincinnati.

"The island isn't as beautiful as it was before."

Those were Evgeni's only words.

"I'll be in touch," the other man said.

The wedding took place in Austin without a hitch. Preston and Trevor were disappointed that another postcard didn't arrive. Gary didn't send an offer of congratulations after his sons had mailed a letter from Austin telling him Preston and Lauren was getting married.

Their father's lack of response wasn't a surprise to Preston or Trevor, nor the man in Cincinnati waiting to make his next move. Things might have settled down in Austin, including Butch Warden, but the forthcoming news would prove that relaxation in the Texas Hill Country wouldn't be possible for those ever involved with Stenson and Rhodes.

THE FUNERAL TOOK PLACE in Columbus. It was a small service. He left behind a grieving wife, but they didn't have children. The man in the casket also didn't have many friends. He was a recluse and quietly went about his business. His wife thought about calling Austin, but didn't want to sadden anyone with the news.

The black iron gates at the entrance to the cemetery were minutes away from being closed. The visitor pulled into the cemetery and drove to his brother's plot. It didn't surprise Helen Rhodes that he failed to show up at the funeral, but she would have been shocked to see her husband's brother kneeling over his gravesite.

Robert's plan had been foiled by someone else and he was happy Evgeni didn't get to him first. He crouched near Ronald's tombstone asking for forgiveness. The letter was full of lies, but having his brother six feet below him changed the way Robert felt. He actually shed a tear or two, the first he had cried since his last child was born.

Jensen was supposed to take out Rhodes, which he did, but it was the wrong Rhodes. He didn't know Robert had a twin. Gary was unaware that Robert reached out to his brother. When Ronald walked out of Mehaffey's Pub, Jensen assumed it was Robert Rhodes and squeezed the trigger. Gary never heard about the mistake. His parking lot conversation with Jensen was all the information he needed. He had duped Ryule years earlier and the old saying "what goes around comes around" came true for Gary. The only man aware of the truth was Robert Rhodes.

He spent a few more minutes apologizing above the ground where his brother's body was buried. It was the first and last time Robert set foot inside the cemetery to visit his brother.

Over the next few months, Rhodes dealt with a handful of former employees from the warehouse and a few who had moved with him to Cincinnati, but had since quit. He avoided paying big money to a lot of people who punched in and out at the Rhodes Tire and Rubber Company because of the briefcase and Gary's program.

It seemed like things were spiraling out of control. A lot of people were scared to seek money because of what happened to those who had, but an ex-employee won a large settlement and lines began forming. Rhodes didn't have a way of getting rid of his current headaches, but refused to continue doling out large chunks of money to "worthless leeches."

In the past, he would have consulted with Stenson, who would have taken care of the problem. He didn't have Big Boy to rely on anymore, nor did he have Gary to hang a number on a shed. He did have a Russian who impressed him with his skills and Rhodes was going to bring him back to the United States at any cost.

He sold all the apartments he owned and went out and purchased three new ones that were spread throughout Columbus. He also bought one near downtown.

The apartment off High Street wouldn't house tenants. Rhodes slightly decorated the cozy quarters. He put a table, with one chair at it, in the kitchen. A visitor would have had a hard time using a screwdriver as an eating utensil, but eating wasn't an option at the abode.

An old couch had been moved from across town and was a perfect fit in the living room. The afghan was also a nice touch. Rhodes hung some old drapes in the window and moved on to his final task in the apartment. He walked into the back bedroom and took off a vent cover from above the doorway.

Evgeni slipped into Gary's room and stole the briefcase and book before ruining a perfect sunset on Canouan Island. Rhodes wanted the items. Number seven shipped them to Robert a few days after returning to Russia.

Rhodes took the briefcase and nestled it into its new hiding place. He grinned as he replaced the vent cover and carried the screwdriver back to the kitchen table. He proudly left the apartment and drove to the library.

Robert had the book tucked under his right arm in between a stack of folders and papers. Rhodes and Stenson had scouted a few places when they started the program. Robert knew he couldn't put it back in its original spot so he settled on another area he and Big Boy had selected.

The tire and rubber bigshot left the library and drove to a warehouse store. He had three keys made to the new apartment near downtown and a trio for the briefcase. Rhodes decided to skip the post office and shed.

Evgeni remained number seven while the new recruits were numbers six and eight. Robert text their number when it was time to get rid of a problem. He borrowed a page out of Gary and Big Boy's book. Each recruit called him on Monday and Friday, asking what time they were meeting for dinner. If Robert had an assignment, he'd immediately text their number back to them. If not, the message went unanswered.

Evgeni recruited two assassins to travel with him to the states. Rhodes also decided contact was allowed, but talking about the briefcase or cases they were assigned was prohibited.

Evgeni had been involved in organized crime since he turned fourteen. He knew people through his travels and ventured to Kamchatka first. He was there to recruit Cheslav. The man was someone who Evgeni deeply respected. They were part of a crew that pulled off a major heist in Moscow six years earlier. After the successful job, Cheslav retreated to Kamchatka for the solitude it provided. It took some work, but Evgeni gave Cheslav his best sales pitch and he was on board.

Rhodes' new right-hand man left Kamchatka by plane and returned to St. Petersburg. Evgeni's next trip took him to Vologda a week later. He got off the train and reserved a room at a hostel for the night. He heard about his next recruit from a reliable source in St. Pete. The incident with Gary made him even more cautious, but the twenty-three-year-old had made a name for himself and had already spent a two-year stint in prison.

Evgeni met him the next day at a small eatery. Jeirgif was attentive and soaked in every word number seven spoke to him. Jeirgif asked numerous questions during their conversation. Evgeni was staring at a mirror image of himself, making the young Russian perfect for the job. They spent three or four hours together before a commitment was made. Jeirgif said he'd be in St. Petersburg the following week.

Jeirgif was an hour or two behind Cheslav. Money was the biggest factor in both saying yes. Evgeni had briefly discussed what they would do in the states. He finished filling them in and explained how they would get in touch with Rhodes.

The next morning, the Russians boarded their plane and touched down in Los Angeles after crossing the Pacific. They had a two-hour layover before catching their next flight to Chicago. From there, they flew to Columbus.

A man was waiting for them when they got off the plane. The gentleman had been Rhodes' driver for nearly two decades.

"Welcome to Ohio. I'll drive each of you to your place of residence."

The quartet walked to a limousine and the foreigners got in the back. Cheslav was dropped off first, followed by Jeirgif and Evgeni. They were happy to see BMWs sitting outside their apartments when they pulled up. Each knew the car belonged to them because their number was written in shoe polish on the driver's window.

Cheslav barely had time to get comfortable in his new digs. The next day, he received a text with the number six after calling Rhodes about meeting for dinner. He drove to the apartment and walked inside. Cheslav didn't know what to expect.

He grabbed the screwdriver off the table and walked into the back bedroom. Cheslav used a small step stool that was leaning in the corner and placed it under the vent cover. He pulled out the briefcase and opened it. The only item in it was a series of numbers on a small piece of paper. Rhodes did away with the map and lighter. Cheslav unlocked the compartment and removed the jump drive. The assassin locked the compartment, shut the briefcase, and put it back in its spot before leaving.

He waited until it was almost time for the library to close. It was another one of Robert's rules. He retrieved the book and hurried to a private booth. He transcribed the series of numbers and put the book back in its secret place.

When he returned to his apartment, Cheslav opened the laptop Rhodes provided and inserted the jump drive. He opened the text document and Peter Thompson's name was the only thing in it. He closed the document and opened the picture. Cheslav studied the man's face for fifteen minutes before removing the jump drive. He took a hammer and smashed it into pieces, placing them in a small Styrofoam coffee cup. Later that night, he drove downtown and emptied the cup's contents into a Dumpster.

Six days later, Peter Thompson's obituary was in *The Dispatch*. Cheslav had performed magnificently. Peter's accidental drowning was questioned by many, but foul play was ruled out.

Jeirgif's first assignment didn't leave anything to the imagination. Rich Leasure was found in his shower with his throat slit wide open. Rhodes wasn't happy with Jeirgif's job, but it only took the young Russian a day to eliminate Mr. Leasure. It was by far the quickest assassination. Rhodes met with Evgeni and wanted him to talk to Jeirgif about his gory methods. The countrymen discussed things the following evening and Jeirgif agreed to tone it down.

Over the next few months, Rhodes' headaches began to dwindle again, but authorities were hot on his trail. They knew he had something to do with the deaths, but they couldn't prove it. Rhodes decided texting was no longer an option. He also knew he couldn't visit his Russian employees because he was being shadowed.

Rhodes fired the landscaping company that had worked for him since the Cincinnati facility opened. Evgeni, Cheslav, and Jeirgif started their own business and Rhodes quickly hired them. The Russians moved to Cincinnati and loved spending time at Robert's Queen City business. The race was on to see who could bed the gorgeous secretary in the rotunda. She still hated Rhodes and his advancements, but each time she was ready to leave, Rhodes gave her a raise—a monetary one. She was by far the most expensive secretary in Ohio.

Rhodes had his office swept for bugs and cameras on a daily basis. He knew it was relatively safe. His new method for assigning cases was simple. He had three magazines sitting on a coffee table and each had an issue number of six, seven, or eight on them. Evgeni was the only one who was allowed to go upstairs to Rhodes' office. Jeirgif, who was somewhat making progress with the blonde beauty, and Cheslav waited downstairs.

Evgeni situated himself on the couch and waited for Rhodes to write a check. If there was an assignment, Rhodes asked how much he owed and number seven grabbed the top magazine off the coffee table. The issue number on the front was who received the assignment.

A year passed and talk of lawsuits died down. Police harassment continued, but Rhodes knew they didn't have solid evidence. A pair of botched trials ended in mistrials again, making Rhodes seem untouchable. Law enforcement sat outside his facility and interviewed several workers, but no one exposed Rhodes because they knew he was capable of hurting them or their families next.

Things were too quiet for Jeirgif so he decided to go back to Vologda. Rhodes didn't object. It was one less thing to worry about. Evgeni knew the kid was trustworthy and gave him his blessing when he left.

Cheslav was also ready to leave, but a letter arrived in Cincinnati and changed things.

Robert,

You know what you've done. Do you really think you're that smart? Have you forgotten that we know everything? There isn't any amount of money that can replace my dad, but you're at least going to try. Two million dollars will cover it. It's a one time fee to keep my mouth shut forever. If I don't receive the money, your days of freedom are numbered.

P.S. I'm sorry to hear about your brother. Helen told me the bad news.

Robert knew the people in Austin would eventually cause trouble, but it wasn't the people in the Lone Star State concerned with his affairs. Trevor and Preston were upset with the news about their father, but agreed he reaped what he sowed. They figured Rhodes had something to do with it, but Preston and Trevor had washed their hands of him.

A few days later, Rhodes was in the middle of making travel arrangements when a second letter from Dane arrived.

Robert,

You might have thought this came from Austin, but it didn't. I'm acting on my own and I want two million dollars. I have everything I need to take you down. I'll be in touch. Until then, watch your steps!

The second letter was too late. Rhodes already blamed his adversaries in Austin, although they didn't have a clue about Dane's correspondence to Cincinnati. Robert wasn't in the mood to play games. He would patiently wait for the perfect time to take them down.

Chapter
Twenty-Five

CHESLAV AND EVGENI WERE summoned to the facility in Cincinnati. Number six was content to flirt, but had special privileges that day. They walked into Rhodes' office and neither would be sent after the briefcase. Robert was neglecting the briefcase and book for his next assignment.

"Read this!"

> *Robert,*
>
> *I'm getting impatient. You didn't put the money into the account. I guess I'll have to leak a little info to the press. You certainly remember one of your assassins being sent to Grove City, don't you? Maybe this article will help you remember. When you're finished reading this, I'm sure you'll be ready to help my bank account swell."*

When the Russian assassins were finished with the note, Rhodes began reading the newspaper article about Melvin Clarke's death. He got to the part about the man being stuck in the right quad with an arsenic-laced syringe and explained that Melvin's boy was out for revenge.

"Here is your next assignment."

355

Evgeni and Cheslav were stunned. Rhodes handed each of them an address, a photo of Dane, and names of the places he frequently dropped by.

"I don't care who takes him out, his head is worth two million. I could send him the money and hope for the best, but he won't stop. He knows his father is dead because of me. His emotions will always stand in the way. I want him dead by the end of the week and then we'll move on to our next targets."

Following his recent discovery and subsequent letters, Dane, who decided Denver wasn't for him, knew he was in trouble. He stopped by the addition near the warehouse a few days before his first letter arrived in Cincinnati. Dane wanted to visit with Ronald and Helen. He was floored when Mrs. Rhodes gave him the news about Ronald's death. He stayed with Helen that afternoon, promising to return often. Dane called Preston and Trevor as soon as he pulled away from Helen's driveway and told them Ronald had been murdered. He deliberately failed to mention his extortion plan.

Trevor's friend knew Rhodes would send someone after him, especially after his recent letter. Dane didn't want to find out if the program was still intact so he moved his stuff to a friend's house in Pickerington. Dane wrote a check for a full year's rent and had a friend sign the lease across the street from his old apartment. The high-tech wizard moved in and began watching the activity below.

Dane wanted to call Austin a second time, but knew his cell phone wasn't safe, especially since he received a threatening voice mail before moving out of his old apartment. He needed to let his friends down south know he had sent the letters to Rhodes. He had screwed up and a simple sorry wouldn't change things.

Slamming car doors woke Dane at seven-thirty on Thursday morning. Peeking through white laced curtains, he looked down to the street and saw two men. They were wearing dress clothes that would have made a 1970s used car salesman look good. Each sported tan khakis, slightly highwatered, and plaid shirts. If they were hit men, they didn't dress the part, but Dane knew how Rhodes' crew operated.

He took several snapshots and watched them slip a pamphlet in the door. They looked up and down the street. Dane stepped away from the window as Cheslav scanned the building. He thought the strange looking man had looked directly at him while he was peering up from the street, but the Russians got in their vehicle.

Dane flipped the laptop open on the small coffee table and sat down on the loveseat he bought for fifteen bucks at a local thrift store. He inserted the memory stick into the laptop and looked through the two hundred seventy-eight photos he had taken.

Dane attached a photo of each man to the e-mail he sent Rhodes.

Robert,

You can certainly do better than that. I don't know who your cronies are, but I'm sure the police would like to talk to them.

You've left me with one option. Two million dollars will be put into a Swiss bank account that has already been opened in my name. If you ignore my deadline—tomorrow by 4:00 p.m.— I will send the news article describing my dad's murder to The Dispatch. It will be accompanied by a small note blaming you and I'll tell them there are people who can testify.

I'll wait until the following Friday. If the money doesn't show up by four o'clock, I'll take them a copy of the article about the house fire—the one started by Gary and ordered by you and Stenson. I'll wait another week and tell them about Steve Birch's death. I have enough on you to keep the game going for a while. The ball is in your court.

P.S. Add another million to my price with each passing week.

Ten minutes after Evgeni and Cheslav pulled away from the curb, Rhodes heard the e-mail alert. He read the message and was furious.

He called his Russian assassins and they immediately drove back to the apartment. Cheslav looked up at the four windows on the second and third floors of the complex across the street. Rhodes had forwarded the e-mail to their BlackBerrys. The photo proved someone had taken the pictures from across the street. Evgeni and Cheslav felt the photographer had been perched on the third floor.

They tried to get into the building, but a code was required. The fire escape ladder on the side of the apartment was an option, but was quickly ruled out. Evgeni ripped off his shirt and wrapped it around his left elbow. He walked over to a window on the first level and smashed his padded elbow into the glass. Number seven unlocked the window, brushed away the glass, and pulled himself into the apartment. As he reached for the lock on the door, a woman who had been sleeping screeched in horror. Evgeni popped three silenced bullets into her and the screaming ceased.

He let Cheslav in and they rushed to the third floor. Evgeni and Cheslav knocked on doors of apartments facing the street. They kicked their way in after no response. Evgeni struck out, but Cheslav found a note from the perpetrator.

"You're a little late and tack on another million to my price."

They rushed out of the building and ran down a side alley to get to their car. The back right tire was punctured. It was obvious they weren't going anywhere. Evgeni quickly secured a vehicle. He went halfway up the block and forced a lady from her car at gunpoint. Cheslav jumped in and they drove three or four miles before ditching the vehicle.

Rhodes' hit men found a bus depot and paid for two seats to a station in Jeffersonville. They stopped for a changeover, but were in Cincinnati by the middle of the afternoon. Rhodes picked them up at the depot and they told him about the note. They drove to the facility and went to Rhodes' office.

Robert sent an e-mail to Dane, agreeing to pay three million, but his offer was rejected. Dane was camped in a mall parking lot and communicating via the wi-fi on his laptop.

"I'm not meeting anyone in person. I won't accept the money being deposited in an area bank. I know you'll have the bank under security and will kill me once I leave. The Swiss account is where you'll put the money."

Rhodes knew he had to track down Dane. He had less than twenty-four hours to generate a game plan. The idea came out of left field. Dane had asked about Robert's brother, stating Helen passed along the news.

Robert and his pair of thugs drove to Columbus later that night. They turned onto Johnson Road and passed the old facility site. The warehouse was caved in and the property was taped off.

They pulled into the driveway and saw a light on in the front room. Helen met Robert at the door and didn't appreciate the intrusion.

"What do you want?"

"The boys and I need your help."

With Evgeni and Cheslav in tow, it was easier for Rhodes to coerce Helen into going inside.

"If you're going to kill me, get it over with."

"We're not here to hurt you. I need a little information and we'll be on our way. Do you know a boy with the last name Clarke?"

"Yes. You better not hurt him."

"We're not going to hurt him. He has information we need. I need you to contact him right now."

"I don't know how to get in touch with him."

"When's the last time you talked to him?"

"Before Ronald was murdered."

"Don't lie to me. He has sent me three letters. In the first letter, he said he had visited you. Either tell me where he is or convince him to come here."

Mrs. Rhodes gave Robert a fake address where Dane was staying. Robert knew Helen was trying to keep Dane safe.

"I want you to go there," he said to Cheslav. "If he's not there, come back and then we'll have a serious conversation."

Cheslav got up from the table and headed toward the front door.

"He won't be there. I don't want to see Dane hurt or killed like other people you've been involved with. I know you had something to do with Ronald's death," Helen said as she broke down sobbing.

"I swear I didn't kill my brother or have anyone kill him. Dane's trying to extort money from me and we're gonna set him straight."

"I'll call him if you make these men leave while he's here."

"I'll agree to that."

Robert accompanied Evgeni and Cheslav to the front porch and gave them instructions. They pulled out of the driveway and Helen watched their taillights disappear in the distance. She immediately picked up the phone. Helen told Dane she needed company and he agreed to spend the night.

Dane would have been a multi-millionaire on the run if he could have made it another day. Rhodes was prepared to pay him the money if his last ditch effort failed.

Cheslav pulled the car sideways on Route 23 near the access road that ran into the backside of the old Rhodes Tire and Rubber Company. Two cars sped down the road and stopped a few feet from the apparent broken down vehicle. Each time, Evgeni climbed out of the bushes, snuck around the bumper, and crept along the driver's side while they watched Cheslav try to block the glare from their headlights.

Evgeni startled both drivers, but they were motioned around.

A third car approached. Dane slammed on his brakes and quickly put the vehicle in reverse. Evgeni darted from the bushes and put a full round into the vehicle. Dane's bloody body slumped over. Evgeni pushed him into the passenger's seat and drove the car halfway down the access road. He snatched Dane's laptop and put the chain back up before rejoining Cheslav.

They drove to Helen's house and waited for Rhodes. He looked back at Helen and turned out the lights. She was discovered three days later.

Robert spiked her coffee with a large amount of strychnine and watched her deteriorate within minutes. Her body went through a series of spasms that advanced to vicious convulsions until she was eventually asphyxiated.

The trio drove back to Cincinnati and the Russian assassins were crossing ocean waters by the time Rhodes climbed into bed. Robert wanted to send someone to Austin as soon as possible. Rhodes was afraid Dane's associates would talk. Evgeni would be summoned once more and the final task carried a steep price tag.

TWO YEARS HAD PASSED and things in the Texas Hill Country were pretty bland. In other words, they were back to normal. There wasn't a sheriff's race to talk about. Butch Warden was behaving himself and nearly half his kinfolk attended Calvary every Sunday.

A stranger or two had passed through town, but a visit to Shick's Gas-N-Go was their only reason for stopping. There had been so much to talk about a few years earlier, but even gossip queens were at a loss for words.

A project at the Alexander farm ended their boredom and captured everyone's curiosity. Excavators worked on the project for two years. Dirt was hauled in, taken away, and moved around. It was a secret until everyone figured out what they were building.

Preston and Trevor were stunned about a year after their father's death. Gary's debts were paid off by the sale of his estate and the remaining money was divided between Trevor and Preston. Each received $5.7 million.

They talked about purchasing an area farm and turning it into a luxurious business, but Preston and Lauren already had a place close to Colt and Jolene. Trevor and Savannah owned a house closer to town. They decided against farming. Preston and Trevor put their money together and purchased land from Mr. Alexander.

Mr. Parson also wanted to sell some land. His wife had died and was buried in the cemetery down the road. Sharon's ashes were buried there and her plot was between Ava and Ellie Mae Hendershot, who rested next to Mrs. Parson. A day didn't pass without someone stopping by the cemetery for a visit.

Preston and Trevor purchased the field where the famous Texas Hill Country pond was located. Mr. Parson still said, "You won't find sharks in that pond, but there still are some biguns." Preston was often teased about his question to Colt years earlier.

People mentioned the dirt moving in passing, but everyone had something to gossip about again when a giant house started being built overlooking the pond. It wasn't all they had to talk about.

The road between the two fields had been a dusty lane since it was carved out by early Texas settlers. Preston and Trevor had it paved. They also paved the road that ran from Mr. Parson's house past the Alexander farm to the state route. There wasn't much traffic before the roads were paved, but once everyone caught wind of it, they went out of their way to catch a glimpse of what was going on.

Locals stopped and tried to chat with whoever was around. They fished for information. Everyone wanted to know who was moving into the new house. Texas Hill Country residents were curious about the roads being paved. They wanted to know when the dozers and trucks would be finished playing in the dirt, especially when they started digging up land that used to belong to Mr. Parson. None of their questions were answered. "Wait and see" was always the response.

Polk's Family Restaurant was at capacity early one morning when Buster Pate walked through the front door with a know it all look on his face. He took his seat alongside Dump Milligan and Old Man Cater, not saying a word.

"So, what gives?" Dump asked.

Buster shook his head, smiling as if he was begging for them to drag it out of him.

"What's so funny at six-thirty in the morning?" Old Man Cater questioned.

Old Man Cater's booming voice woke everyone up. Buster ordered breakfast and remained silent. He stopped smiling between bites, but his joyful mood irritated his companions.

"If you don't tell us what you're smiling about, I'm gonna knock that grin off your face," Old Man Cater said.

"Calm down!" Mr. Polk demanded. "Remember what happened the last time you got worked up in here? Buster, why are you so happy this morning?"

"All right, I'll tell you. You can start calling me Tom Brokaw or Dan Rather. Thanks to my journalistic talents, I found out what's going on at the Alexander farm."

Everyone in the restaurant stopped and leaned closer. The secret was finally about to be out.

"It's a golf course."

"A golf course?" one of the patrons grumbled.

"Yep. The roads are closed again today, but I parked at Mr. Posey's and walked through those woods where "Frenchy" was shot. I saw semis hauling in sand for the bunkers and dozers filled them in. We won't have a new family in town either. That big house is gonna be their clubhouse."

"Are you sure?" Dump asked.

"Positive."

The crowd dwindled in a hurry and cars lined up and down the state route. Sheriff Mulvaney and his boys were called, but they couldn't stop the inquisitive crowd.

Preston, Trevor, and Kurt saw the crowd walking up the road and knew the secret was out. Trevor motioned to a deputy to let everyone through.

Their plan was moving at a slow pace, but once everyone knew what they were up to, things moved rapidly. Volunteers came out of the woodwork. An army of people worked on the course over the next few weeks. The clubhouse received hands-on care and the Parson pond makeover was impressive.

Fairways were sowed and, eight months later, the course was ready to open. The sign on the roadway entrance was covered as were the signs on tee boxes. No one knew what the course was named, but Trevor and Preston planned to unveil it during the ribbon cutting ceremony.

Media members and dignitaries circled around and Preston manned the microphone first.

"As you know, this project has been in the works for a few years. It has always been my dream to work on a golf course. Now, I co-own one. My brother and I are proud of this course and think golfers will enjoy their time here."

Preston handed the mic to Trevor.

"As Preston said, we're pleased to offer a championship caliber course to the fine people of Texas. We've had visitors from golf magazines and they're raving about the course. For media members, the first annual Sharon Talbot Memorial Golf Tournament will take place next month and we have commitments from several PGA golfers, including a few who hail from Texas. Without further ado, it's time to unveil our club's namesake."

Trevor and Preston grabbed a corner of the sheet and slowly pulled it off the sign. Talbot Golf Club of Texas Hill Country was the newest business in the area. The sign brought a smile to those in attendance. Judge Newsome and Sheriff Mulvaney cut the ribbon. Preston and Trevor received a loud ovation.

The crowd assembled in golf carts that were parked along the cobblestone driveway meandering to the clubhouse. The group started at the first hole and the black trash bag tied around the sign was taken off. The par four was four hundred thirty-four yards and was sponsored by Polk's Family Restaurant. Each hole had a local sponsor and the brothers were proud of that feat. The biggest obstacle on the first hole was the creek that ran across the fairway. It sat two hundred seventy yards from the tee box, daring linksters to be brave. The creek offered many challenges as it worked its way throughout the front nine.

Preston and Trevor rode in a cart together, staying close to media members.

"How did you come up with the name of the course?"

"Our mother's maiden name was Talbot. Trevor and I legally changed our last name to Talbot. The Texas Hill Country has been good to us and we decided to honor the land in the name of our club. It's lengthy, but people will get used to it."

The group worked its way to the ninth green and then crossed the road to the back nine. The tenth hole was a par five that crossed Mr. Parson's pond. Technically, the land belonged to Trevor and Preston, but they erected a giant bronze sign with the words "Mr. Parson's Pond" inscribed on it. When Mr. Parson saw it, he beamed from ear to ear.

It took one hundred ninety-five yards of carry to clear the pond and then the fairway was a stairway to heaven. It played longer than five hundred fifty-seven yards, but instantly became a crowd favorite, especially when they reached the green. The back nine could be seen from the green and offered a splendid view of the handiwork.

The fourteenth was the course's signature hole. It was a tight par three lined with woods on each side. The elevated tee box made things tougher. A small pond was on the right side of the green and the left side was protected by a deep bunker. The green was double-tiered and slightly sloped toward the pond. The grumbling carried on for years, but it only played one hundred sixty-five yards and was a fun challenge. Birdies could be had, but double-bogeys were frequently penciled in.

They finished the tour and the Talbots were congratulated. Nearly everyone left and a small party began late in the afternoon. Preston looked out the clubhouse to the tenth tee box and couldn't believe his dreams had come true. He rarely thought about Gary, but chuckled when he thought about the names he used to label him. He highly doubted his "adopted" father would call him a "fairy florist" if he could see their course.

He backed away from the window and headed outside.

"Where are you going?" Lauren asked.

"I'm grabbing my sticks from the bag room. I'm sneaking in nine before sunset."

"You're crazy," she said as she kissed him.

"Hold up bro. I'll join you."

They grabbed their clubs from the bag room and walked outside with their arms around each other. They strolled to the first tee. Trevor won the honors and used his mulligan on the first shot. His second drive was a little better, but only sat two hundred ten yards down the fairway in the right hand rough.

Preston pulled out his Cleveland driver and striped one down the middle. His Titleist waved as it passed the creek.

Trevor hit his second and third shots before he passed Preston's drive. Preston flipped a wedge within nine feet of the hole. Trevor topped his fourth shot, but it rolled to the green. He chunked a chip shot and putted once before Preston conceded a gimme, giving Trevor a triple bogey.

The youngest brother lined up his putt and stepped to his ball. He started it seven inches left and it slowly curved to the hole and found the bottom of the cup. Trevor shook his head.

"Double or nothing on the next hole," he said laughing.

They stopped several times during the round and said, "I can't believe we own this."

The Talbots had indeed made a name for themselves in the Texas Hill Country. The days of looking over their shoulder had apparently ended and so were moments spent thinking about a briefcase.

Their enjoyment continued for a few months, but the forthcoming news wouldn't be well-received.

RHODES WAS TOO BUSY increasing his empire in Cincinnati to worry about the "hilljacks" in Austin. He purchased two floundering companies and merged them with his company. One was in Michigan and the other was located in Iowa. His business was renamed Rhodes Tire and Rubber Industries. He also moved Stenson & Rhodes to Cincinnati and hired several top executives from big firms to help the PR empire grow.

Law enforcement and other interested parties were watching him closely. Rhodes was taking away business from Goodyear and Bridgestone. The company was becoming top dog in the Midwest and no one was happy about it.

Robert was bringing a good light to his companies because of their charitable giving. Everyone at the companies bragged how they gave nearly eight and a half million dollars away the previous year. The companies hoped to double the previous year's figure.

Robert was in Columbus to play in The Memorial Pro-Am. Rhodes Tire and Rubber Industries made a splash by donating two million dollars to the Children's Hospital for research. All the media outlets were there to take a picture of Rhodes presenting the check.

A startling surprise was announced during Rhodes' grip and grin shot. Phil Seevers was there representing Buckeye Health and informed media outlets his company was matching the donation. Stenson knew Seevers well, but Rhodes wasn't familiar with him, other than his name.

Robert and Phil finished their interviews and approached one another. They shook hands and talked about their generosity. The conversation made its way to Stenson and then to golf. Seevers and two hackers were assigned to play with Adam Scott while Rhodes and two other corporate jerks were playing with Rory Sabitini.

As they wrapped up their discussion, Seevers hit him with an interesting tidbit.

"How often do you play in these Pro-Am events?"

"Usually one or two a year. I like to play in this one and the LPGA event near Cincinnati. I'd love to get out to Pebble Beach sometime."

"Well, there is a fairly new course near Austin, Texas, and there's supposed to be a huge event next month. People in the golf industry are ranking it as one of the best new courses in the country. A few pros have signed up for the charity event."

"What's it called?"

"Talbot Golf Club of Texas Hill Country."

"Who owns it?"

"Two brothers inherited money from their father and built it on some old farmland. The biggest problem is that it's in the middle of nowhere, but talk is that a hotel and village is next on their agenda. They're saying they'd like to host a small pro event by 2013."

"Do you know their names?"

"I'm not sure."

"Let me get your number and maybe we can fly down and play together."

They exchanged numbers and went their separate ways.

The event rolled around and Seevers, who had called Robert several times, never heard back from him.

Rhodes was in Austin the weekend of the event. He purchased a ticket to go as a spectator. He wasn't interested in playing. Robert wanted to scope out the course. The crowd was around five thousand and would have been bigger if Tiger wouldn't have had a previous engagement or if the hotel/village project was completed.

Robert watched Seevers hack his way around for a while, but wasn't there to catch up with his associate from Columbus. He was there to see the Talbots. As the event drew to a close, Rhodes saw them on the clubhouse's balcony. They were fraternizing with some of the pros on the enormous deck wrapped around the clubhouse.

Rhodes handed a note to a kid who was walking by and gave him a $100 bill to deliver it to either of the owners. Preston read it first and did a panoramic take of the area. He handed it to Trevor and they excused themselves from the table. They walked inside and Trevor read the note again.

Your course is magnificent! I've enjoyed the surrounding views as well. It's no wonder Kurt kept himself hidden down here all these years. If I didn't have business to attend to in the Queen City, I'd stay a little longer. Preston, it was good to see your face again and Trevor...sorry we couldn't introduce ourselves. I'm asking a favor. Would you please make my friend feel at home?

Preston hopped in his car and drove to the Alexander farmhouse. Jim and Elaine were fine. Preston didn't have time to explain. He ran out the door and drove to his house. Everything was intact. He looked down the road and Colt and Jolene's place appeared to be OK.

He drove back to the course and gave Trevor a report. While Preston was gone, Trevor lapped the course. Neither knew what was going on and they weren't comfortable with the situation.

Several days passed and a plane touched down in Austin. The visitor hoped it would be his first and last time in Texas.

He picked up the car Rhodes rented for him and drove to an isolated motel in the Texas Hill Country. He checked in and headed to a local tonk. It didn't take long for the talk to start. Another foreigner with a weird accent was in town. The owner of the bar went into the back room and called a few of the Wardens. Although 60 percent of their clan attended Calvary faithfully, a few still liked to drop by Roland's for a few swigs.

The front door swung open and Butch walked in first. He was the only Warden who had stopped drinking, but still liked to show his face in the tonks. He was followed by Denny, Sunny, and two younger Wardens. They passed Crystal Wyatt and sat at the bar.

Evgeni quietly ate his food and drank his tall boy. Butch broke the silence.

"Where ya from, boss?"

He turned and stared at Butch for a moment before refocusing on his spot at the bar.

"I'm just trying to make small talk. Are ya from around these parts?"

A second staredown offended Butch and the Warden clan.

"Have it your way Vladamir. Ya see, in these parts we're all friendly and we don't take kindly to folks who ignore us. Ya don't have to talk to us, but we'd like ya to leave our bar."

When Butch finished his spiel, every ruffian in the place stopped what they were doing and stood behind the Wardens. It was evident to Evgeni that he wasn't going to pull a fast one on them the way Filip had a few years earlier.

He downed his beer and asked for his check. He paid his tab and slowly walked to the door. Butch and his relatives watched the

Russian pull out of the dusty parking lot and drive up and over the hill.

Later that night, Butch Warden was sound asleep when the intruder crept into his home. The shotgun beside his bed would have been used had Butch heard him, but Evgeni didn't make a sound. Evgeni quickly slashed the butcher knife across Butch's throat, leaving him gasping for air. He blacked out before he could reach the shotgun. Evgeni ducked into a shadow in the corner of the room and watched the Texan fumble around. As Butch's hand touched the shotgun, a bullet finished him off.

"The name's not Vladamir, it's Evgeni," he said as he stepped away from the corner.

The news spread throughout the Texas Hill Country. One of the Wardens had been murdered. Sheriff Mulvaney, Kurt, and several of Butch's newfound friends took the news hard. Calvary Baptist had a special prayer session for the family and the church couldn't have fit another person inside.

"At least he's in Heaven," Pastor Browne said numerous times.

Evgeni had done his job, but more work was certainly in the future. Preston and Trevor thought Rhodes had sent the hit man for them. They were still targets, but Butch Warden was the first name on their southern "to do" list.

The Talbots were back at square one. They constantly looked over their shoulder and Kurt was also fearful, although he didn't show it. Preston and Trevor gave the note to Sheriff Mulvaney and told them Robert Rhodes had a boy give it to them. However, when they tested the handwriting, it was negative. Rhodes paid someone else to write the message, which looked like a friendly note at first glance.

He also couldn't be questioned for being in Texas because he was there on business. Rhodes attended a convention on Friday and went to the charity event with Texas businessmen he had met. The men said Rhodes was alone for a while, but once again, there wasn't sufficient evidence to pin anything on Rhodes. He was a master at listening to investigators pound on him for hours. He could have been the one who killed those people over the years, but wouldn't admit to anything. He had the toughest skin they had ever seen.

Butch Warden's death became old news and people began to keep their doors unlocked again as months passed.

Preston, Trevor, Kurt, and the Alexander family were never comfortable again. They were always on the lookout. Kurt, Preston, and Trevor thought about starting over again somewhere else, but Austin was their home.

Although they feared one of them could be next, they tried to go back to a normal routine. Kurt and Jim operated fairway mowers. Preston and Trevor planned renovations and expansion. The ladies took care of the numerous flower beds on the course. All seemed to be going well until early one evening.

Trevor had gone home for the day and Lauren, who managed the clubhouse, was waiting for the last group to finish. Preston walked into the clubhouse after completing some work on the putting green and plopped down at one of the tables. He took the opportunity to look through the day's mail before the twosome brought in the keys from their cart.

He sorted it into a pile, but stopped when he saw an unaddressed envelope without a postmark. He tore the letter open and read it. Preston walked onto the back deck and looked towards the back nine, which was mostly nestled below the clubhouse, other than number ten.

"What's wrong?" Lauren asked.

"We have to see what this is about," Preston said as he handed her the letter.

The fellas enjoyed their round today. They said they left you a present on fourteen.

Lauren and Preston didn't wait for the twosome. After locking the clubhouse, they sped down a cart path and cut across the course, ignoring their 90 degree rule. They squinted to avoid bugs that had polluted the early evening air while making their way to fourteen.

Preston drove straight to the tee box and saw it sitting under a bench. He got out of the cart and walked toward it. He picked it up and sat on the bench while reminiscing about his first encounter with his brother at Goodale Park. Preston placed the familiar item on his lap. Lauren put her left hand on his back.

He didn't need a key to open it. Preston also didn't have to go to a post office or a strange apartment to get to it. He opened it and a map was laid out in the old black fuzzy bottom. Preston took the map out and a series of numbers were written on it. The numbers were 4-3-21-11-17-1-25 and 11 was circled.

The book accompanied the map. Preston flipped through the pages. A-U-S-T-I-N. He didn't need to turn to the index, but did so anyway. The 11 confirmed it was indeed a city in the United States.

A key wasn't necessary for the small compartment in the briefcase. He opened it and a folder was inside. A note was stuck on the folder.

Decipher this code—9-16-17-9-10-8-12-23-9-3-12-17-22—before you unseal the folder.

The series of numbers spelled out O-C-T-O-B-E-R-F-O-U-R-T-H.

Preston was finally living out his dream by being on a golf course day after day, but his first thought was how simple things had been while at Stenson & Rhodes. However, he didn't miss much about Columbus.

He unsealed the folder and, for the second time, his picture was inside. The fourth of October started like any other day, but Preston was reunited with an old acquaintance and his photo signaled he was once again the next assignment.

The golf cart was abandoned on the eighteenth fairway. Preston was waiting for lead to crash into his body. A car was still in the parking lot, but there wasn't a trace of anyone. Lauren was hysterical. Preston calmed Lauren and told her to go home. She tried talking him into letting her stay, but Preston convinced her to go. They kissed and Lauren tightly embraced Preston before reluctantly leaving.

Preston retrieved the deserted cart and drove it back to the clubhouse. He grabbed the briefcase and began walking across the front nine. He was prepared for the worst to happen, but was determined to live the rest of his days on a golf course.

He continued walking, enjoying his surroundings, while every step he took was watched by careful eyes.

For the first time in what seemed like an eternity, Preston wasn't worried. He was content walking along in the Texas Hill Country. It was just him, a golfing paradise, and his old pal—The Briefcase!